Behind Those Eyes

Behind Those Eyes

T.P. CARTER

KENSINGTON PUBLISHING CORP.
http://www.kensingtonbooks.com

DAFINA BOOKS are published by

Kensington Publishing Corp.
850 Third Avenue
New York, NY 10022

All Kensington titles, imprints and distributed lines are available at special quantity discounts for bulk purchases for sales promotion, premiums, fund-raising, educational or institutional use.

Special book excerpts or customized printings can also be created to fit specific needs. For details, write or phone the office of the Kensington Special Sales Manager: Kensington Publishing Corp., 850 Third Avenue, New York, NY 10022. Attn. Special Sales Department. Phone: 1-800-221-2647.

Dafina Books and the Dafina logo Reg. U.S. Pat. & TM Off.

ISBN 0-7582-1428-6

First Kensington Trade Paperback Printing: September 2006
10 9 8 7 6 5 4 3 2 1

Printed in the United States of America

For Auntie.
I know you're dancing up there . . .

Prologue

A man whose claim to fame is quarter notes. She could hear her mama warning her now. "Don't get cho' coattail tied up wit' nun a' dem' nickel-and-dime horn players."

She must not have heard anything bad about drummers. Even if she did, Cora was convinced that this one was different. She'd thought long and hard. Couldn't remember feeling like this. When she first met him she thought he was trouble. Met him at a rent party up on 132nd. Carefully trying to make it through that dark, narrow hallway full of people. Talking. Laughing. It was so late. She needed to be in the bed. Rehearsal for the new number at the Cotton was sure to make a mule quit. Plus, there were Colored girl dancers all over Harlem, all over New York for that matter, that would give anything to open for the Duke and his Orchestra. So getting through the hall and down these four stories with the drinks she still had stirring inside her was all she wanted to do.

She paused at the huge picture window at the bottom of the landing and stared out onto the lighted streets. It's amazing up here. What they call the Negro Metropolis. Harlem. 1927. Everything down South closed down almost twelve hours ago. Harlem was still in full swing . . .

"Four-five-nine, man! Combinate it!"

"I got it! Don't rush me!"

"I ain't rushin'—hey, you got a fifth of your specialty on you?"

"Yeah. Hold on. One thing at a time . . ."

After seeing an elderly man purchase a small bottle of vodka from the same person he'd just handed two pink number slips to, I was convinced. There isn't anything that can't be bought here. From whisky, to luck, to Black pride. Culture. Even Whites were buying and selling. In clubs. In hotels. They were selling it to each other. On the black market. I can't say that I've ever seen anything like it. Never saw so many Negros in one spot. Never saw so many Whites wanting to do everything that we did. Be everything that we were. Listen to our music, do our dances, buy our art and books, eat our food. In the South we heard that it was like this up here in the big city, but we thought they were all tales.

I've been up this way for some time now. Still can't believe I'm living this. While I was in Richmond, one of the most interesting men I'd ever met came to town. Selling bootlegged liquor and God knows what else, he introduced himself as Big Franchey DeMadden. Ran into him at the general store. Said he also worked at a place called the Cotton Club. Told him I'd heard a little about it. Tried not to seem so impressed by a man from New York. Didn't know squat about anything but Richmond. He must have guessed that, because he told me all about Harlem. About a man named Langston Hughes, about Colored painters and writers, doctors and lawyers. All walking the streets. *"Just plain happy to be Negro,"* as he put it. Told me about *Crisis* magazine, the NAACP, UNIA, and Marcus Garvey. Then he began to speak about the nightclub his boss owned. Had a full house every night. Its specialty, White patrons, Black bands. Fur coats, and shimmering dresses. He asked me if I danced. I did. Said he wanted me to come up and audition. Couldn't even imagine it. Mama took one look at his nice suit, shiny shoes, slick hair and reckoned the devil sent him. I had to see for myself. That was a year ago. I still can't believe I'm here. I guess I must have been staring out of the picture window for quite some time, because I hadn't noticed anyone standing on the other side of the large velvet drape.

"Excuse me, ma'am. If I might say, you are the prettiest thing in Harlem," the gentleman offered.

"Just in Harlem?" I asked. I was such a sucker for a handsome man. He smiled and tipped his hat.

"Harlem is all that counts," he said assuredly.

"Oh, my . . . well, what about Chicago, Washington, Paris . . . the rest of the world?" I batted my eyes. I should stop. I have someone. He laughed in disbelief.

"I don't know if anyone told you . . . but Harlem *is* the rest of the world! Ask anyone, White or Colored, from here to a hundred and tenth!" He smiled. I smiled back. And we stood there staring. Instantly, I felt warm. Nauseated. Faint. I had to pull myself together. So did he. He was charming. Charismatic. Said he was a drummer. Told him I was a dancer. He played at Small's Paradise after hours. Made extra change running numbers. A hustler. That was all I needed to know. Trouble. Plus, I already have someone. A good someone. When he asked to walk me home, even though I wanted him to, I said no. He did something to me. Something I didn't want to explore. Against my will, I had to do the right thing. Leave him standing at the window. Watching me walk.

The first time we kissed I saw stars. He spent the entire set looking into my eyes. His lips were so soft. A bit hazy, I was somewhere between morning dew and metaphor, walking on a cloud. So high, I didn't ever want to come down. Little by little, my heart began to unwrap. I was worried that if it cracked open, even a little, all the love inside would seep out, and there would be no one around to clean up the mess. He let his fingers, the middle three, touch the back of my neck. Counting hairs. Special. A small bead of sweat traveled down past the small of my back. Made me arch it so as to expose what little was left undiscovered. Share secrets of the heart. Some of this, I wanted to keep locked in. If I would have known that we would be kissing like this, right here, right now, I would have left all of my love at home. In my closet. Underneath my bed.

The rhythmic patterns of his heartbeat helped me fall asleep. Helped me dream. I closed my eyes, sucked his breath, drawing him into me. Saw our children, our peach trees, our stolen moments, and I began to cry. I traced the outline of his lips, tasted his fingers. Touched his face. Wiped away his tears. I saw myself in his eyes. Stretched out in love.

He walked me home that night and returned the following evening with orchids and the most beautiful silver bangle bracelet that I had ever seen. It was simple. Elegant. The outline of a butterfly marked in stones of the earth. Jade, turquoise, amber, quartz. Said it meant more than he could describe at the moment. He took my hand, and we started out into the night. Said he wanted us to go down to the Guild Theater to see *Porgy*. They had an all-Negro cast. He was so confident, so caring. Held my hand as if I were going to fly away. After the show, we headed up to the Savoy. He wanted to dance the night away in my arms. Pretend it was his last night on earth. Love is overwhelming in that way. I leaned in and listened to his heart. He was playing our song. All in quarter notes.

"You feel that?" he asked as he placed my hand over his heart.

"Yes."

"It's yours."

"No, it isn't. It belongs to your woman."

He laughed at me. "My snare is my woman. You are my life."

"You can't serve two masters."

"I serve who gives me life."

We talked a repertoire of rhythm and dance. All for our enjoyment. We walked and talked and allowed our eyes to make love to each other until we'd arrived at the place where soul, tempo, and time took its first steps. At the Savoy. Marble, mahogany, dancing, loving. Painted in oranges, rhythms, and blues. Fletcher Henderson playing. Bebop being born. A cadence in perfection.

"Your timing is bad," I say.

"That's impossible."

"Why is it?"

"I'm a drummer. Timing is everything."

"Nothing's impossible."

"I know what is." He chuckled.

"What?" I asked. Unable to keep the smile on my lips from spreading to my eyes.

"This fight."

"What fight?"

"You're fighting it."

"Fighting what?"

"Love."

"I'm fighting a war. Love, I'm surrendering to."

"War?"

"Yes, war."

"With who?"

"With right and wrong. With time."

"That's a losing battle."

We walked down Lenox Avenue. In the moonlight. Holding hands. I want to tell him about cold nights I waited for him at the window seat. Wrapped up in the rhythm of possibility. And now he's here.

"I have someone," I say to him.

"I know."

"How did you know?"

"Your eyes said it."

"When did they say it?"

"When we danced."

"I was smiling when we danced."

"Yes, you were."

"So how did you know?"

"I am him. I am your someone."

I laughed.

"Are you scared?" he asked.

"Scared of what?"

"Losing the war."

"I've already lost it."

"When did that happen?"

"When we danced."

He smiled that smile. We gazed up at the black sky. Filled with lights. He took my hand. Placed it on his heart again. I did the same. I wanted all of him inside me. His faults, his frowns, his words, his sounds. Tape them up on the walls of my heart and stare at them all night with my feet crossed in the air.

"I want to collect you. Pieces of you," he said.

"Why?" I asked.

"In hopes of getting some of me back."

I paused.

"This is wrong," I told him between kisses.

"Why? Because of your someone?" he asked.

"No. It's unfair. If you die first, you take me with you."

"How so?"

"Have you ever known anyone to live without a heart?"

He paused.

"So. You'll do the same," he said.

"Do what?"

"Take me wherever you go when you leave me."

"No, I won't. Women outlive men."

"I can't live without you. So what does it matter?"

I'm smiling now.

"When did you come to know this?" I asked.

"Known it all my life."

"Impossible. We just met."

"Nothing's impossible."

We continued to walk our walk. Talk our love talk. Through days of fondness and nights of adoration. Through years of sanctity and possibility. And when that war was finally over, when I really knew that this was right, I searched myself for peace. For oneness. For the impossible. And found it lying unscathed at the bottom of his heart. He was my soul mate. My shared entity. And that was as good as forever. While we made love, and I do mean created it, his life force ran through me. It was an energy unlike anything I've ever experienced. Nothing could come between us. Not even death. Not now and not ever. We were married to one another before we met. In love with each other before we knew what love was. The offspring of our souls' affection will tumble together in this playground we call life. Kismet in both hands. Wrestling each other down to the ground, trying to smear it on each other's face. Whether we wanted to acknowledge it or not, it would acknowledge us. When the time was right. Our love was made in heaven. Preserved in pyramids. Painted in murals. Locked in time. So when I got that phone call at four in the morning, that call that changes lives, I already knew. I knew where to find him. Just follow my heart.

When I arrived and saw him lying on his back, eyes shut tight, I didn't scream. I didn't panic. I prepared myself, for I knew my own time was near. Who can live without a heart? We loved in the spirit. Loved as one. And that is as good as forever. So while blue lights danced and sirens blared and cops questioned and mothers cried, I did the only thing I knew to do. I wrapped my arms around him and held him. Until we both stopped breathing.

PART ONE

1

Taiyler

Taiyler Richardson, M.D.
Sunday, forgot the date, 1:15 P.M.
Entry # 110: Free to play

My treasure chest. Love, truth, freedom. Solitude, peace, hope. And understanding. Let's talk love. Sometimes love will curse you with moments. Moments that steal your sanity from right underneath the pillow beside you. Regardless of the gun resting underneath your own. But love is so magnificent, even its moments of root work are blessed. And when this work is done in spirit, no force on this earth can surpass its splendor. For the writer, it's his works displayed in orange covers, with black cursive writing etched on front. A time-share of solitude. Inked in the hearts of those who pen the birth of life-art's mulatto child. For the musician, it's Miles, Bird, Trane, and Monk live from Times Square, New Year's Eve 2065. Free to play in two hundred shades of purple. Freedom to play. For the poet, it's bright shades of blues, reds, and yellows worshiped by the lips of Baraka, Williams, and Care Moore. Drinking the truth of a World Stage Wednesday. One snap at a time. For the dancer, it's Africa under her toes. Stretching her soul over hope's fire. Tracing rhythmic tales of its death up the course of the Nile. Dancing it to resurrection. And for the painter, it's the culmination of resonance and refraction of all color. A mural absorbed in Blacks. Racing for understanding. And being understood. For the activist, it's the call from Alabama alerting you of the bus boycott. So you ride the freedom train. For Palestine, it's your land back. For Cuba, it's the *arrival of Assata and the departure of the embargo. For the lover, it's truth, freedom, solitude, peace, hope, and understanding. Reflected in the eyes of the one you love.*

Let's talk love. I could go on and on. But the force itself laughs at my words in conceit. Knowing that despite my efforts, I will never be able to describe the magnitude of its power.

Sometimes I sit kindergarten style in love's presence. Humbled by the stir in my stomach. Feeling the anxiety of the children of Israel on Passover eve. Wanting to be stronger than I am. But excited to be weak. So at night, I pray to the Allah of my emotions. Thanking him for what has been granted, yet humbly asking for more. Even though I try, a thousand tongues couldn't speak His praises. So I tarry. Wait on the Lord of spiritual love, hoping he'll renew my strength . . .

It's moments like this that I know I'll never get back. I'm flowing. All of the words that I need—and some that I don't—are piled up on the right side of my brain like first graders on the edge of a seesaw. My pen is moving superfast. Writing has always been my passion, even though it's not the career that I chose to explore. I always thought that I would reserve this part of my life for pure enjoyment. Figured that relying on it to create my current standard of living would taint it. Remove it from its purest elements of truth. So I indulge whenever I feel the need to escape this lie we call life. In this case, my sorority chapter meeting is what I'm attempting to leave behind. So I write. And look over my shoulder at the faces of people who bother me. And laugh. Escaping the torture of a steady drip of water from a leaky faucet. Or at least I thought so, until I was violently snatched back to reality by the voice of what had to be an imp to the antagonist of peace . . .

"Order! Order! Sorors! We only have a few weeks left until *DC's Men Are Cooking,* and we need everyone's undivided attention! Now, we've heard from the publicity committee, and they have the community expo spot on WKYS 93.9 FM confirmed for five days prior to and leading up to the event. So . . . what's next on the agenda? Oh. The committee in charge of signing up our male volunteer cooks, do we have our targeted seventy? Taiyler? How's that coming, because if you can't pull it through, Soror Marla has volunteered her services. Her husband is the president of 100 Black Men of Greater Washington and can provide assistance with listing volunteers."

She was the most annoying woman on the face of the earth. And she had to recapture her title. Year after year. Weekend after weekend. Until she plucked every single nerve I owned. They don't tell you about this when you pledge. That you'd rather be on a first-class flight to Baghdad than in the company of your chapter president. At least the one standing in front of me. I swear, sometimes I wonder why I even try. The one thing I hate about sorority meetings is the fact that everyone is the head of this or that, or knows someone who is an expert at something that has to do with whatever, and it always makes these meetings longer than announcements at the end of a Baptist church service.

Every year my sorority heads a number of community service projects and events that help raise money for scholarships, the needy, and just about anything else we can think of. Today we are discussing our progress with one of our annual events called *DC's Men Are Cooking*. We gather up male volunteers from Washington, DC, and the surrounding areas to cook their best dish, and set up shop at the Washington Convention Center downtown. We usually raise a significant amount of money, have an excellent turnout, and much support from the area fraternities, especially Alpha Phi Kappa, our brother frat. So why our chapter president is bitching about every single detail like she's never done this before is beyond me. It's just making an already long meeting ten times longer. Now she wants to know who our volunteers are for this year. Again. That's one of my committees, and you would think that I didn't just call her last week with the confirmed list. So I stand up, give my best bright-eyed, I'm-excited-about-this-shit-for-real look that I can muster up. It's showtime.

"Attention, Sorors, seventy-five of DC's finest have volunteered to cook their best dishes for the event." I measured the *oohs* and *aahs* coming from my audience. I know. I know what I'm doing. I continued.

"Not only that, but Anderson-Tufts and Associates, one of the largest Black owned and operated accounting firms in the country, has come on board as our main sponsor. They will be covering the promotional costs of the event and providing us with a few volunteers as well."

As I sat down amidst the thunderous applause, I shot my chapter president a serious take-that-bitch smirk before I crossed my legs. She and I haven't gotten along since I joined the DC graduate chapter of my sorority. I pledged the fall '92 line of Alpha Kappa Chi Sorority, Incorporated, while in college and figured that I'd stay true to my oath by joining the graduate chapter in my area. Big mistake. I've had more problems with my Sorors and their jealousy, backstabbing, and gossiping than I'd had all through high school and college combined. And believe me, that's a lot to be reckoned with.

The chapter president, let's just call her Sister Mary Clarence, is the ring leader. She always has something to share. An unkind word, rumors, your business. It doesn't stop until she can conjure up enough to fill all that space that going to church and sorority meetings don't. Not to mention she feels as if she is the official moral majority of AKX and doesn't stop to let you know every chance she gets. The bulk of her comments, regardless of how sweet the delivery, tend to make me forget that I'm a physician and put me right back in a Brooklyn state of mind, if you know what I mean.

Even though her condescending attitude and snide remarks sicken me, I let them ride right over my head. It's the glares and constant whispers from the other sorority members that actually bother me. I guess I should be used to it. I just expected more from a group whose claim to fame is sisterhood. They need to pledge these grad hens, too. I didn't have this aggravation from my Sorors in college. They were forced to put aside their preconceived notions of me while we were on line. Well, anyway, you should have seen the look on that wench's face when I sat down. My Soror Shala saw it and signaled for my attention. I saw her, but I refused to look her way for the sake of maintaining my composure. I know she is going to do something outrageous. That girl will make me laugh at a funeral. She's my best girlfriend. My only girlfriend. My only true one. We met in our freshman year at Spelman, pledged together, have been more than sisters to each other ever since.

Mustering up the courage to look her way took a lot. Shala, being Shala, crossed her eyes and stuck out her tongue, mocking our chapter president, who she swears is cockeyed. I couldn't take it and ended up spitting my tea right out. Spraying it all over the table. That's it. That's it. I knew I shouldn't have looked. I know better. I can't hold my laughter, and no one knows that better than she does.

"I'm going to fuck you up after this." I pointed and mouthed between

clenched teeth as she cracked up at the scene that I created. Not to mention Sister Mary Clarence up there had something smart to say about chapter etiquette. I tried my best to ignore her and proceeded to wipe the table clean as fast as I could. Good thing we were starting to wrap the meeting up. Shala and I had plans for brunch this afternoon. Now, *that* I was looking forward to. A soulful heart-to-heart is exactly what I need right now. She is an analytical type just like I am. Put the two of us together and we can solve any problem. Men, finances, family. She is the only woman besides my great-aunt whose opinion I truly value. And vice versa. Plus, through the years, we have been there for each other when it meant the most. She lost her childhood friend; I made her herbal tea, cleaned her house, called her boss. When I lost my grandma, she made me realize that I could go on without the woman that made me.

The one thing that I didn't mention is what makes us truly different. She's batting for the other team. Gay. Or lesbian. Or whatever the politically correct term is for this year. I still can't figure that one out. She can literally have any man in this world that she wants, but she chooses to date women. I don't know. We talk about everything and share many of the same interests, but when she told me sometime around our junior year, I was in total disbelief. No, actually, shock better described it. She didn't fit the bill at all. And she had a man! A fine one at that. Who did anything and everything for her. I always thought that women who liked women—besides that sounding like the title to a Jerry Springer episode—were a little less on the pretty side. Okay, a lot less. With way more of the rough stuff. For example, the women on the talk shows who wear motorcycle jackets and snakes around their necks . . . well, Shala was not like that. She gave absolutely no indication that she was not attracted to men. She was gorgeous. She even had me under pressure sometimes. Not only that. She had her shit together. I mean this was a bad bitch. Always dressed to kill. Hair and nails perfect. You would have thought that she had a live-in stylist. Always turning heads while we're out. Then to turn all that around and not even use it for what God intended? I'll never understand it. But nonetheless she's my girl forever.

I supported her when she made the change, and she still has my fullest support. She's my sister. Closer to me than any of my blood sisters. And I can't wait until brunch so I can smack her ass for making me laugh out loud like that in this meeting.

2

Nathaniel

I'm looking out onto the Potomac, and I'm smiling. I like what I see. I'm watching my life dance across the glare of the large picture window in my office. I'm living the life that my ancestors prayed for while stamping mortar and picking cane. When I pray, sometimes I don't even know where to start. I send thanks for the obvious. Family, shelter, and nourishment. Protection from the perils. Direction toward all that is good. And when this is done, I thank Him for something else. Love.

"Mr. Woods, you have two new messages. First message received today . . . 2:34 P.M.," "Hey, babe, it's me. Just called to say that I love you and to let you know that I have a surprise for you tonight. And yes, it's better than the last one." Beep.

"Next message received today . . . 4:22 P.M.," "What up, dawg? K and Garvin are coming down this weekend, and we're trying to hit that new spot downtown. It's First Friday, and the crew is about to do our thang as usual. For the HU days. Hit me and let me know if Kendra is letting you off the hook tonight. Peace." Beep.

Okay. This is a hard one. Hang with the crew or get surprised by my wife. Not as hard as I thought. The last surprise Kendra had for me ended up with her panties in our ceiling fan and me taking open-minded to another level. Mr. Magic is agreeing with me. Let me call

Derrick and break the news. On second thought, I'll just meet him downstairs after work as usual. Working in the same building as one of your best friends has its ups and downs. It can be cool hanging out at lunchtime, but it's going to be hell walking to the parking lot explaining why I'm ditching my boys for the night. Don't get me wrong. They know that I'm a married man who is very much in love with his wife. But the crew doesn't get together but maybe a few times a year tops.

We were tight in college, all four of us. Through pledging different frats, breakups and makeups with girlfriends, and conflicting personalities that would rip even the tightest of crews apart, we've maintained our loyalties to one another. As a matter of fact, I don't know how we did it without killing each other. Let me give you a little background on the situation. In life people come and go, you make friends, you lose friends, you dust yourself off and try again. After our freshman year at Hampton University—the real HU—I never had to try again. Derrick, K—short for Kalonji; his parents were on that Black Power shit for real in the '70s—and Garvin made that so. Though our personalities were very different, we somehow clicked and never turned back. Derrick's probably the most militant of the group. He's assertive in voicing his opinion. Actually, assertive is an understatement. He can be downright abrasive. Derrick will break you down if your shit isn't tight. He's what we call the Henney and Coke of the group. Intelligent, arrogant, and fuck whoever doesn't like it. That's him. It shows in everything from how he handles his business to how he handles his assets—I mean his women.

K is more of a conservative. Just as smart if not smarter than Derrick, but more unlikely to make a big splash in an argument unless he is pushed to the point of no return. He's probably the better looking of the crew members excluding myself and D. Guess that leaves Garvin. Anyway, the dude is as clean as the board of health. That's why he's my frat brother. K is the objective, detailed, computer science guy. Women flock to him while we're out, but he always finds a way to get taken advantage of. He won't stop until he finds a fine-ass, whiny-ass, insecure chick whose sole purpose in life is to convince him that his friends are shepherds for the devil. Garvin the extreme moderate's life motto is moderation. He has moderate looks, a moderate build, moderate opinions, and women just moderately like his ass. He will always end up in the friend box. Garvin is objective, too, but in a way that borders on indecisiveness. The type of cat that will back up one of Derrick's bitches-ain't-shit speeches and in the very next breath side with K's Black-queen-mother-of-the-earth bullshit. I guess that's why every single girlfriend he's ever had left his ass stranded as soon as opportunity or the mailman came knocking. You would have thought that medical school would have made him a little keener in the problem-solving and logic areas, but he still hasn't figured out how to satisfy his woman.

Me? I'm a combination of all three. I take control like Derrick, revere my beautiful Black wife to K's approval, and I haven't quite figured out what I have in common with Garvin. Whatever the case, when we get together it's all love. Beach houses, ski trips, homecomings, and even a regular weekend is crazy. That's why it's a shame that I'm going to have to pass up this weekend with them. Derrick won't like it, and I'll hear it all the way to the car, but he knows that my wife is my priority. She's my Earth. My queen. My spirit. And they know that she damn near crippled me during our last surprise weekend. So tough, fellas.

I see Derrick as I exit the elevator and begin to walk to our daily meeting place in front of our office building. As soon as I motioned *what up* he started running his damn mouth. He's still fifteen feet from me.

"Did you get the message? K and Garvin are on their way. What's the deal, you rollin'?" he yelled across the lobby. He's the hottest litigator in the city. Guess he can pull his ghetto card out whenever he feels like it. As I began to search for the right words to let him down with, he took a step back, looked at me intently. Here it comes. I'm found out.

"Awwh hell no! Hell no! I know that look, nigga . . . !" As I was unable to hide my guilt, he continued to read right through me.

"I know you're not even about to say that you're not comin' out tonight!" he yelled flagrantly. Okay. Those words finally materialized into a sentence.

"Yo, I'm sorry, man, Kendra has a surprise weekend planned. What was I supposed to do?" Derrick was warming up. I could see it in his eyes. He was going to fry me in his signature burn-you, blame-you rhetoric.

"You bitch ass! Last time it was your balls. What, does she have your dick in her purse, too?" That's the burn. Here comes the blame.

"Tell her you had plans! She knows how we do! The weekend will be fucked up without you, man."

Okay. Now I have to bring him back down. Here goes.

"Muthafucka, first of all, *if* or when you get a wife as fine as Kendra, you can tell me what to tell her. But right now, although I wish that I could come with you guys to the club, you know, to kick it with the gold diggers, and . . . what's that chick's name? The one in the cage? Looks like Bernie Mac in a G-string?"

He tipped his head, thought for a second. Eyes widened. Busted out laughing.

"Lady Godiva!" he spurted between laughs.

"Lady . . . yeah. That remains to be challenged. Well, it seems I'm going to have to pass up *all that woman* for a date with Washington's finest. Is that all right? Can I get that?" Let's see how he comes back from that. He always has something to say. So I waited.

"Well, if you weren't so fucking whipped, you'd know that any real man in this day and age needs a ho and a housewife! Didn't your daddy teach you anything? Every athlete needs a practice round! Especially the bench warmer standing in front of me!" This is Derrick. He won't stop.

"Yeah, you better rethink your strategy pat-na, so your lame ass won't get cursed out tomorrow morning for that sixty seconds you're about to put down on your wife tonight . . . !" He's cracking himself up as usual. And there's more. ". . . hoes, strippers, they keep families together, they're a part of the American Dream!" He got me. Because I busted out laughing.

"Derrick, I swear you're my boy forever, but you need counseling. Forget counseling, you need Jesus!"

"You think Jesus can really change me? He's the biggest playa of all time, man. He has millions of fine single women following him, doing exactly what he says. No questions asked. No compromise. And they *all* know about each other! If that ain't some playa shit, I don't know what is!"

Now I'm in tears. He continued to wallow in his comedic blasphemy.

". . . nah, man, I'll go with the counseling because once I get put on to that game there's no saving me!"

Now I can't breathe. Even Derrick is doubled over. Sometimes I wonder how I ever hooked up with someone this crazy. Damn, I wish

I was going out with the guys tonight. I hope Kendra's surprise is worth it. I pushed that uncertainty back into the hole it crept out of. I know it is. I know my baby. Even with her career and Nile, our little princess, she still makes time to please her man. She cooks, cleans, and can fuck Heather Hunter out of a job. She's my universe. My perfection. It can't get any better. I'll bet my worth as a man on that. No questions asked.

3

Taiyler

I motioned for Shala to meet me outside the meeting area in the lobby.

"So, girl, does that woman make you sick or what?" Shala asked loud as hell. I looked around, made sure no one was eavesdropping. Not that I cared, but I could do without the drama. She continued. "She is determined to work my last nerve, too. How the hell did she make it into AKX? Let alone become president of a friggin' chapter. Did you hear that heifer singing the hymn? Can ten frogs on an ice-cold day sound any more destitute?"

Shala won't stop until she makes me double over. That's usually the case, seeing that she never ceases to say or do the most outlandish things. And just when I think that I've seen or heard it all, she comes with more. It's funny, because she can also be the sweetest and most compassionate person that I know. We passed by Sorors on our way to the car, giving them that generic hug and kiss on the cheek that is so indicative of where we are as sisters that it's sickening. Damn, there's Soror Marla. Nosy ass. Nosy is an understatement. So is wrecking ball or tsunami or any other phrase used to describe what she can do to a pleasant environment in a moment's notice with the right information. I noticed her a few minutes ago. Just standing there, waiting for some of our business to drop out of our pockets. So she can pick it up. Spread it around. Ask if it belonged to anyone else. I can't stand her. And here she comes.

"Smooches, Sorors! Where are you ladies headed on this pink-and-cream Saturday afternoon?" she asked, a little too politely for a woman who prides herself on destroying homes. First response is none of your fucking business. Second response is better.

"Oh, to Georgetown for brunch," I answered curtly. Keep walking. Don't turn your head. Shala. Don't turn your fucking head. I swear. Don't look at her, or it will be hell getting out of here. You know she doesn't have a life, so she has absolutely no problem keeping us here for an extra hour. Shala, no . . . Damn it! She stopped. Now she's talking to her. I waited a good forty-five seconds before I decided to go over there and interrupt. I came in right on Shala's verse of the conversation.

"So what are your plans for today, Soror Marla?" she asked sweetly.

"Oh, I don't have any. Any at all. Just a little cleaning, my husband is away on business." If I were him, I'd be away on business every weekend, too. I can see where this is headed. So I braced myself. Just as Shala began to follow up with one of her sympathy moves, I dropped right in like "parachute man" at a Yankees game.

"That's too bad, why don't you—"

I cut her off in midsentence. Shala is such a softie sometimes. That's another way in which we are different. I don't have a problem telling someone where they can go, especially if it's someone I don't like. So I played my position.

"Uh, why don't you have a great day, Soror Marla, cleaning or doing whatever with—"

Shala shot me a dirty look. I turned it down a notch.

"Well, do whatever you can to enjoy this pink-and-cream day and thanks for the inquiry. We gotta go." Good. That'll do it. I'll be damned if I let any of these stuck-up you-know-whats—I'm trying to stop cursing—ruin my entire day. As I pushed Shala toward the car, she couldn't help but laugh.

"That was signature of you," she said. Although I know she's only half joking, I play along.

"You were going to offer her a spot for lunch. I felt it coming. I know you and I know you were starting to feel sorry for her not having a life, so I had to save you from yourself. Taiyler saves the day. Again."

She chuckled. "I do feel sorry for her, but knowing how you can't stand her, I would not have invited her to brunch, Taiyler. Plus, we have a lot to cover today. We haven't talked in almost two weeks. Before you interrupted, I was merely going to suggest that she curl up with Magnum for the day."

"Magnum?"

"Yes. My vibrator. It's in the glove compartment. It's pink, too. She would have loved it!" Laughter. Third round. And we haven't even gotten to the restaurant. She says that she has something important to bring to the table. A life issue. All I have are updates from my A team and B team. And work stuff to share this time. No major life issues. No major problems. So I'll get mine out first so we can concentrate on her. Whatever it is, we'll work through it today. Well, at least I hope so, because it sounded serious. As we pulled up in front of J Paul's in Georgetown, I was instantly reminded of the parking crisis in DC.

"Just pull into a parking lot, girl, you know it's gay day at Pottery Barn," Shala said sarcastically. Every other sentence of hers is a wise-crack. But I didn't know if I should laugh at that one or not. So I just pulled over to the first parking lot I saw and gave the attendant the key to my car. I always felt funny handing over my keys to a complete stranger. Plus, these lots are so small downtown it would be easy to bump or scratch a car, and truthfully we'd never know. It's funny how I never thought of those things in school when I was driving an '84 Civic. But I'm in a 911 now. And I better not see a scratch on my baby. As we walked into the restaurant, I could see that J Paul's was couple loaded today. But that didn't stop the vultures from swarming. It's amazing how men can be with their wives, girlfriends, or *just a friends* and still make an extra effort to break their necks in order to stare an attractive woman down. It's like they'll risk getting yelled at in public, smacked, or no ass for the night, just for the three seconds of visual stimulation from another woman's cleavage. It's no different today in J Paul's. Shala noticed it, too. She's used to it, though. Even though she doesn't like men, she loves the attention.

"Do you want to sit by the window?" she asked me.

"That's fine. It doesn't matter." I'm hungry as a hostage. Plus, this booth was out of earshot from the general public, and from the sound of it, what we were about to get into was pretty deep. As we removed our coats and took our seats, the server came floating our way.

"What may I get you ladies to drink today?" he sang. Shala wanted a drink drink, so she ordered a martin. I'm like damn, alcohol this early? This must be some serious shit she has on her mind. I wondered if she and Grai, her partner, were having issues. Whatever it is, I'll know in a few. My turn.

"I'll take cranberry juice." As the waiter cheerfully assured us that he'd be right back with our drinks, I adjusted my jacket and bag. Made myself more comfortable.

"I'm going to start because your shit sounds heavy . . ." I suggested. She leaned inward. Ready for battle.

"Let's see, work is going well. I'm getting along with the other three physicians in my practice. It's the office staff that makes my day longer than it needs to be."

She sucked her teeth. "That's because the other three physicians are male and the staff is all female. You aren't slick, bitch. Nothing's changed. Is that one doctor still hitting on you?"

"No. I neutralized him the last time he tried something."

"What did you do?" she asked, obviously amused. She knows what's coming.

"I told him that I hoped his insurance covered sexual malpractice. Because I don't have any experience cutting off a nigga's shit, but I'll grab the first scalpel I see if he so much as puts a hand near my ass!"

She died laughing.

"I don't see why I can't just have a normal day without men trying their luck with me. Sometimes I feel like a slot machine. People aren't going to stop until I break them. And I don't want to have to do that all the time. Well, anyway, work is good, we're steadily getting in new patients, and with the way managed care is cutting costs left and right, we need to see as many patients as we can."

Shala scrunched up her face. Interjected, "Yeah, I read that what used to be an eighty-dollar visit is now worth about twenty on most managed care plans. And that they will only pay for generic drugs. That's trifling."

"Well, it's a little more complicated than that, but yeah, they are some cheap assholes, and I can't stand the way they question every damn 'script I write. If I wanted my patients on the cheap stuff, I'd put them on it. How the hell is a basket-weaving major or cosmetolo-gist turned insurance agent going to tell me what to write for my pa-tients? It makes me sick, really. But that's the job nowadays, and I'm just sucking it up."

My ace of over ten years smirked. Gave me her best Diane Sawyer. "Yeah, so what else are you sucking?"

I raised my eyebrows. "For someone who doesn't like dick, you sure are interested in what I'm doing with them!" We laughed together, and she blurted out something that was labeled obscene before it ever touched her lips.

"That's because what you do with them can only be seen on the Discovery Channel. And I don't have cable, slut."

Oh, she's ready to cut, huh? I have something for that.

"Well, then tell cheap-ass Grai that this is 2003 and the only place they don't have cable is in Cuba. Her licking your shit is *not* as entertaining as she thinks or else you wouldn't be diving headfirst into mine!" Take that. Beneath the belt.

She chewed her appetizer extra fast. Couldn't wait to respond to that. It was a hot one. "Oh, it's entertaining all right. But good girls never tell lest their best friends get turned out."

Too far. So I settle it. "The only one turning me out is yo' daddy. And he's at church with your mama right now. Trickin' the soprano section." Final score Taiyler four, Shala three. Her daddy is her heart. You would think that he spent nine months carrying her.

"Taiyler, take that shit back. Take it back or else I'm calling Lance and telling him that you lied to him about what happened to his mother's pendant."

She wins.

"Okay, okay, you got me. I take it back. It's your brother turning me out. Not Reverend Matthews." We both are cracking up now. Shala is probably the only one that knows that I pawned my ex-boyfriend's mother's pendant while I was in medical school because I was dead broke. To this day, he swears that he left it at one of the apartment buildings he was renting out, when in actuality he left it in my apartment after helping me move in. I thought maybe an old tenant had left it there and took my broke ass straight to the pawnshop. When he told me that he lost the pendant that had been in his family for generations, and that it was the first thing his great-great-grandmother bought as a free slave, I almost threw up. I went back to the pawnshop, and it wasn't there. I even tried to locate the people who bought it, but I couldn't. So since he already thought it was his fault, I let it ride. Trifling. I know. But he would have killed me. Literally. Shala was the only one that I told. And even though we are not together anymore, we're still good friends. So she got that one. After wiping her eyes she asked the million-dollar question.

"So Miss my-coochie-is-overworked-and-underpaid, what are the stats on the A team and B team?"

I shook my head. She will not surrender. I let that one slide. My A team consists of the man I love and another I really like and may learn to love. My B team houses men that I may learn to tolerate. They usually serve one purpose or another. For example, Richard, Nyema, and Simuel are on my B team. Richard is tall, fine . . . and fine. He's a programmer with Hewlett Packard, and you would think that he would at least have the common sense he was born with. Wrong. But he looks good as hell on my arm. And he's attentive to my every need. And we've never even kissed. Nyema is a physician's assistant who I met while he was in the master's program at Howard. Cute, ambitious, funny, and thinks that I'm a goddess. He's just not a class act, if you know what I mean. I'll go to the movies with him, but dinner at B. Smith's is another story. Simuel is handsome and rich. More emphasis on rich. He built his own computer software company from the ground up. He's only twenty-eight. He loses more playing the market than I will ever make in a physician's lifetime. Problem. He's foreign. Before you send out the we-all-in-the-same-gang speech, let me clarify my position on this. I am Black, pro-Black, love my heritage and all that, but that accent is too much material to cut through. I am nowhere near a translator for the UN. Although I speak a few languages, my Yoruba is at best nonexistent. And my dialect detector's battery died with two-toned jeans. He's great, but I can't understand a word he says. Too much work trying to choose a restaurant for the evening. Period. Anyway, I gave Shala the update on team B.

"They're good. Richard just lost out on a great deal on a home in DC because he didn't read the fucking contract right—why am I not surprised? Nyema is taking the boards in a few weeks, so he's under a rock, and Simuel is in Seattle—hopefully with a translator—trying to land a new contract."

She wrinkled her nose. Moved on to a more interesting topic. "What's up with the A team?"

Now, my A team is not to be fucked with. These are some serious Black men. Handsome, intelligent, ambitious, renaissance men who are just my type. The list is a little shorter. There's Lance and Keith. Lance is my ex who has treated me like a precious gem since the first day we met on the train in NYC. I swear I don't know a man on this earth with more class, more finesse, and more culture. He looks, dresses, and carries himself like a runway model and walks like a gangster. He knows all the best restaurants in every city and has traveled the world but is not boastful about it. I used to love to watch him get dressed in the morning when I would stay over. He would slide his beautiful track-built legs through finely pressed suit pants, carefully place his arms in both sleeves of his French-cuffed shirt, and knot his Brooks Brothers tie with the precision of a surgeon. I remember wanting to rip his clothes off as soon as he finished putting them on. And he wouldn't mind it if I did. He loved me almost more than he loved himself. His first "I love you" came before we were even together. And he still says "I love you" even though we are apart. I would never intentionally hurt him. So when I decided to go to Georgetown for medical school instead of NYU, we decided that being apart was the best thing for us both. At least as far as career development was concerned. Now I'm a doctor, and he's an attorney. Classic, isn't it? Well, there's one thing. He's still in New York, and he isn't leaving. He takes good care of his grandmother, mom, and aunt, and I can't knock that. But I'm in Maryland, and New York with its crime, grime, and million-dollar studio apartments can kiss my ass.

So that leaves me with Keith. Met him at a medical conference while at Georgetown. He's doing pediatric neurosurgery plus a PhD. Long-ass program, long-ass residency. Too long for me. I love my work, but I couldn't wait another ten years before I started making money. Hermes and Manolo were calling, and I had turned a deaf ear for too long. But Keith is really in it for the science. I love the fact that I can talk to him about my day or medicine in general and he understands. Although compared to most of my team he's probably the most average looking guy of the group, in spirit, intellect, and personality he's a mirror image of myself. We love music, namely jazz, and not that elevator music you hear on soft 105.9 FM either. I mean hard bebop. Miles, Trane, Bird. The works. He reminds me of Lance without the polish. Problem, he's always getting dumped. In the seven years that I've known him, he's been dumped by three different women. Something's got to be up with that. So we'll be friends until I find out.

"The A team is just fine. Lance's fine ass still isn't moving, and Keith and I still aren't fucking."

"Do you think if Lance moved down here you guys would be together?" she asked. I didn't know.

"I don't know. He's perfect. Well, almost. He treats me like royalty, but we were never friends the way Keith and I are. I'm realizing that I need that in a man. To be able to talk to him and not have him be scared to hurt his girlfriend's feelings, but eager to tell his friend what's really on his mind. There has always been a place with Lance that I felt that I could never get to. He used to say that he didn't want to burden me with his problems or that he wasn't talking because he loved listening to me, but I wanted to him to speak up. I wanted to help him solve his problems. I got sick of pulling teeth for conversation. I'm not Barbara Walters. With Keith, that's never an issue. He'll talk to me about anything. And you know conversation is intimate to me. I just wish that there was more of Keith in Lance. That would be perfect."

"Yeah, girl, I know what you mean. Grai and I talk about everything. It's cleansing."

"Well, then, Grai must be a cleeeean bitch. Because she talks to everybody about everything whether you want her to or not!" Fast one, Taiyler. Way to go. That's for threatening to tell on me. Shala whined as she usually did when I talked about her curly-haired friend.

"Why are you always talking about Grai? What has she done to you besides be courteous?"

"Nothing! I just think that she can talk a hole in your head, that's all. Can I be expressive today? Can I?" I answered in mock exasperation.

"Whatever." Shala sighed. "I just wish my life was as easy as yours. You know what you want."

"And you don't?"

"Let me ask you this, T. You know pretty much everything about me. My likes, dislikes, secrets, aspirations. But looking at me right now, what do you see?"

Okay. I have no idea where she's headed with this.

"Uh . . . I see a beautiful woman and beautiful friend who will touch everyone she comes in contact with in a special way. Literally and figuratively speaking." I had to laugh out loud at that one. That was good.

"Taiyler! Not now! Not now with the jokes! For real, what do you see?"

All right. Time for me to stop playing around.

"Okay. I see a woman who is gorgeous, successful, down to earth, intuitive, intelligent, strong, and loving life."

"See, you left out one important thing."

I wondered what that could be.

"Happy . . ." she continued. "Happy, you didn't say you saw happiness."

Why would I say happy? That is a state of being, not a personal adjective. Sensing that she couldn't possibly be in the mood for my logic, I left that alone.

"I didn't leave it out; I just didn't add it." What the hell am I saying? Oh, good one, Taiyler. You would have thought that you had the martini and she had the cranberry juice. Let's try this again.

"I mean, I know you're happy right now, so it just didn't come to mind. What? Are you and Grai on the outs?" I asked more seriously.

"No, we're fine. Grai is fine. It's just that I'm beginning to think about the future, and it's hard to be happy about what I see. Everyone is getting married, well, not you . . ." She snickered. Interruption.

"Watch that!"

"T, you know what I mean. Not you right now, but we both know that you will have no problems when you've decided it's time. Men worship the ground you walk on. You'll go on to have a wonderful family and live the life you've always wanted to live and be happy. Me, on the other hand, I can't have both."

"Both of what?" I asked. This is making less sense by the second.

"Both happiness and the things that make me happy. I know it sounds weird, but things like marriage and children don't come easy for a gay couple. I'm already Black. And Indian. And a woman. One more minority category and I won't have to ever worry about not having a job."

I chuckled. She's right.

"Being gay or bi doesn't make life easy. Especially since people devote their entire lives and political careers trying to make sure that it doesn't get any easier."

I began to toy with the bracelet on my right arm. My favorite one. Twisting it back and forth, up and down. A ritual of nervousness. She's scaring me. She knows it. Shala glanced down at my hands and released a nervous laugh of her own. I think I know what's coming. I love her to death, but I'm not carrying anyone's baby. Holding my breath, I'm waiting for her to drop the bomb.

"I'm just saying that maybe I'll be happier going back to the other side."

Whoa. I didn't expect that. I know I didn't just hear her say what I thought she said.

"Come again?"

She paused. Heavy thought.

"I'm thinking about crossing back over. Dating men. This way I can have all of the things that I've always wanted in life. With Grai I can adopt, or artificially inseminate, or whatever. But seriously, what happens when the child grows up and starts getting teased in school? Or we start getting hate mail and shit? You know it's okay for homosexuals or bisexuals to date, but once we decide to seal our commitment in marriage or add children to the equation, we become a case for civil rights attorneys across the US, and you know I'm not equipped for that." As the nonconfrontational member of our friendship, she has a point.

"Plus, all these years have passed and I haven't even found the strength to tell my father . . ." As she goes on about how she loves Grai but will never have a life with her, I start thinking. What the fuck has happened here? I pride myself on being a problem solver. An analyst if you will. But this? Oh, no. She can't expect me to work this one out. This decision will affect her entire life. Flat out. Oh, hell no. Hell no. But this is my girl and she's confused. Fuck. We have to work through this. She does make some good points about the children and, uh, wait. She done lost her mind. She don't even like dick. Can't stand it. Says it always felt like a toilet plunger trying to unclog her uterus. Now she wants to . . . Let me finish hearing her out.

". . . so how can I be true to myself and my unborn child if I can't even be true to my family?"

I'm in deep thought, and she wants an instant reply. I'm not through thinking, but I have to deliver, so I do something I almost never do, out of pure shock. Blurt out the first thing that comes to mind.

"Do you even remember how to do it?" Bad move. Now she thinks I'm not taking her seriously.

"No, I don't get as much practice as you do."

I deserved that. But I didn't mean it in that way. So I tried my best to clean it up.

"No, seriously, do you remember how you used to say it felt?"

"Like a toilet plunger unclogging my/your uterus," we sang in unison.

"And you're willing to go back to that for the sake of what you perceive to be the general formula for happiness? A husband, house, and two point three kids? Two out of three cause more trouble than they're worth, Shala. Yes, your father is a reverend. But he loves his little girl too much to discard her like a used condom on account of her sexual preference. Tell him. Let him splash a little holy oil on you if it will make him feel better and live your life, girl. Don't change because of what others' expectations are of you." There. That sounded good. For now. We're going to have to come back to this one. I need time to sort it out. Pro and con it. Shala took a huge bite into one of her spring rolls.

"Sounds good. But there are two things that I have been my whole life. American and my father's daughter. I'm not trying to fuck with either of them."

4

Nathaniel

"Yeah, sweetie. Uh-huh . . . Yeah, they'll be disappointed because we don't get together as much as we used to . . . So what? You're my baby and I want to spend this time with you. . . Don't feel bad. You sure you don't want me to bring anything home? I'm on the Beltway . . . fifteen minutes tops. Okay, sweetie, see you in a minute."

That's my baby. She is so considerate. She actually felt bad that she was pulling me away from the crew tonight. Can you believe that shit? She never ceases to amaze me. While other wives hate for their husbands to blow the night away with their boys, she actually encourages it. She says it gives us a chance to miss each other. I swear I couldn't have married a better woman. As I pull into my driveway, I take a look at my beautiful home and the beauty waiting for me on the inside and send up a quick thank-you to the Lord above. No man should be this lucky. Usually, I come in through the garage door, but I decided to switch up and surprise Kendra by coming in through the back. Instantly, the smell of vanilla and spice berry filled my nostrils. Candles were everywhere. I found a piece of my linen stationary folded up neatly on the kitchen table. Located a fresh bowl of cherries sitting right next to it. She wants to make love tonight. I'm down with that. Last time I walked in for a surprise night, the ambience was different. Nine Inch Nails blaring over the sound system. That kind of let me know that she wanted some thug lovin'. I do what I can. The note was penned in calligraphy. Creative, babe, I thought as I unfolded it.

> *Kendra is not here tonight.*
> *She can't please you the way that I can.*
> *I'm waiting for you upstairs.*
> *Come to the guest room . . .*

What the hell does that mean? Aight. This better not be some tricky shit. I'm not in the mood. I just want to bust a nut and get Kendra to do the same, before I pass out tonight. She better not be putting me up to one of those female what-would-you-do-in-this-situation bullshit scenarios. I headed up to the guest room. Didn't see her. Instead there was another piece of linen paper, with a pair of boxers lying in its company. This note read something different.

> *Kendra told me that you look good in these.*
> *Put them on for me.*
> *Then meet me in the guest bathroom . . .*

So now I'm doing as men do. Going along with the plan. I took my clothes off and began to put the boxers on, when I swear my mind started playing tricks on me. I heard more than one voice coming from down the hall. Two female voices. Neither one of them Kendra's. Nah, I'm imagining shit. Finish putting the boxers on, man. I made my way to the bathroom, which was hard as hell because it's dark. But I made it. There's one candle and one note. This one was handwritten.

> *Sit on the toilet.*
> *There's a remote on the floor to the left of you.*
> *Pick it up, press the play button, then blow out the candle next to you.*
> *Spread your legs,*
> *Relax*
> *and wait for further instructions . . .*

All right. Sounds simple enough. I'm sitting in the dark, not knowing what to expect, when all of a sudden a woman's voice comes pealing through our bathroom cube speakers. Actually, it's two women's voices that I hear. So I wasn't hearing things before. They are moaning and whispering and groaning, and one is telling the other how good it is, and it's turning me on. In the background I hear the chorus to Janet Jackson's "Would You Mind" dripping out of the cubes while the sounds get louder. Okay, Kendra, that's all it took. Come on out, baby. I'm ready. Suddenly, the moaning stopped, and I heard another woman tell me that Kendra was sorry that she couldn't be here tonight and that she was going to be my host for the evening. Sounded like an older woman. She said that she was going to give me some instructions and that if I broke the rules, it would all be over in an instant. What would be all over? I'm waiting . . . As soon as I hear Janet's sexy voice switch over to "Ooh baby, ooh baby . . ." my dick loses all sense of rationale. He's demanding attention right now, and I'm not about to put up a fight. Then rule number one is stated. Damn, she sounds good.

"At no time are you to touch yourself, or the person serving you."

Serving me, huh? I decided to test the waters. I grabbed myself one good time from the base up, and guess what? The fucking music stopped. No joke. She can see me. How? The voice started again.

"I repeat . . . rule number one, at no time are you to touch yourself or the person serving you. Rule number two, do not attempt to remove any items used to restrain you or to restrict your vision. Rule number three, do not call out Kendra's name at any time during your night. Rule number four, you are not to come to orgasm in any other room except the master bedroom . . ."

I'm losing track.

"Rule number five, if at any time you break any of these rules, the night is over. Period."

She goes on to tell me to place one hand on the towel rack and the other on the edge of the sink and not to move them. Then she commands me to close my eyes. All right, they're closed. Shit, Mr. Magic is hard as Chinese algebra. Between Janet telling me to lick her thighs and all of the mystery, I can't wait anymore. Suddenly, I feel someone slip something over my eyes. While the material is being adjusted, both of my arms are being lifted. They're being tied to the metal rack over where I'm sitting. I've been straddled from behind because I feel two soft breasts sinking into my back as two of the softest hands in the world are caressing my chest . . . Now she's kissing my ear . . . now my neck . . . this feels good. Omigod! Ummmmmmh . . . What . . . UHH-HHH! . . . the mmmh . . . fuck! Oh, shit. She's licking the tip . . . now she's got me all the way in her mouth. One, two, three, four deep throats . . . Ahhhhhhhh! She's sucking the hell out of my shit. Keep going, doll. Keep going. Uhmmmh! Wait! How is she kissing my neck and sucking my dick at the same time! I'm losing it. Damn rule number three or four or whatever. Oh, my God. There has to be more than one woman in this room. I'm squealing like a bitch. Come on, Nat. Take this like a man. Owwwwwwwwwwh! I can't! One of them is playing with an area that I'm ashamed to say feels this damn good. The other's lips are on my neck and chest, and this one right here is sucking me into oblivion. I'm half strapped, half standing now. Somebody's hair keeps brushing my thighs. That feels so good. Deep throat number twenty-one. Damn! My heart can't take this. I'm going to bust. Janet's moaning. I'm going to bust. How many people are in here? Don't do it, dawg. Hold on. Wait. What just happened? The music stopped. Everything stopped. My hands were untied. The host's voice came back on.

"My friends love you, Nat. They all want to entertain you tonight, but only one of them will be able to have you. Which one do you want?"

I heard a few giggles in the background.

"Remove the blindfold and turn on the mini monitor in front of you. When you see the picture of the woman you want for the evening, press the stop button on the remote. She will be waiting for you in the master bedroom."

At this point I am in shock. I have never had head that good in my life. I feel like a punk. I have never been so . . . out of control. Wait. Is my birthday coming up or something? Shit, I can't remember anything right now except for what this woman is telling me to do. I am *so* willing to cooperate. I removed the blindfold and was surprised to see the bathroom in perfect shape. Nothing out of place. Candle burning. Not a person in sight. Is this some crazy shit or what? I do what the voice instructed me to with the remote control, and when the monitor flashed, I saw pictures of three beautiful women dressed in different outfits. One had long black hair like Kendra's and was dressed in a sexy nurse's uniform. The other had short wild hair like Halle's in *007*, with the swimsuit to match. The last one was dressed in . . . in nothing, and I couldn't make out what she looked like. However, I could make out the pleasant sight of her masturbating on what looked like my living room floor. That's all I needed to see. That's the one I want. I couldn't care less about what she looked like. Her body was all I needed tonight. So I pressed stop. And what I guessed to be number three's voice came oozing out of my speakers like warm honey.

> *"Thank you for choosing me. I am yours for the evening. I will do anything you want me to. Kendra will never know. Meet me in your bedroom."*

No problem. Suddenly, I got the feeling that I was cheating on my wife. My dick began to deflate. No, she set this shit up, Nat. Do the damn thing. Stop being a punk. Okay. Carefully, I made my way down the long dark hallway leading to our master bedroom. After about four slow steps, I was pushed up against the wall by what seemed to be two different people. One massaged my dick and the other licked my nipples. Whew! This is some movie shit! I hope I don't get in trouble tomorrow 'cause I'm taking this all the way, baby! If I could, I would kick up my fucking heels. This is good shit. They let up, and I walked a few more steps toward the master bedroom. Preparing to be molested again, I tensed up, but nothing happened. So I continued toward our room. When I opened the door to the bedroom, there she was. The woman in the video. On my bed. Naked. Touching her beautiful body in ways that even I couldn't imagine. She had me captivated. I just stood there like I was at the free throw line.

As she beckoned me with her index finger to join her, I wondered—almost out loud—what was next. Those looked like Kendra's breasts, but with what I think just happened in the bathroom, I'm not assuming anything. With the way the light flickered off of her body, I just wanted to plunge into her right there. She had what appeared to be a satin mask on, keeping me from seeing her face. This is absolutely nuts. Inviting me to join her, she's stroking herself, squirming, and everything else in between. Watching her body quiver is too much for me. Okay, stop staring, man. Playtime. Moving my hands up and down my shaft and watching this beauty please herself is all I need. I came all over her after about a good eight strokes. She didn't even wipe me down. She immediately put her lips on my shit and went to work. Get the fuck out of here. Ummh. She's a bad ass. She had me back up in no time. All right, let's do this, baby. I'm ready. Come with your best. She flipped me on my back and stood directly over me. She told me how good I tasted and that Kendra didn't know what she was missing. Then she slowly slid the mask off, unpinned her hair, and as I watched those soft black curls cascade down her back, there was my beautiful wife looking at me with the most devilish grin on her face that I've ever seen.

"Are you going to tell your wife?" she asked coyly. I decided to play her game.

"Only if you are better than she is. And believe me, no one is better than her."

She sat down on Mr. Magic and let the tip of his head inside her already extremely wet soft spot. As if that wasn't enough, she started to contract and relax her vaginal muscles right on his head. He lost his mind. She won. I'm going to die. Just as I started to call out Kendra's name in agony, she stood back up.

"Kendra is not here tonight. And I *am* better than her. Say it. Say that I'm better."

At this point I will do whatever. Fuck the game playing. Looking at her standing over me with my dick pulsating into my stomach has brought me near tears.

"Baby, you won. I love you, I want you, I need you to breathe. Please don't make me wait any longer. I love you, I love you, I don't care . . . baby, let me have you . . . pleeeeeeeeeese!" A tear slid out of the corner of my eye, trickled past my ear, and slid down my neck. She broke me. I guess she felt sorry for me because she just grinned that sexy grin of hers, slid down on it, and rode me like a jockey. Uhhhhhmmmmm. Yeah, baby . . . baaaaaaby. Then she started to moan. That look on her face always does it for me. She looks so good, so soft, so sensual when she is about to climax. I have to look away. Concentrate.

I want her to get hers. Okay, she's there. Damn, baby. You did it this time. I love you, I love you, I love you is all I'm thinking as I feel one of the biggest orgasms I've ever had start to pull from the center of my stomach and radiate to the tips of my fingers and toes. Before it shoots from the center of my back, through my pelvis, and out of my penis, I yell . . . "Kennnndra! Kennnnnndra! Ahhhhhhh! Kennnnnie!" Fuck the rules.

I woke up to the smell of bacon, eggs, and I think I smell grits. Shit, my entire body is sore. Did what I think happened last night actually happen? If I weren't so weak, I would have thought it was all a dream. I don't think I had an official ménage à trois. I don't know what I had. All I know is my wife did her thing last night. That was pure voodoo. I know she's a psychiatrist, but she took that to unfair and unforeseen levels last night. Let me see if I can make it downstairs. One step at a time. Like an elderly man with prior vertebral fractures. I'm down here. I go over to hug her fine ass, and my dick is getting hard just thinking about it. She lets me know that breakfast is ready and proceeds to tell me that our five-year-old daughter Nile's soccer game was cancelled today and that she's at her mom's house.

"So, honey, what did you do last night? You know Nile's recital was yesterday, so I was there. Did you keep yourself busy here at home?" she asked nonchalantly. Now she's playing games. I was victimized.

"No, you kept me busy, and I'm scared to ask about what happened in the bathroom."

She gave me that are-you-crazy look. She knows damn well that I'm not.

"What happened in the bathroom? Did you flood the toilet again?"

All right. I'm not up for this psychological shit this morning. I want to talk about how she turned me out, ruined me for life, and that how if she dies, I will never be able to remarry because no woman in this world can take me where she did.

"Kennie, enough with the games. I don't know how you did what you did last night, but I love you for it. I am a better man because of it. Baby, com'ere. I want to thank you on the table." She threw her head back and laughed. I eyed her Hopkins degree sitting comfortably next to my own Columbia MBA. I wondered when she would stop using her maiden name Henderson as her professional name.

"My husband is so appreciative. Although I don't know what you're thanking me for, if it involves me being on the table, I'll accept that thanks." Oh, she's slick, all right. That's what I get for marrying a shrink. She's running circles around me this morning. Aight, baby. You got this. This is your house. I'm just renting space. She goes on to say that Derrick called and said that they were going to do dinner tonight and wanted to invite Kendra and me. He also said that the DC grad chapter of our frat was providing volunteers for *DC's Men Are Cooking,* our sister sorority's annual fund-raiser and that he submitted my name as a volunteer. I know him. Payback for sticking him with Garvin and K by himself. That's all right, muthafucka. It was well worth it, dawg. As I look over at Kendra pouring my OJ and her herbal tea, one thing comes to mind. The woman of my dreams.

5

Taiyler

"**D**r. Richardson. Dr. Samuels wants to know if you can squeeze a few more patients in today between what you already have on schedule. He's running behind and doesn't want to reschedule them. Plus, he has to speak at one of the drug programs tonight and doesn't want to be late. What should I tell him?"

Another freaking Monday morning and the bullshit is starting early today. Dr. Samuels, one of the physicians with whom I'm in practice, is always trying to push his patient load off on me. Like I don't have my own work to do. It kills me that people with families—the all-American version, a spouse, two point three kids and a dog—feel as if being single means that you don't have a life. Or that it can't possibly be as full as theirs. They expect you to work late nights and early mornings, cover meetings, and fill in for them just because they think that you couldn't possibly have anything else to do with your time. It starts with a simple *"I can't make this staff meeting because lil' Charlie has a recital, or soccer practice, or a science project due . . . Do you think that you can . . ."* I hate that shit. When I tell them that I have plans, they give me that what-the-fuck-else-could-you-possibly-have-to-do-more-important-than-work look. It's a new form of discrimination. And if they keep pushing me, I swear I'll have Ed Gordon, Al Sharpton, Jesse Jackson, and Kwesi Mfume up in this bitch. The only bad thing in this case is that if the practice doesn't get paid, none of us do. But you know what? Ask me if I care. Nope. Not this time. He's going to have to handle this on his own.

"Tell Dr. Samuels that I would love to squeeze them in, but I have a full load today."

"I know, Doctor, so I took a look at your schedule and figured out how we could squeeze them in without you getting too far behind."

Bitch. Can't stand her. She is determined to make my life harder than it needs to be. I know I could have taken a few more patients on, but damn it, I didn't want to. And this heifer knows that. So because I'm still new here, technically anyway, I decide to go with the flow. For now. But this has got to stop. So I give mega nurse my pageant's best.

"Thanks so much for being proactive about it, Lucy. I'll take a look at what you have. Just know that I'm seeing Ms. Daniels today. You know that I spend a little more time with her than the average patient. So whatever you have worked out will have to be worked around that." Everyone knows that Ms. Daniels is one of my favorite patients.

Everyone here loves her. I had to fight with Samuels to take her on as a patient. I'm the only cardiovascular subspecialty in the building and the only African American physician. Although I didn't offer that as a reason for the switch, I know that she suffered from occasional high blood pressure and her cholesterol was high as a kite. I also knew that Samuels was so pressed to squeeze in patients that he seldom took the time out to treat what he calls "little things" like high cholesterol. The majority of our high-lipid profile patients were African American, Ms. Daniels included. So we made the switch, and I've been taking care of her ever since.

Lucy said that she understood and would send one of the assistant admins back here with the revisions. Damn. This means that I'm going to be here for an extra hour or more, and I have that meeting tonight with the *DC's Men Are Cooking* male volunteers. I guess stopping home to unwind is out of the question. Okay. Let's get this day moving. First patient, mild asthmatic, two puffs of Advair *q.d.*, Albuterol as needed. Send in the next one. Mr. Joseph. Diabetic, glucose and blood pressure normal, titrate him up from Lipitor 10 to 20 milligrams to get his cholesterol down from 151 mg/dl to below 100. Patient number three. Take a little more time, Taiyler. This is a new one. Coughing, tight chest, nighttime awakenings and light headedness: asthma. On second thought, order a chest X ray on this one to check for any walking pneumonia or bronchitis.

"We're going to get you a chest X ray, all right, Ms. Farley?" Shit. I don't think her insurance will cover it. Fuck it, do it anyway. Her insurance can kiss my ass. Next one up.

"Hello, Mr. Francois, how are you? What seems to be the problem today?" Pain in left shoulder. Says it's not piercing, it's throbbing. Burning. Took aspirin, it didn't work. All right. Sounds like more advanced form of arthritis.

"Any history of ulcers?" Nope. No cardiovascular problems either. Perfect, I'm giving him Celebrex, 200 milligrams once a day. Note to self: write him a referral to a rheumatologist.

"Lucy, where's the chart for my next patient?" I'm getting dizzy. I'd better slow my ass down before I end up on the examining table. Patient number five, Ms. Daniels.

"Hi, Ms. D! How are you? You're looking good as usual! What are you, forty-five now?" I always joke with her about how young she looks. She gave a hearty laugh.

"Oh, naw, girl. Is you the docta' and I the patient, o' is it da otha' way 'round? Nah, I know you knows this ol' body is older than it look. It's about as ol' as it feel." We both laughed out loud. She brought me a lemon pound cake. Right on point, Ms. D. Okay, get a grip. Yes, you love her to death T, but you have to stay focused. Let's go.

"Ms. D., how are you feeling? Is the medicine I gave you working on your arthritis?"

"Shol' is, I been able to get down in ma' garden since then. I 'preciates it." Her Georgia drawl was sincere. Made me smile.

"Great. Are you still walking and eating the things we talked about?" I looked through her chart. She has to be. She's lost weight, and at least 30mg/dl on her LDL. I'm proud of her.

"Yeah, I started cuttin' the skins off my meats like you said, and I ain't hardly fryin' nuthin' no mo'. Plus, me and my grandchile walks around the block every day. You know I got a nice nephew for you. You still sangle, pretty as you are?"

I'm blushing. She's always trying to hook me up with a nephew or two. This is how we get off track. Let's see, her lipid profile is finally looking the way I want it to look. LDL and triglycerides are down below 100mg/dl, blood pressure is normal, and her HDL is up. She is ready to roll. Gave her a topical to rub on her joints for the "rainy weather" as she seems to feel like her arthritis "acts up" right before it rains. Big hug and kiss good-bye, and she's taken care of.

Next patient in. Wait. It's lunchtime. I think we have a lunch scheduled with a pharmaceutical company rep. I really don't have time for
that shit today, but I'm hungry as hell, and since I'm going straight to
the meeting tonight I won't have time to eat. So I stroll into the lunch
area as soon as the rep begins to pull out the promotional gifts he
brought in for the office. Pens, notepads, damn. These are nice pens.
He said his manager was on his way in. Great, two of them pushing
this drug information down my throat. At least we're having Italian
this afternoon. We began to talk about the company's drug and how
it compared to others in its class. Every company thinks that their
drug is paramount and that it's best for every single patient that I
have. Wrong! Just as I was about to tell the rep about the side effects
that one of my patients experienced with his beloved drug, one of the
must beautiful men in DC walked through the door. He had creamy
caramel-colored skin, dark thick lashes that almost made his lids stick
together when he blinked, and the type of lips that made you wonder
what his favorite pastime was. Taiyler, get it together, girl. The word
for today is *focus*. Focus. So where was I? That's right. Side effects. We
continued to talk about side effects and other aspects of the drug
throughout lunch.

Some of my partners came in to grab a bite and ask questions. All
the while this rep's manager is watching every word that rolls off of
my lips like he wants to catch any excess saliva that may escape my
mouth before it hits the table. He seems to be trying to play the professional role well, but I know. I know men. Now, I could be imagining
this, so I decide to give it the old litmus test. I take a deep breath and
lick my lips while he's in midsentence, just to see if he'll break stride.
Top one. Bottom one. Stutter. Yeah, Mr. Manager. You are not that
damn professional, are you? I chuckled at his attempt to regain his
composure. He did try, though. That's what counts. As they wrapped
up the presentation, I silently shot ebony man a look that let him
know I was paying attention. He knew it well because he took the bait.

"Excuse me, Dr. Richardson?"

"Yes?" I already knew. The mojo. It'll pull you in if you let it. I
smiled inside. As the pharmaceutical wordsmith groped for words.

"Uh, I—I just wanted to comment on the beautiful bracelet you're
wearing. It's very interesting. Exotic. If you don't mind me asking,
where is it from?" he probed. I held my arm up and examined it as if
I had never seen it before myself.

"Oh, this . . . this I've had for years. I bought it in New York at a festival in Harlem. I believe it's Egyptian," I said as I played with the heavy silver bangle on my wrist. I know he's not really concerned in the least with my bracelet. So I waited. Like clockwork, he struck.

"This is going to seem very unprofessional of me, but may I ask you a question?"

"What, the thousand questions that you just asked me during lunch were not enough?" I answered jokingly. He seemed to take lightly to my sarcasm. Good. A sense of humor is important.

"My apologies for the lengthy session, but all through lunch I wanted to ask you where your family was from. You almost look South American, but I just couldn't figure it out."

"No, I'm not South American. I'm African American. My family's originally from the South," I answered promptly.

"You probably hear this every day, but you are gorgeous. Are you sure you're not mixed with anything at all?"

Okay. I hate this. I just told this man that I am Black. Not South American, not mixed, just Black. Which part of that did he not understand? So I find myself having to clear something up. Again.

"Would it make you feel better about your judgment of beauty if I told you that I were anything other than Black? I mean, you seem to be a little disappointed in the fact that you can't attribute my features to a race of people other than your own." That may have been a little harsh, but I already said it, so fuck it. He looked at me intently. The look that I got from him was the same one that I usually get when a man, Black or White, approaches me with the same dialogue. That *you-are-too-beautiful-to-just-be-Black* commentary. They give the same look that most ignorant people give when they realize that they have issued an insulting comment to someone outside their race. They somehow figure out that it wasn't appropriate, but they just can't understand what made it so. So they apologize, not knowing fully what they are apologizing for. You don't want the apology. Instead, you'd rather have them take an introspective look at solving the problem. Expand their horizons. Here it comes, the apology.

"I'm sorry if I offended you. It's just that it's not every day that you'll find a Black woman with features like yours," he replied.

"And what features are those?" I asked. Clearly with the tone in my voice indicating that I'm losing patience.

"You know, unique features. Your auburn-colored hair, walnut skin.

Plus your eye color. I just figured that you had to be mixed with some-thing, that's all. Believe me, you are still beautiful."

Oh, and what an apology it was. Not realizing the depth of his ig-norance, or the shallowness of his retort. You are *still* beautiful. As if he had to reassure me, and himself for that matter. Don't get me wrong. I don't have a problem with the question he asked; it was the implication behind it. Too many times have I run into men who refuse to give up until they have pinpointed my nationality, as if it were impossible for me to be Black and beautiful at the same time. Or as if these features, *my features,* aren't inherited in members of my race. At all. I didn't borrow my hair or my eyes from someone else. My people were here first. Why couldn't *they* have borrowed them from *us?* My features belong to me. And to my mother. And my grand-mother. And hers. Yes, my eyes are charcoal. Yes, my hair is red. Yes, I am Black. I'm annoyed. I want him out of my face.

"Thanks for lunch, and the cross-cultural commentary, but I have patients to see, with and without unique features. Have a good day." And I left him standing right there in the lunch area dazed, confused, and completely unaware of the impression that he'd left on me—that he was a living example of what our men have morphed into with the help of music videos and magazines. Idiots.

On my way to the meeting with our volunteers for *DC's Men Are Cooking* I had to stop and give myself a quick six-point check. This is a meeting full of DC's finest men, and I look an absolute wreck having worked all day. So I pulled over and ran through the program that my grandma always said worked when you're in a rush. Hair, face, nails, clothing, shoes, spritz. My hair was a mess, so I brushed it and pulled it into a ponytail. I've always wanted to cut this mess, but never had the guts. It's been well past my bra line my entire life, and I've always envied the bold sisters with short, sophisticated cuts. However, on days like this I wondered what they'd do when faced with a few min-utes to get their shit together. Neither one of them can pull a ponytail off without looking like whodunit.

I moved on to my face. I don't really wear makeup. Foundation and blush are a little much to do every day, so I thank God and my mom that I have her skin. I do wear gloss, a nice eyeliner, and shadow, de-pending on the day. Today, it's gloss only. Maybe a little liner under the lids. That's it. I don't have time for anything else. On to the nails.

Perfect. Just had a manicure this weekend. Next up, clothing and shoes. Uh, the lab coat and Pumas have to go. I look like ultranerd. I keep the gray slacks and button-down that I had on and just add the gray matching blazer and my Ferragamos. Great. Now for the spritz. I get out of the car with my favorite bottle of Marc Jacobs in hand and hit all of the pressure points. There, a different Taiyler in less than five minutes. I get back into the car and begin my drive to the Marriott in Greenbelt, Maryland. I reserved a meeting room there for tonight. Shala offered to meet me there to help out. I told her to relax. Save her energy for the actual event. She's always there, whether I need her or not. That's my girl. We still haven't even begun to work through the bomb that she dropped on Saturday, but I'll set aside some time to think about it before the end of the week. Damn, my phone is ringing.

"This is Taiyler." Great. It's Simuel.

"I thought you were in Seattle. Why are you calling me from a 301 number?" I asked.

"Ahm eha tasmouvayo fuha few days."

"Oh, my God, I'm so sorry."

"No."

"What?"

"No, be-be."

Obviously I heard him incorrectly. Shit. I don't have time to try and dissect this accent today.

"What was that, Simuel? You're doing what again? . . . Oh, you're here to smother me for a few days? I thought you said you were here because your brother had AIDS. Sorry about that . . . well, I can't get together tonight because I have a meeting . . . Uh, no, you can't meet me afterwards because I'll be tired . . . Yes, I want to see you . . . no not tonight . . . Tiffany? You got me something? Thanks, we still won't be getting together tonight, though. Whatever it is will have to wait until another time . . . Don't sound so sad . . . all right, me, too. Later."

What am I going to do with this man? He's smitten. I can't blame him. A twenty-eight-year-old man who's never had oral sex before. Then he links up with me, and now he's in love. Go figure. I can't control that. He's buying me gifts left and right and has proposed on more than one occasion. He said that if I lived in his country, we'd be married already. I have to keep reassuring him that this is not his country.

He has showered me with everything from Hermes crocodile bags to three-carat diamond earrings. I keep telling him that it isn't necessary, but he won't stop. I refuse to pick out anything while we're together, so he sends it to me while he's away on contract. Shala calls him Prince Akeem and wants me to place a few orders for her. She's crazy. I fumbled with the CDs in my visor. Found the one I wanted. Rachelle Ferrell. I need to unwind. I'll be pulling into the Marriott parking lot in a few, and if I don't calm down, I'll still be in bitch mode from working like a slave today. I threw my head back, relaxed my shoulders, exhaled, and listened to her sing like her life depended on it. I'd really love to see her live.

I believe . . . there's a doorway to me . . . inside you . . .
I perceive . . . a sure way to love . . . inside you . . .

Sing, girl. This is just what I needed. I continued to let the words envelope me in an array of relaxation. Possibility. Dang. That's deep. Sometimes I wonder if I will ever feel what she's referring to. That oneness. I know I've been in love and I'll fall back into it, but somehow, I've always felt as if there was a stretch of love that I hadn't discovered. I mean, I love my great-aunt more than I've ever loved anyone other than my grandma. I love Shala. I love Lance. But still, this love . . . my intuition tells me that it's different. Rare. And that I'm destined for it. I can't put my finger on it, but it's the type that makes you feel what Rachelle is singing. Seeing yourself in someone else almost seems impossible. Especially for me. I'm too complicated. Whatever the case is, this is not the time to analyze it. I'm here. From the looks of it, so are some fine as hell brothers. Mirror check. Let the games begin.

6

Derrick

"So what we really have here is an opportunity to make a serious difference in the lives of underprivileged children who are intelligent enough to get into college, but just don't have the funds. One hundred percent of the proceeds will go to the Alpha Kappa Chi Scholarship fund. That's the best thing about this fund-raiser. Making a difference. If you look over to your left, you'll see a table with applications, my contact information, and directions to the Convention Center . . ."

I'm sitting here listening to the event coordinator for *DC's Men Are Cooking* tell us how we are going to make a difference by cooking up our best goods, and all I can think of is how I want to cook up her goods. Really. I walked in here prepared to be bored to death by a not-so-attractive, high-strung, highly annoying AKX sister with a high-pitched overly accommodating voice. Instead I'm watching the most beautiful woman I've ever seen in life walk from one side of the room to another as if she doesn't want to leave any one of us out of the conversation. When she came in, I must have been on the phone with . . . It was the doesn't-think-that-I-know-she-wants-to-use-me-to-floss in front of her high-post, low-class friends. I was making an appointment for some ass tonight disguised as *"Yeah, I'll go to church with you on Sunday."* Lord forgive me. She's one of what I'd like to call my talented ten. Educated, well dressed, upwardly mobile, and very easy on the eyes. Because she knows these things she considers herself a good catch and acts like it. She has her way with most men, but clearly I'm another story. Only I don't let her know that, though. She thinks that because she is doing her thing careerwise and goes to church after shaking her ass on Saturday night at the club—oh, excuse me, the "lounge"—with her educated buppie friends, she is different.

My troupe is filled with women just like her who don't realize that the Black college sixteen-to-one ratio of women to men triples in the professional world. These chicks are a dime a dozen. And they are all looking at me. Salivating. Wanting to prove to me that they can be good wives. Wanting to pass me off as their boyfriend or fiancé to their self-righteous, judgmental friends to prove that they are the better woman in the group for having a man that everyone approves of. Honestly, this *tour de femme* that I've been on since undergrad has less to do with me being a renaissance man and more to do with the way women just outnumber us these days. I could go on and on about how great of a catch I am—and most of that would be true—but no bullshit, women are forcing themselves on the brothers right now. We'd be idiots not to indulge. No matter how much some of them get on our nerves. This one, the coordinator for the fund-raiser . . . I dunno. She seems different. Has a certain air about her that says she has absolutely no fucking idea how beautiful she is. So I must have been on the phone when this wonderful creature waltzed in because I'd never let something like that pass me by. I couldn't have seen her come in. Lord knows, if I had, I would have put my thing down right then and there.

Taking a look around, I assessed what I was up against. Normally, there's no real competition for me. But tonight, I'm in a room full of brothers who have their shit together. Just out of the few in here that I know, I've counted at least five physicians, three or four brokers, a federal judge, and a record company exec. That's not counting the brothers who aren't members of the frat. You can't waste time in a situation like this. Some of the guys are married, some aren't. Some wear their rings, some don't. I know one thing; all of us are mesmerized right now. I can tell that my boy Mike, the label exec, is liking what he sees, because he's been smiling ear to ear the entire time like he just bumped into the prince of Zamunda at a basketball game.

This woman walked in, and all the volunteers, frat included, started loosening up their ties, fidgeting in their seats, and concentrating on

her like she was the hardest question on the Virgina State Bar. She
even has Mr. Humphrey, the judge, rocking back and forth like he's
about to tell an old war story. For some reason, she seems to have the
room on edge, sort of like the feeling you got waiting for the OJ ver-
dict to come down, or while listening to the minister Farrakhan's
challenge at the Million Man March. It's like we're in here, intently
focused on this woman. Waiting for a chance to outlet this kinetic energy. Waiting for a change of some sort. Wondering if she takes off
those dark-rimmed frames, will there be a big ugly mole there to
buffer some of that beauty? A wart? Damn, something. That's what
we're waiting for. Something to tell us that what we're seeing isn't
real. In the meantime, she gives us nothing but perfection. While she
transitions from one thought to another, she pauses, exhales, and
licks her lips just enough to tie *Miles Kind of Blue* as the eighth wonder
of the world. It's such a genuinely beautiful act that you want to frame
it and pair it against the perfect picture of apartheid. Just to maintain
the balance in the reality of life. Brother Harris broke the one-sided
dialogue by asking her a question.

"So do we need to put down what we are cookin' on the application?" Dumb-assed question from a dumb-ass muthafucka. Why else
did he think that there was an entire section specifically reserved for
that? Hold up. Not so dumb, though. This will give us the opportunity
to spend just a little more time watching her walk. He's on the other
side of the room. And if luck strikes us hard, she will strut her . . . yup!
There she goes. Good ol' Brother Harris. An old school playa. My
bad, partner. As she walks from her side of the room to his, Mike is
cheesing even harder, and it takes the young brother sitting next to
me all he has not to belt out our traditional "DAAAAAYYUUUMMM!"

While holding his fist to his mouth, he leaned over and whispered
loud enough for the bruhs in Zimbabwe to hear him, "Now *that's* what
I'm talking about! Hey, frat, have you ever seen anything like that before?"

Even though I've been trying to figure out from the beginning of
the meeting whether I have or haven't, a playa can't give that type of
information up voluntarily. Especially to a young buck.

"Yeah, man. She's fine, but a brother has finer in stock." Let's end
that shit right now. The brothers know me for two things. My dedication to the frat and my dedication to pussy. They live their lives
through tales of my nights with different women from all over. Pussy

in Peru. Vagina in Vermont. Coochie in Cali. It's all the same. So I couldn't possibly let a young brother down by giving this woman the credit that she deserved. As I surveyed the guys in this room, I noticed that they didn't seem to be watching her ass or anything in particular. They were piercing the space around her. Interrogating it. Almost as if they didn't think that it was good enough to contain her. There's something about this goddess that I can't figure out. She's an Alpha woman, so I know that she's a good one. Smart. Pretty. Successful. But she seems to be different somehow. Okay, maybe she knows how fine she is, knows she's intelligent, and has gotten over it. Doesn't even notice it. It also seems as if she actually gives a shit about the cause. Now, that would be a first. But that's still not it. The power that this woman has over this room—me included—is coming from somewhere else. Whew! I'm beginning to sweat. Hold up, playa. Get it together. No woman in this world, no matter how beautiful, will throw you into a frenzy like some fat chick at a Ginuwine concert. Make you break stride. Hell no. So much for the pep talk. I'm wiping my brow. How in the world is she doing this to an entire room?

The guy in the corner must know her because he is the only one in here that isn't ready to tell his wife to go to hell or his girl to fuck off. He raised his hand and complimented her on getting the Convention Center this year instead of having it at their usual hotel. As we clapped, she blushed, thanking him for the compliment. Bashfully tossing her ponytail over her shoulder, she assured us that we could call her with any questions at the number provided in the application packet.

Meeting adjourned.

Fuck me for sitting in the back. Now I have to fight my way through fifty hardheads just to get a good look at her. This means that I need to prepare my A game, because if I know these brothers, she will be worn down with cheap one-liners and side comments alluding to her beauty. By the time she gets to me she'll be immune to the game, aggravated, and snappy. I'll have to unravel that ball of worms and then try to get some information out of her. Fuck it. I'm Derrick. It won't be that hard. Still, I can't help but think that I should have worn Miyake tonight instead of Polo Sport. Whatever. Almost my turn at bat. Quick review of the vitals. Don't tell her how beautiful she is, don't compliment her on any part of her body, don't ask for her information until she asks for yours—my thoughts are interrupted by a tap on my shoulder. A guy whose breath smells like fried rice is trying to kill me. A halitosis-cide. I chuckled at how corny I could be. Had to pat myself on the back for that one.

"Uh, I think she's trying to get your attention, frat." Uh-oh. He's right. She's looking this way. She's smiling. Motioning for me to come over to where she is.

"Excuse me, excuse me . . ." I say as I make my way to the front of the room.

"Umm . . . you wanted me?" I offered, a little too clumsily for my taste. But, boy, did I want her to say yes. She cut her eyes at the brother directly behind me, pulled me toward her, and whispered in my ear. Oh, my fucking god. If one of those lips brush my ear one more time, they're going to have to handcuff me. Gat dayum. Keep talking, sweetie.

". . . So I told that pervert that I was with you so that he'd stop telling me how much of my bathwater he wanted to drink. Do you mind?" she asked earnestly. I swear, I saw her mouth moving, but I didn't hear anything coming out of it. All I could gather was the smell of Marc Jacobs and something about bathwater. So I said yes. Yes to whatever it was she wanted, because at that point I couldn't possibly deny her anything in this world if it was her heart's desire.

"Yes?" she replied incredulously while raising her perfectly arched eyebrows and transmitting the look Black women use in abbreviation of the phrase *"I know he didn't just fucking say what the hell I thought he said."* What's her problem?

"Well, I apologize for wasting your time. Don't flatter yourself, it's just not every day that I get harassed by fifty men at a time. Usually there's an intermission of some sort, you know, a break between ignorant comments. Since I've noticed that you won't stop until you outdo the masses . . . please, don't let me get in your way." Now those gray eyes were cutting my way, and I couldn't help but imagine that she gives the same look when she's about to . . . I wanted to see that for myself. I got the weirdest feeling in my stomach. I almost asked her to do it again. Wait! She's walking away. What did I say? All I said was yes. Damn, what did she ask me? I can't chase her. I won't. Not me. Not in front of the bruhs. Fuck! I don't know what car she came in. I didn't get a chance to say shit. Another tap on my shoulder. Fried rice again.

"Dayum, man, what part of your ass did you pull that lame shit out of? You gon' let her get away, dawg? If that were me, I'd be jumpin' her beautiful bones down I–495 right now!" He huffed and puffed, slapping five with one of the other dudes in proximity. I can't stand nosy-ass bruhs. I'm pissed and he's annoying me, so I have no choice. Gotta lay him straight.

"Nigga, you ain't me. If you were, you wouldn't be wearing those cheap-ass shoes, and it would be your face your woman saw every time she touched herself." That one got some *oohs* and *ahhs* from fellow bruhs. Put me back on top. He looked like he was ready to slit my throat. Fuck it. I have more to worry about than this. I need to get out of here, find that woman, and fix whatever it was that I did to piss her off. I need to call Nat.

7

Nathaniel

"Church! Somebody hep' me say . . . Jeeeeesus!"
"Jeeeeeeeeeesus!"
"I said Jeeeeeesus!"
"Jeeeeeeesus!"
"Call his name . . . I said you (ah) . . . Don't know (ah) . . . a what
he's done (ah) . . . fuh me . . . Heyyyyyyyyy!"

I can't help but chuckle as Reverend Matthews, who has to be at least sixty-five years old, almost knocks the floral arrangement over up front as he leaps and sprints from one side of the church to another. No wonder he's healthy as a mule. Sundays at Washington Tabernacle are as entertaining as a P. Diddy performance at an awards show. As the drummer cracks the snare and high-hat, it sends a simultaneous jolt of energy through the already electrified crowd.

"Noooo other name ah know!" the reverend hollered as various church members answered in the standardized call and response fashion of the Black church.

"Jeeeeeeeesus!" they answered to the beat of the traditional stomp and clap rhythm found in almost every Black church in the country. Women and some men, too, are in the aisles jumping and shuffling their feet to the groove of the bass line, organ, and drums. I swear, Washington Tabernacle isn't sending any of their members home without sweat pouring down their necks. Even sitting down I'm sweat-

ing. It may also be from what I like to call the six-hundred-to-four ratio. Six hundred people in this place, to the four extra-large motorized fans that don't spread air past the fourth pew, and contain enough dust to start an asthma epidemic in a matter of minutes. It's okay, though. Church wouldn't be the same without it.

I look toward where the choir is sitting. My wife has her eyes closed and has one hand in the air. She's singing a solo today. That's why I'm here. To hear her sing. I'll get a couple of thank-yous in, too. God has blessed me many times over. Kendra wishes that I came to church more often. If she knew how half the soprano section was trying to give it to me when I did come, she'd never want me here. Church hoes are the worst type. They're the home-wrecking type. Kiss my wife on the cheek, pat my daughter on the head, and pass me their number on the way out. None of them can hold a candle to Kennie on a bad day, let alone a regular one, but you never know what desperation has up its sleeve. So to avoid the drama that can come with regular attendance, once a month is enough for me. As the music starts to calm down a bit, I watch the reverend wipe his face, take a sip of water, and place both of his large hands on either side of the podium. Or as my wife calls it, the pulpit. He begins to tell us that upon the trumpet sounding we will be changed and . . . Who's tapping me? I look over my shoulder, only to meet the nastiest grimace I've ever seen on an old woman. What is it with these church ushers? I don't get it. They get a uniform, an extra set of white gloves, and the authority to separate families and friends at will, and they still grit on you the entire service. She's motioning for me to get up. For what? I wasn't sleeping! Was I? No, I know I wasn't. Who can sleep with the production of *The Wiz* being recreated in the pew right in front of me?

"Why?" I mouthed to the old lady tough enough to be a navy SEAL. I'm not getting up. That shit is embarrassing. She rolled her eyes, gave me that boy-don't-you-make-me-come-over-there look and motioned for what I perceived to be backup. Backup at church. Aight, lady, bring it on then. In a matter of seconds, another usher, a younger one, walks right up to where I'm sitting. The ushers are like gangsters here.

"Your daughter is acting up downstairs in children's church. You need to go and get hu-r'. Now." This one, with earrings the size of cowbells, looked like she just rolled out of the club and came straight here with the same Opium perfume she sprayed on her twelve hours ago.

"Why can't my wife get her? I'm listening to the sermon!" Clearly I'm annoying her by keeping her from moving on to inconveniencing the next unsuspecting victim. After a broad huff and puff, she replied.

"Your wife is in the choir stand, Mr. Woods. You are not. Now, will you please go downstairs and get your daughter before she drives the teachers down there crazy?" Embarrassed by the scene, I silently wished that I had complied with the orders of the first usher as I humbly made my way down the center aisle to the vestibule. Where is children's church again? Obviously waiting for me to ask her, the mean usher vigorously points to a stairwell to the left of me and then shakes her head, as if the church would burn to the ground if I ever set foot inside again. Making my way down the stairs, I was pleasantly surprised by the sound of children singing.

"Yes, Jesus loves me . . ."

As I scan the room looking for Nile, my five-year-old daughter, I find her sitting in a corner looking like Jesus hated her. Not to mention that one of the volunteer teachers almost broke her neck trying to get over to where we were just to tell me that Nile wouldn't stop knocking her feet against the chair and that she was distracting the other children. Whatever. My little princess isn't ignorant. She knows how to conduct herself in public. I bend over and scoop my juju bean up into my arms.

"Baby, what's wrong? They told me you were acting up. Why? You don't like children's church?"

She cuffed her hand around my ear and whispered in her top secret voice, "Daddy, I like it, but I'm tired . . . and Ms. Dawson smells like poo-poop."

I busted out laughing. I could never really control my laughter. In fact, I was laughing so hard I had to put her down. Her face lit up as she continued.

"I want to be with you, Daddy. Why do I have to stay down here?" she proposed as she batted the same eyelashes her mother does when she wants to break me down. They get me every time. I couldn't really come up with anything substantial, and she wasn't going to let me go back upstairs without her even if I had brought NATO's peacekeepers down here with me. Nile is unequivocally a daddy's girl. Wherever I am, she wants to be. She only throws these tantrums on the Sundays that I come to church because she knows they'll tell me to take her upstairs with me. Smart girl. I have to do some chastising. Or it will look like she ran the okeydoke on me.

"Princess, Daddy's not going to come down here and get you every time you decide that you don't feel like staying." There. That sounded good. Kendra is so much better at this than I am. She fingered one of the damn-near hundred-dollar bracelets we got her for her fifth birthday. She's not buying it.

"But you al-ways come to get me, Daddy." With that, she placed her hand in mine and with the confidence of an Olympic diver turned toward the door and waited. As if to say, *you know the routine, old man, don't question the process.* Baffled, I did what any other father would do in that situation. I took her little ass upstairs and pretended that she didn't just boss me into it. She is truly her mother's daughter.

After service, we stood outside and waited for Kendra to come outside.

"There's Mommy!" Nile squealed. There she was indeed. She looks so . . . so . . . pretty. The caramel-and-cream suit that she wore with the scarf and shoes to match gave her such a pure and clean look. She refuses to wear anything too tight or too revealing to church. Totally unlike her spinster choir friends who are hell-bent on cuffing the first man they can find here who didn't make his own outfit. And she still looks like a supermodel. Makes me think of things I shouldn't be thinking of right now. Bible in hand, she makes her way down the stairs and over to where we are standing. Placing a quick kiss on my cheek, she looked as radiant as ever.

"Hi, honey! Did you enjoy the service? Reverend Matthews really preached today. Did you hear me sing?"

After eight years of marriage, I'm still mesmerized by the way she looks after church. Snap out of it and answer her, fool, she's waiting. Blushing, she asked again.

"Sweetie, did you hear me?"

Lying, I squeezed Nile's hand. Our signal to shut up and let Daddy handle it.

"Oh, yeah, I heard the last part . . . you were great as usual, babe." I planted a fat one on her cheek. As Nile giggled, I shot her a look that would have tranquilized a wild horse.

"Are you sure?" Kendra asked, raising her right brow. "Because a certain usher said that a certain little girl made a certain grown man, who will remain nameless because he caused a scene today, rescue her from children's church just as the choir was about to go on. Is this true, little girl?" She gave Nile that knowing look that kids translate into *spill the beans*. Oh, she ain't giggling no more, huh. Don't crumble under pressure, princess. Don't tell her you punked me again. Please. It'll be bad for both of us. Nile did what she usually does when found guilty. She hid behind my leg and sang in the sweetest voice that she could find.

"Sorrrrrry, Mommy!"

"Nat, what did I tell you about spoiling that girl like that?" Kendra asked disapprovingly. "She only does that crap when you're here. I can't believe you allow her to walk all over you like that. And you, young lady, know better." She looked down at Nile. Grabbed her chin with one hand, grabbed mine with the other.

"Anyway, are you ready to go, hon?"

Am I! I was ready when that usher looked at me like I had leprosy. Just as we were walking to the car, my cell phone rang. Looking at the screen, I could see that it was Derrick. Damn, I know he wants to talk about the weekend I missed, and I really don't feel like hearing his mouth. So I hit the END button on my phone to silence the ringer. It rang again. Derrick again. It must be important because he'll usually just leave a message.

"What up, D?" I asked.

"What up, Nat?" he replied. Started before I could say I was busy.

"Yo, you're not going to believe the shit you missed last weekend . . ." As he began giving me the rundown on the weekend, I couldn't help but notice how uneventful it sounded. I'm really glad that I'm married. These guys really believe that the bullshit they run in the clubs and jumping from woman to woman is better than coming home to Kendra every night. Don't get me wrong, I do have fun with my boys. I just wish that they would engage themselves in a different kind of fun. Instead of the same old routine. Get dressed, go to the club, drink each other under the table, fight over the five pretty faces in the club out of the five hundred women there, and come home drunk, funky, and with no love to show for it. I can count on one hand the number of women that they have gotten in clubs. Derrick doesn't even pick up chicks at the clubs. His women are the snobby, educated types that only go to the clubs once or twice a year on invitation. So I don't even know why he goes at all.

"Did you hear me, man? I said she was the most beautiful woman I've ever seen!"

"From the club?" I asked. I hoped not.

"Naw, dawg! Have you heard anything I said? The event coordinator for *DC's Men Are Cooking*! I met her at the meeting. She had every man in there under her spell. Even me, man. I'm telling you! It was like watching that around-the-rim shot MJ made during the '91 championship. Niggas were just sitting there watching her with their mouths open. Un-fucking-believable! I'm trying to get at her. But she doesn't seem like the type to fall for the usual," he said. This sounds good. He hasn't referred to her as a bitch once. The last time I remember Derrick getting this excited over a woman was back at HU. He continued.

"Then she leaned over and whispered something in my ear, but I was so into her that I couldn't make it out. Anyway, to make a long story short, somehow I ended up screwing shit up, because she made some smart-ass comment to me, then spun off like I was the most ignorant person she'd ever met. So, Nat, you're good with situations like this, or you used to be before Kendra opened a can of whip-ass on you. What do I do to get in good? I mean, she could be the future Mrs. DeCosta."

At this point, I'm confused as hell. She must be finer than the women he has on staff. With Derrick, it's never deeper than that.

"I don't know what to tell you. I'm still trying to digest this. You met a fine-assed woman who didn't sweat you like a bill collector. She had you so fucked up that you couldn't get right to work your mojo on her, ended up looking stupid, and you want me to help you turn things around. I would say that this is monumental. Most of your women pretend not to like you at first, but you have never *ever* been at a loss for words in front of any of them," I reviewed.

"I know, man, I know. That's what I'm saying. I'm out of character, Nat."

I thought for a moment.

"Why don't you come by for dinner? Kendra cooked as usual, and we can talk about it then."

"Aight, man. Good looking out. I'll swing through in about an hour and a half." We hung up. I leaned over and kissed my beautiful wife on the cheek. I hope she doesn't get upset.

"Baby, can Derrick come by for dinner?"

She sucked her teeth. Inhaled. Uh-oh.

"That's funny, I thought that he was already coming by. Why would you need my approval?" she replied with the sarcasm of a Neiman Marcus salesperson talking to a sixteen-year-old Black girl. I deserved it. I should have at least run it by her first, even if I knew she would say yes. So I retreated to my apologetic voice. The one I use when she wears heels with nothing else but . . . heels.

"Sorry about that, honey. Really, I am. It's just that he needs help with a situation he's in."

"And you just happen to be the only one who can help on a Sunday afternoon."

I looked at her with a look that spelled *Taa-daaaa* on my face. "That's right."

"Oh, has Shelly stopped giving it up to him after years of being run amuck? Or did he get caught with his pants down again?" she asked.

"No, this is actually different. He said that he thinks he met his future wife at the fund-raiser meeting last week and that he needs some advice on how to get at her. None of his player shit worked. Can you believe that? Derrick, babe. Derrick. This woman must have put something in his food. Anyway, is that okay?" I asked.

"Yes, that's fine, sweetie, I'll just whip up another steak. Besides, I'd love to hear about anyone who can hold Derrick's attention for more than three minutes," she said as she smiled and locked Nile into her seat belt. God couldn't have created a better example of a woman.

"Nat! Nat! Honey, I need you to run to the store for me! I've run out of frosting!" Dang. What is it about women that they always seem to pick the most crucial moment in a game to ask you to run somewhere or do something?

"Ken, I'm watching the game, sweets! You checked all the cabinets?" I yelled in frustration.

"Yes!" she yelled back. "I need frosting if you want this lemon cake today. It will only take a few minutes!"

Shit. Why me?

"Okay, I'm on my way. Write the brand down so I don't forget!" I hear her coming downstairs. We have a five-bedroom single-family home in which this room—the basement—is the only room in the house that belongs completely to me. Kendra set it up for me with a pool table, autographed, framed jerseys from my favorite ballplayers, and a sixty-inch plasma screen television. As if that wasn't enough, she bought that leather recliner from Brookstone that massages your entire body from head to toe. I have my own little pantry with snacks and a mini fridge. The crew calls it the boom-boom room because of the serious surround sound system she had installed. The best thing about it is that it's soundproof. I can play my trumpet down here without disturbing anyone. When I'm stressed out, I trot down here, pull Lucille out of her case, start out with "In a Sentimental Mood," and end with something that rivals the torment of "Bitches Brew." I head back upstairs feeling cleansed. Time down here is time well spent. I'm sure it was money well spent, too. I was scared to ask how much all of this stuff cost, and Kendra never brought it up. She just said "happy birthday," and we christened the massage chair the right way. Now she wants me to leave all this in the middle of the Wizards' game to get some damn frosting? Women.

"All right, baby, I'm gone. When Derrick gets here just tell him I'll be back in a little bit."

When I arrived at the grocery store, I was immediately reminded of the fact that I hated the supermarket with a passion. Noisy White kids telling their mothers what they ain't gon' do, noisy Black mothers telling theirs what they ain't gon' get. The way it takes forty-five minutes to locate small things you need like frosting or toothpicks, while a huge lawn mower or extra-large-sized aluminum pot is advertised right up front. I finally found the brand of frosting that Kendra wanted. Seeing that it was the last one, I went for it. Not realizing that I wasn't the only one grabbing for it, I bumped elbows with a woman who seemed more than a little annoyed with the fact that we were aiming for the same thing.

"Uh, excuse me. I was going to grab that," she said nonchalantly.

"Uh, yeah, I was, too," I replied.

"That's great, but I was here first. Maybe they have some more in stock for you," she said with the same finality that my daughter used when bossing me around earlier this afternoon. Okay, to borrow a phrase from Derrick, this bitch is reeeeeeeeally bugging me. Let's replay this. She was standing here looking for something in her purse, I walked up beside her, we both reached for the frosting, bumped into each other, and drew back. Technically, I could be a gentleman and offer her dibs on it, but she's so fucking arrogant, I think I'll pass on that. So I let her know the obvious.

"Why would anything in a stockroom be of my concern? Better luck next time," I said as I grabbed the container off of the shelf before she even realized that I had it. She was fuming.

"Wow, and they say chivalry is dead. Such a fucking gentleman." She took a quick glance down at my left hand. Aimed her venom at my ring finger.

"God help your wife."

As I was about to verbally sting her ass, something weird happened to me. I took a look at this woman. A good look. Something about her seemed so . . . familiar. Her eyes were like two blades cutting off my already limited supply of oxygen. I couldn't tell if this was how they were naturally or if they were just like that because she was pissed. Her hair was red. Like an auburn color. My stomach started turning, and I started to sweat a little. I must be coming down with something. Whatever this is it's making me feel really weird. It was an energy flow unlike anything I've ever experienced before in life. You know that feeling that starts out as a minor pinch at the center of your being and radiates out to every extremity it can find? I was stuck at the beginning of that feeling. The shit was ripping through me. Cutting me up. Open. I feel nauseated. Nervous. Like I'm about to present in front of the seniors at work. I need to get out of here and get home so I can lie down. I'll just let her know that she can have the shit. That's what I'm going to do.

"Umm . . . you can have the frosting, miss. I'll go to another market."

She blushed. I felt worse. What the fuck was that? She looked away, as if ashamed for cursing me the hell out. I wanted to somehow save that frame of her, the way she looked when she just did that . . . made that face . . . She looked like . . . I can't describe it . . . I can't look. Breathe. Gather yourself, Nathaniel. Give her the container and walk off. Just walk. She licked her lips, said something else, turned around, and hurriedly walked away from me. And there I was, left standing there with lemon frosting in my hand watching her walk away. Watching her walk.

8

Taiyler

"So are you going to meet up with Simuel while he's in town? You know he acts like he's being deported if you say for a second that you can't see him while he's up here. Plus, I know he's got some outlandish gift for you. What will it be this time? The friggin' Hope Diamond? Shit, ask him if he wants to see two lesbians get down. I need my credit cleared . . ."

I'm laughing so hard that I almost have to pull over. I can't believe this girl has me cracking up like this. Actually, I can believe it. My stomach is in knots, tears are running down my face, and she just will not quit. Between sniffles, I mustered up a response.

"No, girl, I told him that I'd check with him later. I was on my way to the fund-raiser meeting and didn't have the energy to deal with him at the time. Besides, I'm not in any real need for dick. In fact, I just got some a few days ago, so truthfully there's no need to rush seeing him."

"Bitch, pleeeze. You better get downtown to see Prince Akeem and stop acting like you don't care that he has something for you," she said, chuckling slyly.

"I don't." I sucked my teeth. Really, I don't.

"What if he got you that bracelet you wanted, girl? You know he doesn't let a word you say hit the ground."

Hmmmh, good point. That is a possibility. Light decisions.

"What, do you think I should get with him, get my bracelet or what-ever, and be out? That's kind of trifling, but that would have to be it because I don't feel like giving him any conversation or coochie, and I know his starving ass can't even look at me without his abnormal-sized penis giving me the ol' salute." I can hear her snickering in the background. She rates my sexcapades as pure comedy.

"I don't know how you deal with that. Even when I was having sex with men I couldn't take 'em too big. It was just uncomfortable. Well . . ." She paused. "If you don't feel like being with him, at least get your shit. Because all he's going to do is end up sending it to you anyway. At least give him the pleasure of seeing you." Shala the softie. Feels sorry for everyone. She has yet to understand my point. The man works my nerves.

"It's not just that, Sha. It's all of the talk about him making me his wife and how he wants to take me to Nigeria, and frankly, I just don't feel like dealing with that today. Or tomorrow for that matter. He knows I can afford my own. That just turns him on even more."

"Well, then, why do you deal with him at all?" she asked.

Good question. I can think of more than a few reasons. But I want to change the subject. I just have something against giving this much mental energy to someone or something that I don't really care too much about.

"I don't know, Shala. But let's not waste any more time on Simuel. We have more important issues to tackle. Have you put any more thought into what we discussed last weekend?"

She paused. Thought. She wants to avoid it. It's too important. So I'm not letting her. Not this one.

"What are you talking about? We discussed a lot last weekend." She toyed.

"Bitch, don't play with me. You know *exactly* what I'm talking about. You were claiming that the key to a better life is through heterosexu-ality and that you wanted to make a change for the better."

She took a deep breath before replying as if I just reopened a wound.

"Yeah, I've thought about it. I don't know what I'm going to do. When I got home, Grai had this whole spa thing laid out for me. She had candles lit everywhere, some relaxing music playing, girl, the works. As if she knew just how stressed I was. I took a hot bath, and she gave me a full body massage. You know what happened after that.

She reminded me of why I was with her in the first place. So needless to say, we had a good night. I had stopped thinking about it until you brought it up . . ."

As a woman who loves men, I can't stand it when Shala gets into these descriptive moods where she wants to give me a play-by-play analysis of her escapades with Grai. As her best friend, I just grit my teeth, bear it, and listen. She listens to me when I feel like painting an all too vivid picture of my sex life, so I give her the same respect. Even if it makes me sick to my stomach sometimes.

"Can we change the subject, T? I know that I need to deal with this, but today I'm not in the mood to analyze anything," she said dejectedly. I felt bad. This is really messing with her. So I complied.

"No problem. Whenever you want to talk you know I'm there. I tell you what, though. You're not going to believe this shit. At the fundraiser meeting last Monday night, why, I did meet the *Essence* Man of the Year."

Hand over mouth, she let out a gasp to rival any Emmy Award-winning drama queen. She's such a girl.

"Ahhhhh . . . You did? Get the hell out of here! How was he? Was he stuck on himself? If I remember correctly, he was exceptionally handsome, and you know that's a lot coming from me," she said excitedly.

"Yeah. When he walked in I thought he looked familiar, but of course you know I wouldn't dare say anything to him. So I kept racking my brain, trying to figure out where I'd seen him before. Then all of a sudden it hit me. The *Essence* Man of the Year. Live and direct. He was fine as shit, girl. I mean better than he looked in *Essence*," I told her.

"Stop it! So what happened? I know your ass didn't leave without putting the business on him! Did you run the 'give and go' on him while you were giving your presentation? I know you did something serious because if what the article says is true, then that's urgent material right there. From the looks of it, I'm sure every woman in the city is after him!" she exclaimed. Of course I did. The shit just didn't work.

"Now, Sha. When have I ever been concerned about the competition, huh? Really, give me a break," I issued more confidently than I felt. She didn't make things easier.

"When have you ever tried to buckle down the *Essence* Man of the

Year? That's like me meeting Ms. Halle in person. I wouldn't know
what to say if she sat her fine ass in front of me at a meeting." She did
have a point. Women probably do flock to him. I went on to tell her
about how I called him up front to shield me off from the vultures
and how his arrogant ass played me. She was surprised.

"Damn, girl. He said that even after the hand on the neck and the
whisper in the ear and everything? I don't know about him. But on
the flip side, you did say that he was staring at you the whole time,
right?" she asked in confirmation.

"Yes. Shala, I'm telling you, I haven't been wrong about something
like this in a while. But when I spoke to him, he just stood there looking at me like I had two heads. Then when I asked for his help, he
acted like I had asked him for directions to the damn welfare office.
So I left. You know I don't overexert myself for anyone."

She sighed. "I don't know, did you see a ring on his finger?"

"Hell no! If I did, I wouldn't have said anything to him! You know
how I am about marriage! My grandma and grandpa were married
until death—" She cut me off before I could get one foot on my soapbox.

"I know, I know, T. I was just saying . . . anyway aren't you going to
see him at the fund-raiser?"

"Yeah, but *Essence* Man or not I'm done. I'm not doing anything
else. If I was right about him, he'll come around. I'm not putting too
much energy into it. Listen, I'm almost home. I'm turning in to my
subdivision now. I'll call you later on," I said as I approached my
street. Damn, phone ringing. "Hold on Sha." I pressed the FLASH
button on my cell phone. These damn buttons are too close to each
other.

"This is Taiyler . . ." I say, naturally. Almost sounding like my
mother. I didn't hear anything, so I repeated the greeting. Suddenly a
male voice emerged. A sexy one.

"Hello, um, is this Taiyler Richardson?"

"Depends on who wants to know. Who is this?" I decided to humor
him.

"Uh, this is Derrick DeCosta, one of the volunteers for the fund-
raiser next weekend. Is this Taiyler?"

"Yes, this is, hold on, Derrick. I have a call on the other line."
FLASH.

"Shala, that's one of the volunteers from the fund-raiser. I'll call you right back."

"You gave a bunch of men your cell phone number?" she asked in disbelief.

"Yeah, I had to give them something! I gave them my decoy, you know, the one for the B team and other bench players. The only others I had were home and office. And the decoy never rings at night, because folks think it's my daytime number. Remember who you're dealing with, chica."

She laughed. "I forgot this was your decoy number. All right, girl, call me back," she said. I hit the FLASH button again.

"Hello? I'm back. What did you say your name was again?"

"Derrick," he replied confidently. The name sounded familiar as hell. Well, what did he want? Not waiting for him to let me know the reason for his call, I advanced the conversation myself.

"Were all of the instructions clear in the packet, Derrick?"

"Yes, they were. I just had one additional question for you."

"Shoot," I answered bluntly. Determined not to make this a fifteen-minute conversation, I edged him on a little more, "I'm all ears, Derrick."

"Well, I just wanted to be clear on a few things. The event starts at twelve in the afternoon, but the packet is not clear as to what time the volunteers should arrive. Also there is no information regarding chafing dishes and whether or not they would be provided to warm the food or if we needed to bring our own."

I know I went over this.

"All volunteers should arrive no later than ten A.M. for registration and setup. As for the chafing dishes, you'll need to supply your own. Sorry that wasn't in the packet, but I think I went over those items at the meeting." As a matter of fact I'm sure that I did. But men don't listen, so why did I figure that I'd be getting more calls like this for the next five days up until the event? Slightly perturbed, I asked him if he had any more questions. He sounded like he wanted to say something else, but decided against it.

"No, that's all. See you on Saturday," he said. As we hung up, I couldn't help but think that his voice sounded a little more than familiar. I'll figure it out later. For now, I need to get out of this garage and into my house.

* * *

Peppermint tea. Coltrane. All two hundred and forty-one pages of Jenoyne Adams's first epic tale. Stretched out on the lamb's wool rug in my living room, sipping, listening, and reading on a Sunday evening is the life. It can't get any better than this in terms of relaxation. My home is comfortable. I did all of the design myself. From the exposed brick to the honey-colored wine room and lounge area, I'm proud. The house was built from the ground up last year, and I'm the first to break it in. Feels good as hell. I'm still doing some work on it, but I am pleased with what I've already done. The skylights illuminate even the most dismal areas. The glass walls are functional as they are artistic. Being able to look right out from my living area to the ink-colored pool adds a sense of tranquility that can't be bought. And my favorite addition is actually on the exterior. They say that you can take the girl out of Brooklyn. You can't take Brooklyn out of the girl. They're partially correct in that assumption. I decided that I would bring my hometown along with me to Bowie. The huge brownstone-style steps were the icing on the cake.

Bebop . . . da, da daaa duh . . . bop de de be bop . . .

Trane is the man. Art, music, and reading are my passion, so all of my accent walls are covered in contemporary canvas oil and acrylic prints by some of my favorite African American and international artists. Sometimes I get emotional thinking about where I am in life and how hard it was to get here. People see me get into my car, or walk into my home, and somehow get the impression that this was given to me on a silver platter. That I didn't work like a dog to get it. They are one hundred percent wrong.

Sinking into the chaise in the reading room of my living area, I allowed the herbal tea to soothe me. A perfect way to buffer the beginning of another hectic workweek. Not to mention *DC's Men Are Cooking* is this coming weekend. So I'm going to savor this time to myself while I can. Sometimes I take a look at all that God has blessed me with and wonder why he hasn't struck me down for playing hooky from church all of this time. At least put me out on the street. Well, as my grandma used to say, "Thank God for life." Speaking of, I need to call my great-aunt. Although we speak almost daily, Sunday evening is our teatime.

She along with my grandmother took my sisters and me in while my mother was going through a really rough time. They had just retired from years of working for one of the best mental health hospitals in New York and still took us in. I was five, and my sisters were ten and three. They clothed us, fed us, cared for us when we were sick, put up with our fresh mouths as we were going through adolescence, and attended all of our school functions no matter how many buses they had to take. They made sure that we grew up with all of our cousins and instilled in us a value system that only comes through that traditional Southern upbringing, even though we were in Brooklyn. At twenty-nine years of age, I still say "yes, sir" and "no, ma'am" to anyone with a speck of gray in their hair. We never went to school without a full breakfast and never went to sleep without a hearty dinner. I don't know how they did it with their incomes, a mortgage, bills, and us three, but they did. And I am so thankful to them for it, because I would not be who I am today without them. Due to their endless love, teachings, and values, I developed a serious work ethic. Graduated from high school at sixteen. Spelman at twenty. And now I'm here. I wish my grandmother could see me now. She passed right before my high school graduation. If that wasn't one of the worst days of my life, I don't know what was. It took me years to come to grips with it.

After that day, my great-aunt stepped up big-time. She was already a huge force in our lives, but she pressed even harder to make sure that my sisters and I had what we needed to make it through. When Lance got my car towed because of the tickets that he didn't pay, she gave me the money to get it out. The summer before college graduation, I came home broke as a joke, with a part-time job at Banana Republic and the remainder of my chemistry courses left to take in summer school. She gave me train fare, made breakfast and dinner, and made sure that I had everything I needed to pass those courses and get my *"narrow behind"* out of school.

My sister Andrea, the oldest, was always in a jam. Usually, because of one guy or another. I remember one situation in which she had moved to West Virginia, of all places, with a man who was known to beat her to a pulp if he felt she was stepping out of line in any way. My aunt wouldn't let him stay at the house, and Andrea got pissed. She disrespected my aunt in ways that caused me to drive to New York from Georgetown right in the middle of exams with all intentions to whip her fucking ass down. She called her names, threw things around in the house and all, just because my aunt was doing something that was best for her. My youngest sister, Dion, called me in tears to let me know about the commotion. I put on my sweatpants, packed some Vaseline for my face, and hit the road ready to knock Andrea what we call the fuck out.

When I got to the city, Drea was packing her shit en route to West Virginia with her "Ike Turner" boyfriend. Regardless of everything that Andrea said and did, my aunt still wouldn't let me get at her. Out of respect I complied, but I made it clear to her that if I ever caught her on the street, her ass was mine. How dare she disrespect my aunt like that? After all she and my grandmother sacrificed for us. A few weeks later, my youngest sister called again, saying that Aunt Mae had just left for West Virginia to pick up Andrea. She was in trouble again and wanted to come back home. My aunt said that what Drea did at the house a few weeks prior didn't matter. What mattered was that she needed help now, and if her family wouldn't help her, then nobody would. When they got back, I called to talk to Aunt Mae. I let her know that she needed to put her foot down with Andrea and that I was coming back up to help her do it. She responded in a way that made me feel as if she were beginning to lose her mind. She said that everybody needed help. No matter who you were, or what you made out of yourself in life, everybody needed it. She relayed that God was the only one she answered to. She didn't need an apology from Andrea or orders from me. God took care of her, and she would do the same thing all over again even if she was treated worse than Andrea treated her.

I really didn't understand how she could qualify the fact that she let a young lady who she loved, raised, and fed disrespect her more than a stranger on the street ever would, without smacking the shit out of her. But I listened and didn't dispute her. The conversation ended with her reprimanding my attempts to get her to cut Andrea off. But with Aunt Mae, it never did sound like she was chastising you. Even when she was. I remember her words clearly.

"Taiyler, baby, everybody makes mistakes in life, and everybody needs hep' sooner o' later. They'll come a time when you gon' need it, too, so you hep' those in need so that God will hep' you when you need it."

Speaking of help, I'm going to need Aunt Mae's help with some of the dishes that I'm cooking for next weekend. Even though the event is called *DC's Men Are Cooking*, the women usually make a few dishes themselves. This year I'm frying catfish, making potato salad, and devil's food cake, and I need her help with all three. As I headed toward the kitchen to finish unpacking the grocery bags, my mind began to form the image of the man I bumped into at the market. I got such a funny feeling inside when I looked into his eyes. I usually stare people down when I'm giving them an earful. He was arrogant and selfish, but his eyes said something else. When he looked directly at me, I felt a rush. Dizzy almost. It got so strong that I had to divert my eyes from his. I can't explain it. He was handsome, but not nearly as fine as most of the men that I'm drawn to, so I can't say that this was a physical attraction. I don't even think that attraction is the right word to describe it, because he didn't look like my type at all. It was more like an energy of sorts. Whatever it was kind of scared me, because the only way I could gain control of it was to walk away from him. Talk about weird. Oh, well. This shit isn't worth analyzing. I have bigger fish to fry. Literally.

9

Derrick

Pissy-assed mattresses. Free lunch. Long lines for government cheese. Basketball goals made from milk crates on telephone poles. Games made up. Hot peas and butter. Red light/green light. Hide and go get it. Televisions running on the outside. So that everyone could watch. Fiends shooting up on the inside. So that no one could see. What we had. Opportunity for failure. What we didn't. Opportunity to succeed. What I remember, all of it. What I don't . . . how I made it out. As soon as I hit Alabama Avenue, childhood memories flooded my mind like a dam held together with wood glue. Some are great. Some aren't. All are unforgettable. No matter how much anyone who grew up sandwiched in ghetto life tries, they can't remove the imprint that it leaves on your being. We are who we are because of these experiences. Good or bad. I cherish them all. Which is why I do what I do. Stay visible. Keep my key to the hood on the same ring that houses the key to my Rover. Listen to them jingle songs in the key of life over and over again, until I've memorized each note. It's a long song, but it's the only one that describes who I am. A man who owns mutual funds diversified to fit his lifestyle. Home in Georgetown. Still at home in the hood. As I pull up in front of the barbershop that my father took me to for my first cut, I let out a deep breath. Parking is a bitch around all of this broken glass. Kids are playing football in the middle of the damn street, and a crackhead is trying to sell me an electric toothbrush. Georgetown is nice. I love where I live. And despite the customary and inconvenient activity of the hood, I have even more love for where I grew up. So I park, hand Tony a five to watch my truck, and head on into the shop. My heart will always be here. Plus, I can't get a decent haircut anywhere else.

"I done said it, and ain't no more to be said about it! Halle won that Oscar 'cuz she was fine and fuckin' dat fella like a rabbit in that movie! I saw it, I saw it all, and if she would'a gave me some like that, I'da gave her ass a Oscar, a Emmy, a Grammy . . . A NAACP award, the Nobel Peace Prize . . . a Purple Heart . . ."

As the shop erupted in hysterics, I shook my head and couldn't stifle a laugh if I wanted to. Willie Lee, or Wil-a-lee as some of the older guys call him, is a nut. Between him cutting and splicing verbs to his liking or simply making up words of his own, he kept all the younger cats at the barbershop in stitches.

"And I'll tell you another thang!" he continued even louder. He was on a roll now. "That Puff-diddy, or P-daddy, or whatever he call himself is a homo-ses'ual!" Another round of wild laughter. The young guys laughed the hardest. Wil-a-lee is known for employing as many Howard University students as he can. He always wanted to attend what's referred to as "The Mecca of Black Intellectualism." To him, that's the only school there is for Blacks to attend in the country. I don't even know if he's ever been on another campus. One of the Howard boys slid the towel from around his neck and threw it at Willie while cracking up.

"How did you get from you giving Halle the Nobel Peace Prize to Puffy being a homo?" the young buck asked.

"I seen it in one a dem' magazines y'all read and be leavin' all over the shop. The *Extra Large* . . . or something like that. It was in nere," Willie explained. As the fellas tried to figure out what the hell he was talking about, he continued. "It don't matter where I seent it. The boy prances around like Lil' Richard at Harlem Boys Choir practice!" Willie shouted. And he was serious.

As run-down as this shop is, with the door barely on the hinges, the brownish green paneling on the walls hanging off, and the wood literally coming up off of the floor, you still couldn't pay me to get my hair cut at another shop. I've been to barbershops all over, the ritzy ones that offer you cognac to the ones that even have live jazz performances. I still choose to come into South East to get a five-dollar shape-up or an eight-dollar haircut in my old neighborhood.

Coming here once a week keeps me grounded and close to the issues that are keeping my folks in what seems like a never-ending slump. It kills me to see the kids doing acrobatics on those nasty mattresses. It's a constant reminder of what I need to do here. I mean, at least stay visible so the kids will have some hope of getting out of this shit hole.

But visibility isn't all. My heart is in investment. Real estate. Commercial and residential. I've made some pretty decent strides financially in rehabbing and reselling old homes downtown. Now that I have the means, it's time to do what needs to be done. Knock these projects down. Build affordable housing for my people. Open up a recreational center. A real one. Not one of those tired-assed project community centers. There's a difference.

Real rec centers have equipment for all sports available. They have computer training courses for young people, sewing and knitting for the elderly. They have qualified karate and basketball coaches. They have swimming pools with water in them. There's a huge difference.

I drive down here every week since I came back home for law school, and I'm going to keep driving down here until I get something done. So that I won't lose touch. I'm not letting the Range and the plasma TV go to my head. Never. So I'm in the hood. Plus, no one does a better job shaping up my shit. When you come out of this shop you leave with your jaws or stomach hurting from laughter, and your cut looking like a million bucks.

Kane, my barber, summoned me to the chair. "You up, man. Whatchu want?" he asked like he really didn't give a shit. Customer service in the hood. We're still working on it.

"Uh, I want a close Caesar—not too close, though—and round the back, don't square it. My regular. And line my tee up."

"Aight." He nodded and went to work. Meanwhile, one of the patrons managed to figure out that the magazine Willie was talking about was *XXL*, the hip-hop magazine. Before the guys could discredit Willie's story entirely, dude spoke up for him.

"Oh! Nah, y'all, hold up! He means *XXL*! It's like *The Source* magazine except it has better articles. He just called it extra large!" The patron along with everyone else in the shop is laughing so hard that his barber has to shut the clippers off. Willie defended himself.

"Damn it! Tha's what I said! When ain't extra large and XXL been the same gat'damn thang! And it don't matter where I got it. That boy got sugar in his shoes and can't nobody 'spute dat!"

They commented, interrupted, and disputed one another with antics that ranged from comical to almost violent. Then all of a sudden Tyrone, or Ty-Ty as I refused to call him due to the fact that he's a grown-assed man, signaled for my attention.

"Yo, D! I'm starting a business up, and it's mainly gon' be targeted toward women. I need you to holla at some of your shorties for me." This is the fifth business he's started since I've known him. I met him last year.

"What kind of business? Because you know what happened the last time I hooked you up. And why do all of your business schemes involve women? Especially mine?" I asked him.

"First of all I'm insulted. Truly, dawg. This ain't no scheme. It's a sure thang, and I know that you tend to have women on call, and fine ones at that, so I'm asking you to hook a bruhva up. Is that so hard? We ain't all ballin' like you, playa!" he said jokingly.

"Damn, Ty, you say 'on call' like I'm pimping these women. I can't make them do anything they don't want to," I said, wanting to believe that myself. Why did I even set myself up for that one? All I heard were snickers from the guys. Willie glared at me with a don't-even-try-it look on his face.

"Boy, don't make me come over there," Willie said. "You, me, and everybody else knows you need to settle down with a nice lady, ya hear me, fella? One, not twenty. Yaundastand?" Since he acted like he wasn't going to finish cutting his customer's hair until I answered him, and he's known me since I was starting fires in garbage cans, I muffled a simple, "Yeah, I hear you," so we could dead the issue. I was about to finish inquiring about Ty's business when the young Howard boy raised a pretty good question.

"Hey, D. I see the women that come to get you from here sometimes or meet you here on the way to wherever you're going, and they're all gorgeous. Wifey types. Plus, they seem smart. And nice. And paid. You ain't seen *nothing* you want in any of them to make you wanna marry one?" he asked innocently. Why am I under fire today? Since he looked like he really wanted to know, I obliged him with the truth.

"It's not that none of them have anything, but not one of them has everything. I'm a picky man. With a short attention span. A woman has to have everything I want in one package or else I won't be able to stay focused on her. As soon as I meet another woman who has something that she doesn't, I start to lose interest. I just haven't found the one." I was as sincere as I could be with him.

"Or if you hit it." He grinned.

"Or if I hit it." I grinned back. Got up. Paid Kane for the cut. "But when I meet that special one, you'll be the first one to know. Aight?" I dapped him up.

"Aight, man. Holla at me later, D," he replied.

I said my laters, gave my pounds, and walked out into the cold with one thing on my mind. I do need to settle down. I know that. I can't ever let on to the guys that I really want that right now, or else I'll look like a failure for not being able to put it together. Truth be told, I know that I'm doing my thing as far as the ladies are concerned. Most guys don't even have one good woman to choose from, and I have at least nine or ten. I don't even know how I ended up with that many. My mama would kill me if she knew what was up. God rest her soul.

The truth is, it's her fault that I haven't found a woman to suit my standards. She was an exceptional woman. The longer she lived, the more beautiful she became. My pop says that she just came down like an angel and rescued him from himself. He used to run the streets, in and out of the clubs, running numbers from pool hall to pool hall. Shit, he had more women then than I do now. And those are the ones he can remember.

I remember one day when I was about seven, while thumbing through those old albums, I came across a picture of my mom in her late twenties. All I could say was wow. I knew I wanted to marry a woman just like her. She was intelligent, too. Excellent with numbers. My pop never had to write a check for anything. She respected him as the man of the house, but didn't let him walk over her. She was just the right type of independent. Not what these so-called independent women are today with their nasty attitudes. She worked for Macy's in the fur department for thirty years, we never missed a meal, and you could eat off of the floors in our house.

We had prints and original pieces by African American artists before buying Black was "in style," even though we lived in what's so neatly referred to as the "inner city." I used to see pop swinging her around in the living room, and they still kissed on the lips when they thought I wasn't peeking through the holes in the banister from the top of the stairwell. Nobody's mama was as beautiful, as smart, and as sweet as she. So I decided a long time ago that I would marry a woman just like her. Not because I was a mama's boy. Because I wasn't. I'm much closer to my father. But because she was the total package. I won't settle for less. I'll die a bachelor before I do.

As I placed the key into the ignition, a thought of Taiyler, the coordinator for the fund-raiser, skipped through my mind. At Nat's house on Sunday, I told him about how she was at the meeting. Flawless. Although he laughed throughout the duration of the recap, especially at the part where she left me looking stupid in front of the bruhs, he encouraged me to pursue this one. He said that he hadn't seen me this excited since college.

Well, I wouldn't say that I'm excited. That's pushing it. So far she's just another pretty face. No, fuck that. A gorgeous face. But for all I know, she is just like all of the women I end up putting in the fuck-a-friend box. Beauty and brains, no common sense. Brains, common sense, no confidence. Confidence and beauty, no culture. They always start out with a lil' sumthin' that turns into a whole lot of nuthin' by the time they give it up. Then they fuck around and start talking that *"why didn't you call me last night"* or *"my mom is cooking this Sunday and I was wondering if you . . ."* bullshit, and I get aggravated. It only takes me one date or one fuck to figure out what I want to do with you. If the pussy is good, or at least different from what I have in stock, she's a keeper. If it isn't, then it's a wrap. Simple as that. That's what I was trying to explain to the Howard young buck at the shop. So I really can't say that I'm excited, but I am curious. I haven't met a woman that piqued my interest like this in a while. Shoot, my body hasn't reacted like that since I was in school. Sweating and shit.

It was more than just the physical with this woman. The way she walked with her head tilted back, the way she raised her right eyebrow while she listened to comments and answered questions. She seemed so poised. So smart. She was dressed very neatly. Very chic. Ferragamo loafers. Tapered charcoal blazer. Like she knew exactly what type of power she would have on us, and in efforts to spare us, she dressed down. I can appreciate that. But it didn't work.

Usually, when a woman is expecting to be in the company of one successful man, let alone seventy men, you better believe she is going straight to Ho's Heaven Outlet to get her low-cut blouse and tight pants. Oh, don't forget the designer bag with the on clearance tag. As if that's going to help an already helpless situation. Help make them look less transparent. We see right through that shit, and we're still going to fuck you, even though hell will freeze before we make women like you women of ours.

Taiyler evidently couldn't care less about that shit. She seemed to know she would do more damage in there than hurricane Gloria with or without the hype. I still don't know why she flipped me off, and when I called with those bullshit questions, she didn't remember me. Shit, she didn't even recognize me from the *Essence* article. So I don't know. I was going to wait my normal week out to call. Nat said not to waste any time calling her up and getting her out before the fund-raiser this Saturday because he knows all the brothers there are going to be on her like she's the last woman on earth. I agree. As a matter of fact, I'm calling her again. Right now. Using my knee to steer the wheel, I reached over to grab the information packet she gave us with her number on it. As I dialed, a minor burst of adrenaline ran through me. I dismissed it. I'm too cool for that shit, and she's just another woman.

"This is Taiyler . . ." she answered on the third ring. Damn, she sounds good.

10

Taiyler

"Just because a man is well dressed or fashion conscious doesn't mean he's gay. There are a whole lot of thugged-out mutherfuckers who are bending over just as quickly as the pretty boys. Just like Dre on the football team from school, remember? He had a girl and everything, and his ass was straight out of an E. Lynn Harris novel. Now, tell me I'm wrong, Shel. Tell me. You can't because I'm not wrong and you know it . . ."

Solange, my college girlfriend, and Michelle, my fair-weather friend, were going back and forth about the Black male gay crisis. They are both strong, opinionated Black women who, in the ten plus years we've known one another, never seemed to agree on anything. I think they do this shit on purpose. Shala, Solange, Michelle, and I attended Spelman together and stayed tight through it all. We became friends for life during our freshman stay at Abby Hall. Although Shala and I were the closest, all four of us stuck together like glue. Solange was the first person I'd met at Spelman, and I had determined that I couldn't stand her stuck-up ass. She was from Georgia and didn't stop to make it clear to every girl in the dorm that she was a fourth generation "Spelmanite," as if those of us who were first generation students were underclass citizens. She pranced around the dorm in Chanel sandals, Hermes scarves, and hired help to clean her room. She was too much. Being from Brooklyn, I thought she was a fake bitch that I would never speak to let alone become friends with. Life had other plans. Since we both were biology majors, we had almost all the same classes. Each day, she would whiz by in her silver 328i and wave to the rest of us "financial aid cases" as we pounded one foot after another into the pavement, cursing all the way.

I refused to taint my ghetto authenticity by befriending her. I did, however, find out that she was smart as hell and had been all over the world. I discovered this in a botany course we shared where she spoke candidly of plants and trees that bloomed in countries that I'd never even heard of, let alone traveled to. I figured she was just bragging and paid her no mind. That is, until we were paired up at the end of the semester for our final. We had to list as many flora and fauna on campus as we could and place them into their appropriate classifications. I just knew that I would die partnering up with "Whitley," as everyone on campus referred to her. Determined to show her that I was less than ecstatic about the arrangement, I marched right up to where she was sitting and gave it to her Brooklyn style . . .

"Okay. How are we going to do this? I don't want to waste any time because I have other finals to study for, so let's get this bullshit over with."

Cynicism never wore a more uncaring set of eyes. She reviewed my hair, nails, outfit, all in a matter of milliseconds. I wasn't Taiyler Richardson, fly girl from New York. I was a bum who'd just asked her for spare change.

"I'm not starting anything. I'm going to the mall. I already have the final. My cousin did it a few years ago. You can either come with me or not. I'm leaving in five minutes."

I remembered thinking that she couldn't possibly be serious. And sure as hell, in five minutes she had that Prada knapsack packed, and we were cruising in her BMW to *Illmatic*. Shocked the shit out of me that she even had it in the deck. We've been friends ever since.

I've learned so much from her. Things that I couldn't learn from my grandma and Aunt Mae, even though they did their best to expose me. That first day we went shopping, or rather I went with her, I learned that the Prada bag she used to tote her dirty textbooks cost more than my first car. We used her family's time-shares to trek Europe in the summer, St. Martin and Ocho Rios on spring break. I learned to speak fluent Spanish, Italian, and Portuguese from summers spent in the Dominican Republic, Italy, and Brazil. I studied languages that I didn't even know existed. All on her parents.

She's learned a lot from me, too. I exposed her to the world as it was. Minus the butlers, the maids, and the Benzes. I took her home to Brooklyn with me and watched her cry when we rode through the projects. I observed proudly as she debated with my homeboys on who the best MCs were and why there were so many young Black men in prisons. Although we are different, she being one of many physicians in her family while I am the first, the experience and knowledge that we have exchanged through the years have been priceless. It's made us better women. We're not as close as Shala and I, but we're good girlfriends. She's still stuck-up, and will always be, but she's balanced and well-rounded. Michelle is . . . well, let's just say she's Michelle. She went to Spelman to find her a Morehouse man, and she found one. That's all there is to her.

"Well, anyway, let's change the subject," Solange interjected.

"Taiyler, how's your sorority fund-raiser going? You got everything together, girl? You were in charge of gathering volunteers and publicity, right? Because you know the Links have many radio and television contacts that I'm sure I can get forwarded to you," she mentioned. That's her. Always willing to help.

She's the only one out of the four of us that received an invitation to become a Link. I think you have to do so many community projects and be of a certain stature professionally. The rumor is that family name and funding weigh heavier than the former. I'm not sure about that, but seeing that Solange hasn't accomplished anything more than I have professionally, my guess is that my family being from the straight-up hood taints my chances. She says I'm crazy for thinking that, but I've read *Our Kind of People* by Lawrence Otis Graham, and that shit was made quite clear. Most of the Links were involved in Jack and Jill, spent summers at Oak Bluffs on Martha's Vineyard, and went to prep school together. Solange included. I was a card-carrying member of the BRC—for those who don't know, that's the Brownsville Recreation Center in Brooklyn—spent most of my summers jumping in and out of hydrants or down South digging for worms in my aunt Marie's backyard, and went to PS 183. So I guess I'm missing a few checks on the application.

Solange keeps assuring me that I would be a great candidate, and I'm sure that I would be. But the Links are some of the most bourgeois women that I've ever met, and I'm sure that one of them will probably have me lose my damn medical license up in that bitch. I have a hard enough time dealing with Sorors. Many of the Links are also AKX Sorors, so I already know what to expect. Plus, Alpha Kappa Chi is all I need. And sometimes that is too much.

As for them assisting with *DC's Men Are Cooking*, I'm okay on this. It's my first time heading a graduate chapter fund-raiser committee, but I was the publicity chair of AKX at Spelman, and we sold out every event we had on and off campus. So I know what I'm doing. I thank her anyway. "Thanks for offering, girl, but I have this under control. We have radio promo and corporate sponsorship. All the vitals. Plus, we have more than enough volunteers."

"Oooh, I want to hear about the volunteers, how fine and how rich?" Michelle probed. That's all her gold-digging ass was ever worried about. If she put as much energy into formulating her own success instead of picking through the garbage of every man she meets to find his pay stubs, she might be able to support herself without her ex-husband's alimony check. My answer reflected my apathy to the issue.

"I mean, they were your average group of successful Black men. Some were good looking, some were okay, some weren't," I answered evasively. Before she could begin her traditional behavior of annoying me, my phone rang. I waited my usual three rings before blessing the recipient with the sound of my voice.

"This is Taiyler." I watched Michelle mouth to Solange, "This is Taiyler," with that half-I'm-joking-half-I-really-can't-stand-her-ass face that she never hides as well as she thinks she does. Solange just shook her head and chuckled, thinking the girl was actually joking. I know better. I know haters. The voice on the phone sounded familiar.

"Hi, Taiyler. This is Derrick. I spoke to you yesterday. I called with the additional questions."

What could he possibly want now?

"Yes, Derrick. I thought that everything was made clear at the meeting. What else wasn't made clear in the packet, at the two-hour meeting, or on the phone?" I was being a bitch, but I couldn't help it. I have an extremely low tolerance for ignorance and an even lower one for stupidity. He's straddling the fence on both right now. Either that or he's just using this as an excuse to call me. Whatever it is, Derrick seemed to blow right by my sarcastic comment as if he didn't even notice it. I guess it was because he had one of his own.

"Brains are hilariously unreliable. Sometimes the voice of reason up there goes hoarse. Why would I call again if I was clear on every-thing? Or I hope you don't think that I'm making excuses to call you. You'd have the wrong man for that right there. There is, however, one question that I didn't ask during our last conversation . . ." He contin-ued without even the slightest inflection of his voice. All the while I'm thinking to myself, damn, did he just nip me?

The girls are giving me that confused who-is-that look followed by an even more serious look from Shala saying, *"Do I need to click in and rescue you?"* This guy has my full attention at this point, so I shot back a general glance that women use to say, *"Don't worry, I have this under control."* It's amazing how we can have a complete conversation in a matter of seconds without ever opening our mouths. As I prepared to curse this Derrick the fuck out for implying that I was being flippant for no reason, his next comment stopped me dead in my tracks.

". . . So the thing that I was not made clear on, Ms. Richardson, was what I said while we were speaking at the meeting to piss you off so much that you stomped off like a kid who'd just dropped their ice cream face first on the pavement," he said playfully.

At this point, I was frozen. I know who this is. Fucking *Essence* Man of the Year. Oh, shit. On my phone for the second time in two days. Why didn't I figure out who he was the first time he called? Probably because he was such an asshole that I didn't expect or even care to hear from him again. I rose from the sofa and headed toward the deck. I needed privacy for this one. No wonder he sounded so famil-iar. His fine ass . . . Whew! Gather yourself, girl. Get your A game on. Breathe. Go.

"Well, Derrick, I only reserve pointed comments like that for peo-ple who deserve them. What did you do to deserve it? Or do you re-member?" I asked coyly.

"If I remembered, I wouldn't have to ask you, now, would I?" he replied. I could see his arrogant smile plainly. He won't win this.

"Well, I guess short-term memory has become a luxury item these days. Listen, why don't you call someone else and play games with them? I'm entertaining company. Okay? I'll see you at the Conven-tion Center Saturday." Reverse psych 101. I hope he doesn't hang up. I really want to see what I can do with this one. I thumbed through my virtual rule book for blaringly handsome arrogant assholes. I can not and will not let on that I know about his article in *Essence,* nor will I act like I give a fuck that he's calling. Best case scenario, I initiate the hang-up. He either A, impedes it by bringing something else up, or B, hangs up and calls back after the one- to three-day wait period men reserve for returning calls to women they want to see, but don't want to sweat. Either way, I win. I'll see just how much he wants it.

"Oh, really? You'll see me, huh? So I don't get an explanation at all?"

I could hear those conceited wheels turning.

"What if I told you that I don't want to play this game, Taiyler? You're beautiful and I want to see you. I'm not going hang up and call you back in a week to prove a point. I want to see you as soon as possible. And definitely before the fund-raiser this weekend. You can tell me what I did wrong over dinner," he said as confidently as Colin Powell addressing the press.

Right now I'm thinking to myself, damn. He's blowing me right now. But if I know his type, he probably gets his way with women, especially the professional, educated types who are on the hunt for a man like him. I'm not on the hunt. I have to draw him out of his box a bit. So I can't give him his way. At least this time.

"Derrick, I'm sure you charm women with the direct approach— believe me, we love that in a man who's expressing interest—but I have work to do this week. Lots of it. I appreciate your initiative, but if, and I do mean *if,* we were to get together for dinner, it would have to be when my schedule lightens up a bit. You can understand that, right?" There. Play with that one, smart-ass. He wallowed in what seemed to be deep thought. There I was, positioning myself for either a clever comment, sarcastic retort, or an indicator of how much of an asshole this beautiful man probably is, and to my surprise he delivered neither.

"When your schedule lightens up, huh?" He chuckled. "Listen, Taiyler, please don't make me beg. Or you won't get any sleep tonight. I'll just have to call you every five minutes until you agree to see me this week," he replied.

What surprised me the most is that in a matter of minutes he went from that clever, confident, I-know-you-want-me attitude to one that was so sensitive in nature that I started to have doubts as to whether or not I was still speaking to the same person. Even though it's probably all bullshit, I did want to get to know the man behind the mask. I just have to make him work a little harder for it.

"Derrick, really, I'm flattered. But my schedule is really packed for the week. Why don't you call me Tuesday afternoon? I'll be able to give you a better picture of when I'll be available. Is that okay?" I asked with a sweetness in my voice that I didn't even know had seeped through.

"All right. So you're going to make me beg. Fine. I can do that. It's been a while, but I can do it. I'll call you then," he said dejectedly.

"I'll look forward to your call, Derrick," I said to soften what seemed like a blow to his ego. Why was I even feeling bad about it? I do this to every man who wants to see me for the first time. We hung up, and instantly, I wanted to call him back and say fuck it, let's get together tomorrow evening, et cetera, et cetera. But Lord knows I can't. It's just not me. So I'll have to wait until he calls me back. Just as I began to step back into the living room, Shala met me on the deck.

"Grai just called. She's not feeling well, so I'm going to head out. Was that Lance?" she inquired.

"Nope. Guess." I must admit, his call left me a little on the giddy side.

"Ol' boy in Richmond?" she tried again.

"Nope."

"Well then, who, damn it! I have to go, T, stop playing!"

"Okay! Okay!" I prepared myself for the reality of my own news. "Who was just featured in *Essence,* is volunteering for us on Saturday, and fine all over?" I riddled. She got it in less than a second.

"Ahhhhhh! You are lying! You are lying, girl! That was him? I thought you said that he was a complete asshole at the meeting! What did he say?" she exclaimed. As I began to give her a play-by-play synopsis of our conversation the phone rang again. I couldn't believe my ears. It was him. Again. Glancing at the hands on my Jaeger proved his punctuality precise. It's exactly five minutes after we hung up. His voice made me smile.

"Taiyler, this will be the first of many calls tonight if you don't say that you'll give me the chance to take you to dinner this week, gorgeous. So what is it going to be?" Something about the way he said the word *gorgeous* made me think of things that I shouldn't be thinking of at the moment.

"Do you always stalk the women you ask out?" I asked him.

"No. I don't even call them to ask. They usually call me. So if you'll forgive me, I'm a little rusty. I just remember that the calling-every-five-minutes thing got me a spot on the frat line when I was at HU.

Persistency has its perks. I'm just hoping that it'll work with you."
Either he is an extreme ladies' man or he's really being honest right
now. I'm trying to gather up the strength not to give in. It's hard.

"I see. Persistence, huh?" I chuckled. "Well, if it means that I'll be
able to get a good night's sleep, I guess I'll take you up on your offer,"
I said reluctantly. Completely in opposition of how I felt.

He laughed. "What, is that a charitable contribution, or do you actually want to see me?"

He's backing me into a corner. A formidable opponent. He wants
to know how badly I want to see him. How much of a woman's game
I'm playing tonight. If I say that I do want to see him—if I abate—he
has me and he knows that. If I continue to play it down, he won't be
so sure of himself, and he'll work harder. I have to get control of this
thing. I'll give him some of both. A little confusion makes the male
heart grow fonder.

"Well, since you've made it painstakingly clear to me that my phone
will ring all night if I don't accept your proposal, and I need my
beauty sleep, I guess it is more of a selfish gesture than a charitable
one. How is Tuesday at six? You can pick me up after work . . ."

11

Shala

"Yeah, I'm turning in now. Can you come down and open the door please? Shit, I forgot just that quickly. All right, I'll use my key. Yeah. I have them . . . What? No, you didn't . . . You didn't say Tylenol, you said Motrin . . . They're the same thing, Grai, damn. Yes, I have the ointment, too. I'm turning the key as we speak."

Damn. I hate it when Grai is not feeling well. She can be such a worrywart. Did you get this, can you get that? You would think I was taking care of a man. I didn't know women were this needy. I placed my keys on the kitchen table, put the groceries up, and started a pot of tea. I don't know why she hasn't bought a real kettle. I don't know how many times I've burned myself spilling over-boiling water from this sauce pot to a tea mug. Good. She got her new issue of *Essence* in. While I waited for her tea to boil, I thumbed through it. I need to get a subscription and stop buying mine off of the stands. I'll save a lot more money. Let's see, this one looks pretty interesting. Not too many advertisements. The articles look good this month. Ananda Lewis has her own talk show? Get real. What else is popping in here . . . *YOU MAY BE SLEEPING WITH A GAY MAN . . . see page 74.* I guess I don't have to worry about that one. I chuckled as I thought to myself. Nia Long's in here. Edible as usual. She and Halle can get it whenever they want, especially Halle. With her you can't go wrong. When Grai and I went to see *Swordfish*, I sat there watching her slide into those black panties with all the intention of sliding right out of mine before I snapped out of it and realized I was still at the theater. Shit! The water is boiling over.

As I turned off the gas and grabbed a bag of wild-berry tea to take to Grai, who oddly hasn't yelled down the stairs for anything yet, I thought back to my junior year when I first became overwhelmed with these feelings that I have for women. I was with Bruce Correra, one of the finest football players at Georgia Tech. Or so everyone thought. He had a beautiful copper complexion, almost like he had a year-round tan. His family was from the Dominican Republic and moved to New York when he was five. His dark curly hair and lashes to match drove all the girls in Atlanta crazy. You could wash a load on his chest and stomach. He was known as a ladies' man, but when we met in our sophomore year, all of that changed. He did everything for me without me having to ask. He used to call me his little Indian princess, and from the outside looking in, he looked more like my servant than my boyfriend.

Much to everyone's disbelief, he'd make public displays of his love for me. His football buddies used to tease him about the effect I had on him. While they were on the road, girls were throwing themselves at him left and right, and all he wanted to do was call his lil' "Pocahontas." Sometimes I just wanted him to get out and have a good time with his boys. I wasn't insecure at all. Plus, I needed some space to sort some things out of my own that were starting to trouble me. One thing in particular. As I searched the cupboard for the honey, it rang crystal clear in my mind . . .

"Shala Matthews? Shala Matthews, your appointment was for three today, right? Is this your first time here?" the receptionist asked me. Why she was yelling from behind the desk was beyond me. I'm right in front of her.

"Uhh, yes, it is," I answered sheepishly. Taiyler and Solange are regulars at this spa. They come in just about every two weeks. I felt so corny saying that it was my first time here. I just didn't think that college students did this type of thing. The only reason that I'm even here is because I'm stressed out, and Taiyler swears that this is the answer to all of my problems. I told her about letting Solange's bourgeois ass hook her up into spending money that she didn't have. Her answer to that was if she's going to be a doctor, she'd better start doing things that doctors do. I told her that was great for those who had doctors' money to spend. I happened to know that she didn't. Knowing T, she had some dude paying for this shit every single time.

"Shala? You can come back . . ."

I got up and walked toward the massage rooms in the back, cutting through the salon stations and organic body product shelves. Noticing the prices, I couldn't help but think that this had to be a crock of shit. Fifteen-dollar shea butter. Six-dollar lip balm. A stick of Queen Helene's cocoa butter only costs you ninety-nine cents at CVS.

When I arrived at the entrance of the massage area, I was instructed to step into a small, private changing area. Here, I would take off my clothes, shoes, and put on the robe that was provided. Dang. Forgot to make sure that my panties and bra matched. I think my masseur is a guy, too. My guess was that it didn't matter, because I think I'm supposed to be underneath the cover on the table for the duration of the massage. Well, at least that's what Taiyler said. I wandered into the massage room thinking, damn . . . this really is relaxing. The lighting was dimmed, and there were candles all over. Plus, the music was so soothing. I didn't know they played Sade in day spas. I thought I was going to have to sit through one of those dumb-ass wildlife tapes of birds chirping and water running. Okay. Two points for ambience. Now, let's relax. How am I supposed to lie on this bed? I guess I'd better wait until the massage therapist comes in. He'll let me know what to do.

"Shala? Are you comfortable?" The voice from behind startled me. The receptionist again? Where the hell is my masseur? Why don't Black people ever do anything on time? He was supposed to start working out my kinks like ten minutes ago! I have a four o'clock class! As I spun around to give whoever this was a piece of my mind, I was stunned. Literally. Right before me stood the most attractive woman that I had ever seen. She wasn't the average runway model type; she was truly a natural beauty. Golden curls, pulled back into a thick ponytail, cinnamon freckles screaming to be touched and tasted by hungry fingertips, and a smart nose, being bullied by a set of lips that needed their own playground. Or a new group of playmates. I could help her with that. I felt parts of me responding to this woman in ways that I thought only came about in my dreams. It had never happened for real before. Why was this happening now? The very thing that's stressing me out popped up while I'm supposed to be getting relaxed.

"Shala, did you hear me?" she asked with her head slightly cocked to the side. Uh-huh, I wanted to say, but I can't answer her right now. My heart is beating too fast.

"Are you okay?" The girl with the beautiful teeth wants to know if you're okay. All right, Shala, snap out of it.

"Yeah, uh, I mean yes, I'm fine. Uh, what did you say again?" I figured she must think I'm the densest person she's ever met.

"I'm Zadia. I'll be filling in for Mark today. He called in sick. Do you prefer oil or lotion?" she offered. Oil or lotion. Oil or lotion. The million-dollar question. If I answer either way I'm fucked.

"Shala!" She raised her voice. Shit, I must be staring. I can't believe this is happening.

"Uh, lotion," I mumbled as I turned around. Pretended to be admiring the art they had hanging on the walls.

"Lie down on your stomach and pull the cover completely over you. I'll be right back," Zadia said. As I removed my robe and climbed up onto the massage table, my mind traveled to the dream I had just a few days ago. The brown-skinned girl with the bob haircut. Doing things that I was even ashamed to imagine. I woke up sweaty, panicked, and scared to go back to sleep for fear of having another dream. I've been having dreams like that since I was fifteen. Each time I would tell myself that it was only a dream. That I would never feel anything like that in real life. That I couldn't be gay because I had a boyfriend and we had sex on the regular and I liked it. Or that if I didn't place myself in the position to be tempted, I would have nothing to worry about. Well, I hope all that shit stands up now. Because all I can think of is Zadia's hands going places that would make my father want to drown me in a tub of holy water.

While in midthought, Zadia waltzed back into the candlelit chamber. Told me to slide up onto the top of the table and to place my face inside the round apparatus below. No problem. She instructed me to take my hair out of the ponytail. Done. She rolled the crisp white linen down, right beyond the small of my back. My weak spot. Hope she stays away from there. My masseuse squeezed a large mound of lotion into her hands, rubbed them together, and started working every knot and kink out of my back that she could find. I was doing quite well. In my dreams things are usually out of control by now. But I'm doing all right.

Her hands felt good, but they weren't making me crazy. Probably because I wasn't looking at her. Maybe this attraction thing isn't what I'm cracking it up to be. Getting through this would be so good for me. It would prove that I'm normal. That would relieve me of so much stress, and I can concentrate on my midterms. Just as I was about to give myself a gold medal for hurdling this today, something happened. Ummh. She's . . . she's heading toward the small of my back. Circular motions . . . uhhhm. One, two, one, two . . . damn, that feels so good. I can feel my mouth starting to water. God help me. My head is starting to spin. This shit feels too good. She started to massage the back of my pelvic bone, slowly bringing her hands around to the sides, a little to the front . . . I felt her breath on my neck as she whispered in my ear.

"Turn over and let it happen, Shala. Turn over and let me . . ."

No. I can't. I'll go to hell. Once I turn around it's all over. All of the energy I've spent fighting this very thing will be wasted. Nope.

"Free yourself, Shala. You know you want me . . ."

Okay! Fuck it! I give up! I give up, damn it! I lifted my head, preparing myself for pleasure. I felt dizzy. During midturn, Zadia stopped massaging me. What? Didn't she just say turn over?

"Shala, put your head back down; you have to relax for this to work. Try not to move, okay? You have a lot of tension in your lower back," she said seriously. At this point, I don't know what the hell is going on. Obviously I'm losing my mind. I have to concentrate. If I put my head back down, my imagination will run wild, and I'll start throbbing again. As she continued with my massage, I heard myself moan out loud. A sensual moan. I don't know if I'm going to make it. This is more like torture than anything. I know it's just a massage, but her hands are relieving much more than just physical stress right now. I'm aroused like shit. As she continues away from my pelvic area and heads back up toward my neck, I can't help but think that if she feels this good massaging me, I can't imagine what she feels like . . .

That was probably the day that I decided I would explore the whats and whys of women and how they made me feel. What I didn't know was that I would meet a cute philosophy major that would answer all my questions in the best ways. I ended up breaking things off with Bruce and having to make what was the biggest decision I've ever had to make in my life. Although I was scared shitless, I knew that what I was doing had to be done. It was the best thing for me and I had procrastinated with it for too long. When I was with India, I felt complete. Mentally, emotionally, and physically. I felt liberated. Appreciated. Not to mention that with her, sex without an orgasm was unheard of.

I went back and forth between men and women for a while, kind of comparing the two. And when it was time to sink or swim, the person who made it easiest for me was Taiyler. That's why I love her so much. That's why she's my best friend. I could tell that she was a little shocked by the changes that I was making, but she didn't change. She encouraged me to do what was best for me. She didn't judge me. She stuck right by me. More than any sister ever could. She helped me analyze the pros and cons to following my heart. She gave me the courage to do what I needed to do. Embrace my sexuality. As I finished up with Grai's tray of sick person goodies, I heard her call me from upstairs.

"I'm coming! Hold on, I'll be right up!" I yelled back. While heading up the stairs with my hands full, I thought about another life decision that I've been putting off. Whether or not I want to expose my family and future children to my life. Will I be able to raise them in a normal, unhostile environment? If not, am I even capable of having a relationship with a man after all of these years of loving women? It's just not something that I want to deal with now. At the top of the stairs, I navigated through the hallway holding the tray tightly, making extra effort against dropping this shit on me. When I rounded the corner to the master bedroom, Grai was sitting upright in the bed watching Wesley and Sanaa make Terry McMillan richer, with a glob of tissue hanging out of her left nostril.

"Would you do something with that?" I asked playfully.

"What took you so long?" She smiled and said softly. "I'm about to die over here. I feel like I'm suffocating. Did you get the Afrin?"

"Yeah. I got everything. Hold your head back and sniff," I told her. I handed her the medicine, slipped out of my clothes, and crawled in bed beside her. Watching Grai sip her tea, her lips folding the way they were over the tea mug, her wild curly hair all over her head, I felt my mouth watering a little. A little dizzy, I started tapping my foot the way I usually do when I'm horny.

"No, Shala. I'm sick! Stop being selfish," Grai said pointedly. Damn, I'm busted.

"I didn't say anything! What are you talking about? Just drink your tea and watch the movie!" I answered, laughing.

"You didn't have to say anything. I know you. And I'm saying no," she replied, cutting her eyes at me. She's smirking. She's not serious. She can't be. As if on cue, the scene that everyone lives for in this movie played. Wes, Sanaa, and the refrigerator.

Say no now, Grai. I dare you. As a matter of fact, I double dare you. I already know I'm not going to make it through this scene. And judging from the look on her face, I know she won't either. As I dove under the covers, I thought to myself, *I'll never be able to give this up.* And then I did what I was born to do. No objections, no questions asked.

PART TWO

12

Nathaniel

We take baths together almost every week. It started on Valentine's Day when I was a senior at HU. Didn't have a pot to piss in. I knew that Kendra had gotten me something. I, on the other hand, couldn't even buy her time. I was still waiting for my refund check to come in, and everyone knows that Hampton is quick to collect their money, but slow as hell in dishing it out. So I had to figure out something. It wasn't like I had to do something expensive; I had already made my impressions. That's how I got her to be my girl in the first place. But I did need to be creative. And at three o'clock in the afternoon I still hadn't thought of anything.

If I remember correctly, I only had a few hours to pull this one off. All I could think of was fuck me for procrastinating. So I sat down on the sofa and thought. Thought so hard a sweat broke out on my nose and upper lip. When all was said and done, I had a night of comfort planned for my baby. Borrowed twenty dollars from Derrick and hit Wal-Mart like a tornado in La Plata. Bought a bag of tea lights, bubble bath oil, and one of those plastic spongelike balls that I always saw hanging on the shower racks in the girls' dorms. Seven dollars and forty-seven cents. Added some baby oil. Eleven sixty-two. On to the grocery store. A box of spaghetti, three small red cans of Hunts tomato sauce, a head of lettuce, a cucumber, a sleeve of Italian bread and a package of strawberries. Five dollars, ten cents. About three dollars left. Went over to the Korean place on the way back, got a brush and a bottle of clear nail polish. By twelve o'clock that night, I was the fucking man.

I told Kendra to call me when she was a few minutes away from my apartment so I could meet her outside. I always met her downstairs and walked her up, so she didn't think anything of it.

When she stepped out of the car, I took her bags—you would have thought she was spending a week in Istanbul. Standing behind her, I moved that black ponytail from her back to her breast. As I kissed the nape of her neck, I tied one of my old frat tee shirts around her eyes. She giggled, surrendering to me without reservation. Like an elder that has lived his three score and ten walking with Christ, she trusted me.

I led her to the middle of the living room and removed the make-shift blindfold. Since I had managed to light all fifty tea lights, the house glowed. It was comfortable. Loving. No one is more romantic than Luther. To her left was dinner. Spaghetti, garlic bread, and tossed salad. A college student's gourmet meal. Fresh roses from outside of the Marine Bio building were cut and arranged perfectly on the table. Beside it was a small handmade card that read, **Welcome to Kendra's Spa Paradise.** I introduced myself as her host for the evening and began to deliver our list of available services. Dinner, sponge bath, massage, dessert, et cetera. From the look on her face, my twenty dollars was well spent.

We ate dinner, proceeded to what I called her "Nile water awaiting." I sponged her. Kissed her. And kissed her. As she blew bubbles in my face, I took each one of her fingers and savored it. She surprised me by standing up, lifting my shirt, unbuckling my pants, kissing me deeply. Couldn't describe the feeling that I had then. First time I'd felt it. It was only duplicated when I saw her walking down the aisle. I continued to sponge her. She returned the favor. I knew she was it. I knew then what I still feel now.

Lotion on her beautiful body, I placed her on the sofa and massaged her feet. Using the clear nail polish I'd purchased, I painted each one of her ten toes. Tried harder than a three-year-old to stay inside the lines. Her eyes thanked me a million times. I was investing in an hour from now. "Superstar" began. She threw her head back. I wanted to take my sweetie upstairs for her body massage, but she looked so tranquil lying there. I had just turned over my sheets, as my grandma would call it, and sprinkled a little powder in between them.

I could've left her down here in relaxation's temple, but I wanted her to see how much work I'd put into the night. So I carried her upstairs to my bedroom. Her grip on my neck tightened as I laid her down onto the bed. Told her to turn over. She gave me that mischievous grin that she still does to this day to let me know when she wants me.

"Dar me beso . . ." Kendra spoke two languages. One of them she uses when she is aroused. That drove me insane. Only because I knew how ravenous she was when she was pushed to that point. I looked down and was reassured by my man down there that all signs were a go. But I had bought that damn baby oil and was going to use it if it killed me. So I told her that I would do whatever she wanted, but I was under contract to complete the spa services selected for her. I could tell she was getting impatient. So I turned her over and worked out all of those neurology, bio-chem, and physiology exams with my hands. I had honestly massaged plenty of girls on campus before, so I considered myself an expert. However, Kendra's body was so perfect that I didn't think that I would make it through this with me straddling her. She obviously knew this, because she wasted no time tempting me with her back arched, waving her ass in my face. Torture. But I'm strong. So I leaned over on my side and continued to knead her troubles away.

I remember thinking that a girl shouldn't be this beautiful all over. It could cause the type of trouble that forces a man to have to plead temporary insanity. It was then that I decided to make sure that she never wanted for anything. I'm sure plenty of guys were lurking like Lucifer was with Jesus on the mountaintop, waiting for the opportunity to offer her the world. Just so he could have the pleasure of claiming that she was his. I'll never forget the look on her face. She was in her most vulnerable state. Naked. Unveiled. True.

How the hell my dog ass ever got through to her was beyond me. Took four long years. Persistence pays off. I was an undercover male ho. A testament to how a good upbringing and a sixteen-to-one female-male ratio could tear the spirit. The type that never would admit to treating women like they were pieces of meat, but had a revolving door to my bedroom. Made every girl I was with feel like she was the love of my life. For one night, or one week, or a month if they lasted that long. I was a trumpet player. Moved to my own tune. One resonance, one philosophy. My own. Would fuck you on Saturday, take you with me to church on Sunday, and act like I didn't know you on

Monday. Kendra saw right through me from the day I introduced myself to her on the steps of Ogden Hall in our freshman year. Made me work for her. Slaved for almost four years. Did whatever she wanted. No man gives up anything that he worked like a dog to get. Wrapping up her massage, I pulled the sheets up over her and placed the oil on the nightstand.

While looking for the cap, I felt her soft hands wrap around my chest and my stomach. Spanish. More Spanish in my left ear. She moved to her own conjured rhythm. Full of slow, seductive motions that left me forced to compromise my own. She became my wife that night. In my imagination. In my dreams.

As I continued to reminisce, I felt her thick nipples pressing against my back. Like berries. Can't draw the line between memories and reality. Her voice does the same thing to me this morning as it did years ago.

"*Quierdo tu mucho. Nessisito mi amor ahora . . .*" Same language, same ear, same yearning. Does wonders for my ego. Makes me want to conquer for her. Lay my conquests at her feet. I turned, tilted my head upward, so that I faced her. I want her to see in my eyes what I hear in her voice.

Pleasing my wife is my weakness. I want to give her the spoils of Egypt. So I placed my hands around her waist and lifted her wet body out of the bathtub. Onto the bathroom sink. She knows. It's ritualistic. I can't help myself. Massaging her lower back, running my fingers along the imaginary creases of her panties, and tracing her softness with my tongue makes me want to lean like an addict. Kiss, caress, pressure, lick. My wife let out a soft scream that lets me know that she's addicted, too. This is our crack house. The bathroom sink.

She tastes so sweet. Times like this make me wish I could crawl inside her and fall asleep. Using my entire tongue, I kissed her lips with the same tenderness and care as I would if they were on her face. She taught me that. How to slightly cock my head to the side, place my lips inside hers, and softly run the length of my tongue up and down the essence of her womanhood. She loves it. It weakens her into a state of utter confusion.

Right now, she's trying to break away from one of the most euphoric feelings on this earth. Claiming that it's too much for her. Maybe it is. But I won't let her go. I can't. I'm just as addicted as she is. Heart racing, I continued to inject full doses of pleasure into my baby without ignominy. Her squirms, gasps, curses, and scratches make me a cannibal. And just when the look on her face says that she's hurting with pleasure, that she's overdosed on ecstasy, I devour her flesh with the desperation of a man eating his last supper.

She does more than moan. She sends a shrill through the air of a Rastafarian lover hearing the first few notes of "Redemption's Song." She's high. She's long. She's stretched out in love. It takes all of me to keep her sweat-drenched body from slipping off of the sink. But I hold her. Love her. Watch her body twitch and jolt as she commands me in the language of a sailor not to lay another hand on her. She's too sensitive. It's okay, though. I need this time. I'm still licking her sweetness off of my lips.

Upon her orders, I lift my queen into my arms and carry her into our bedroom. Threshold crossing is a practice initiated on that Valentine's night years ago. I'm her warrior, I'll carry her. Carry her from Mooréa to Guanacaste to Morocco. From the bathroom to the bedroom every weekend is minute. I lay her down on our bed with the care of a first-time father handling an infant. She usually goes to sleep after our baths. My baby. Assuming the fetal position, she beckons for privacy. I pull the duvet over her and slip downstairs to allow her that hour and a half she usually spends in that place where no men are allowed. I love Saturday mornings. I love pleasing my wife.

While my beauty is sleeping, I make way into the hallway. I have to start getting ready for the rest of the day. I almost head into Nile's room to wake her up for morning cartoons. Forgot she wasn't here. My daughter usually spends Friday night and some Saturdays with her grandma. Kendra's mother. Bless Mrs. Henderson. While I'm handing out blessings, I ask God to bless what I'm about to prepare for this afternoon's fund-raiser. I had already prepared the spicy fried chicken which was directly out of my mom's cookbook. Onion powder, garlic powder, pepper, onions, a quarter cup of butter . . . she could put the Colonel out of business. Kennie made my favorite collard greens with cornmeal dumplings and red rice with cayenne. I know that's cheating, but no one will be able to turn down those greens. Technically, *DC's Men Are Cooking* volunteers are only supposed to make one dish. I don't think anyone will mind me adding a few to the list.

At the moment, I'm cutting and peeling sweet potatoes for dessert. Honey-glazed sweet potatoes and apples. Yams, sweet apples, a cup of honey, apple cider, unsalted butter, ground cinnamon . . . Lord, bless this food. Let it be nourishing. It's from my kitchen and from my mama's soul. Bless me not to mess this up. Thank you. Amen. I open my eyes and take a quick look around. My prayers are short and said standing. I've never really felt comfortable with my eyes closed for prolonged periods of time. Kendra says it's because I don't trust in the Lord with all my heart, mind, and soul. I don't know about all of that, but I do know that a Black man kneeling with his hands clenched and his eyes closed usually signals danger. Given the current state of affairs in America, God should understand my sentiments. Hopefully.

For the next hour, I cut, peel, mix, pour, measure, and stir my way into deep thought. I see Kendra's and my honeymoon in Papeete, her father giving me his blessing on his deathbed, and the first glimpse I got of Nile's beautiful head during her birth. I hear our sweet vows being traded, the beat of Kendra's heart quicken when I tell her that I'll die for her, and the pitter-patter of my daughter's little feet as she runs through our house. I feel the tears of my wife on my neck after I cracked open her ring box, the joy of watching Nile's first steps, and the warmth of knowing that I am loved without reservation. I place the knife on the cutting board and feel that familiar feeling. It's overwhelming. Looking at all that He has blessed me with, especially my wife and daughter, chokes me up at times. This is one of those times. My two main arteries. Kendra's my left and Nile's my right. I'd kill myself before I'd allow anything to come between that.

With my hands soaked in a mixture of butter and cinnamon, I'm forced to use the back of my sleeve to wipe my eyes. I only hope that my boys experience this. I can't explain it to them. I think each person, if they're lucky, has to discover it on their own. There's nothing like it. Hearing her shuffling upstairs prompts me to get my shit together quick. Can't let Kendra see me this way. So I leaned over and ran some cold water over my face and eyes. Grabbed a kitchen towel and wiped away the evidence of my moment of weakness. Love is a mutherfucker.

"Baby! Honey! Are you almost finished down there? Didn't you say that Derrick would be here at ten?" I heard her yell down from the bedroom.

"Almost! He's never on time anyway!" I hollered back up. Just as I was putting the dish in the oven, she sauntered down the stairs in her favorite after-bath, all-white terry cloth robe and placed a fat kiss on my cheek. Invaded my space. And I loved it. Loved everything about it.

"Look at you . . ." I said for lack of anything better to express my wonderment of her beauty. I love her hair when it's messy and all over her head. Makes me want to grab it and bury my face in it.

". . . How is my sweetness doing this morning?"

"Like . . . you . . . wouldn't believe . . ." she answered in between placing kisses on my face.

"Can . . . I . . . do . . . anything else . . . for my lady?" I offered while stamping her eyelids with kisses of my own.

"No, you've done enough for the morning, thank you!" She laughed mischievously.

"Are you sure? Just say the word . . ." I say, owning the look of a shamefully amorous dog awaiting to fetch the slippers of his master. I grasped the space underneath her shoulders and swung her around to the opposite side of me. I just wanted to touch her again.

"Thank you for this morning, sweetie," she said, disregarding my last statement and smiling like she does every Saturday morning. As she made her way back up the stairs, I stared at my wife with starvation in my eyes.

"Thank you for the last eight years, babe," I answered back. And I meant it.

13

Taiyler

"Aunt Mae! I did exactly what you said! It's not my fault the fish is breaking apart in the pan! Yes, I let the oil get hot . . . Yes, the batter is thick . . . uh-huh . . . I did that, too! . . . So why does my catfish look like eggs! . . . No, for real, Auntie . . . This thing is today and . . . Yes . . . the fund-raiser . . ."

I was frustrated, running late, on the verge of tears, and she was laughing at me.

"Gal . . . ha, ha, ha . . . you . . . ha [cough] . . . sure you let the fire get hot enough?" Aunt Mae asked me in between rounds of laughter. I could just see her petite frame rocking back and forth, shoulders slumping up and down, and her leaning over to grab a clean tissue to wipe her eyes.

"I think so . . ." I whined, sounding like a three-year-old who just skinned her knee.

"I'll never be able to do this, Auntie. I can't cook like you and Grandma," I said, damn near tearing my wrist apart, pulling at my favorite bangle while wiping my eyes. I really was crying then. I had to be downtown at the Convention Center in a few hours, and I didn't have a piece of catfish to boot. I should have gone down to Negril's on Georgia Avenue and just picked something up.

Aunt Mae is used to this. Me calling her in the middle of cooking—or attempting to cook something—and bawling about the fact that I can't pull it all together. I think the last time it was my macaroni and cheese that came out tasting like pound cake. Bottom line, I can't cook anything without Aunt Mae on the phone giving me play-by-play directions. As long as I don't call her during *Jeopardy* or *The Young and the Restless*, she is more than happy to deal with my tantrums and pitiful vernacular. She does the same thing each and every time. Laugh for about five minutes straight, ask me if I followed the recipe she gave me, and then tell me to take everything out of the pots and pans, or *panes* as her thick Carolina accent described it, and start all over. She'd then assure me between sniffles and a long ol' "wheeew!" at the end of her laugh that I would be able to cook just as good as she one day, if I kept on trying. If my older cousin Ella was visiting, she'd put her on the phone and have me describe the mess I'd made all over again. While both of them cracked the fuck up at my expense. She began the ritual of walking me through the recipe as she walked me though life.

"Well, then, do this fuh me, Muppet. First take the pieces of fish in nere, out da pane . . ." She called me Muppet. Damn, she must really feel sorry for me today. ". . . you gots you a fresh piece, baby?"

"Yes," I answer solemnly.

"Good. How high is the fire?"

"It's on medium-low," I replied astutely.

"What in the world is medium-low, Taiyler? Is the fire big, small, or flickerin'?" she asked me, sounding slightly agitated. Obviously medium-low wasn't the term she was looking for.

"I don't have a fire, Auntie, remember? I have an electric stove."

"Well, dat's your problem nere! How you gon' watch the fire if day ain't no fire to watch! You can't cook no good batch of nuthin' on dem lek-tric stoves!" she scolded.

Okay, I have to get her past the electric stove thing. I have got to have twenty pieces of fried catfish coming out of this kitchen in an hour. I forgot that I'm talking to a woman who still uses a rotary phone.

"Aunt Mae, uh . . . I meant the fire is small. It's electric, but it kind of looks like a fire when you stare long. It's small."

"Oh, whatever, chile, I didn't just fall off the watermelon truck yesterday. I know how it looks! Anyway, turn nat fire up high and get that grease hot. Yo' grease ain't hot enough. You ain't got the patience to let it git hot neither. I know you. While the grease is lettin', start cuttin' up those taters for the tater salad. That'll get yo' mine off of watchin' the grease steady like you used to when you was lil'." She continued to give me instruction after instruction. So well, in fact, you would've thought that she was in my kitchen frying catfish and making potato salad instead of in her flowered housecoat sitting in the leather recliner I gave her two Christmases ago.

It's this type of insight that I can't ever perceive of having myself. Knowledge beyond belief, patience beyond imagination, and peace beyond faculty. The ability to make good from bad. To calm the spirit and soothe the soul. I don't know if I can live without this. Without her. Even though she's getting old, I try not to think of the inevitable. She always says, *"We all have to go that way . . . ,"* and I'm sure we all do, but when I think of her going, I become hysterical.

I remember once as I was driving back to Maryland from Brooklyn the thought crossed my mind. My auntie passing away. I fucking lost it. Started crying and heaving so hard that I had to pull over for an hour. My eyes were so swollen that I could barely see the road. So it took me double the time to get home. That's happened on more than one occasion. Just the mere thought sends me into a frenzy. I'm in a constant state of paranoia about this. I probably should have started seeing a therapist right after my grandma passed. I might not be a nut case about it now. I guess that's why I'm so hard on her doctors. Every visit, every prescription, every opinion has to go through me. Shoot, I just stopped driving up there to go with her to the doctor. I know that I'm Dr. Shalom's worst nightmare. But this is my auntie. *My* aunt Mae. God is going to have to take her like he did Elijah if he wants to bring her home. Because left up to me, she'll never be sick.

"Taiyler, baby . . . you listnin'?" Aunt Mae asked. Startled that I had been zoned out for that long, I answered a hasty, "Yeah, Auntie," and kept my eye on the grease. This grease looks ready. It's hot.

"Should I put the fish in now?" I asked.

"Naw, chile, be patient!" she yelled, as she went on with whatever she was talking about.

". . . So the boy called me and told me he was doin' fine in school 'cept fo' math . . . I tol' him put his book up underneath his pillow and he'll do betta' . . ."

Damn. I haven't heard a word she's been saying.

"Who called you, Auntie?" I asked, eyes still on the grease that's popping so hard that I'm sure it'll ignite any minute.

"Your nephew, gal . . . you been listnin'? He says he's doing well in his lesson, 'cept fo' math. And Drea, well, she's doing as best as she can. I know if it wasn't for you helpin' nem boys of hers, they all would be in a world of trouble, 'cause she ain't got a pot to piss in . . ."

Oh. She's giving me the lowdown on the family. My sister Drea will never have anything. She's too busy chasing dick to even think about her sons. They're both smart, responsible, and don't want to be anything like their mother. So we have everything in common. And I take care of them. Made sure they got into and attended the colleges of their choice, put clothes on their backs, et cetera. It's not their fault their mother is selfish. She can't stand it either. How can you not stand that someone is helping your sons accomplish their dreams? Jealousy is irrational. She's a selfish and self-centered bitch if I've ever met one. Just like my mother. I guess someone had to inherit the bad genes. This grease is fucking scorching. My kitchen is going to go up in flames if we don't drop a piece of fish in there.

"Auntie."

"What!" she yelled, seemingly agitated that I was interrupting her.

"Can I put the fish in now? The grease is going to catch fire."

"No, it ain't, gal. Start on the salad," she answered with the nonchalance of a man in front of a John Madden football video game. She went on. About cousin Ella's barbecue, about the lady down the street who just passed, about how terrible the neighborhood has become, about how foreigners are buying up everything they can grab in Brooklyn, about anything and everything except the damn fish grease. I'm pulling my hair out watching this grease smoke.

"Did you hear me, Taiyler?" she asked.

"No. What'd you say?"

"Put the fish in now. Lay it down easy or else you gon' be in the 'mergerncy at DC General."

I did exactly what she said. One piece at a time. Watched it bubble and fry just like I used to when I was little. She was right. The grease wasn't hot enough. I swear, the things she knows.

"Now, don't turn it over till it frys hard on this side here, you hear?"

I let out a sigh of relief. Aunt Mae to the rescue again. Looking at the clock, I'm running a little behind, but I'll be okay. Shala volunteered to get there early to oversee the setup for me. I got caught up at the hospital last night and didn't get in early enough to start cooking. Plus, I like my food fresh, so I figured I'd just get up early and hit the kitchen.

"Have you talked to your mother yet?"

Silence. I know where this is going.

"You know she's the only one you got, Taiyler."

Here we go again. Aunt Mae and my grandma must have been campaigning for sainthood all their lives because they're the most forgiving people I know. Either that or the biggest pushovers I know.

My mother is probably the only one who is more selfish, reckless, and irresponsible than my sister Drea. My motto: Let them knock each other out. I can't be bothered. She has done more dirt . . . I mean, stolen shit from her own mother. And this is my flesh and blood. When it came to me, her "property" as she must have perceived our relationship, I guess I was fair game, too. When I was fifteen and decided that I would go to college hook or crook, I had given her nine hundred dollars that I had managed to save during summer break. I worked as a camp counselor during the week and at my uncle's store on weekends. Gave all my earnings straight to my mama for what she called safekeepin'. Came time to use the money for books first semester at Spelman, the shit was nowhere to be found. She'd spent every dime on some jailbird-assed man she was dating. That was one incident of many in which she found the time to put a man before her daughters. So, no. I haven't talked to her lately. I could really fucking care less. I have to somehow make that sound more congenial. Aunt Mae isn't having it. All right, be clever, T.

"You're my mother. I talk to you every chance I get," I said. And I meant it. She sighed heavily.

"Chile, call her. Don't let bad blood sit for too long. It'll start to rot and stank," she warned.

"Auntie, I don't see why I should; the phone works both ways. Why can't she call me? She's the one in the wrong," I whined.

"Two wrongs don't make a right. You call her because she's your mother and God wants that. You worry about cho self and let the Lawd worry about cho mama. You da only one that gots ta stand fo' Him in heaven and take a report fo' yo' self," she scolded. I can't argue with that. I don't want to, either. Plus, I need to finish this fish and start getting ready. I give her my defaulted "okays," tell her I love her, and turn this fish over. I have to get dressed.

At times like this, I wish my Carrera would turn itself into an SUV. For what I spent on this thing, it should covert into a 737 equipped with a stewardess and snacks. I don't want this food in the front seat, and my grandma would turn over in her grave if I put it in the trunk with my workout clothes and tennis rackets. There has to be a happy median. My phone has been ringing off the hook, and I've been ignoring it. If I'm to deal with all the hustle and bustle of the *DC's Men Are Cooking* volunteers and patrons like a champ today, I can't be stressed before I get there. Or else it will be as my nephew says "all bad" for the rest of the day. My phone rang for the fourteenth time in a row. It's Shala.

"Hey, girl . . . how far are you from downtown?" she asked.

"Ten minutes or so, how is it down there?" I'm lying.

"Everything is good. Most of the men are here already. I had them sign in like you asked, and I gave them each a booth number. So people are really just setting up now . . ."

Good. Everything is going according to plan. I wasn't worried anyway. Shala and I have the same blood, bones, and gray matter. I'm sure she's handling things exactly the way I would down there. It feels good to know that. I was more worried about the fish. She continued the rundown.

". . . yeah, so everything is okay so far. Sister Mary Clarence hasn't started working my last nerve yet. But then again, she's probably saving it all for you."

I laughed. She was probably right.

". . . and what time did Mr. *Essence* say he was getting here?" she said slyly. I could see her beaming through the phone. A true friend. Happy when I'm happy.

"I don't know. We only talked twice yesterday, and we didn't talk about the fund-raiser." Now I'm beaming. The last few days with Mr. DeCosta have been wonderful. That's the other reason I was just getting around to cooking for this thing this morning. We've been together every day since Tuesday, the first day we went out. Despite my apprehension, he was the perfect gentleman. I'm not officially letting my guard down, but between his ideal amalgamation of class, culture, and just plain fine, he's starting to lean a little toward my A team. Quickly. It's almost scary. He loves art. Has an appreciation for music. Everything from Jay-Z and Common to Jaco Pastorius and Coltrane. Said his best friend played trumpet. I told him I was a writer by heart, a physician by trade. He loved that. He reads. And not just *Whoreson*, *Flyy Girl*, and the *Autobiography of Malcolm X*. Not that there's anything wrong with those books, but we were able to compare notes and ideologies on *The Future of the Race, The Souls of Black Folk,* and *Under a Soprano Sky.* Men almost never read Sanchez.

What also stood out was his ability to make the smooth transition from Octavia Butler and Toni Morrison to Sista Souljah and Teri Woods. His versatility was outstanding. He cares about his people. I could go on. Derrick impressed me. And that's hard to do. I wanted to fuck him right there on the table at Filomena. Right on top of his Chicken Parmesan. Especially after he told me what it was like growing up with modest means and how he struggled through law school and made it. A litigator. No wonder he's a little arrogant. Self-assured. That happens when you're self-made. A man after my own heart. We're so much alike that it's nerve-racking. It seems too good to be true. So I'm playing the bench right now. Watching him make his moves. Cheering him on.

"Sha, there's so much that I could tell you about this man that attracts me to him, we'd have to do a day at B Natural and lunch at Maggiano's. For right now, let's just say that I am very, very pleased with Mr. Derrick DeCosta."

She squealed. The high of the moment was shattered by the blatant blaring of horns and sirens.

"Hold on, Sha, I'm turning left on Ninth Street now. I should be inside in about five minutes. Let me concentrate, you know how DC traffic is," I offered.

Shala chuckled. "Yeah, tell me about it. Okay. See you in a minute, T."

Upon arrival, I was amazed at the fluidity of the event. Even for myself, who is well-organized, this event went astoundingly well. The booths were divided into sections based on cuisine type. There were Southern and Creole cuisines. Caribbean and South American. African and Middle Eastern. Italian, Indian, and Asian. There were so many people here walking the floor, tasting everything they could get their hands on. Shala and I worked my booth. Sorors pulled through on everything else. They were all over the place. Collecting money at the door, at the information desk, at the lost and found, giving shout-outs during WKYS's live broadcast, just everywhere. Even our chapter president had to come down off of her high horse and acknowledge that it was the most successful year we'd seen with this event. I was ecstatic.

I hadn't seen Derrick yet, but he called and told me that he was in the Italian area of the event. I couldn't wait to see him. When the catfish was gone—not too many can turn down Aunt Mae's catfish fry recipe—Shala and I abandoned our booth and headed out to sample food from the other stations. This place was packed. I felt like I was bobbing and weaving through the MCI center at halftime.

"Oooh, T! Look over here, empanadas!"

"No, Sha, let's get some escovitch fish!"

"Damn, girl! You smell that gumbo?" shala exclaimed. That was one of her favorite dishes. We were like kids in a candy store. The gumbo won. We both picked up a miniature bowl of gumbo and headed down the soul food aisle.

"Oooh, Taiyler, look! Honey-glazed sweet potatoes and apples! I didn't think people up here knew how to make those!" Shala exclaimed. As we headed over to other areas I remembered that Derrick was over in the Italian section. I hadn't seen him all day.

"Sha, hold on, let's go over to Derrick's booth. I want you two to meet. He said some of his close friends and frat were in that area, too—I mean, not that you actually care."

Shala laughed out loud.

"Hey, you never know . . . I may need a sperm donor." We both laughed at that one. I spotted Derrick talking to one of his frat brothers.

"Hey! The woman of the hour!" he and his frat yielded in mock homage to me.

"This event was great, Taiyler! I'm proud of you. They'll probably want you to do this every year . . ." He always knows what to say. "Is this Shala? It's nice to meet you, I'm Derrick DeCosta." He bent over and kissed her hand. Such a charmer. He looks good in his fresh white tee shirt and white-on-white Nikes. I want him to kiss my hand. I want him to kiss something else.

"Yes, I'm Shala . . . It's nice to meet you, too! Taiyler has tol—" I nudged her in her side hard enough to make her fart. She knows better. She was about to say Taiyler has told me so much about you yada yada yada. Taiyler hasn't said a damn thing about a man she's been seeing for only a week. She caught on quickly.

"Owwh, T! . . . Taiyler said this was the best Italian food over here. Mind if I try it?" she asked him while making an I'm-going-to-fuck-you-up-for-that face at me. While she dove into his shrimp alfredo,

Derrick proceeded to introduce me to his frat brothers and friends as if I were a superstar. It was flattering, but I couldn't help but be a bit embarrassed. There was the judge, the guy from Arista, one of the attorneys he worked with on a few cases, some young guy who kept staring at my breasts, and finally, his best friend.

"Hi, I'm Nat. Derrick's boy from way back. He's told me a lot about you."

The twinkle in his eye. His piercing stare. Made me uncomfortable. And then it came to me. That warm feeling. Started at the base of my wrists and ran like molasses through to the center of my body. Leaving my hands cold and sweaty. I know this feeling. He and Shala were talking. All the time his eyes were on me. Like he was trying to figure me out. I heard Sha say something about me. Something that I would have ordinarily laughed at. But not this time. I'm feeling weird. Shit, Taiyler. You're a physician. Get to the bottom of this. Now, I demanded of myself to no avail. I felt . . . like I was spinning out of control. I wanted to hold idle chat. Do what Sha was doing. But I couldn't. I couldn't do anything other than what I was doing. Staring. Like an old white couple at dreadlocks. I felt like an idiot. I just want to go. Shala must have sensed this, because she grabbed her food, did the same to my elbow, and we were off with her yelling over her shoulder, "We'll be right back!"

I was off in another time and space. Thinking.

"Taiyler! Girl, you hear me! Taiyler Richardson! . . ."

I better answer her. She only uses my first and last name when she is getting aggravated.

"Huh?" I answered clumsily.

"What the hell was that about back there? Do you know that guy?" she demanded to know.

"No, no . . . we don't know each other. I just thought that I'd seen him before . . ." Actually I had, but this feeling was so hard to describe. And I don't have it near figured out. Sometimes lying is easier. Even when it's unnecessary. ". . . and I can't think of where. He just looked familiar, that's all. That's it." We both know that I'm lying. I always use qualifiers at the end of each lie. Like "that's it," or "see?" I can't help it. I'm paper thin.

"All of that drama for someone who just looked familiar? Whatever,

T. Let's go over to the Caribbean area. I heard the curried shrimp over there'll make you wanna pack up and move to a third world country."

I busted out laughing. Shala's antics. Her sarcasm. It'll make you laugh at shit you wouldn't ordinarily find funny. Most people think pretty girls are too stuck up to be funny. She's obviously an outlier.

"Are you going to stop stuffing your face anytime soon? Grai isn't going to want your ass all fat, sitting on top of a sweet potato," I teased. She glanced at me through the corner of her eyes, raised her hand to her temple like Malcolm in that picture hanging in every bean pie station and Black barbershop in the country, and gave an overly introspective response.

"You're right. Grai will want my ass all fat, *naked,* and sitting on a sweet potato." She's cracking herself up. I had to laugh myself.

"Whatever, Ellen Degenerous."

"Okay, Heather Hunter!" She threw a piece of shrimp at me and took off running. She knows I'm coming after her ass. The stain on my blouse is the only sign she needed. Shala made a break for it. Not before I did, though. She's dodging and faking through the sea of Black faces. Laughing her ass off. I heard Soror Marla yelling something about slowing down and twelve year olds, and that just made me laugh harder. Shala darted off toward the left side of the Convention Center. I can't believe we're running around like children. Then it hit me. Shit, I'm the coordinator. I'd better slow down.

"Sha! I'm going to get you later on!" I threatened. I bent over, placed both hands on my knees and gasped for air like a teacher's pet in a Lamaze class. I located a bench to the right of me and sat down. Thought about the day's events. Everything was perfect. We raised a record amount of money, the food was great, and people were genuinely happy. Derrick was still as fine as he was when I left his house last night. The only thing I couldn't figure out was the series of events surrounding me meeting, or officially meeting, Derrick's friend Nat. The warmth. The peculiar mood. The way he stared directly at me, caught himself and quickly looked away. As if he'd just seen his mother naked. His hand was cold and clammy. But when I shook it, it heated up my entire left arm. The same way I felt in the grocery store. Woozy. Out of sync.

"Trick, you made me drop my food," Shala said walking towards me. All I could do was chuckle. We must have run a mile, knocked over a few kids, and all this heifer is worried about is her damn shrimp.

". . . so I had to get another plate." She smiled guiltily and put her head down. Greedy ass. She knows something sarcastic is about to float right off of my lips. She intercepted the remark with one of her own. "Oh. By the way, Derrick asked me to tell you to call him right after this."

"Okay, I'll call him." Half of me was here; half of me wasn't. And she knew it. She looked at me the way she does when she's waiting for me to spill my guts. Eyes tight, lips pursed. I can't deliver. Not right now. Shaking her head, she went right back to her shrimp alfredo. And I went back to trying to figure out why I felt awkward every time I ran into the man from the grocery store.

14

Nathaniel

What the hell is Derrick listening to? What the fuck is this? You've got it bad? I'm flabbergasted. Sitting in D's truck, the harshest of the harsh reality hit me. This mutherfucker is strung out. Whipped. In a record amount of time. I wish he'd hurry up and get his ass inside so I can banter him about this shit. I chuckled to myself. You've got it bad. As my grandfather used to say, "Gat day-um!" Shit, *she* got him bad. Just as I was raising the aluminum pans off of my lap to place them in the backseat I heard Derrick shout.

"Ahhhhhh! Nooooooo! Nigga! I know you ain't about to put that greasy shit all on my butter-soft leather! This ain't no damn school bus, Nat! It's a 4.6!"

Shit, I forgot about how Derrick worshipped this truck. I don't know why he worries. He makes enough to buy five of these at a time. They look like little houses on wheels if you ask me. He needs to get a real truck. A Cadillac.

"Damn! Okay! I apologize! I just didn't want this shit leaking on me," I answered.

"So you'd rather have it leak on my Coach leather? You know how much money women pay for one Coach bag? Ask your wife. As a matter of fact, I dare you to lay a fucking greasy-ass dumpling or whatever the hell you have in those pans anywhere near one of her bags and see if she doesn't make your ass sleep in the basement," he chided.

"All right, all right. I hear you, man. Calm down. I'll hold them up front with me. Pass me one of those tee shirts in the back of the truck that you use to play ball in," I asked him. Wait. Recap. I know he isn't saying what I think he is. Let me kill it just in case.

"And by the way, chap . . . Kendra will never have my ass in the basement doing anything other than watching the game. *I* run my house." There. Just in case there was a misunderstanding up in here.

"Yeah, whatever, man." He glanced over at me, smirked, and held the steering wheel with his knee just long enough to grab a CD from the holder on his visor. Clearly he doesn't believe me. Now I'm pissed. I don't know what it is about men and their friends, but opinions count. More than anything. Especially when it comes down to handling your business with women. Or more importantly, them handling you.

"Aye, man. While we're on it, don't be so into, you know . . . not being whipped that you miss Garvin's birthday party at my house. I already sent out the E-vite."

"His birthday is like two or three months from now. Why all this so early?"

Derrick looked at me like he had all the answers that life never gave me.

"Why do you think? Do you know how long it'll take for even a playa like myself to round up respectable honeys for Garvin's birthday?" He has a point. Garvin isn't exactly on the Cosmo Top 20 list of men women want. I don't know. Does he want an answer?

"Nat, think of that new SUV Kendra wanted and you said it looked like a fake-ass station wagon on fifteens."

"Infinity?" I asked. And he just looked at me for a minute and smirked.

"Hell yeeeeah, Infinity!"

I had to laugh at that one. Derrick is a clown. When he gets to this point, he's almost amusing himself.

". . . So two or three months actually has this nigga right here under pressure!" Make that a circus. He's a freaking circus.

I'm laughing to myself. Feel bad about cracking on our boy but Derrick is telling the truth. "Aight, man. You sent me the E-vite, right?"

"Yeah. Yesterday."

"Cool. You know I'll be there." We sit in silence for a while. Watched Route 50 go by us in a collage of trees. No traffic. Doesn't even look the same. It's Saturday. Catch this Monday morning and you may shoot yourself in the foot for driving to work. Or shoot someone else for driving you up a damn wall. I decided to break the silence.

"So, man . . . how long have you and Taiyler been going out?" This question's loaded. He's not getting away from his pussy-whipped comments earlier. I'm just slicker than he is.

"We went out four times in four days," he answered with his usual aggressive male bravado.

"And in that four days . . . just that four . . . you let her unscrew your dick and uh—how'd you put it a couple of weeks ago when I told you I wasn't going out with the crew—put that shit in her purse? Damn, dawg. At least with Kendra it took eight years." I had to hit below the belt on this one. I'm smiling. Daring him to lie. Come on, D. I dare you.

"Nat, now, you know me better than anyone. Ain't no woman on the face of this earth putting my dick nowhere but in her mouth. That's policy, man. That's policy," he retorted.

"Yeah. Whatever. Come on, D. You've got it bad? Get real. I'm your boy," I said between failed attempts at stifling my laughter.

"You don't have to lie . . . It's okay, D . . . 'cause yo' dick ain't comin' home . . ." I'm laughing hard as shit now as I sing along with the track that's rotating. He can't help himself. Biting his top and bottom lip, he lets out a few stifles against his will. He knows I'm telling the truth.

"Nat, hustle man gave me the Usher CD last week at the shop. It was free. And so what if I am listening to Usher. That doesn't mean shit." We stopped for gas at the Exxon on the corner of New York and Bladensburg.

"Okay, D. All right. Do me a favor."

"What?" he asked as he lifted the nozzle on the premium pump.

"Call her a bitch."

"What? For what? She isn't one. And that's no way to talk about women. I'm surprised at you," he scolded. Damn. He's for real. As he continued to pump the gas, I fell right the fuck out. I was laughing so hard that I couldn't breathe. People were looking at me, chuckling to themselves. I guess it was contagious.

"Come on, man . . . say it. That bi-atch . . ." I mocked his usual antics.

Derrick started laughing, too. "Aight, man . . . aight. I guess you would have seen me bitch out today anyway."

"Whew!"

He shook his head from side to side like a dog shaking water off its ears. He grunted. Then whispered almost as if he were talking to himself.

"She's the woman of life, Nat. I swear, it defies depiction . . ."

I'm laughing even harder now. Sitting on the pavement with my hand on my stomach. Tears flowing. Trying to keep my face from splitting in two.

". . . I mean . . . I've never felt this way in my life."

I stopped laughing long enough to look at him. He looked pitiful. Happy pitiful. It was a hell of a combination. I had to ask him.

"Did you dig her out? She put her voodoo on you?"

"Nope," he replied quickly, with the dumbest look I've ever seen plastered on his face.

"Nope? Nope?" My eyes bulged with disbelief. "So what were you doing the other day at your house when I called?"

He pulled the receipt from the pump station, slid into the truck, and closed the door. He's evading the question. I walk around the truck in amazement. Almost walked right into the crash bars.

"You heard me, nigga! Y'all kissed or something, damn it!" It's amazing that at thirty, we still trade stories about women like we were thirteen-year-old pubescent boys.

"We talked," he mumbled under his breath.

"You what?" I asked for emphasis.

"We talked!" he confessed. That did it. I really fell out. Laughing harder than I did before. About two minutes later, while wiping the tears from my eyes, I mustered up the strength to tell him what I really thought.

"I can't fucking believe it! Derrick DeCosta. Dig 'em out D. Dick 'em down Derrick. Alpha Kappa Chi's Most Valuable Player. Does she know that you've fucked half of her sorority?" I swear, if I didn't know Derrick, I would have thought that he was a little embarrassed by my last few comments.

"We don't talk about that sort of thing . . ." he said quietly. This was indeed something new. I decided not to be as abrasive. Shit. He's met his match.

". . . we talk about important shit. Politics, the state of the race, religion, art, music. She's into writing, her poor patients . . . her Black patients . . . AIDS in Africa . . . She cares man . . . she cares," he said.

I'm blown. He told me that this woman was gorgeous. And that is a lot coming from a man that usually dates the crème de la crème. I thought he was smitten by her beauty and left it at that. A few things about Derrick. He never chases a woman for anything other than pussy. CEOs, attorneys, sorority women, churchwomen, congresswomen, the works. He almost never has them over to his place. Never shits where he eats. He always gets bored. She always ends up in the bitch pile. I need clarification.

"So you took her out, on Tuesday, had her over on Thursday, and never saw her panties? Once?" I asked incredulously.

"Never even tried. I lit the fireplace, poured some Clicquot, and just enjoyed her presence." He smiled, obviously still satisfied.

"And guess what, Nat. And you better not tell anyone this! . . ."

I'm still staring at my boy in disbelief.

". . . I cooked for her. Myself. Dinner. A good one, too. Jerked chicken, rice and peas, salad . . ."

Awwh shit. Now I'm two minutes from a coronary. Dinner? I've had enough. I couldn't even laugh. As we dodged the potholes and orange flags from the never-ending construction on Seventh Street and turned onto the block facing the Convention Center, one thing came to mind. Damn.

Derrick and I walked into the Convention Center with our arms full of food. The place smelled like a Black family reunion. I wondered how long we had to be at our respective booths. I wanted to eat as much as I could today. As we stood on line awaiting registration, I couldn't help but notice the sisters that were taking names and handing out numbers. All damn near tens. Alpha Kappa Chi turns out some of the most intelligent and best-looking women on the face of the earth. All wife material. As we approached the front, I noticed one of the women—I guess she was the organizer—had a face like an angel. I'm married but not dead. Dark, shiny black hair. Parted down the middle and braided on either side. Dark features. Damn beautiful. Looked like an Indian princess. A modern-day Pocahontas. I wondered if Derrick saw her. He isn't even paying attention. Obviously she's not Taiyler.

"She said that she would be at the front desk. I guess she's tied up," he said, looking like a boy who lost his puppy. I gave the beautiful sister my name, she scanned the list, handed me a booth number, and directed me to another nice-looking sister who pointed me in the direction of my area. I'm glad my wife's beautiful. And smart. And sexy. If she weren't, I'd have a hard time keeping it together. She changed me for sure. Before we met, I would have already devised a plan on how I was going to get lil' Indian girl to rock my teepee. Five minutes was all I needed. Southern charm is a muthafucka. I gave Derrick a pound and headed over to the Southern Cuisine section. He was in the Italian area. I agreed to meet him at his booth when we were done. My booth was right in the middle of the floor. In the center of everything. Sorors, elders, children, and teenagers were peeling into the Center by the droves. The place was packed.

"Excuse me? What kind of chicken is this?" a good-looking woman who looked to be about in her mid-thirties asked me.

"Southern spicy fried chicken. It's my mama's recipe," I answered. I hoped she wasn't going to interrogate me on this. Women will have a thirty-minute conversation on flour, sugar, and marinade. I'm not in the mood. I already had to cook the stuff.

"It sure smells good. What's it seasoned with?"

"My mama's stuff."

"Oh," she answered before taking a huge bite. Her mouth was big as hell. Seemed like she could take in that whole piece at once. I wondered what else she could take in all at once.

"Your mama's stuff, huh? I'm more interested in your stuff . . ." she flirted. I know she sees my band. She has to. Just in case she didn't, I picked up my Snapple with my left hand. You know, to give her a little help. She sees it now.

"Your wife must be a very, very happy woman. Are you a very, very happy man?" she asked with no shame. I can't believe this woman. This is right about the time I wish Kendra was here to come over and bust this desperate bitch's bubble. I'm hip to the game. It usually takes about thirty seconds for the transaction to go through, but it's worth it. I'll call Kennie over, and whatever home wrecker that happens to be in my face at the time studies her in that series of I'm-not-looking-but-I'm-looking glances that women seem to navigate so well. It usually takes about thirty seconds for them to finish evaluating her. Her flawless skin, well-kept hair, manicured nails, and conservative attire followed by that big-ass rock I put on her finger. And then I smile. Plant a fat one on her sexy lips. Ah-hah-a–ha-ha, you can't fuck with her, is usually the song that's going through my head. And just like that, it's over. Kendra never has to say or do a damn thing. Right now, I'm not in the mood for this shit. Have to nip it quick.

"Ma'am?"

"Yessss?" she answered, damn near pushing her titties down my throat.

"Do you mind me asking you for your age?"

She must have thought that to be the beginning of a come-on because she readily answered me.

"Thirty-five. Why do you ask?" she cooed.

"Because I assume that at around the age of seven or eight, your parents kind of explained what this was right here . . ." I said as I held my ring finger in front of her face in plain view. ". . . and I would hate to think, given your age and all, that it has been *that long* since you've seen one of these . . . I mean, you do remember what it is, right?"

Obviously stunned, she looked at me with the eyes of a woman scorned.

"I'll have you know, you self-centered bast—"

I'm not about to let her get ignorant in here. "No, it's okay. Sometimes we all have to be reminded of things that are easy to forget. Like the sanctity of marriage and shit like that. You know, the little things. Have a nice day, ma'am." If looks could kill, I'd be deader than a rapper working for Suge Knight. If deader is a word. She gritted her teeth, prepared to deliver a snide remark, and I guess thought otherwise, because she stomped off leaving a trail of smoke behind her. I laughed quietly to myself. And women say that men are dogs.

The rest of the day was cool. People loved the honey-glazed sweet potatoes and apples even more than they did the spicy chicken. I got an occasional gesture, but the Sorors are too classy to embarrass themselves like ol' girl did earlier. Well, some of them anyway. The last piece of chicken was lifted by the cutest little boy. He had to be at least Nile's age. Dark hair, big brown eyes. He was so polite. Made me think of what it would be like for Nile to have a little brother. He finished the chicken before they got ten steps from the booth. Mama's food is always good to the soul. Great. I'm done. I figured that I'd grab whatever was left of the food at the various stations. I did want to head over to the Asian area; that Mongolian barbecue smelled good as hell. Just as I was headed in that direction, my cell rang.

"What up, man? You done?" Derrick asked, excited as hell.

"Yeah, I'm done. I'm going to grab some food, and I'll meet you over where you are after that."

"Nah, man. You have to come over now. Taiyler is here, and I want you to meet her. Her girlfriend is fine, too. I mean, not for you, but you know what I mean," he said, sounding like a schoolboy. I have to get used to this.

"Aight. I'll be over there in a minute." I made a U-turn and started heading toward the Italian section.

"Booth fifty-three, right?" I asked.

"No, booth fifty-five, man. Booth fifty-five. If you're coming from up front, head left, and then north, as if going toward K Street . . ." Derrick directed.

"Okay. I'm in the Indian area. Now what?" I hate looking for shit.

"Aight. Look up at the pink AKX sign. Now, do you see the lady in the orange head wrap? Walk toward her."

"Head wrap? I don't see a—oh, okay, I see her now." I hate this.

"Now look over here to your right. I'm waving. Keep walking . . ." he said. I think I see him.

"Okay, man, I see you. I think. It's you, Brother Harris, Terry . . . I see you, I'm coming." At about ten feet from the group my quick stride came to a complete halt. Derrick and some of the bruhs came over to say what's up and exchange handshakes. I couldn't even hear what they were saying over the noise in my head. I can't stop looking at her. And then it came. The most peculiar feeling washed over my entire body. My heart has got to be arrhythmic, because I don't feel normal. I feel warm . . . nauseated. I'm glad I didn't eat. Derrick tapped my shoulder and pointed in the same direction of my intense stare.

"That's her, man. That's her." He looked so proud.

"That's who?" I asked, still unable to focus on my surroundings.

"That's Taiyler, man!"

"Which one? There's two of them over there." My hands are getting clammy. I feel like I'm going to be sick. I need to sit down.

"Red hair, man. Long red hair. Introduce yourself. I'll be right back," he said and darted over to another booth. Introduce myself. Introduce myself. To the woman from the grocery store. I don't even know what the fuck is going on. My body is doing flip-flops. My dick feels hard. I glanced down there. It's as soft as ice cream. What the f—? Okay. Get yourself together, Nathaniel. Why is this so hard, damn it!

Why do I feel like this? Walk over there and introduce yourself. Correction. Walk over there without falling flat on your face and introduce yourself. I took one step at a time as if I were walking a chalk line at three in the morning in Birmingham. The closer I got, the harder it was to focus on anything but her. I stopped. Stuck my hand out. Said what I think resembled *"Hi. I'm Nat. Derrick's boy from way back."* Or at least that's what was supposed to have come out. Pocahontas said hello. Introduced herself as Shala. Taiyler said nothing. I couldn't say anything else. Shala started doing the talking. Much to my relief. She started laughing. My guess was that I was supposed to laugh as well. So I did. With my eyes still on her. I felt like a fool who had no control over his body. I was so glad when Shala pulled Taiyler away, and I didn't even know why. All I knew was that this was some weird shit. As I stood there, watching her walk away, Derrick scared the shit out of me.

"Where's Taiyler?" he asked.

"Uh . . . I dunno. Her friend said they'd be right back."

"What did you think? Beautiful, right?"

"Uh . . . yeah, D. No doubt. A real beauty." That's what I said. What did I actually think? That I'd better figure this shit out. Immediately.

15

Shala

"You have thirty-six new messages. Message number one..." "Good morning, Shala, this is Dr. Johnson's office... we're out of Zocor 20mg's. We really need it badly as Dr. Johnson's starting a lipid clinic in a few weeks..."

Fuck. I'm sick of this shit. God only knows why I went into pharmaceutical sales. Well, I know. The money. Someone should have warned me. Cash the check, sell your soul. Even as a CV specialist, these mutherfuckers must think that they own me. As the thunder clapped, I turned over and looked at Grai. She's still in dreamland. I could never sleep through a thunderstorm. Scared the heck out of me when I was little, and they aren't far from doing the same now that I'm grown.

Two more jolts of tremendous loudness shook the house. Grai snuggled up closer to me and threw her arm haphazardly around my waist. That's funny. She must be able to sense that I can't sleep. Or that I'm nervous. Or one of the two. I hate these things. It's four in the morning, and I'm checking my damn voice mail at work. This is what storms do to me. Falling back asleep with all of this in the air is a definite no. Which means that I'm going to be dead-dog tired tomorrow. I mean today. That won't be good. When I'm tired, I'm bitchy. Beyond bitchy. Picture taking barbwire to my neck. That's what I'm sure I'll be doing while trying to get through the day. I have a breakfast appointment in four hours, a lunch with a top area physician to follow, and a dinner program at seven. Not to mention the three reports that I let sit over the past few days because I just couldn't bring myself to do the work on the weekend. All due by tomorrow at the close of business. Shit. I have too much going on. I need a vacation. A serious one. Alone. And Lord knows, I can't bring myself to funnel through the rest of these messages.

"Third message . . ." Shut up bitch. I hang up the phone and place my thumb and forefinger at the bridge of my nose. And pull. The unrelenting thunder has made its way back onto the roof of my house. Back into my bedroom. I swear this is God practicing for the end of time. My grandma used to say that thunder is nothing but the devil beating his wife. An old wives' tale. If that's the case, then she should be dead already. Anything that makes that much noise getting hit should be gone by now. Maybe God spares her.

Listen to me, I'm delirious. God. God. The lamp against my feet, the light upon my path. Or the light against my feet, and the lamp . . . oh, forget it. I haven't been to church in so long, He probably doesn't know that I still exist. Who am I kidding. He knows. He just probably turns his face to me. Probably in disgust. Or shame. A girl raised by one of His own flock. And a mother who is damn near a saint. I know Him. Know the Word. Profess to love Him. Don't claim to understand Him, though. He could have made me into what my parents raised. I wanted so badly to become that. A woman who will marry underneath her father's words, with her mother shedding tears of happiness and rejoicing. But He didn't.

Instead, I'm a soul engaged in a marriage of wills. Unwilling to cooperate with each other. The will to do what I think and feel is right, and the will to do what my heart knows is right. I'm fighting a losing war. The tears that I shed when Grai loves me—the right way—are monumentally different from the ones I shed while praying to the Savior. Who must hate me. Love is supposed to be God's gift to mankind. It's cursed me. And that's wrong. I am in love. Truly. With many ideas. Family, marriage, peace, solitude, freedom . . . truth. And with this love, I'm conflicted into a season of vicissitudes. Family, marriage . . . those come with the price of freedom and truth. And so it stands for solitude. Peace is ambiguous. I am at peace being true to myself. I am free loving Grai. Allowing her to love me. Grabbing the sheets while she manipulates her tongue to make my spirit rise out of my body. Kissing her in the places that worship my existence. However, I am also in love with the idea of living a life of society-based normalcy. Children. Christmases. Cookies. The idea of one day being able to live in a way that pleases God, my father, and my countenance gives me peace. At the expense of solitude. Of truth.

So you see my dilemma. This losing war with right and wrong is killing me. Spiritually. If I live right, I advance spiritually in God and family and portray the life of my ancestors. If I live wrong, my spirit dies a slow, tedious death anyway. I'm just not sure which is which. Which is right, which is wrong. Right used to be what was felt in the heart. Righteousness will cause me to rip my heart apart by the seams. Forsake what feels good to the soul. A woman alive without a heart. Has it ever been done? Don't think so. So I'm caught in between life and death either way. I don't know which way to move. I try not to overanalyze it. But it's fucking with me.

A flash of lightning illuminates my bedroom. The rain continues to pour. I pulled the covers over my head and slid in closer to Grai. I'm trembling. She kissed me beneath my ear. Wants to know if I'm okay. I want to know how long she's been up.

"Long enough to see you almost jump off of the bed when the thunder hit," she said softly. My lashes are wet. I'm tearing.

"Shala, why are you so scared? Everything will be okay. Storms don't last long," she said meaningfully. Another tear fell. She doesn't understand.

"I've been dealing with this since I was young, Grai. I don't know how to make it go," I mustered in a barely audible whisper. She still doesn't understand.

"I know, but it's just a storm . . . it's just a storm," she reassured me as she pulled me even closer to her.

"I don't know why I'm like this . . . I don't want to be . . ." I relayed quietly between sniffles.

"You'll be okay, sweetie . . . com'ere. I love you . . . stop trembling, okay? Everything will be okay." She held me close and rocked my body back and forth, nursing my iniquity. She really doesn't understand. Grai's family has always been liberal. Her mom and dad were at Woodstock celebrating freedom in love, peace, and truth while mine were in Memphis righting wrongs in the name of God. They accept her the way that she is. And so does her god. So does her god. I cry. Hard. She knows this is about more than just the rainstorm. She has to. She can feel it. Because she loves me. In spirit and in truth. Loves me enough to want to steal all of this pain away. I feel it leaving with every stroke, every lick, every tease. She's making me forget. With the skill of a surgeon, she removes the tumors growing inside me. The self-hate, the doubt, the pain. I can feel it all leaving me.

"Damn . . . mmh . . . Gra . . . Gr-a . . . sh-it . . ." The confusion, the feelings of betrayal . . .

". . . uhhm . . . Oh, my God . . . oh . . . fuck! Shit . . . I can't take this, baby . . . ple . . . pl-eeeese . . . ummh . . ." I know she's hurting. Hurting just as I was a few minutes ago. I know this because she has all of me right now. Every aspect of my being is being experienced by her at this moment. Every touch lets me know how much of me she has become. I can feel it on her face. As her lids brush the insides of my thighs. She's hurting. Just because I am. And trying to love it all away. Just like me. I grit my teeth and let out a hoarse moan. She's licked and sucked and moaned, caressed and kissed and loved me away from this world.

"Wh—wh-at are y-y-ou do-ing [breath] to . . . me . . . ahh . . . oh, Lord . . . mmhm . . . Grai baby . . . yes . . ." I'm crying out in Jesus' name. Hoping God turns a deaf ear. I feel her tears fall between the creases of my thighs. She's fighting this war with me. God only knows I can't do it by myself.

"So as you can see, Zocor offers your patients a complete package. It's been proven in the most legendary clinical study ever to lower LDL, triglycerides, and raise HDL without compromising safety or cost. Now, let's talk about Statins, C-reactive protein, and the new study just published in the *American Journal of Cardiology* not too long ago."

I am almost done. Breakfast went well. Well meaning I delivered my clinical presentation without my head hitting the table. Or without cursing the receptionist out when she asked me if I could wait in the patient area for the doctor to come in. This morning I came to work in a state of utter lethargy. Not only due to the lack of sleep I received, but mostly to Grai's relentless means of therapy. I feel the corners of my mouth curling upward as I think about it. Not bad. Not bad at all. I left for work this morning optimistic. Now I'm at lunch with one of the top cardiac surgeons in DC. With a tension headache.

They say he's one of the best. I didn't totally believe it, because all of my cardios have major egos. They all feel that they are the best. When I saw Dick Cheney walk out of the examination room, and Dr. Johnson signal for me to come into his office, I knew that today would be a day for extra questions. I heard our vice president had enough chemical and molecular compounds in his medicine cabinet to throw CVS under a bus. Dr. Johnson is all ears. They all are after seeing a difficult patient.

"So, Shala. What's the percentage of patients in these studies that experienced rhabdomyalgia? What about the contraindication with Amiodarone? . . ." He's firing away. I'm not as quick as I need to be today. But I get him the answers he needs. Pushing through the rest of my day was a piece of cake after that. Just as I was placing the drug samples into the trunk of my car my cell phone rang. Daddy.

"How's my little sweet pea today?" In a Louis Armstrong voice, his velvety singsong cadence vibrated through the fiber optics with all intention of lifting my spirits. And it did just the opposite. Somehow I have to muster up the energy to be Daddy's little girl today.

"Hi, Daaaa-deeeeee! How are you? Aren't you supposed to be getting things ready for the conference at the church this weekend? I've been hearing it all over the radio. TD Jakes, Kirk Franklin, and who else?" Figure that'll get him started. The only thing he loves as much as me is the church.

"Oh, yeah, sweet pea! We gon' have a sanctified time in the Lord! I don't know if we gon' have enough room for it all! Yeah, there is quite a buzz about it, ain't it?" He's proud. Wish he were proud of me. He says that he is all the time. Only he isn't talking about the me that I am. He's proud of the magna cum laude Spelman grad, the Merck Cardiovascular Sales Specialist, the Boys and Girls Club volunteer, the soprano section choir girl. Daddy's little girl. Not the one who uses the Lord's name in vain four ways from Sunday.

". . . they got some of those new gospel ballerinas—this I gots' to see—and the young people's choir will be singing, too," he exclaimed. I know he wants to ask me. Doesn't want to force it.

"Did Mama get the choir's robes ordered on time? I know she was worried about that," I asked, playing dodge ball with the issue at hand.

"Yes, you know your ma, she stayed on those robe folk until she got 'em all in," he said triumphantly. That's my mother. Three hundred robes in two weeks. Silence. I know he wants to ask me. I oblige him this time.

"Dad, I can't come this weekend." I hear him sigh. The same sigh he sighed when I told him I couldn't come last time. And the time before that. I'm hurting him. It's hurting me. He doesn't want his daughter to burn in hell. He doesn't know that it's too late.

"Oh, baby, you gon' miss such a blessing . . ." His voice is begging to understand. The fire-baptized preacher of decades. Leader of thousands. Counselor of generations. Reduced to the inadequacy of a daughter who flirts with sin, despite the reverie of a saint. He's wondering what happened to turn me away from his church. From church in general. How did the preacher's kid become the prodigal? I haven't been to church since my goddaughter's christening a few years ago. And even then I thought I smelled sulfur as soon as I hit the vestibule.

"I know, Daddy. I know. I just have so much work to do—"

"God gave you that job, Shala," he interrupted. Oh, now I'm Shala. I guess sweet pea goes to church on Sunday.

"I know, Daddy. I know. And I thank Him for it every day. I just can't make it this weekend." Or any other weekend until I figure myself out. I won't defile my father's church. I just won't.

"All right. We'll talk about it another time . . ." He sounded dejected. I hate that. "I have to go and check on the delivery for the kitchen. Deacon Tufts isn't here. Baby, your father is here for you if you need him. The one you're on the phone with and the one smiling down on you. Just call Him. Okay? He'll help you through whatever is keeping you from His house."

If he only knew. I hang up feeling hungover. Sitting in the driver's seat with my head against the steering wheel. Driving myself insane with similar thoughts. Phone rang again. I let it. Curiosity gets me. It's Taiyler.

"Hey, chica . . . how's your day going?" she asked cautiously. Almost as if she were afraid for me to answer.

"It's going. Had a breakfast, a lunch, and have a dinner tonight. You coming?" I asked with a pain in my voice reflecting the mood of Coretta Scott King's veiled photo in *TIME*. She disregarded my answer and my question.

"It stormed last night. You okay?"

"I could've done better. Nothing I couldn't handle." There's nothing like a best friend who knows you so well that she doesn't have to ask for details.

"You wanna talk? I know you were probably thinking about—"

I cut her off midsentence. If I start this, I'll never make it through the day.

"Nope. Don't want to talk about it, T. Is that okay?"

"That's okay, Sha. Just know that I'm here," Taiyler said empathetically.

"When haven't you been?" I asked her. She sighed. The same one she sighed when I told her that I couldn't be with Bruce anymore. I couldn't continue to lie with men. Lie to myself. It's the same story. Same sigh. Different person. Different love. Same turmoil. It's so funny that the only thing in life that changes is time. Back when we were in college, and a terrible Georgia storm hit, I would jump down off of the top bunk and hit the ground running. Straight to Taiyler's room. Jump in the bed and cry. She got so used to it that she would just make room for me in her twin bed at the slightest hint of a rainstorm. Something about thunderstorms that always made whatever emotion I was sitting on at the time rise to the top. Ever since I was a little girl. This morning was no different. She sucked her teeth. This thing is fucking with her, too. I hated to be the cause of that. I heard the wheels of her brain turning. I felt bad. For the second time today. I can't help that right now. Shit, I can't help myself.

"Shala, just be true to your—"

"T, I meant it. Not now. Are you coming out tonight?" I asked impatiently. Damn. I just bit her head off.

"No. I'm heading down to the International Gallery of African Art tonight with Derrick. I won't be out too late, though. So if you decide you need me, just ring."

I like Derrick. Glad she met him. Wish my life were that simple. I'm coveting. One step farther from heaven. Making my bed in hell. After I hung up with T, my head throbbed. That tension headache has become a migraine. Fuck this dinner. I called my business partner, asked if he could cover for me. He owes me three or four anyway. No problem. I'm going home. Grai's still there. Writing. Her book signing at Karibu isn't until later tonight. She's signing her third novel. A story about true love. In the spirit. The more I think about her, the faster I drive. I pulled into my driveway, hit the button on the garage opener, and damn near totaled my mountain bike. Kicking my shoes off, I began unzipping my skirt. Where is she? She's not in the kitchen . . . not in the sunroom . . . not in—oh, here she is. In the office.

"Hey, sweet—"

I don't even let her finish greeting me before I do the same with a kiss. And another. And another. And I send a silent prayer of thanks to La Perla. And she knows what I need.

"How was your da—"

And I don't let her ask.

"Sha-la, baby . . . what's wrong?"

And I don't answer. She knows what I want. This is not about sex. It's about the spirit. I need to know that mine is still alive and kicking. That I haven't lost it in this war. That it's still a reflection of me and that it's still wanted. Needed. Loved. Holy. Even if it's not in the eyes of the Most High. I don't have to answer her. She knows. She has to. She can feel it. When two people love like this, love spiritually, then that is all that their love can be measured by. So she succumbs. Throws her head back, grabs her hair with both hands, and lets me understand her. That's an understatement. She lets me become her. Complement her strengths, compensate for her weaknesses. Until I know all that she has learned. Until we dance the same dance, shout the same shout, sing the same songs. Until we are one in spirit. Until the truth is told. Solidarity is spoken. Until peace allows my heart to be still. If only for a slice in time. And when I'd licked and stroked and loved my way to her core, to the part where nothing else exists other than truth, other than the spirit, I find myself there. Understanding peace. Gazing at it in amazement. Lying on my back. Staring at the walls of her love all night with my feet crossed in the air.

16

Derrick

I stare out at the rain, balancing the scales of life on the bridge of my nose. The left side tips, making the right appear as lightweight as an anorexic teenager. All of the lies told, lives destroyed, and dirt done to women haunt me like a haint in a Carolina graveyard. The math does not add up. There is no logic to the rules of karma except what goes around will surely come back around. So amidst my calculations, Taiyler Richardson should be the last person that I'd be blessed to know.

The past few months have been filled with a sweetness that I've only read about in Channer novels. I want to reach out to my past and hide every untruth ever told through my eyes to a woman. Tuck them neatly underneath my bed. Because if this is what I've put at risk—this feeling—then I'll never forgive myself. I can't deny it. At first, I was just taken by her beauty. But today, it's the beauty of her spirit that overtakes me. I'm supposed to pick her up tonight. We're going to the International Gallery of African Art together. But as I sit in my office chair and think, I get scared. If this is what I'll lose because of my foolish ways, I won't be able to bear it. Surprised, myself, by my intensity, I close my eyes and focus. On the God of Israel. Who forgives. Who led them into the promised land even after their murmuring and complaining. Sinning and strutting. He forgave them. Please forgive me. Please don't let this be a sample of what I would have been blessed to experience if I had not treated the ones before her with such depravity. I'm sweating. I must be praying hard. Praying for those scales to shift weight. Let the good outweigh the bad. So that I can partake of the milk and honey that is Taiyler. Damn. I didn't know it would hit me like this. My thoughts were interrupted by a knock on the door. "Come in." It's my secretary.

"Mr. DeCosta, the Board of Education is on line one, they want to know if you've filed the motion for the enforcement of the code, and Mr. Woods is on line two. Says it's important."

I think. Hmmm.

"Tell the board that my response is in the mail and that I will talk more on the matter once our original agreement is resolved, and put Nat through." As she turned around, sauntering out of the office with my instructions, I couldn't help but notice one thing in particular. I'm not looking at her ass. In fact, I've been looking at the picture that Taiyler and I took at the Roy Hargrove concert a few weeks ago. And I never even looked up. Midthought, my line lit up.

"This is Derrick." Damn, I'm answering the phone like my lady.

"Hey, D. What's up, man? Listen, I have a favor to ask of you," he sounded stressed.

"Shoot. What's the deal?"

"Tonight is my night to pick up Nile from dance rehearsal. But I have a business review tomorrow, and we are not halfway through with the components of our presentation. I need you to pick her up at around five-thirty."

Just as I was about to tell him I could do it out of habit, I realized that I was picking up Taiyler an hour later. Shit.

"Kendra can't do it?" I ask like an idiot's idiot. Knowing that if she could, he wouldn't be calling me.

"No. She's at the hospital on rounds. If she could, I wouldn't be asking you!"

Point taken. This is my boy. My boy who happens to trust me with the care of his only daughter. I'll just have to call Taiyler and let her know that we'll be a little late.

"All right, Nat. I'll get her. Where is the studio? And what time are you going to be home? Because Taiyler and I have a date tonight downtown," I told him.

"Oh, I'll be at the house by seven. And actually, Kendra should be coming in around the same time. It's just that neither of us can get all the way to South West to pick her up," he explained.

"That's cool, just call the studio and tell her instructors that I'm coming, so they won't be staring me down with the police on one line and Child Protective Services on the other."

He laughed. "Will do. Thanks a lot. I appreciate it."

"No problem, man," I answered. It's nothing.

"You find out what time K is bringing Garvin down this weekend? Better yet, just tell me what time the party starts and I'll be there. Those guys are always on major CPT. We'll fuck up a whole day waiting for their asses."

I'm a little confused. Make that a lot. Why are they coming this week?

"What are they coming down for? I didn't know anything about us hanging this weekend." Thoughts of the last boys' night out at Dream haunted me. And I have plans with my lady this weekend. Nat started laughing that annoying-ass laugh of his.

"What's so damn funny, patna?" I asked.

"What do you mean what's so funny? Nigga, you know just as well as I do that Saturday is Garvin's birthday and the shit is at your house."

Oh, shit. Oh, shit. Yeah, yeah, he's right. How could I forget that? I invited like fifty people. This is tomorrow night. Where's my head? Can't believe I forgot. Can't let Nat know that.

"Yeah, nigga, I knew! Just wanted to make sure you were on your *p's* and *q's* seeing that you missed it the last time we got together. Some of us don't forget about our boys." Hope he buys that bullshit. But if I know Nat . . .

"Muthafucka, please. Your ass forgot. Yeah, you have never let a woman fuck you up this badly," he says to himself. I can see him shaking his head.

"And I ain't whipped this time either. I'm still Derrick. Remember that," I said. Attempting to salvage the small piece of my manhood that Nat insisted on taking with him.

"No, *you* remember that," he spewed playfully. We say our aight thens, and holla backs as we prepare to hang up. Just as I was pulling the receiver from my ear, Nat yelled out.

"Yo, D! Yo, D!"

"Yeah?"

"Uh, how's your new girl? You've been incognito for the past few weeks."

I can feel his laugh coming on through the optics. He's happy for me. A true friend.

"She's fine, man. I'm learning something new about her each day. And I'm still captivated. So I guess that means I'm fine, too." I know I sound sheepish. But for some reason I don't care. At least for right now I don't. I can tell that Nat is still getting used to this. Shit, I am, too. I know he expected some of my bullshit rhetoric. He didn't get it this time. He's surprised. I can tell by the way he answered.

"Okay, playa . . . that's good . . . real good. So, uh . . . has she let you hit it yet?" he asked more carefully than he usually would. I guess he's still fidgeting with my changes. What he doesn't realize is that this has always been Derrick. What he'd known all of this time was my alter. The ego I prayed to in order to keep my innermost desires and fears from surfacing. It's funny how you can become empowered with a personality that will allow you to build a bridge over the weaker or more fragile you.

"Nah, man. Not yet. And I'm kind of glad about it. Because I'm not thinking of her in that way anyway. I want to save it." Now, I know that floored him.

"Save it?" he reiterated.

"Save it, Nat. The deeper I get into her self, her likes, her dislikes, her fears, her foes . . . the better I think it'll be." And that's all I give him. I don't want to cheapen his image of her by reducing our inter-action to a series of dick and pussy. I don't want to kill him either. I can tell this is a lot for him to digest. Nat's quiet. I chuckle. He didn't know I had it in me. I didn't know either. I suppose it takes the right woman to bring it out.

"All right, D. You're scaring me, man. But that's cool, I've always wanted you to experience a good woman, but damn. This is drastic. Well . . . keep up the good work." He encouraged me. I needed it. Because I'm way more scared than he is. I'm petrified. I've never felt this way before. I don't even know what to do.

For now, I pick up the phone and dial her cell phone number. With each digit pressed, I'm closer to hearing her voice. My heart races. Under my arms I can feel that little pinch of a sweat breaking. Her voice mail comes on. Damn. I forgot she turns her phone off dur-ing patient time. So I lean back in my chair, more so in an effort to relax than anything else, and listen to her beautiful voice tell me to leave my name and number at the sound of the tone and she'll get back to me. Sweet nirvana. Only I do one better than leave her a message. I leave her my heart. And I hope she gets it back to me in one piece.

I always start with the shoes. She had on a pair of black leather sling-backs that made her legs look as long as a summer day. She doesn't usually wear jeans, so imagine my surprise as I watched her strut across Georgia Avenue and slide those sevens into my truck like she owned the street and everything on it.

"Hi, babe. You ready to go? I'm really excited about this exhibit . . ." She was talking to me. Looking at me. But she might as well have been speaking Yiddish to a wino playing dominoes on a New York City street corner. I'm caught up. I can't even hide it. And she knows this. Dr. Richardson is not right.

"Derrick. Derrick! Earth to Derrick . . . come in, babe . . ." she teased. I'm stuck. No shame in my game. I didn't realize she was bow-legged. Still trying to rewind and play that image of her crossing the street. I'm two seconds from asking her to do it again.

"I'm here . . ." I say, showing teeth from every angle. "You didn't tell me you were, uh . . . changing your clothes."

Taiyler looked at me and smirked. It's a damn shame she's this beautiful.

"When you told me you were going to get Nile, I went home and changed into something more comfy. You don't like me in denim?" she asked, delivering a look that let me know she already knew the answer to that question.

"Yeah . . . uh . . . yeah, I'm just a little surprised, that's all. I almost always see you in business casual attire. Slacks, button-downs, you know . . . clothes that don't show your . . ."

"My what?" she asked coyly. Shit, I'm not really prepared to have a conversation. I just want to look. I should have pretended that I had something on my mind and let her drive, so that I could stare without looking like a voyeur.

"My what, Derrick?" She tightened her eyes and repeated in mock anger. I want to fuck her right now. Right in the back of my truck. Save making love for later on. Control yourself, man.

"Your . . . uh . . . your *anatomy and physiology*, Dr. Richardson," I said, using the tone of a sixty-plus-year-old professor. She obviously thought that was hilarious because she threw her head back and let out a loud laugh. I'm counting her teeth.

"You are a mess, Mr. DeCosta."

I really am at this point. We head south on Georgia, past Walter Reed, past Howard, and hit the stoplight on Florida. She rode with her right hand in her lap and her left hand caressing the back of my head and neck. I love that.

"So how was your day? No emergency surgeries or ambulance rides today?" I asked in jest. She chuckled. Cleared her throat.

"No, not today. I actually had a good day. My presence was requested at a pharmaceutical conference in Aruba today. As a part of a physician marketing study or focus group for a new category of heart drugs coming out. Happy about that. Saw a truckload of Patients. Most of them are doing well. A few aren't. Usually my hypertensive and hypercholesterolemic patients. Those are the ones that I spend the most time with. They usually aren't taking their medications correctly. Which reminds me, have you had your cholesterol tested?" she questioned.

"No, I haven't," I answered flatly. I hate going to the doctor.

"I know you're young, and handsome and all, but you need to get that tested."

"Yeah, but I hate going to the doctor. No offense, baby."

She smiled that understanding smile that I remembered from the fund-raiser meeting. I'll do whatever she wants.

"I know, Derrick, but you have to get over that fear. This is important. Don't worry, I'll take care of you." That smile is a seductive one now.

"And just how do you plan on doing that, Doctor?" I raised my eyebrow in mock interrogation.

"I have my ways. Don't worry, just have your secretary make an appointment. I'd be happy to show you."

I'm quiet. Nodding my head. Teeth over my bottom lip. My phone rang. Fucked up my mental quickie. Shit. It's Sherry. All-star Sherry. Ass-smells-like-strawberries Sherry. Decisions, decisions.

"Are you going to answer that?" Taiyler asked, not the slightest hint of jealousy or annoyance in her voice. But I know better. Fuck it. I have to do this anyway so . . .

"DeCosta . . . Nope . . . No, I can't see you this weekend . . . not then either . . ." I glanced over to the passenger side. Taiyler's mind is dancing to the rhythm of the wiper blades. This is a test. All right, playa, rip that card up.

"I am seeing someone . . . yep. Other than you. I want to make her the love of my life . . . yeah, eventually . . . no, I'm not kidding . . . don't know if that will be possible but I'll run it by her. Hold on . . ." Asshole. Do your asshole thing. A lesson in life, when in the presence of two, choose one, fry the other one like a Popeye's crispy chicken wing.

"Taiyler, baby, this is Sherry. I used to date her before I fell so help-lessly for you. It was nothing serious. She wants me to escort her to a company dinner next week. I told her that I thought it was a bad idea, but I'd run it by you. What do you think?" I know she's stunned. But she's not showing anything that resembles surprise. And then that smile shows signs of amusement. Or disgust. Depends on how you read it.

"Don't involve me in your heartless drama . . ." She threw her hand toward me in a tsk. And then that smile turned mischievous. ". . . and ask her what part of *no* didn't she understand?"

So I did just that. One down, a whole lot to go. She can't believe my crassness. I can't believe I've never showed it to her. We continued our conversation. Outside of the fact that it's pouring rain out, my night is perfect. As every night with Taiyler has been for the last few months. As I pull up in front of the Gallery to let her out while I parked, I realize that I couldn't care less about the pieces inside the building waiting for us to appraise them. My priceless piece of art is sitting right beside me looking like a shooting star. Feeling her lips on my cheek and watching her slide out of the truck and open my um-brella was every wish granted. Then I wondered if this was what Nat felt with Kendra. If it was, no wonder she always came first. It's not for her, it's for him. This shit feels good.

We walked around the Gallery, hand in hand, admiring works by some famous and not-so-famous artists. Playing hide and kiss in the confines of cubbyholes stationing pricy sculptures. I bought a limited edition print by Haven Gordon. Taiyler was still looking at a warrior mask from Ghana. I forgot. She collects them.

"Derrick, this is wonderful," she commented in awe. "I just don't know if I have space for it on my wall, but I have to get it." Just as she was turning around to signal for someone's attention, a young college brother with locks came up to us. He works here. As they conversed on everything from the origin of the mask to the type of wood used to carve it, I became increasingly clear on one thing. I don't know shit about African warrior masks. Made a mental note to stop at the bookstore this weekend and grab a book or two on the subject. I'm sure about one thing, though. I swear I heard him say that piece of wood was twelve hundred dollars. I must be hearing things.

"How much did you say it was?" I asked him.

"Uh . . . it's on sale for eleven hundred ninety-five dollars. It's thirty percent off."

This shit is nice, but it's not twelve-hundred-dollars nice. I moved over to the picture window and watched U Street pass by in a whir of lights and water. Still in heavy conversation with the young buck, Taiyler whipped out her gray American Express card and placed it on the table without so much as a breath between sentences. They are beyond talking about the mask and into his art history major at Howard. She never even broke a sweat. She applied her John Hancock and made arrangements to have the piece delivered to her home. She's obviously doing better than I imagined. I almost got a touch of the "insecure bug," but I let it go. My father's words echoed in my mind, *"Beware of what you pray for, you just might get it."* I took a look at her. A good one. And shook that little insecurity bug off of my sleeve. She's exactly what I want. Confirmation that I'm wanted. Not needed. She doesn't need me for a damn thing other than love. And I'm ready to empty my pockets for her until I'm pulling out lint. Interrupting my thoughts with a kiss, she lets me know that she's all done. And that she loves my print. And that she's having a great time. And that she's pleased with me. And it does wonders for my ego. I want to make her world perfect.

"Taiyler, I'm going to get the car. Stay inside until I pull around." I sorted keys from various vehicles. I have to get rid of some of these cars.

"Noooo! I want to walk with you. I like the rain. It's romantic."

I was about to tell her that this was non-negotiable. Until she shut that down.

"A little wetness never killed anyone," she said matter-of-factly as I watched the corners of her mouth form something short of a Hawaiian sunset. Forget seductive, that smile is sinful now. Enough said. One day I'll practice saying no to her.

* * *

We rode back to Bowie in silence. Her with the passenger seat leaned back to capacity, counting raindrops, putting every tenth one in her pocket of thoughts. Me watching her watch the water. Wondering why she's not speaking. Wanting whatever is diverting her attention away from me dead. Our usual post-date commiseration consists of talks that would make Oprah and Tavis jealous. I love to hear about her trips to Tokyo, Ibiza, and Ipanema. She cross-examines me on my cases. Challenges my decisions. Makes me wonder if she was an attorney in another life. Makes me realize how empty mine was before she came along. And now she's quiet. Disrupting our short-lived ritual. I pulled up to a four-story home. With huge brownstone-style steps. We're here. In her driveway. Behind her Porsche. Next to her X5. I love her style. She didn't move.

"Baby, we're here. You want me to help you out?"

Still no answer. With her eyes fixed on the windshield, she tugged at the silver bangle on her arm.

"Derrick, these past few months have been wonderful. You are so much of what I want and need in a man. I just want to make sure that I'm all you wan—"

"You are," I interrupted. I couldn't say any more than that. I've never been good at verbally expressing myself. So I'll show her. I got out of the truck and walked around to her side. Sans umbrella, I lifted her up, let her wrap her legs around my waist and lay her head on my shoulder like a toddler being carried off to the sandman. With her feet crossed behind me, she held on tight. And I massaged the muscles at the base of her neck. I carried her over the threshold, past the living area, up the stairs, past the balcony, up the second flight, the third, and onto the top floor. The master bedroom. My master's bedroom. I lay her down on the bed. And get on my knees. And wait. I'll wait forever. Do whatever. It doesn't matter. I don't think she knows that. She's groggy. From the massage. Eyes half closed, she whispered questions that I was prepared to answer.

"What are you doing, Derrick . . . why are you down there?"

I can answer that. Pausing just long enough to capture her beauty, I lick my lips and trace a psalm of love onto her shea-covered skin.

You are everything that I want in a woman. And much more than I need. I've taken women everywhere, yet you're taking me places that I've

*never been. I've had more sex than one man could ever want. Yet I want
to preserve your love in mummy tape. Wrap myself in it and live longer
than the Pyramids . . .*

I'm speaking from the heart. In the spirit. And now she's wide awake.
Kissing me softly. I'm still writing, hoping she can hear my thoughts.

I want to dig to the center of you, pose with your wonder in National
Geographic, *and tell tales of how your discovery changed my life . . .*

She's kissing me harder. More passionately. More intense. I light a
candle. Remove her bra. And continue.

*You don't know what you do for me . . . I want to roll your scent up,
set fire to it, burn it in incense, and pass the ashes down to my grand-
sons . . . Taiyler . . .*

Her arms are wrapped around me. Holding me in place. Keeping
those scales balanced. I want to love her until I break everything except her heart. My soul speaks to this woman when my mouth can't
find the words. Our experience at this point is so euphoric that I almost think I've crossed over. Passed out. Seen the light. Died an old
death and lived a new life. We're naked. And I'm inside her love.
Feeling the love of my ancestors. Tracing the tale of the scarab up
through the inner walls of her womanhood. Hoping to be reborn. I
look into her eyes. And I want to tell her how I've named a star for
her. And how I'm going to build a pyramid that will stand tall at the
very point on Earth where that star shines light. And that I've inter-
preted the writings on her walls. And the hieroglyphs that configure
the phrase *"How can a man be born again?"* And I donate my hypothe-
sis. And she agrees. And trembles. And tightens. And breathes short
breaths. And curses me to a lifetime of love.
    "De-rr-ic-k . . ."
    And I lose track of my thoughts for a moment. As I wrestled with
prolonging the ceremony of emptying my livelihood into her womb,
every woman before her became faceless. Taiyler's raising me. Making
me from boy to man. With each stroke, I am closer to shaving my
prince's lock and becoming Pharaoh. Whom God has forced to
soften his heart.

"Tai-y-ler . . ." My voice is four octaves higher, but my love is ten thousand leagues deeper. Amidst the parting of the seas, I tell her that I'm in love with her. I know that she can't hear my heart speak. But I'll continue. Continue to deliver these words in the way that Moses delivered his people. In silence and in truth.

17

Taiyler

If I had to write about last night, I would be on my second novel by this morning. There's so much to be said about a man who can love me the way Derrick did. So many words are paired up, holding hands, skipping, singing a song of love in my head. Intense and tender. Passionate and euphoric. Timeless and wonderful. Times like this make me wish that I was fanatic about my writing. One who slept with their pen and notepad underneath their pillow. Taking record of their dreams as they occur. Wish I had the strength to do that while he was taking me to places where the sun sets twenty-four hours a day. Just in case things didn't work out, I would have a marker. Directions for the next one on how to take me to Paris, Ethiopia, and Cairo without leaving my bed. Can't say that I've had this experience before. That's why I really need to lie here for a little while longer and process all of this.

When Derrick woke up this morning and wanted to cuddle, I couldn't. I didn't want to be touched. At all. Anywhere. I needed time alone to let my mind and body communicate. Let one tell the other what it felt. Some of it I actually don't remember. When a feeling is too overwhelming, good or bad, mentally I tend to block it out. Don't remember how I felt when they called me at school and told me to come home quick because my grandma was sick. Don't remember how it felt when I was accepted into Georgetown. Don't remember how I ended up in orgasmic shock this morning. So this time with myself is important. Hope Derrick understood that. He got up and, I guess after several tries, decided to talk to me later. He looked so pitiful. Probably thinks that I didn't like his little me-Tarzan, you-Jane performance last night. Picking me up, carrying me upstairs, and devouring me like a hostage does a boxed lunch. I liked it. He took charge.

He's actually a very good lover. Now that my memory is slowly coming back. Okay, yeah. The picking me up part was nice. The oral sex was nicer. Damn. It's all coming back now. Whew! I must have had at least four orgasms. Wow. That's why I'm lethargic. He kept saying my name over and over. It was driving me crazy. And he was so soft. Moved so slowly. It was damn near unbearable. At one point, he just stopped. Right on my spot. And lay there. Kissing me. Thank God I wasn't inebriated. Because my bladder was full. Let's just say this. I felt so good. And so relaxed. It wouldn't have been pretty. Damn. The day is slipping away. I need to get my satisfied ass up and go through some charts.

Something tells me that getting up is going to be hard. I try. I was right. My legs feel like they're stuck in molasses. All right, Taiyler, let's try this again. This time, I gripped the wrought-iron bars of my bed, thinking that was a good idea until it started to feel like I was doing pull-ups on the windowsill of the Empire State Building. God damn you, Derrick. His pretty ass is on his way to get his hair cut without a single muscle ache. From what I could tell, he is in pretty good shape. All right. Last time. One . . . two . . . three . . . up! Made a little progress. Now all I have to do is . . . damn it! The phone is ringing. Thinking about reaching for it gives me an instant headache. Leaning over to grab it leaves me a little short of a coronary.

"This is Taiyler," I answer with the enthusiasm of a Catholic priest without an altar boy in sight.

"Mornin'," she says just as dryly. Great way to ruin a heavenly night. Greetings from Lucifer's star student.

"Why are you calling me at this time of morning?"

"What, you ain't up doin' heart transfers and hip replacements?" I heard her laugh out loud. She wore sarcasm like a pregnant woman wore bootie shorts. Already, I want to reach through the phone and strangle my bitch of a sister.

"What do you want? . . ." I began. Forget about being the star student. Only Lucifer himself would cause me this much aggravation this early in the morning. Damn, I can't stand her. ". . . and no, I don't have it," I auto-answered. She sucked her teeth. I could bet on her rolling her eyes. Thought that went out in the eighties. I know this routine. She's about to get ignorant.

"Bitch, you ain't the only one that got . . ."

She's about to get her ass whipped. My eyes are tightening.

". . . so don't think that you is."

Amazing. At her age, she still amazes me. I have to answer that.

"Are. The proper word is *are*. But I wouldn't expect you to know that. You were too busy inhaling dick in the third grade to notice anything that ran across a chalkboard." I know that stung. But it's too early for this shit. I need to put a stop to it before it ruins my day.

"Taiyler, I'm gonna say this once. You ain't the only one with a education. Get that through your thick skull."

I could hear the steam peeling out of her head. That's one war she won't win. I'm smarter. Figured out how to aggravate her with that a long time ago. I know. It's wrong. But she aggravates me. So I continued.

"You're going to."

"I'm what?" she asked incredulously. I chuckled like the pompous bitch I could be.

"You're *going to* say this once. Not gonna. Two words. Not one. Now, what do you want?" I asked in a tsk. Like she was a fly hovering over my salad. She's pissed.

"You're such a bitch. What I want is for you to stop giving Mike money every time he asks for it. Especially when I tell him he has to earn it. He's not your kid. He's mine. Remember? You don't have any." Andrea brings out the asshole in me. She doesn't have to try hard at all.

"Uh, and if I remember correctly, it's not your money. It's mine. Remember? You don't have any. And I am putting Mike through Hampton just because of that right there. I know you have a better life envisioned for your oldest, but unfortunately he doesn't want to spend the rest of his life in Brooklyn stuffing viles and baggies. He's smarter than that. Maybe smarter than you. So if I want to send my nephew a few dollars, I'll do just that."

She wants to say something. But she's enraged. Can't talk. Hate has her tongue, and it's eating it for breakfast. I'm not the one. I go on.

"The day you send me a check for eighty thousand dollars . . . no,

I'm sorry, you have two sons at Hampton, make that one hundred sixty thousand, you can tell me what the fuck to do with my checkbook. Understood, Andrea?" I can't stand her. Always a director. Never contributes. She can't stand me either. The only thing we have in common. I expect her to hang up on me as usual. But she doesn't. As a matter of fact, she's calm and cool. It's almost surreal.

"You sent him two thousand dollars. *Two thousand.* For what? How is he supposed to become responsible with money like that to blow?"

I shook my head. Reached over to grab a Celebrex from on top of the nightstand. Forgot that I was sore. I need to make this go away. All of it. Somebody does. Andrea doesn't understand that books, fees, food, and other miscellaneous shit add up. Ignorant ass. She doesn't know because she doesn't ask. Doesn't care.

The only thing that gets her attention is me sending the boys money. Making her look bad. Her image. Selfish bastard. She's nowhere to be found when professors need to be contacted, financial aid counselors need exacting, tutors need to be found and hired. Tests need to be studied for. Majors need to be chosen. Condoms need to be sent. Internships applied for. Pictures taken. Games visited. Recitals attended. Shit. She better quit while she's ahead. She has no idea. The boy works his ass off. Gets excellent grades. Doesn't ask for shit. It's the least I can do. She doesn't know her son.

"Andrea, he didn't spend it on freaking Play Station games. It was needed. For shit your ass won't ever understand. Understand? Now, this conversation is over. Period."

"Don't send him no more money, Taiyler. I mean it," she snapped. Jealous of her own sons. Damn.

"Sign a check, bitch. Until then, it's a dead issue." Click. Line's dead. Good. At least I didn't have to do it. I stared up at the skylight and tried to wish myself back to that feeling I had minutes ago. It's hard. My nephews and I are close. Maybe too close at times. People do think I'm their mother. As I prepared to write my oldest nephew another check, I thought about how we were both cursed with mothers who gave a damn about themselves and damned us. But we still persevered. Out of spite, I added another zero to the amount on the check. Take that, Drea. Now he has more than you.

I swung both legs over the edge of the bed and slid my feet into my slippers. I'm full of energy now. Adrenaline is a bitch, isn't it? All right. First things first. Wash my face, brush my teeth. Or as Grandma used to say, *"Wash yo' teeth."* Have to get this after-kissing taste out of my mouth. After I clean up, I'll go downstairs, make something quick to eat, and separate my clothes for the cleaning lady to wash. Wait. I need to make a list. Saturdays are the only days that are totally available to me. So I like to get up and take care of the little doodads that are overlooked during the week.

Constructing a Wal-Mart list is a must. Gotta have one before you get trapped in there. Go in for a bottle of house cleaner, come out with a new barbecue grill and bathroom towels. Oil change. Post office. Grocery store. Wine for Derrick's party. I took each one of the stairs carefully; my legs are still weak from trying to hold in that last orgasm. Cracking the door to the deck open, I took a sneak peek outside. God. It's beautiful out. My sprinklers were moving back and forth, back and forth. Making that sound that will always remind you of the suburbs. Comfort. Security. And then it happens. That damn phone rings again. Ahhhhhhh! It's upstairs on my bed. Why I only have one phone in this house is beyond me. Note to self. Phone. Add it to the Wal-Mart list. Taking two steps at a time, I sprint upstairs. Trying to make myself forget that I have sex legs, I jet down the hallway and dive for the caller ID like an outfielder. It's Shala.

"He-y . . . g-i . . . rl!" I sounded like a fat boy running behind the ice cream truck. Desperately gnawing the ice cream he already had in his hand. Silence. Must have missed it. Just as I hit the Call Return button, it rang again. Loud as shit. Scared the B-jeezus out of me. Sha again.

"Hey, girl," I answered, still a little out of breath. Gotta get back into the gym.

"Hey, T! What's up? Why do you sound like that? Awhhhh, sheee-it!" She's laughing. "We're close, but we ain't that close!" She's in a playful mood. I need to laugh. We've been operating on this type of telepathy for a while now. I'm thankful for it.

"Yeah, whatever. Your girl Drea just called. Fucked a good morning right on up. Other than that, I'm okay. A little out of breath. But okay." I'm smiling. She senses that.

"Well, what is the Washington Sports Club doing with your hundred fifty a month? Because they sure as hell aren't doing anything for you."

"No, this is not a sports club issue. It's a Derrick issue."

She gasped. I swear she is overly dramatic at times. It's funny.

"What! Hold on. When?"

"Last night."

"Planned?"

"Nope."

"How?"

"I don't know. One minute we're driving home from the Gallery, the next he's auditioning for P.E.K.O.Y."

"Huh?"

"You forgot, Sha? PEKOY, Pussy Eating King of the Year."

She pulled the receiver away from her ear and screamed.

"What? Oh, my Lord. He ate you out? How was it? I know you're picky," she said. She's right. It usually takes everything I have not to shout out orders like a drill sergeant. Men just don't get it sometimes. Dogs bite, snap, and gnaw food. Men kiss, caress, and lick the you know what. Derrick was good down there. Soft. I liked it. So that's what I tell her.

"I liked it. He was gentle. You know I like to be barely touched."

"I know. So on a scale . . ."

"Eight," I answered quickly.

"Wow. The highest rating. Interesting. Are you sure? Because Lance was a seven point seven. And you called me plenty of times ranting and raving about him."

She's right. I think it over. Yup. Eight. "Yeah, he's been the best. So far."

"Categories, please." She must be surprised. We haven't done categories since college.

"Okay. Let me think. Tongue . . . excellent; surrounding area contact . . . good; simultaneous activity . . . fair; orgasmic height . . . excellent, excellent, excellent. I had at least four."

She gasped again. I can see her right now, sitting cross-legged on her bed, hand cupped over her mouth. I giggled.

"Wow . . ." she said in amazement. And amazement is right. I haven't had multiples since I was with Lance. And he was holding the record with three. She's reading my mind.

"Lance is holding the record with three. And you said Derrick gave you at least four? At least? Wow. I mean, that's all I can say."

"Oh, you can say something else," I chided.

"Uhhh . . . congratulations?"

"Nope. Men can do it, too." I take her back to an old conversation we had about men not being able to be as gentle with women as other women are.

"Men can do what?" She forgot. I'll remind her.

"Oh, so you forgot now? Let me refresh your memory. A man will never be able to touch a woman with the gentleness of that of another woman. They just can't. If they could, there would be no lesbians . . . remember that, miss?"

She busted out laughing.

"Yeah. And that is the truth. If Derrick gave you four, Grai could give you eight," she said matter-of-factly.

"Whatever. You know I'm right. And anyway, since we're on the topic of old conversations, why don't we finish one that we started a few months ago?"

"All right. Shoot," she said enthusiastically.

"What are you going to do, Sha? I mean, you can't just go flying back to dating men full-time. There has to be another way to handle this." Silence.

"Hello?" More silence.

"Sha? Are you there?" I asked softly. No reply. I know she didn't hang up. Then I heard what sounded like a sigh. More like a moan. She's frustrated.

"Shala. You have to address this. It won't go away. We're not getting any—"

"I know! Damn it, T! Why do you keep pressing me to talk about it! Shit! I'm fucking tired of evaluating the situation! Either way it's a no win. No compromise. Why do you insist on reminding me of that? I mean, damn, is it not enough for me to be confused and frustrated? Do I have to feel doomed as well? I can't think of anything to help the situation, so I don't think about it! Is that a fucking crime! I mean, damn . . ."

Whoa. I just cracked open the dam. She's angry. Hurt, confused. I can hear it. She's talking superfast. I let her curse me out. Until she starts to cry. Until I'm crying right along with her. I have to help her with this. Even if I just let her use me as her personal punching bag. This is her life we're talking about. Serious business.

". . . so I mean I can't figure out anything that will work . . ." She's slowing down. I wipe my eyes. ". . . and evidently love has nothing to do with this. My happiness doesn't matter. So fuck it. The only thing I

can think of is to move to a third world country and live off the fucking land. Eat fresh crawfish and shit for breakfast. Then find out that
I'm being stoned for going against the tribal laws. Women and Men.
Adam and Eve. Where the hell did it mention anything about Eve's
lesbian lover?" She stopped. She needed that. I'm quiet. Don't know
if she's done for sure. She takes a long, deep breath. So do I. This is
hard. Silence again. I decide to break it.

"Sha. You can be happy. I'll help you figure this out," I say for lack
of better verbiage. She started back up. This time calmer. As if watching her words scroll across a teleprompter.

"All I can feel is relaxed. Whole. Helped. Unconditionally loved.
When I'm with Grai. And it's not about the sex. Fuck the sex. It's
about wrapping my legs around her and talking till four in the morning. Waking up in the middle of the night and laughing our asses off
due to either one of us acting a damn fool. It's about rubbing each
other's shoulders when they're tense. Crying on each other's shoulders when we're weak. Brainstorming ideas. Critiquing music. Art.
Food. Her laying out my pajamas for me when I come in late from a
program. Traveling. Living life with someone you love more than
your own."

Damn. She sounds so relaxed. I want to find that place. Where she
is now. While she's talking about the love of her life.

"I have tried to leave, T. I've tried to. You know that. For reasons
other than this. The kids and family thing. But every single time I've
tried, I've failed. Couldn't stomach not having her love in my life.
Couldn't imagine it."

I don't want to ruin her Saturday with this. But I do want her to get
this stuff out. I've always believed that there is a solution to every
problem. They're hidden in the energy of life. Waiting to be found.
Some just take longer than others. This one is hidden well. But I'm
not scared to look. We'll find it.

"Sha. Look. I didn't mean to ruin your day with this. You know I
just want what's best for you."

"I know, T," she sniffled. My eyes are welling up again. We've always
been that close. She cries, I cry. And vice versa. I got us here. Now I
have to turn us around. At least temporarily.

"Hey, what are you doing tonight?" I ask, a little too cheery for my
own tastes. I've never really been good at making segues.

She chuckled. "Oh, now, since you've fucked up my morning, you want to take me out?"

She knows me. I forget how well sometimes. "Uh . . . yeah. Didn't know you would fly off the handle like that. You know." I'm kidding. My dry humor. It cracks me up sometimes.

"Yeah, I cursed you out, didn't I? You weren't ready. If I weren't so upset, I would have cracked up. You? Silent? Please. You were shocked." That's an understatement.

"You got that right. But listen, we'll pro and con it the way we usually do. This one will just take a little longer. Okay?"

"Okay," she answered solemnly. "So what do you want to do later?" she asked.

"Derrick is having a small birthday party for one of his college boys. I won't know anyone there."

"Yes, you will, T. Remember his boy? You know, the one we both met at the fund-raiser?"

Nat. I remember. The feeling. The weak feeling. Hadn't thought about it since then.

"Oh, yeah. I remember. Well, I'll know one person. Whoop-de-doo. Either way I don't want to head up there by myself. Derrick has a lot of friends. Male and female. And you know the routine." I know she knows. We go through it all the time.

"Yeah. The men flirt, the women hate. We'll split the attention as usual. I have your back, sista." She always does.

"Yeah, I'm too tired to cope with all of that myself."

"Don't mention it. Call me and let me know what time you're coming by."

"Why do I have to drive?" I asked. She always makes me drive.

"One, I drive all day, every day, for work. Two, you invited me. And the third is obvious."

"Not that obvious," I replied.

"This is your first time meeting his college boys, plus, knowing him, probably some of his exes. Shine that Porsche up. We have to shut those bitches down."

I laughed out loud. She's right. Car detailed. Add it to the list.

I swear, I hate driving in DC. Traffic is always enough to make you want to hang yourself. Trying to get from Bowie to Georgetown is a disaster. Especially in the rain. People act like they're in the middle of the second coming. Everything in slow motion. There is no reason for a Saturday night to look like a Monday morning. No reason at all. This is a mess. I look over at Shala, who for the umpteenth time is in the passenger side mirror, adjusting the pins holding her curls up.

"Sha, why do you keep messing with those pins? You're taking them out in a few minutes." Pin curls. The only way to preserve our hair in the rain. Something I learned getting my hair washed at the Dominican salons in New York. Something she evidently won't let go of. Such a Miss Priss. You walk out of your house dressed to kill, with your hair bundled up in what seems like a thousand pins, looking like corporate Minnie Mouse. Talk about ghetto. It's funny. However, it really is the only way to keep our hair from doing the wop in one hundred percent humidity. She looks at me like I'm twisting her last good nerve.

"Listen. I'm trying to keep those awful pin lines from showing up in my hair. Can I do that? Can I?" she answered in mock exasperation.

"Yeah, as long as you keep that big-ass head of yours out of my way. Can't see. Do you mind?" I answered back, smirking. I know she has a thing about her melon head. The one thing keeping the perfectionist from perfection. She looks over at me, and then out of the rearview mirror.

"How far are we from his house? We've been in Georgetown for a few minutes now." Good question.

"Uh . . . I dunno. He lives on 31st and N. On the corner. But with all of the construction, I think we have to take the detour on Wisconsin, which will put us only God knows where. So bear with. Okay?"

"Okay." She paused, the weirdest look spreading across her face.

"What?" I asked.

"Did you say 31st and N? The corner?"

"Yeah." She tipped her head, leaned back in her seat, and looked my way again.

"The huge white house? Looks like a building? Pool, outside deck, et cetera?"

I laugh. Her eyes are the size of saucers.

"Yup. That's it. Why?" I already know why. My baby is doing it. Doing well. One of the best litigators in the city.

"All right, heifer. You've been holding out. I'm not one of your little freak associates that you keep things like this from. He's paid, T!"

I pull onto N Street, check my reflection in the rearview. Never know who's out.

"Sha, uh, don't you want to do something with those pins? We're right down the street." Trying to divert her attention.

"I'll get to my pins in a minute. You're not getting off this easy. That house is worth at least three million. At least." She's amazing herself. I have to admit, I was a little shy of amazement my first time there. It wasn't the size of the house that got my attention. It was the design. The windows, the art, the Italian furniture, the accent walls. I knew he had excellent taste, but damn. Besides, having good taste is not what will keep me interested. Good dick, maybe. Culture, class, education, definitely.

"Girl, when have you ever known me to be wooed by bullshit like that? I take care of me. I wasn't holding out. It just wasn't important." And that's the truth. It wasn't. Well, not that important. We slow up right in the middle of 30th. As Shala frantically undid her pins, I pulled up front. Saw lots of cars. People walking toward the house. A few men stare. The women pretend that they don't want to. I chuckled. So does Shala. We know the routine by heart. The Porsche answers quite a few questions. We don't have to say much. Sha takes a brief glance around.

"Dang. Parking is serious out here. You sure Richie-Rich doesn't own any parking lots around these parts? I mean, it wouldn't be out of the question." Two smart-asses. No wonder we get along so well.

"I wouldn't know about that," I say as I pull the garage door opener off of my visor. "Derrick doesn't let me park on the street." As the garage door retracted, I could see at least three women all wearing the same expression that my girl had on her face. Utter fucking disbelief. Or shock. Whichever you prefer. I pulled up right next to his truck. A perfect pair. Shala let out a laugh that said she's had enough.

"Oh, this is going to be good. A former playboy who won't let you park on the street. Who has at least those three women over there . . ."

I watch her point to a group who is obviously not over the fact that my Carrera is sitting in his garage, and that I'm taking my keys out and headed for the door.

". . . here to see your highness chew his food." She's crazy. I'm glad she came with me. We enter through the gourmet kitchen and make a stop at one of the guest bathrooms to freshen up.

"T. Oh no, he doesn't have a powder room in his freaking bathroom! This looks like a lounge! Who the hell is watching a plasma TV while touching up their makeup?"

As I prepared to answer her, something stopped me dead in my tracks. I hear him. And that warmth surrounds me again. The feeling from the fund-raiser. The one from the grocery store. I feel my face flushing. I hear my heart pounding. I hear Nat. Ask me how I know it's him. The sound of his voice is barely above a whisper. But I know. Somehow. It's freaking me out.

"Taiyler, everything okay?" Shala asked.

"Yeah. Why do you ask?"

"Because your hands are shaking."

"Are they?" I looked down. They look fine to me. My stomach is queasy, though. I hear him laugh. Then I hear Derrick. I shake the feeling off. Whatever it is.

"I hope you are not nervous. No, I know you're not. You are his woman. And a bad bitch at that. Get your shit. Let's go meet the press." Shala. My backup. The bad-bitch thing. We used to say that before we went to a sorority set. Before the big sisters would use our self-esteem as punching bags. Stomp on our personalities. Make wine of our security. It never worked with Shala and me. Because we were bad bitches by our own standards. As we prepare to leave the bathroom, I'm attempting to gather myself, and I don't know why. This is some shit.

"Which way?" Shala asked determinedly. I point over to the great room. Where the noise was coming from.

"Let's go," she said, pulling me like a teenager does her toddler sister. Walking into that room was an experience. Everything moved in slow motion. Like Saturday night traffic. Derrick smiling ear to ear. Shala smiling back. Hellos. Good to see yous. Derrick's kiss on my hand. Shala's kiss on his cheek. Kalonji's sweet introduction. He likes Shala. His girl doesn't. Eyes from me to Sha, back to me.

"Oh, so you're Rick's new girl . . ." The sharks, how they do swim.

"Don't know who Rick is, but yes, I'm with Derrick." My baby shows up. Takes me by the waist. Kisses me on my cheek. Says he's glad I came. Stick a fork in her. She's done. Mad as shit. At the punch bowl. The house-party office cooler. Gossip central. Showdown number

two. Used to be the life of the party. Just ten minutes ago. Right before we arrived. Now she's not. Wants to know who ruined that.

"You're the one who came in the Porsche, right?"

"Yeah. That's me."

"Nice ride."

"Thanks."

"How'd you get in?" She's a bold one.

"What do you mean how did I get in? I walked."

Shala busted out laughing.

"Obviously. So, ummmh, how do you know Garvin?"

Too many questions. I'm getting tired of this one already. "I don't.
I know one of his best friends. The host."

"Oh. Well, Derrick invited me, too. We work together. I'm a paralegal." She's smug. Shala loves this. I hate it. She's waiting for me to
drop the bomb. With professional women the evaluation goes . . .
let's say very professionally. In order of priority, looks, education, occupation. If you are prettier, they win if they are smarter. If you're
smarter, they win by being prettier. If you happen to tie in the former,
occupation is the tiebreaker. Who's doing it. And doing it well. For
example. An accountant wins over a teacher. Unless she's a Ph.D.
Top-ten company exec is always acceptable unless you're up against
an attorney. She'll win that. Owning and operating your own company is another undisputable. CEOs can't be beat. But they're never
out. And never insecure enough to engage themselves in this type of
competition. The only thing that breaks all ties and takes all trophies
is the physician. Ten-plus years of school, surgery, the works. You're
smart. And paid. No question. A tiebreaker like a mutha. And it'll
shut a woman like this down in a heartbeat. I let her dig herself into
that hole. Hope she can pull herself out.

"So what do you do? If you don't mind me asking." Can't imagine
she was bold enough to cough those words up. I must be winning the
looks category by a landslide. My girl looks at me, beaming. She
knows what's up. Wants me to put the nail in Ms. I'm-a-paralegal's cof-
fin. Talk about excitement. Shala's on the verge of choking on her
martini. She enjoys this way too much. Derrick gets both of our attention by blowing me a kiss as he passes by with two new bottles of cham-
pagne.

"I make Derrick happy," I answered. I'm twisting the knife. Answering like a bimbo without a real job. Set her up for the kill.

"Oh, really. That's sweet. I didn't know Derrick had a girl. Is that your day job?"

Oh, yeah. She's asking for it. Just then, just as I was about to make this chick feel smaller than a penny looking for change, I got it again. Weak. Warm. Nauseated. Shala's nudging me. I left her hanging. Waiting for her favorite part. Get it together, T. Slam the bitch. I can't. I'm stuck. In the kitchen. Well, I'm not in the kitchen; I'm at the punch bowl. He's in the kitchen. Stuttering in a conversation with myself. How poised. Way to go, Taiyler. Don't know what happened. But I'm walking over there. Shit. I don't feel good. But walking over there does. He extended his hand.

"Enjoying yourself?" he asked.

"Yes. And you?"

"I am."

"I remember you."

"I know. Aisle three," he answered.

"Yeah, that's right. Frosting." I blushed. Why am I blushing?

"Your temper needs work," he added playfully. He's smiling. So am I. And seeing colors. Reds, purples, blues. Damn.

"And you're arrogant. Work on that." I'm pulling on my bracelet. Nervous. I shouldn't be. But I am.

"I know. My apologies."

"Likewise," I replied.

I stood there in the kitchen. Right in front of him. Staring past him. Focusing on the flow of the party. Trying my best not to look uncomfortable. Shifting the weight of this feeling from foot to foot. Trying to figure out where it was all coming from. Wanting it to end. Wanting it to begin again.

He's humming. I know the tune.

"Coltrane. 'A Love Supreme.'" I answered my own question.

"'Pursuance.' Not 'A Love . . .'"

"I beg to differ."

"Begging does not become you," he answered while turning his back to me. Arrogant mutherfucker. Pouring OJ. That's his excuse. I want him to look at me. I happen to know that he doesn't want to do that. For some reason, I make him.

"Face me."

"What?"

"Face me and tell me that isn't 'A Love Supreme.'"

He turns back around. Looks at me. Eye to eye.

"It's what I said it was," he answered.

But he doesn't turn back around this time. He just stands there. Half glass of OJ in hand. Looking at me like he's seeing something he doesn't want to see. My hands are sweaty. And I'm slicing lime.

"Go get the CD case. Derrick has it. Play it," I challenged him. Just to do it.

"It's a love song. Not appropriate for tonight," he assessed.

"Why not? People here are in love. What, are you scared to lose?"

"Never."

"Never what? Never scared to lose or never in lov—owwhh." Cut my finger. Going too fast. He grabs a paper towel.

"Wash it." He takes my hand. Guides it underneath the faucet. Wraps it in the paper towel. Holds it. Eye to eye again. It's too much. Wish I would have stayed out of the kitchen. Followed Aunt Mae's words. When it gets too hot.

"Hey, babee!" Derrick's here. Just as jubilant as he always is when I'm around. To my rescue. I swear he must have ESP.

"You okay, honey? What happened?" he asked. Looks at me. Looks at his boy. Back at me. Nat's still holding my finger. Doesn't realize it. Drops it like a hot potato. Paper on the floor. The stuff that starts my heart running all over the place. See the panic in Derrick's eyes. See the same in Nat's. Different reasons.

"I cut my finger slicing lime, sweetie. I'm okay. Really. I'm a tough cookie," I said and smiled. Kissed my baby on the cheek. When I hurt he hurts, and it's all over his face.

"Oh, shit. You're bleeding, Taiyler. Com'ere. I told you that you didn't have to do anything. Just relax and have fun. Don't lift a finger. I'll be back with some Neosporin and a Band–Aid." As Derrick made a mad dash up the stairs, a wave of something that resembled guilt ran through me. For what? I haven't done anything wrong. At least I don't think so. I don't want to think so. Well, just in case I'll stay away from ol' boy. Sweaty palms are never a good thing.

18

Nathaniel

I love my wife's lips. They're like heart-shaped melons. And this morning, she is using them for what God intended. Sucking the life out of me. Literally. Saturday mornings are ours. Love that. It started out while I was in that half-here-half-there state of unconsciousness. Sunlight streaming in. Kendra moving closer to me. A bump here. A grind there. Tossing. Turning. Until finally, we're both awake and aware. Moving to each other's rhythm. Her hand on it. Where it belongs. Today she doesn't want sex. I love when she's in these moods. The generosity is unbelievable. Give it to me, babe. I'm doing all I can not to look down. Her hair on my thighs. Lips stretching to the point that they almost look like they're inside out. And she likes doing it. I've never had to ask. Beg a few times maybe. But only when she's being a tease.

I take a quick glimpse down there. Feel like a heart attack's coming on. That's what I get for being nosy. Her head bobbing up and down. Slow. Circular. Shutting my eyes as tight as I can helps. Sometimes. I don't want to do it right now. Don't want to come. Ten more minutes. Okay. Five. She's starting that moan of hers. Okay. Two minutes. And that's my final offer. I let out a punk-ass whimper. Punk mutherfucker. I hate myself sometimes. Stay strong, Nat. You're not comein' when she wants you to. Have some control. Heart beating faster. Faster. She's in a rhythm. My leg's shaking.

"I-I-don't wan-wanna come yet..." I mentioned to no avail. She doesn't care. I tried everything. Counting to ten, counting sheep, nothing's working. Until I feel it stirring in the deepest part of my stomach. My son. Or daughter. Or whoever she's about to bring out of me. I give up. Punk out. The usual.

"Ba—be. Baaaaa—beeee! Ahhh. Right there . . . right there . . ." Who am I telling? She already knows. "I'm almost . . . it's coming . . . uhhmmmm . . . Damn it!"

She stopped. What th—! I have heaven in my stomach, and she stops?

"The phone, honey. Get the phone." She looked up at me with saliva all over her cheeks.

"What?" I answered in disbelief.

"Sweetie, the phone. At seven in the morning it has to be important," she said as she reached over me. My dick jumped. He's wondering what happened as well.

"Honey, it's Derrick. Said it's urgent." She hands me the phone. I picture my hands around D's neck.

"What up?" I know I sound the way I feel. Fucked.

"Yo. You got the platters for tonight, right?"

Urgent. I'm going to kick his ass.

"The what?" What type of person calls this early about a platter? Selfish bastard.

"The food. Platters. Whatever. For the party tonight. You said you had it. Was just checkin'."

Oh, shit. Damn. I mentioned that to Kendra weeks ago. Forgot to remind her. Caterer won't do it same day.

"Uh, hold on a sec, man." I put the phone on mute, turn around, and face Kennie. Maybe she can whip something up real fast for tonight. On second thought, she's out with the girls today. No can do. Damn!

"What's wrong, honey?" Flashing those doelike eyes at me reminded me of where we left off. I toss the thought.

"I forgot to put in the order for the food tonight. Who takes same-day orders, babe? I have to make this happen or the food will be shitty."

She looked at me and rolled those beautiful eyes. I know. I'm sorry. Sometimes.

"Didn't you look in the fridge last night?" she said. Her eyebrows raised.

Rapid blinking. Up to something.

"Yeah. Why?"

"Everything's there."

"Where?" I asked. She looked at me like the president of Brazil looked at Bush after that how-many-blacks-you-got-here comment.

"Downstairs, hon. I knew that you would forget. So when I called Vitality to place the order for the staff meeting next week, I placed one for you as well. Veggie tray, international cheeses, chicken, everything you mentioned. It's downstairs."

What can I say? She's my other half. Literally.

"Whew! Thanks, babe." I kissed her forehead. There is not another woman on this earth that can love me the way she does. I let out a huge breath. Unmute.

"D, yeah, I have everything. Got some chicken, veggie trays, cheeses, and some other stuff." Oh, I'm energetic now.

"Good. Thanks, man. I was just checkin'. Got a few errands to run. K's bringing the liquor, Chelsea's on the flatware, Taiyler's bringing the wine . . ."

Big gulp. Feel like I gotta go to the bathroom. Stomach swirling. And they say blue balls is a myth. Feeling light-headed. All of a sudden. As soon as he said it.

"Aight then, man. I gotta go. Was kind of busy when you called."

He's laughing. I'm not.

"Cool, Nat. My bad. Was just checking on things for tonight. See you 'round eight." He's still laughing. I hung up. Back to business.

"Thanks for real, babe. I really did forget," I said as I curled up under her. Trying to get her back on top. Get me back on top of the world. We can make a deal. All she has to do is let me put it in. That's all. Don't even need all of the extras at this point. Yeah, babe. Back that thang right up. What do I have to do to get her back there? Kiss on the back of her neck. Oh, yeah. Her ears. Forgot. Lick. Suck. Pull. Yup. Move those hips, Kennie. Move 'em. What you want, girl. I got it. You sure you know who your're messin' with? I'll make you wetter than Seattle. Your man'll get you there. She's moving her ass so slow and deliberate that it's boring a hole in my stomach. Next step pull it out. Keep the rhythm. Slide it in. One. I can hear her breath bounce off of her pillow. I pull her closer. Two. A gasp. Love that high pitch. Thr—she popped up like a jack-in-the-box. Almost ripped my shit off.

"Owwh! What's wrong now!" I'm almost screaming.

"Lower your voice, Nat. Your daughter's at the door." She's right. Those petite knocks. Kitten paws. My little princess.

"Mommy . . . Daddy . . . I can't sleep. The bogeyman is under my bed," she purred in her perfect little princess voice. Bogeyman must not be getting any. Because he's making damn sure that I don't. Kendra slid into her slippers. Opened the door. I smile. Can't help it. My little beauty. Her pigtails looking like acute angles. She took off. Nosedive. Right under my butt. How she gets under there I will never know. I started to tickle her. Her squeals make me smile again. Make me laugh.

"Daadddy! Stop! Ewwwwwh!" She screams loud enough to wake up all of the Gold Coast. Kendra peeks her head out of the master bathroom.

"So . . . are you going with us to church tomorrow?"

Where we differ. I'm good with once a month. No more. No less.

"No. I'll be at Derrick's almost all night. Need Sunday to run some reports. What about you, coming tonight?"

"No, sweets. Thought I told you. Rehearsal for the concert, remember? Kirk Franklin, Yolanda Adams. It's coming up. Reverend Matthews wants us to lift the house." Lift the house, huh? I chuckle. How about pay for the house? But that's a dead issue. I hear her pager go off. She races out of the bathroom, grabs it, pulls it right up to the bridge of her nose, and lets out a huge sigh. She works way too damn hard for my liking. I make enough for her to stay home, but that's not what she wants. I pull my wife onto the bed. Give Nile the signal. She sits on Kendra's lap. Play's her position. I massage her shoulders. Nile does her temples. We're an excellent team. Our ritual for Mommy. Kendra draws a huge breath, lets it out slow. I can feel her mind decoding whatever bullshit was left with that page.

"Honey, I know it's my turn to take Nile to school next week, but I'm on rounds, and I'm taking appointments in the early morning and evening. Do you think you could take her?" she says as she pops up, kisses her little clone on the forehead, and skips back over to the bathroom. I'm thinking . . . something's up next week. Oh, yeah. Our annual meeting. My firm is one of the many sponsors of a big biotech conference that gives top physicians from all over the country a chance to preview new FDA approved therapies and advances in medical technology. We are a finance company, but we do what we can to stay connected.

"No, babe. I have to go to that meeting next week, remember?"

"That's right. Damn. I'll guess Ma will have to do it. You want to see Grandma next week, sweetie?"

"I don't like grits, Mommy," Nile says, looking like she smelled something rotten. I'm cracking up. Nile isn't. She doesn't see anything funny. Kendra shot me a look. Shut me up.

"You don't have to eat grits, baby . . . Mommy will pack your breakfast and lunch, okay?" Kendra glanced over at me. Teeth over her bottom lip. We're both on the verge of tears. Her mother's grits are . . . let's just say thick. Nile pops back up on the bed with me. I cross my eyes. Stick out my tongue. Turn her frown upside down. Kendra's back in the bathroom. Sticks her head out again. Hears us laughing. Hears all the commotion. All the love. Nile and I are playing footsies. I'm winning. Kendra's smiling. Nothing but giggles.

"Nat. Nat! Be quiet for a minute," Kendra pleads. We both stop. Nile gets a kick in on the sneak tip. A fast one. I taught her well.

"Please, you two! Nat, you are old enough to know when to stop!" Kendra's mock scolding us. Another Saturday morning ritual. She goes over the regulars. Take out the meat for tomorrow. Clothes in the washing machine. Put them in the dryer. The cleaning lady will be here at ten. Oil change for the truck. How she keeps up with all of this is beyond me.

"Got it?" she asked while she pulled her Hampton sweatshirt over her head.

"Got it," I answered. I have it right now. After tonight, let's just hope that I have all my senses after the guys get to me.

I hit I-495 feeling good. Trunk packed. Sunroof open. Windows down. Wind hitting my face. Roots Crew blastin'. Excited about hanging with my boys. When we get together, it's all hell. We don't care about who else is coming out. As long as all four of us are there, we'll make it pop. Tonight, I know, will be great. Derrick's parties are one of a kind. He's like the Black Hugh Heffner of the DC area. Once he puts the word out, chicks with top-dollar jobs and swimsuit calendars on their resumés pour out by the dozens. Partially because he's pimpin' them. The other part becomes more obvious when you get to his house. The shit is beyond phat.

Derrick will boast and brag about his conquests with women, but he's really humble about his professional and financial accomplishments. So if you're not ready, walking into his house can mirror an out-of-body experience. Five floors, four stainless steel balconies, three gourmet kitchens, two loungelike guest bathrooms, one glass elevator. His cook and cleaning lady are finer than the art show he has going on in his main foyer. The best part about it is that you can look straight up from the first floor to the sky. Glass roof. Even better view from the fifth floor. Stars and everything. Fireplace the size of the Lockness Monster. Master bedroom has two floors. Like a separate apartment. Let's not forget the movie theater that makes my daughter and her friends think that "Uncle Derrick" is the coolest thing since the big purple dinosaur came to town. The recliners are so comfortable, you'd be damned to make it through to the end of a movie without visiting the sandman first.

I'm thinking that tonight will be crazy. D seems to have everything in order. Even though this is Garvin's birthday, it's special for Derrick, too. This will be the first time in the history of our friendship . . . let me think. Yup. First time ever he's introduced a woman of his as his woman at a gathering like this. The funny thing is that I am the only one who believes it. Kalonji said that Shirley Caesar had a better chance of singing background for Lil' Kim. They won't buy it. K nor Garvin. They haven't seen how he's been over the past few months either. Like we've never seen him before. Thoughtful, generous, self-sacrificing, you name it. It took a while for me to digest it, but the man is blown. Gone. All because of her. Her. *"Taiyler's bringing the wine . . ."* The echo's running chills through me. The woman from the grocery store. Beautiful. That he was right about. And even more so at the fund-raiser. Horns blowing.

"Fuck you, too, asshole!" Middle fingers. Mine out of the window. His through the rearview. "Well, then, get in your lane, you blind-ass mutherfucker!" I'm in the wrong. I know it. No room for deep thought on a Saturday night on the Beltway. Need to pay attention to the road. These people will kill you out here. Taking a look at my watch, I'm late. Supposed to be there around eight. Before the guests were scheduled to arrive. Shit, Derrick's going to have a stroke. I followed the split off of New York Avenue to Massachusetts. Around the circle, past the Wyndham. Down M Street. All the way to Georgetown. Gat dayum! They need to fix these roads! If I crack a rim, it'll be like the return of bin Laden out this mutha. Turn up Wisconsin. Construction. Right on N. Slow down at 30th. Looking for a spot to park. As a matter of fact, I need to call D and tell him to come down and help out with all this shit. Speed dial 6.

"D. Yeah. I'm out front. Bring ya ass down here. Yeah, for the food. No, I didn't. You said Taiyler had it . . ." Felt like my ear was being tickled with a feather. I have to get to the doctor. ". . . no, you didn't. Well, then, I didn't hear you. Whatever, nigga . . . aight then." Click. He's on his way down. Asked me if I brought some vintage bottle of something. I hadn't the slightest idea of what he was talking about. Fuckin' bourgeois ass. I chuckled to myself. I didn't grow up rich, but I grew up exposed to cabarets, fine wine, and cigars. He didn't. I don't know or care to remember any of that shit. He knows it all. Down to a tee. Life is funny.

Watching him stroll out of the front door, stop to talk to a group of women headed for the house, see them smile, shriek and purr at his comments, makes me remember my freshman year. James Hall. Giving him a pound, overloading the trays and platters onto both arms, and knowing he's right back there to catch me if I fall reminds me of our frat years. Pledging. Maneuvering through the cars in the garage, walking through the first-floor kitchen, and entering what he so lovingly calls the Great Room reminds me of how far we've come. Together. Of the twenty dollars I borrowed from him on that Valentine's Day that made Kendra look at me differently. Made her say yes. Of the tests that we cheated on together. The party I threw to make the money for his tuition balance. So that he could graduate. Start law school. Of the time that I kissed another girl during Senior Week at Hampton and she told Kendra. Almost ruined my life. Derrick spent two whole days calling Kendra every hour on the hour. Convincing her that it was him and not me. Even though it caused his own girl to leave him. Yup. This is my boy for life. The only man that I trust with the care of my only daughter. Her godfather. My back.

"Yo, Nat! Wake up, man! Ain't no time for no daydreaming, deep-thought shit. Put that over there. Take the lids off. Hurry up, man! People are here! Thought you were going to be here by eight!" he yelled. Derrick does not like to be unprepared. I need to calm his ass down.

"Hold up a sec. Rushing never accomplished anything. Just wait. I'm moving as fast as I can," I answered calmly.

"You ain't movin' fast enough!" he said as he rushed back out to my car to grab whatever was left of the food. Taking a quick look around the Great Room, he's right. People are arriving. By the packs. Don't folks like to be fashionably late? Guess that's old school. On my way to the kitchen, Danielle, one of the women who went to school with us, grabbed my arm and pulled me in for a big hug.

"Heyyyy, Nat! How arrrre yoooouu!" Why women sing questions that don't belong to songs will always be a mystery to me.

"I'm fine, Danni. How's life treating you? What has it been, a few years since we've seen each other?" I asked. I think so. I hope so. I have a terrible memory. Hope I didn't see her recently and don't remember. Seems like women take offense to that. Seems like they take offense to a lot.

"Uh . . . let me think . . ." She placed both hands on her hips, threw her head upward, and rolled her eyes to the sky. So dramatic. The differences between men and women. Drama. One of the main ones. ". . . yeah, you could be right. Uhmm, I think it was last year at Kalonji's barbecue. Memorial Day."

I remember that. I almost had to break this dude's neck for trying to holler at my wife.

"Oh, yeah, you came with Nicole. How's she doing?"

"She's fine. Working on that MBA up at Columbia. First year is the toughest. I'll tell her you asked."

"Cool. And you? You get scooped up yet? I know some lucky guy has his hand in the pot." She's cool. Smart. Sexy. Paid. Private wealth management at Morgan Stanley. Hampton sure does turn out the good ones.

"Hand in the pot?" she asked incredulously. "Hand in my pocket without a pot to piss in is more like it!"

And funny. Forgot about that. I let out a loud laugh. Still laughing. She joined in.

"Nah . . . it can't be that bad," I replied between breaths.

"Only if you're a single, multidegreed, independent woman in New York City looking for someone who isn't dressed like his twelve-year-old son in a throwback jersey and matching head gear. Or a college graduate in English who thinks that 'you know what I mean' can be summed up in a matter of two words. Ya mean?" she answered between laughs of her own. ". . . all the men are down here."

I'm cracking up. Danielle is great. Forgot how cool she was. A class act. But not so much that her nose is stuck on top of the Empire State Building. She can't be serious, though. She's a hell of a catch. The

NYC bruhs can't be that ignorant. There's some good ones up there. Not all of them are rolling on dubbs and fucking hoes in hot tubs. She made her way back to the Great Room and left me in the kitchen.

Just then, the bathroom door opened. She walked right by me. Didn't look up. Didn't say hi. Nothing. Pocahontas gave me a hug. Took a carrot stick right out of my hand. She's a mess. I like her. The other one just kept going. No acknowledgment at all. And I'm stuck to the floor. At the end of Candy Land. In the Molasses Swamp. Sweating.

"See you later, Nat," Poca said. I nodded. Or I think I did. My eyes are fixed on her scarf. Light. Delicate. I find myself wanting to remove it. Discover the shape of her neck with my fingertips. I watch it all. Derrick's kiss. Her smile. I shake it off. Those thoughts. Invading me like British soldiers do African villages. I placed my head in my hands. For a moment. What is going on? All right. I'm back. Hooking up the veggie tray. Despite my will, I'm not in the kitchen anymore. I'm at the punch bowl. My eyes are. Where she is. Watching the interrogation. Watching her gracefulness. Watching her laugh. Wondering if she sees me. Watching her walk. Headed over here. Or is she? No way to tell. My judgment's off. I'm outside of myself. Watching my heart beat. Watching me extend my hand.

"Enjoying yourself?"

"Yes. And you?" she replied. Me? I don't know if I am. I don't know me.

"I am," I answered. I am nervous. I am woozy. I am a lot of things. Feelings mostly.

"I remember you," she said.

"I know. Aisle three."

"Yeah, that's right. Frosting."

"Your temper needs work," I said. I have to lighten this up. I'm feeling heavy. In the wrong places. She laughed a little.

"And you're arrogant. Work on that." Pulling on her bracelet. She's nervous. Or not. How in the hell would I know?

"I know. My apologies."

"Likewise," she replied.

I stood there in the kitchen. Feeling big and small. Having to try too hard not to stare. Trying my best not to look uncomfortable. Trying to figure out the last digit of pi. Thinking of infinity and probability. Wondering why I'm thinking about it. Vertigo invading my senses. Spinning me around. I hate it. I'm wanting it to end. Wanting it to begin again. I'm humming. She knows the tune.

"Coltrane. 'A Love Supreme,'" she answers like a prize student. She's wrong.

"'Pursuance.' Not 'A Love . . .'"

"I beg to differ."

"Begging does not become you." I force myself to turn around. It's rude. My back to her. I know. But her scarf is bothering me. Pulling me in. I don't want to be pulled in. Somehow she knows that I don't want to look at her. But she makes me anyway.

"Face me."

"What?"

"Face me and tell me that isn't 'A Love Supreme.'"

I look at her. At them. Those eyes. I think I can see past them. See what's behind them. See what's making me sick.

"It is what I said it was."

"Go get the CD case. Derrick has it. Play it." She put me on the spot.

"It's a love song. Not appropriate for tonight," I answered sheepishly.

"Why not? People here are in love. What, are you scared to lose?"

"Never."

"Never what? Never scared to lose or never in lov—owwhh!" she yelled. Blood running down her pointer. Think fast, Nat. Don't want it to hurt her. I look toward the sink and grab a paper towel. Grab her finger and place it under running water. Wrapped the paper towel around it. Applied pressure. Eye to eye again. I don't know where we are. Don't know this feeling. I don't know me.

"Hey, baabee!"

I do know that voice. It's Derrick's. It's echoing. I look down. What the fuck? Her hand in mine? Drop that shit. What am I doing? Not good. Not on purpose. She cut herself. I was helping out. I was here minding my business. The feeling was good. No, it wasn't. It was bad. I'm explaining it all. Derrick doesn't hear me. I don't hear myself.

"Oh, shit. You're bleeding, Taiyler. Com'ere. I told you that you didn't have to do anything. Just relax and have fun. Don't lift a finger. I'll be back with some Neosporin and a Band–Aid." Derrick is damn near in a panic.

"Nat, look out for Garvin. He's fucked up already. Sorry ass. I'll be right back. And these chicken kabob thingys are good as hell, man." While D made a mad dash up the stairs, I made a similar one toward the great room. When in doubt, get the fuck out. This queasy shit has to go. The store, the fund-raiser, and now here. Derrick needs to tell Taiyler that her perfume is not good for people with bad allergies. Like myself.

The party progressed naturally. Women scrutinizing women's clothing, hair, and credentials. Men scrutinizing women's faces, asses, and tits. Lots of laughter. Music. Musiq. Badu. Jay-Z. The Roots. Fifty Cent. Twenty-one questions. Do you remember Senior Ball? Isn't Envy doing well? Remember The Showcase? They did what? Tear down the Union? Yes, I've done France. But not Greece. London but not Ibiza. Who's pregnant? She was doing what with who? Yes, she works for *Essence*. No, he works for *VIBE*. They still fucking? Brian married who? Bastard. Wasn't he in med school while we were freshmen? And he's still there? You going to homecoming this year? Were you at Derrick's last party? See him in the *Post*? Et cetera, et cetera, et cetera.

Same shit, different toilet. But we love to do it over and over again. It never gets boring. We always look good. And are always doing better than we were the last time. Nobody understands us like we do. We're not elitists. Or exclusive. Just sisters and brothers. Sharing the same experiences. Hampton-bound as high school graduates. Success-bound as Hampton graduates. Living life. Loving it. Like clockwork the conversation changes. Politics. The state of the race. Who helps, who's an Uncle Tom. Who cares. Who doesn't. Rap. Influence. Videos. Jail. Percentages. Black male to female. White to Black. Causes. Effects. The works. I glance over by the fireplace, and my heart skips a beat at the sounds bouncing off of the walls. She's involved in a hell of a conversation. Half the party is tuned in to the debate. Politics as usual.

"See, that's the problem with the so-called Black elite. You get your degrees, single-family homes and Benzes, and start feeling yourself. Creating lines of separatism. The 'hood' as you put it doesn't need or want your money. It needs direction. Visibility. Not your holier-than-thou attitudes." Taiyler makes an excellent point. Deborah, one of Derrick's so-called exes, constructs a counter.

"When my ass was struggling with two and three jobs to give Hampton that advanced deposit, your beloved hood didn't do shit for me. I studied for those tests. I made it through. I did it. The only help I had was from God. So, no. I don't feel obligated to give my money away. God helps those who help themselves."

Wow, is all I can say to myself. The blind leading the blind. And to think. She has children. Taiyler is obviously not impressed with the soapbox routine. She cleared her throat. Placed her forefinger and thumb underneath her chin and prepared her attack. I'm impressed already.

"On this planet here we call Earth, and at that university, sometimes college, sometimes institute you call Hampton, visibility and direction do not translate into throwing your dollars at the less fortunate like raw meat to a pit bull. That wasn't my point. Too often are our kids, and yes, I do stress *our,* misdirected. 'I failed the SATs.' There is no failing the SATs. That's nothing but twelve years of misdirection. Underqualified teachers. 'I don't have money for college.' That's being intimidated by the lengthy financial aid process, which includes forms and deadlines that are so stringent, they are often missed and misinterpreted even by the ones that have a clue. Misdirection. 'I'm not good in math.' How about my math teacher barely passed her certifications? Or my math teacher is upset that he has to teach in an indigent neighborhood filled with Blacks and Hispanics, so he flies through the shit like the lazy bastard he is? How about my mom is working until twelve midnight, and fuck money for tutors . . . we have to get the electricity turned back on . . . ?" Whoa. Taiyler is rolling like Malcolm X. Passionate. Intense. Derrick is beaming. ". . . so if they saw more of us on a regular basis, had more direction, maybe they, too, could afford the opportunity to stand here and act like no one helped them become who they are." Silence. Ahem. Clearing of throats. Extinguishing of future dumb-assed comments. Or so we thought.

"Where are you from, Taiyler?"

"Brooklyn."

"Oh. That explains it. Your closeness to the issue." Deborah is a bitch. For real. "And what did you say you did again, Taiyler?"

"Actually, I didn't. But since you won't feel complete until you know, Cardiology and Internal Medicine, private practice. So I'm not as close to the issue as you think. You're actually closer. Paralegal, right?"

Shala fell the fuck out. Right on the sofa. Cracking up. Taiyler's killing this chick. She's a pro and she knows it. Derrick jumps up. Almost knocks my glass out of my hand.

"Okay! Okay! This is a party. No more politics. Baby . . ." he says as he looks at his woman. Who's ironically cool as a cucumber while her opponent has steam coming out of every orifice of her body.

"My love . . ." He grabbed her hand, took her by the waist, pulled her to him, and planted a fat one on her lips. In front of at least five or six exes. No games tonight. Kalonji and Garvin both look at me in sheer disbelief. I nod. I told them. He's a goner. We eat. Dance. Talk. Laugh. Till the cops come knockin'. Or dawn. Whichever comes first. People shake hands, give dap. Hugs. On their way out. New friends made. Some for the night. Some for life. And then I see her pick up her coat. I don't want her to leave just yet. I have something to say. I just don't know what it is.

"You leaving?" Obviously she is. I'm such an idiot.

"Yes. Been here for too long. Had fun, though."

I want to help her slide her jacket on. But I can't touch her. Can't move from this spot.

"Hey, uh . . . we're glad you came into Derrick's life."

She looked at me strangely. "We who?" That look. I know that look from somewhere.

"Uh, the guys. Me, K, and Garvin."

She smiled. Licked her lips. Lord help me.

"Really. Well, he's a good guy," she said, finally getting that jacket on. Then we just stood there. Quiet. Staring at nothing and everything.

"Well, you have a good night. Drive safely. Take care of Pocahontas."

"Poca-who?" She raised her eyebrow. She's amused.

"Shala. We call her Pocahontas," I said. She threw her head back and laughed. Music to my ears.

"I will. She's been in worse condition. Until next time."

"Until then. Good night."

And I stood there. Watched her slide into her Porsche. Watched her throw her hair into a ponytail. Watched her adjust the rearview mirror. Watched her watch me. And I stood there, making sense of nothing. Enjoying the energy flow. Not knowing where it came from. And not caring. The lack of control. The weakness. It's all a part of me. I want to talk. I think I know what to say. But I can't find the words. I'm the cousin of weakness. Standing outside myself watching me walk toward her car. Watching her walk in my mind. Wanting to erase it. But rewinding it instead. As she pulled out onto N Street, I stood there. Feeling full. Feeling empty. Overwhelmed. And wondering why I couldn't shake the feeling this time.

19

Nathaniel

Somehow or another I always end up on cleanup. Derrick's cleaning lady is coming in tomorrow, but from the looks of this mess, she'd have to bring all of DC Sanitation with her just to be able to see the tabletops. So I usually help clear out some of the heavy stuff and leave the wiping and washing to her.

My mother cleaned homes that were way too large for any one person to handle. I hated watching her blacken her knees, scrubbing floors and wiping moldings. White folks weren't the only ones cracking the whip. My mama cleaned the estates of rich Black people. Johnson's, DePaul's, Whitaker's, and McQuerry's. Quinones's, St. Paul's, Carter's, and Grant's. People who couldn't remember whether or not they had slaves in their lineage. Folks who have never set foot on any Martin Luther King, Jr., Boulevard in any city in this country. The ones with good hair. Good genes. Born dark, marry light. Born light, stay that way. You would have thought that we were of two different races.

The only difference between some of the misters my mom cleaned for and the massas my great-great-grandma cleaned for was that one had an excuse for degrading their staff. Excluding them. Making them feel like less than three-fourths. They were ignorant of their asinine behavior. They weren't us. They were the enemy.

Well, what happens when you work your fingers to the bone for your own? And they turn their nose up at you like you didn't purchase goods from their stores, visit their private practices, support their causes, and put money in their collection plates? What's their excuse? What do you say to the fifteen-year-old brother that calls your mother by her first name when she could have had him after she had you? I don't know. But I'm glad my mother doesn't have to lift another finger for anyone again in her life. If I die tomorrow, I would have lived to accomplish that one thing, and I'd pass into the next life with a smile on my face. I think about those old days from time to time. Sometimes it makes me mad. Tonight, I'm just glad to be able to help out in any way that I can.

As I continued to fill the extra-large Hefty bag with plastic containers and other garbage, I took a look around. Everyone's knocked out. I'm up. With something going on inside of me. A stirring. I want to think about what happened earlier. But I'm afraid to explore it. Afraid to even touch it. Want to summon the ability to wish it away. Wanting more than just that. And it's scaring me. There's something so familiar about her. Like visiting the home of an elderly Black woman on a Sunday afternoon. The level of comfort is invigorating. Smells like Grandma's house. Feels like Grandma's house. Even though you've never been there, you know your way around. Pot of coffee on the stove. Fruit magnets on the refrigerator. Old photos posted on even older frames. Plastic on the sofa. Radiator blasting. Sheets fresh. Evening news on. You fall asleep. And you don't even know it. Because you're comfortable. You know that place like the back of your hand. Even though you've never been.

That's where I was today. Grandma's house. Wanting to leave. But stuck to a feeling that I don't want to recognize. I headed over to the linen closet, which is actually the size of a small bedroom, and grabbed some pillows for my boys. These guys are all over the place. On the floor, hanging off of the sofa, slobbering, and drooling. I threw the pillows behind their heads and adjusted their feet so that they wouldn't wake up in a drunken panic talking about how they couldn't feel their legs. Surprisingly, I'm okay. Didn't drink too much. Thinking about hitting the road. Getting home. Getting some air. Getting her out of my head. And then my phone rang. Four in the morning. Has to be Kendra. Hope everything is all right.

"Hello."

Silence. Shit. Now I'm worried.

"Kennie? Baby, is that you? Everything okay? I'm on my way home . . ."

More silence. I look at the caller ID. Private.

"I just wanted to say good night. I-I kind of rushed out . . . and . . . I . . . uh didn't get to say it back."

My heart stopped. I know the voice. And somehow, I knew she would call. I look over at Derrick. At the smile on his face. And I know who put it there. She does that well.

"Did you make it home okay?" I asked. I have no morals. No feelings. But the ones I'm fighting.

"Yes, I did. Thanks. Are you still there?"

"Yeah. Walking out now," I said as I keyed in the code for Derrick's house alarm. Damn. I have like thirty seconds to get out of here, and I haven't put my shoes on yet.

"So did you have a good time?" she asked.

"I did. I usually do." Shoot. These are the wrong shoes to be trying to rush on. I almost kill myself in the process. End up in the garage. Can't leave through the front when the alarm is activated.

"You're doing it wrong," she said.

"Doing what wrong?"

"The door. You'll set the alarm off. Remove the sensor first." Oh. That's right. The sensor. Forgot about that. Wait. How did she know?

"How did you know that I was in the garage?" I asked. Silence. I asked again.

"How did you know to tell me that?"

"Turn around," she said.

"Do what?"

"Turn around. That'll answer your question."

I did just that. And when I did it, only God could account for what I felt at that moment. Only He knows how truly beautiful she is.

"You're here . . . You're back." That was all I said. All I could say. She looked like a goddess in plain clothes. Tugging on that bracelet. Pulling me farther away from myself.

"Made it home. Made it back. Wanted to say good night," she said, eyes focused on mine. Searching for something true. Searching for understanding. Well, at least I was.

Her eyes were a mirror to my iniquity. Through them, I could see it all. Fear. Confusion. Wonder. Pent up inside like boiling water in a kettle. Waiting to make its presence known to the entire house.

"The good night. You've said it. And you're still here."

"I know. And so are you."

"So what does that mean?"

"I don't know. I was hoping you did."

And there it was again. Grandma's house. In all the wrong places.

"What . . ." She wants to know what I'm staring at. It's her scarf. It's hypnotizing me.

"It looks so soft. Mind if I do?" I asked. All I wanted to do was feel the softness. The familiarity. The sting of the scorpion. She nodded her head. Looked away. Like she did in the grocery store. As if that would do it. Control this. We are the same person right now. A mask of symptoms looking to be diagnosed.

"So you feel it, too," she said. More so as a statement to herself than to me. Sometimes it's good to know you're not out there by yourself.

"Sometimes."

"When are your sometimes?"

"When you are around."

"What about the weakness?"

"Yes."

"The nervousness?"

"Yes."

"The confusion?"

"Yes."

"The fear?"

"Uh-huh."

I'm hearing her breathe. Feeling her breath on my neck. My fingertips on the back of her. We're dancing to the rhythm of adrenaline and dopamine. Her fingers moving down the middle of my back. Tickling my soul. Guiding me into a frenzy of overwhelming emotion. I'm dizzy with pleasure. Spinning with the type of euphoria that comes with highs bought with priceless gems. Wondering how I got here. Not caring. Inside her is where I want to stay. Slow dancing to nature's song. Feeling what was created in our minds the first day we met.

Her kisses feel so good. I don't know what to do with them. So I give them back to her. Spread them all over her body. Watch them run across her most sensitive spots. Her most feminine ones. Watch them make her scream out loud. Make her move like she's always imagined she could.

In this garage packed with heavy hearts, I'm light-headed. And she's light. So I pick her up. Hold on to her. Love her. Lover. Listen to her moan. I want to be the sound of pleasure that escapes her. I want her to be the mouth that speaks for me. That tells her how good she feels to me. That moans for me. That whispers strawberry kisses in her ears. On her neck. Her shoulders. And when she told me that this was as good as I'd ever felt, as great as I'll ever be, I let her tell me something else. On top of me. My hands around her waist. Pushing her down on me with a softness that was so intense, I couldn't hear myself groan. Couldn't hear her moan. So I asked her to tell me something. Anything. Because I wanted to speak, but I couldn't find the words. And with my worth as a man inside of her, she said it all. Amidst short breaths and light curses. That her love would never leave. And my body answered her in a way that I'd never experienced before. I was spinning so fast my stomach hurt. Spiraling backward on the autobahn. With her on my lap. Legs wrapped around me. Her body was all I needed to survive.

"Pl-please . . ." was all that I could muster up. If we don't stop, I won't make it. Anything that feels this good will surely kill you. My heart is about to implode. From the inside of my pelvis. Her eyes are half closed. She's in our own world. Beads of sweat on her brow, I wipe them clean with my lips. Lick them and swallow them whole. Don't want to waste anything that will bring her closer to me. Then I feel her. Shiver. Shudder. Hold on tight. Or is that me? It's so hard to tell. Now that we've slowed down, it's even harder.

"You're so intense," she said.

"Never been this way before. Not that I can remember." And that's the truth.

"Yes, you have. But a long time ago."

"A long time ago?" My eyes are still closed. My mind still open.

"Yes. The first night we made love. Valentine's Day."

"Valentine's Day?"

"Valentine's Day, Nat. Stop playing around. You remember."

My eyes popped open. The look on my face said it all. I fucked up.

"Nat, honey, what's wrong? Why are you looking at me like that?"

Oh, my God. No. I didn't. I couldn't have. The sex. Taiyler. The garage . . . the way I felt. Goodness. I was saying her name over and over and over again. And then another feeling took over. Complete fear. I hope Kendra didn't hear me.

"Baby, what just happened?" I asked carefully. She must think I'm a damn fool. But I have to know. How I got from Derrick's garage to my bedroom with my wife lying on top of me, my dick still pulsating inside of her.

"Stop acting up, Nat. It's too early for that. Especially with how my body's tingling right now. A-plus, sweetie. A-plus."

"No, for real, Kennie. How'd this happen?" I'm serious. She thinks I'm playing around.

"All right. I'll play your little game. You came home this morning. A little out of it. Like something was bothering you. You didn't want to talk about it. Got right in the bed. Hit the sack as soon as your head hit the pillow. I woke up to the feeling of you. Your hands on my waist, moving like you did on our honeymoon. Like Valentine's Day. I must have had about four or five orgasms. Two in a row. There. Happy now? Mr. Macho. Wants to hear how he's ruined his wife. Okay, fine . . ."

As she went on, I pretended to listen. Pretended that I understood what was going on. What had happened. Pretended to understand me. Shaking my head, I sat upright.

"Nat, what's up?" Kendra asked. I couldn't say anything. Couldn't do anything. But sit there shaking my head from side to side. It could not have been a dream. My hands are still shaking. But then again, why wouldn't I want it to be? I don't know if I'm disappointed because I dreamt of my best friend's woman giving me the type of life that I couldn't have ever imagined, or if I'm disappointed that it was only a dream. Either way, I'm feeling like less than a man for even having the experience at all. What kind of control do I have over myself? How could I allow this to happen? My wife is still talking to me. She knows something's bothering me. Doesn't know what. Doesn't know what it's doing to me.

"So, baby. Talk to me. Did you have a nightmare? We can talk about it later if you want . . ." She's so supportive. I really feel like a faggot. Not in the homosexual slur connotation, but in the true meaning of the word. The low-down dirty version, that so appropriately rhymes with maggot. I have got to fix this. I can't and won't have any more of those dreams. If I have to, I'll stop drinking alcohol altogether. Even though I didn't have much, I'm sure that's the reason behind all of this. From Derrick's kitchen to the garage to my bedroom. Yeah, I'm bugging the fuck out. I lie back down and hold on to my wife for dear life.

"I'm okay, babe," I answered her. "Just got a little distorted. I'm not drinking anymore. I don't know what I had, but it fucked me up. And I didn't even drink a lot."

She looked at me, chuckled, and smoothed over my eyebrows with the tips of her fingers.

"Well, whatever it was, put me down for three cases of it. If it'll make you move like that, honey, I'll buy stock in it!"

She's feeling good. Laughing. Joking. And I'm feeling like a runaway train.

20

Shala

"Sha. Shala, get up."

"I don't want pancakes . . ."

"Pancakes! Girl, get your drunk ass up before I have to call Grai down here." That did it. I'm up. Grai hates to see me drunk. Well, I'm not drunk, but you know.

"Shala . . . I'm not playing; it's like two in the morning. And I still have to drive to Bowie. And we have a chapter meeting tomorrow. And you're getting on my nerves!"

That's good. Because she's getting on mine. Doesn't she see that I'm up? I'm moving. My head is still lying on the window. Isn't that funny? Look at the smoke on the glass. I'm a dragon. No, I have dragon breath. I burst out laughing. Maybe I'm not up yet. But she doesn't need to trip like that. She's not my mother. Damn, she's pretty. Okay. I really am drunk.

"I'm calling Grai." That did it. Again. Don't feel like hearing her mouth. Feel like feeling it, though. So fuck it. Call her down. A three-some never hurt nobody.

"Damn it, Shala!" Taiyler's really irritated. She got out of the car. Huffing and puffing and shit. Two dragons. Ain't that a bitch.

"Sha, this shit ain't funny. If I knew you would have gone this far, I would have left your ass here."

Now, I may be a little *"under the tonic"* as my Grandpa used to say, but she ain't gon' talk to me like I'm some . . . Oh, this bitch done yanked me out of the car. I'm going to curse her out. I gotta spit up. Never mix dark and light. My stomach . . .

"Ewwwh, Sha, damm. You're sick, girl. Here . . . over here. So the street cleaners can get it." Okay, she's being nice. And my face feels like it's retracting back into my lungs. So I'ma curse her out tomorrow. She's laughing at me. Some friend.

"Nah, normally y'all know I don't do this . . ." I'm really laughing at my corny-assed R. Kelly impersonation. "We off up in this jeep . . . we foggin' up the windows . . ."

Taiyler sucked her teeth. My father is like the R. Kelly of Washington Tabernacle. Doesn't want to face the fact that all girls aren't worth having. I'm one of them. Not worth his perception of me. If he knew me, he'd wish he never had me. I throw up again. Taiyler dries my face with her scarf. My girl. No cursing out for her. Not tonight. Not tomorrow. I wish they would stop talking over my head. Oh, shit. No, T. No . . . Grai doesn't know about the whole thing. The back-and-forth thing. I'm not really going back. Don't tell her, T. That's between us. I love her too much to hurt her. Don't tell her why I'm crying. Hold on. If I can just get my shit together . . .

"I'm okay," I said. They're still talking over me. I hate that shit.

"I'm okay," I say again. Taiyler's getting in the car. Giving her a remedy that Aunt Mae used for drunks. Oh, yeah . . . soak my feet in hot water and Epsom salt. I try to tell Grai.

"Epsom salt . . ."

She looks at me like I'm really bugging. Epsom salt, that must be the wrong one. Think that's for soaking feet. What was the one we used to use for sobering us up? Dunno. We walk up the stairs. Shit. We're in my house. How did Grai get here? Thought she was at home tonight. I looked over onto the bed. My shorts and tank top. Laid out like my mama used to do. Grai think she's my mama. I think she's fine as hell. She washed my face. Rinsed my mouth with Listerine. Made me drink water. And something else. Eat bread. All this shit never worked. I always end up feeling bad in the morning. Took a Celebrex. Would know that four dollars a pill anywhere. Bet Taiyler gave her that. Chapter meeting tomorrow. Mutherfuckers. We should meet during the week. Sunday is for rest. And church. I'm on my bed. Sitting on the edge. Swinging my legs. Think I might jump. Think I got all of the vomit out. Hope so. Because these are my Banana sheets. Nice thread count. Whatever. I'm tired. I'm going to sleep.

*"It's the power . . . of His name! King of Kings . . . Lord of Lords . . .
Ruler of all that is! Alpha and Omega! Beginnin' and the end! Chu'ch!
Let me hear you say Jeeeesuuuus!"*

I have to be at least twenty-five feet from the entrance of my father's church. And I can hear him just as clearly as I would if I were
sitting on the front pew. As I got closer to the large stone steps, an extreme sweep of nervousness takes over. I have to pause for a second.
It's taking everything I have not to turn my sinning ass back around,
hop in my car, and hit the Beltway. I know every single person in this
building. And if I don't know them, then they sure know me. I'm the
only daughter of one of the most powerful men in the country. Every
organization from the Congressional Black Caucus to the NAACP
calls on him for one thing or another. Comus, Boule, Masons, you
name it. He's in it, associated with it, did it, done it, and a part of it.
Which makes my absence in church damn near a freaking topic for
Jet magazine.

Today, they're hosting a huge conference. The Who's Who of
gospel are scheduled to make their appearances. Told him I couldn't
make it as usual. Changed my mind after I woke up hungover in the
middle of the night in tears. Grai made orange tea, massaged the
bridge of my nose, and kissed my eyelids until I fell asleep again. I feel
bad. Poor Grai doesn't know what to do with me. I guess we're having
the same problem. Damn. Hope I can rectify that today with God. If
not, I would at least have made my father happy. Well, at least one of
them.

I gathered the energy in the pit of my stomach. Placed it on the
first of many stairs leading to the entrance. Moving like molasses. One
step at a time. Twelve-step program. Only way to cure an addiction. I
hear the organ. Brother Sam racing up and down the keys. Hitting
chords as recklessly as a drunk driver. The sound. It gets to me. Forget
it. I can't do it. Answer a million questions today. Where have you
been, chile? What are you doing with yourself, young lady? Can I give
you my daughter's resumé? Are you joining the choir? We need good
sistahs like you! When are you gon' settle that pretty face of yours
down and get married? All the while I'm thinking, Would you pleeeze
let me get in the front door before the press conference begins?

And then the worst of the worst. The smile on my father's face
when I walk down the aisle. No matter where he is in his sermon, he

always notices. He always stops. He always smiles. Then all five thousand people always stare. Point. Whisper. Wave. You would have thought that I had been fighting Sadaam and all of his sons on a dingy street in Baghdad. He looks so happy. So proud. Like I'm all that's missing to make his ministry complete. Too much pressure. Especially after I had Grai's face in all the right places this morning. It was the only way for me to get back to sleep.

I approached the front door slowly. Put my ear up against the piece of wood tall enough to be a Douglas fir. Hear the drums. Hear the cymbals. The tambourines. And take off in the opposite direction. I can't do this today. No sooner do I reach the bottom of the steps than I hear her. The voice from my childhood. So distinct. So devoted. Sister McCullen. The only usher that could whoop my little behind when I was acting up. An old wise woman who will cut you down in a minute if you act like you want her to.

"Baby . . . Is that you? Is that my Shala?" She grabbed my arm. Turned me around. Her grip is like the Jaws of Life.

"Yes, Sister McCullen. It's me. How are you?" I asked for lack of anything better to say. I'm unprepared.

"Oh, I'm blessed, sweetie! And sooo happy to see you! You still down in Atlanta? You here visitin'?"

Now, I love her to death. But she is a nosy one. She knows damn well I graduated and that I live here, because she was at my graduation party. In other words, she wants to know why my Black ass hasn't been in church for the past few years. So instead of asking, she gives herself the most logical response. That I must not live here anymore. Because that's the only thing outside of death or disfigurement that could keep her away from her Lord. Sneaky, but not that sneaky. Chapter meeting, church, same difference when it comes to nosy old Black women.

"No, Sister McCullen. I just don't go to church anymore." That solves that. The look of shock on her face was enough to make me crack up. But I know better.

"Oh. Well, okay. I'm prayin' for you," she said as she looked at me like I was lying in a hospital bed with a thousand tubes running through me. She pities me. She doesn't know the half.

"Your father know you here?" she asked, as we both made our way up the huge stairs leading to the vestibule. She knows how long it's been.

"No. He doesn't. I figured I'd just slip right in. You know, surprise him." Hope she gets it. I don't want her to tell him. I'd rather do it myself. The last time she walked me in, she took me right down the trail of tears. Straight through the middle aisle. Right up to the first pew. I was mortified.

"Okay. Well, I'll let you be. And remember, honey . . . your father loves you. God does, too. Don't be a stranger here, this is home. Okay?"

"Okay," I answered back. Feeling like more of a stranger than I did a minute ago.

She turned around, lifted her chin, placed her chest in peacock position, and hit that legendary strut that those dignified ushers, deacons, and trustees own in churches all over the country. I had to let out a laugh. She's the shit.

I'm left standing in the vestibule, ingesting my surroundings. The stairs that lead to the balcony. The cubbyhole that I used to hide in when it was time to go home and I wanted to stay. The extra choir robes hanging in the hallway. The smell of freshly fried chicken, and sweet potato pies, yellow cakes with just the right kind of white cream frosting. The things that love made. The things that made me. Pushed me to go to Spelman. Pushed me to become what my ancestors couldn't.

I noticed the side door where I used to sneak into church when I was late. Think I'll take that option today. Sliding into a seat in the back, listening to my father speak words that ignite hearts and motivate minds made me think of what ignites me. What motivates me. And how hard it is to merge them. Make them acceptable. Make them normal. I've been looking down the entire time. Reading the program. Avoiding eye contact. Trying to take in all I could in peace. Without being noticed. It doesn't matter. He still knows that I'm here. It's like he can sense it. He tells the church how happy he is to have his daughter here with him today. And that the day is truly blessed by God. Does everything but call me a saint. Sometimes I think he loves me more than he does my mother. Sometimes I think she thinks the same thing. As soon as I looked up, a young girl whispered to me.

"Nice to meet you. He talks about you all the time. You went to Spelman, right? I'd like to go there, too. Maybe we can talk later. Is that okay?"

I nod my head. Listen to the choirs sing. Watch the collection plate being passed. Feel the spirit of love and unity being shared. Wishing I could share this with Grai. I hate leaving half of me at home. As the service comes to a close and folks start getting up, I feel someone pulling on the hem of my skirt. A little someone. I look down. I know that I'm smiling. Because I'm looking at a little angel.

"My mommy said she's happy to see you . . ." she said as she smiled a mile wide. I take a good look at how much she's grown, give her a big hug, pick her up and swing her around. Keep her on my waist.

"Where is she?" I asked as I blew air into her cheek. Made her giggle.

"Over there!" The little angel pointed over to the choir stand. I smiled again. Had to. I was looking at a good friend. One that I hadn't seen in a very long time. The only person besides Taiyler that helped me deal with my sexuality. Dr. Henderson. And the little angel on my hip is Nile, her daughter.

"Well, well, well . . ." she says as she hugs me tightly. Feels good to be home.

"Yeah, yeah. It's me. The prodigal daughter in the flesh. How are you?"

"I'm fine. The question is, how are *you?*"

"Honestly?"

"Honestly."

"I'm having some issues."

"Still having the nightmares we used to talk about?"

"Yeah. They started up again."

"Crying spells?"

"Yup."

"You were doing so well, what happened?" She looked concerned as hell. More than a psychiatrist should be. It made me feel like I was talking to a friend. Made me feel good.

"I started thinking about marriage and having a little angel like Nile, and well . . . things just got bad again." I'm tearing. I don't want to. Not here.

"You want to come back into the office?"

"I'd like to. Just so that I can sleep."

"Come tomorrow at four." She looked around like a slave about to make a run for it. I know what she's about to ask.

"Uh . . . your father see you yet?"

I was right.

"Yeah, but we haven't talked. He's been busy greeting the members," I answered.

"You know that'll be all day. He has to shake everyone's hand. Twice." We shared a laugh.

"I know. Your father is such a person for the people. And he adores you. You may not have to put yourself through this, Shala. If you just talk to him. Feel him out. You know?" She looked over at Nile, who was playing with another girl her age. Running around the pews, having the time of their life. Reminding me of when times were simple.

"I hear you but I don't think I can. We can talk tomorrow, right?" I asked as I extended both arms toward her.

"Yes. At four," she replied, doing the same.

We hugged, and I took off to complete my mission. See my father. Have him smother me in a big bear hug. Give him the opportunity to be daddy and not "pastor" or "reverend." Free him for a minute or two. As I make my way over to the exit, all of the people standing in line awaiting the chance to shake my dad's hand to tell him how great of a sermon he preached move to the side in order for me to get to the front. I guess they want to see his reaction, too.

"Hi, Dad." I'm here. Face-to-face with a mogul. Heart to heart with my daddy. I see his heart melt right in front of me.

"My baby." He kissed me on the forehead. Again on my cheek. A signal that he's pleased. "Thought you said you couldn't make it. Although I sure am glad you did, you caught an old man by surprise."

I couldn't help feeling bad. It's been so long since I've seen him. Here or at home. He has more gray hair than I remember.

"I know. I worked something out. The visiting choir was great. Karen Clarke Sheilds can blow." I'm bullshitting. Unprepared again. All eyes are on me. How am I supposed to handle that?

"Yes, she sure can. I am so glad to see you. You have made my day, princess. I know you must be hungry. Go downstairs and sit at my table. There should be food ready for you. I don't know what's down there, but the sisters will fix whatever you want. We'll talk down there." He's emotional. Playing it off. I guess powerful men have to do that. The bear hug almost suffocates me, but I know he can't help it. I'm thinking . . . I have a chapter meeting this afternoon. Then Taiyler and I are having our normal brunch. I can't do both. Eat and make the meeting. Quick decision. I head downstairs and call T. She picks up on the first ring.

"Hey, Sha."

"Hey, girl. You won't believe this, but I'm at church. And my father wants me to stay for a minute. So I'm not going to be at the chapter meeting. But we're still on for brunch." I can hear her mind clicking. Wondering what got me to church after all these years.

"Uhm . . . okay. Well, where do you want to meet?" She's in shock. Didn't ask me one question about why I'm here.

"How about McCormick and Schmick? Three P.M."

"McCormick it is."

"See you then."

I make my way downstairs, sit at the table with all of the major fixings. China, crystal, fruit, drinks, excess food, special napkins. And I notice my seat. The one next to my dad's. With my old napkin. The pink one with my initials embroidered on it. Stood out like a sore thumb. How appropriate. Dang. My life has changed so much. If my father knew about me, would my pink napkin be in the same place I remember it being all of these years? Or would it be thrown out in the trash. Discarded like any other dirty item on this table would be. Don't know if I know the answer to that. Don't know if I want to find out.

The hustle and bustle of M&S reminds me of what the other half is doing on Sunday. I navigate my way past the hostess station, to our favorite table. The one facing Ninth Street. Facing the world. I see Taiyler sitting there, menu in hand, legs crossed, bouncing her foot to a contrived rhythm. So feminine. So classy. Our eyes meet. She tips her head to the side. Shakes it slowly.

"You're holding out on me."

"Can I sit down first? Before the interrogation, counselor?" The sarcasm. We do it well.

"You're holding out. Split-second decision to go to church. You're having nightmares and shit. And you're not telling me."

Whoa. She knows me too well.

"Sometimes, yes. Not all of the time. But if I'm going to do this switch thing, I should at least try to start going back to church. You know, doing the right thing." I don't believe myself. So I know she doesn't believe the shit.

"Why are you doing this to yourself?" she asked.

"Doing what? Going to church?" I'm playing stupid. Buying time. I don't know why.

"No. Going to praise God is great. Going in hopes of finding the strength to leave the one person you've loved with all of your heart because it doesn't fit into society's plan is another. Make the decision on your own. And for the right reasons." She's making sense. I'm hating that right now.

"What are the right reasons? I love her. That's it. It'll hurt for any reason."

"Then why do it? People get married, cheat, give each other AIDS, fuck their kids, and call it love. Do you think God honors that? So much that you'd leave the love of your life to stand in front of him with some dickhead proclaiming a love that you don't feel? I'm not an expert on religion or anything, but doesn't God hate liars?" Good point.

"As far as Sodom and Gomorrah is concerned He hates homosexuals, too." Good counterpoint. We're here. Where we've been so many times before. An analytical war. Trying to single out a needle in a haystack.

"Weren't those people guilty of so many other sins? You're guilty of what? Being a positive role model for your mentees, giving to the needy, volunteering at nursing homes, and let's see . . . uhm . . . loving someone who loves you back. Who happens to be a woman. Wow. If that's not cause enough to burn, I don't know what is."

"It is just cause."

"Then we're all going to hell in a handbasket."

"Not all of us."

"None of us are perfect. We all sin."

"All sins are not an abomination."

"All sins are the same. At least that's what it says in the good book."

"That's not what my father will say."

"You serve one Father. Your father is a representative. He is not God."

"I'm not saying that he is. But I know him. His image. It won't work any other way." I'm losing this war.

"And what would he say if you knelt before God spitting straight lies?"

"I don't have to be attracted to the person I marry. That's not in the vows."

"You're going crazy. And I'm not going to let that happen."

"I'm not."

"You are. You'd rather kneel at the altar face-to-face with God, and challenge Him in a session of lies. Your arms are too short. And you're fighting to get into the ring. Sounds crazy to me." She makes another good point.

"Either way I'm fucked." That's the way I feel. Taiyler let out a huge sigh.

"I don't know. I'm just not for you living a lie of a life. You know how much of a bitch you are when you're not happy. You'll pass that energy to your children. And that won't be good at all. You'll surpass the point of bringing them into this world. Cancel it out."

We sat quietly for a few seconds. Eating our salads. The issue at hand eating us alive. I want to change the subject.

"Dance Theater of Harlem is in town next week. Grai will be touring for her new book. You up for it?"

She gave me a knowing look and cut her eyes at me. She knows I'm tired of talking about it. She adapts to the change.

"I have that pharma thing, remember? I told you the Pfizer rep invited me to that big cardio conference. That shit crept up," she said, as she took a huge bite out of her chicken Caesar.

"I forgot. Where is it?" I asked. If I remember correctly, it's usually somewhere nice.

"Oranjestad."

"Connecticut?"

"No, Aruba, honey! You know Pfizer isn't cheap like y'all are at Merck." She has the biggest grin on her face. Shoot, I may go with her. I need a vacation.

"You're kidding." I know she's not.

"I have to get some new bikinis. On second thought, maybe not. I forgot I'll be in a sea of old white men who never get away from their old putrid wives. I don't want to be responsible for any heart attacks." Talk about modest. She busted out laughing.

"They would be in the right place, wouldn't they?"

"Maybe. Half of the medical population doesn't know what the hell they're doing anymore. So maybe not. Depends on who they get. But either way, they're not ready for all of this!" she says, as she forms the shape of an hourglass with her fork and knife. Now we're both laughing. If were in the mood, I'd crack a few. But all I can think about is getting home to Grai. Getting in the bed. Watching Larenz and Nia.

Turning the air-conditioning up, snuggling under my comforter, and twisting my legs around hers like a pretzel.

As I listened to Taiyler speak, I wondered if she'd ever feel like this. Caught up in a whirlwind of indecision. Fighting a war of wrongs and rights. Losing sight of what makes them different. Driven by love and logic. Both of them pulling you in opposite directions. Until they rip your heart right down the middle. By the seams. I glanced at her twirling her fork and rolling her eyes while she talked about crackers, mutherfuckers, and assholes and got my answer. I don't think so. She's way too strong for that.

PART THREE

21

Derrick

"Baby! Come upstairs quick! I wanna show you something!" I yelled out at the top of my lungs into my master bathroom.

"Derrick, I'm right here. Why have intercoms if you're still going to yell like that," Taiyler replied calmly from inside the bedroom. Call it a crime, but I just wanted to see her before she went to work.

"I wanted to show you this rash that I have on my stomach. It just popped up," I whined. I know I sound like a spoiled five-year-old, but I'm vying for her attention right now. I do that sometimes. Can't help it. I want her all the time.

"Okay, I'm here," she panted, rushing into the steamy room. "Now, what's the problem? You have a rash where? Let me take a look," she said in that sexy doctor's tone I've grown to love so much. She has on those dark-rimmed frames. The ones she seduced me with at the fund-raiser meeting. My jimmy acknowledges them as well. He likes what I like.

"Right here!" I said, pointing downward, a huge grin covering my face. "See it? It keeps getting bigger and bigger, babe! I need a doctor! Fast!" I said as I whisked her into the shower with me.

"Owwh! Derrick! Damn it! I just got my hair washed! You play too damn much!" she whined as I held her close to my soapy body, while the water ruined her clothes, curled her hair, and spotted those new Manolos I just shelled out six hundred dollars for. A moment with my baby next to me is worth six hundred. No doubt. She's pissed, though.

"Derrick. I'm going to be fucking late for work! *You* make a cabil-lion dollars a year. *You* can go in when you feel like it. You. Not me. I have patients to see in a little while, and they don't give a fuck about you or your little . . . your little rash!" she said frantically.

"Ain't nothing little about this here!" I defended, pointing to a swelled penis that wanted her almost as badly as I did. "See, feel it for yourself!" I said, waving my manhood in the air. I am cracking myself up. Watching her expression morph into a Jack Nicholson scowl. She looked like she wanted to kill me. I changed gears. Quick.

"My love, you were on the phone with those messages this morning and up all last night with those charts, and well, I'm jealous. I know we both have to work, but baby, I need you. Damn, I need you so much sometimes. Please take a shower with me. Pretty please?" Am I begging? Oh, man. I'm a sorry mofo. She spun around on her heel, stomped out of the bathroom, and slammed the door. I fucked up. Guess I could have done it a little differently. Hey, I'm not used to having to do all of this shit for a woman's attention.

I lathered up and continued to do my thang in the shower. When the lights went out and "Addicted," the belly dancing striptease theme, oozed out over my speakers, I had to catch my breath. Somewhere be-tween that sexy music and all of that steam emerged Taiyler. Naked. Side view. Strip show. With nothing to strip except her shoes. Her hips following her navel. And her navel following her hips. Arms in the air. Winding her wrists to the melody. My eyes traveled up, then down, then back up. Perfect little red triangle down there. Pretty ass. Pretty lips. Both pairs. And she's working it like a pro. Whew! Note to self, cancel all upcoming trips to the strip club. I done fell for a professional. *"It's so contagious . . ."*

I was in a trance. I guess she likes to hypnotize her prey before she strikes.

"You were saying something, Mr. DeCosta . . ."

Right now, I'm not saying anything. I wanted some attention, but I also wanted to be able to go to work today. If she continues, I don't see that happening.

"What were you saying, sweetie? You wanted me. Is that correct?"

Why is she doing this to me? I think I'm nodding my head. I know I'm stroking my dick.

"I want you to say it, babe. Tell me." She did this thing that made her belly look like it was a warm wave of liquid, crashing lightly against her pelvis. My strokes got a little more intense. I think she liked that.

"Say it, baby." She has the naughtiest look in her eyes.

"I n-ee-d you," I managed to say between strokes. My dick is about to burst wide open like a ghetto hot dog. She's doing her hoodoo, staring me in the eyes.

"Uhm-hmm. What else?" she said as she twisted her ass in a hot rhythm of sexiness. She was pouting, dancing, stroking herself almost into a frenzy. I could feel it on this side of the shower door. I didn't know what I was getting myself into.

"I want you, baby. I want you soooo much."

"What else?" she said, obviously unsatisfied with my answers. I felt feverish. All of this steam and her hot ass. I should have just taken a regular-assed shower this morning. If she keeps this up, I'll come. And I wouldn't even have touched her. I started to get desperate. Like a sex maniac locked in the hole watching the live version of *College Girls Gone Wild*. I'm fishing for words.

"What else do you want, baby? The house? Yours. My cars? Yours. What, Taiyler? Anything you want. Just come closer to me, baby. I want to touch you." I am so gone. About to break the latch on my shower door trying to get at her. When animals attack. It's never a pretty sight. All of a sudden, she came to a dead stop. Cut the music and everything.

"What, T. What? What's up?"

She's cracking up. Every time I open my mouth she laughs harder. Doubled the fuck over. She's inching closer to the door. Wonder why.

"Gotcha!"

She screamed. What the hell does she mean gotcha?

"Got what?" I asked, obviously unaware of the joke. She couldn't stop laughing enough to tell me. Finally, between breaths, she managed to cough something up.

"That's what your ass gets for playing! Next time you want to drag me into the shower, kill three hours at the salon and one of my favorite suits, you'll think twice, won't you, Rambo?"

What? I swear to God women push us to domestic violence. I'm mad. For a minute. Can't be upset at my baby for longer than that. Even if I tried. So I made a break for it. Sensing it, she took off. We're tearing through the house like two whirlwinds. I didn't know she was this fast.

"Sorry, hon!" She panted as I chased her from floor to floor. Just when I thought I had her, she hopped the fucking balcony. Talk about surprised.

"All of that fancy track shit ain't gon' do nothing for ya, sweets! You're in trouble!"

We're ripping and running, through the great room, around my art, until she ran straight into the guest lounge. She's trapped. There's one way in and one way out of this room. So here we go. Around the sofa. That game you played when Grandma was one step from whipping your ass good. Wear her out running around the couch. It's a last resort, but a good one.

"You're trapped, babe. Give up. You did me wrong. Now you have to pay the piper," I said to her. I can see those logical wheels spinning. It doesn't matter. She can't think her way out of this one. I'm smiling ear to ear.

"Now, you can throw yourself upon the court's mercy, or you can plead guilty and take life behind my bar . . ."

She rolled her eyes at me. She still won't give up.

"I'm pleading self-defense," she said defiantly. The cutest smirk on her face.

"Nope. Can't do that. It would have had to be in direct response to the crime, babe. In the heat of the moment. You can't get off on that. So what will it be, my love? Life behind my bar isn't that bad. If it were me, I'd opt for life in the hole where it's nice and damp. But to each his own."

She let out a loud laugh.

"You are too much, Derrick. Com'ere. Life behind your bar, huh? I guess I'll have to deal with that," she said as she pouted and headed over to me with her arms stretched out. I'm not falling for it. She's from the hood. I know she's going to try to make a run for it. That's just how we do. And that's just what she does. Tries to knock me out of her way while I'm defenseless. Ghetto children. I tackled her onto the bear rug. Tickled her until those charcoal eyes turned red. She let out a high-pitched scream. I'm getting her good.

"Now, what do you say?" I asked.

"Okay! Okay! I'm sorry!" She surrendered. My tickles turned into caresses. Then to light kisses. Then to deeper ones.

"De-rri-ck . . ." She likes that. I like her.

"Taiyler, guess what?" I say in between kisses.

"What . . ." she replied between breaths.

"I want you to know something before you go into the office this morning."

"What is it, honey?" She tried to sit up. I wouldn't let her. She feels good where she is.

"I love you."

"Huh?"

"I love you. I'm in love with you." I could see her heart jump. She was speechless. "Don't say anything, just know that, okay? All I want you to do is know it."

She kissed me all over. My cheeks, my chest, my stomach, my—oh, shit! I'm just going to do the bitch thing and pass out right here on the floor. I hate to think about how she got this good. Oh, my God. The room is spinning. Had I known that this was all I had to do, I would have said it earlier. Love is what it is. I'm not ashamed. I've loved her since the moment I saw her.

This is the second time this week she's been tossing and turning in her sleep. Sometimes she's smiling. Talking to someone. Like she is now. Mumbling and moaning. This happy dream has me wondering if I'm in it. If she's dreaming about me. I hope so. I watch her tell whoever it is how much they mean to her. God, I hope it's me. I notice something that I didn't notice the other night. She's crying. Smiling, but crying. A tear rolls down her cheek. She throws her arm around me and buries her head into my chest. Ahh. Sweet nirvana. She's dreaming about me. I feel so good inside. She's kissing me, mumbling something about her heart. I kissed her back. On her forehead. Guess that woke her up.

"Good morning, sweetie. You're dreaming again."

She opened her eyes, jerked away quickly, and looked into my mine. The look that she gave scared the shit out of me. Fucked me up. She looked like she hadn't the slightest idea of who she was sleeping next to. She shook her head like a puppy with water on its ears, squinted, and made a face like she was trying to remember the content of the dream.

"Taiyler. It's me, Derrick, babe. You were having another dream. Do you remember it? It must have been good, you were smiling."

She looked at me again, yawned, and slid in as close to me as she could get. Hugged me tight. Threw her leg over mine and went right back to sleep. Knocked right the fuck out. I chuckled as I wiped some of her saliva off of my chest. She sleeps so hard. She has hard days. And we don't exactly get a lot of sleep when we spend the night with each other.

I thought back to the last dream she had that woke me up. Same setup, except she was moving in her sleep as if she were trying to dance while humming a tune. The next morning, when I asked her about it, she said she couldn't remember the details. Then she didn't say anything for the rest of the morning.

As perfect as my baby is, if I could change one thing, it would be her occasional despondence. The way she withdraws from the world when something is on her mind. I asked her about that one day, while we were shopping together, and she said that she's always been that way. Pretty much that it was the way she dealt with issues good or bad. She was just quiet until she figured them out. Said if I thought she was being antisocial now, I should have met her before she went to Spelman. She claimed that Shala and her girlfriend Solange opened her up. That she didn't talk to anyone in Brooklyn except her great-aunt about anything at all. Told me not to take it personal. I can't imagine her shutting down any more than she already does. I hope that'll change with time.

Well, she seems to have gotten out of that dream and into a good-ass sleep. I'm trying to follow suit. I have to take her to the airport this morning. Some medical conference in Aruba. Shit, wish I could get clients to pay for me to go to Aruba. Something about new heart drugs. No wonder drugs cost an arm and a leg. What's wrong with having conferences in DC? Last time I checked, there weren't any shortages in hotels, conference rooms, or entertainment. Oh, hell no. Hell no. I know that isn't the fucking alarm clock. Can't be. Arrgh! Shit. Time to get up. Get her to her flight.

"Taiyler, wake up. Get up, baby." Kissing her on her forehead always manages to wake her.

"It's time already?" She looked defeated.

"Yeah. We have to start getting ready. What time does the flight leave?"

"Eight-thirty. Can't I get like fifteen more minutes?" She sucked her teeth, looked at me like I'd just rained on her parade. I wondered what she did when she slept alone. Suddenly, the phone rang. She reached over me, picked it up.

"Yeah, I'm up, Auntie . . . I know. I know . . . No, I'm not lying back down . . . I know you know . . . Eight-thirty . . . Yeah, I'll make sure I eat breakfast . . ." she chuckled. ". . . and no, not those candy bars with the nuts and grains. I know they ain't no good. Nothing like your bacon and eggs. When are you coming back down to cook, then? . . . I have some, but not like I did when you came down . . . mostly at restaurants because I don't have time . . . Okay. I will . . ." She let out a loud-ass laugh. Too loud for five in the morning. "No, I can't take the terminator. They don't let cans of mace through security . . . yeah, if I see anyone that looks crazy, I'll take my shoe off and do 'em in, ya hear? . . . Love you, too. Call you when I get there." She sat up. Stretched her arms. Yawned. Now I know what she does when I'm not here. Auntie. I watched her stretch. I want to get her a flight out tomorrow. Spend the day with her today. I don't want her to leave. I run my hands through her messy hair. Mess it up even more. She smacked my hand away.

"You're a brat when it's time to get up," I said.

"I know, babe. I'm used to my aunt waking me up." She looked bashful. Like she'd been found out.

"She calls you every day?" I asked.

"Every single day. We never had alarm clocks in our house. If you needed to get up at a certain time, Grandma or Auntie would wake up at the right time. We were never late for school, never missed a job interview, or a test. Doesn't matter if I'm in Brooklyn, Georgia, or DC. She wakes me up every morning." She's beaming.

"You're spoiled."

"I know I am. I was raised by old people. Breakfast every morning. Dinner every night. What can I say?" She swung both of her long, gorgeous legs over to the side of the bed. "All right, we have what, an hour?" she asked.

I turned on the plasma. "Looks like forty-five minutes if you count the accident on I-97. I'm glad you don't live too far from BWI."

It didn't take us long to get ready. As usual Taiyler was well prepared. No last-minute stops. No rushing. She was packed up. We showered, ate, and hit the road. She makes my truck smell good.

"Got everything?"

"Think so. If not, I'll find out. I'm not tripping; they'll give us everything we need anyway."

I nod my head.

"Hey, you know you had another dream last night. It didn't seem so bad. But you kind of cried a bit. You dream a lot, don't you?"

She leaned her head back, let it fall toward the window.

"I dream when something is bothering me. I usually can't remember them when I get up. It's probably just stress."

"From me?" I hoped not.

"No. Not at all. Probably from work or who knows. Can we stop at 7–Eleven on the way? I need some gum. Don't want to get it at the airport." And that was it. No more talk. No more anything. Guess it was a dead issue. Silence was the only noise that accompanied us to BWI. Through the departure terminal. To the front of US Airways.

"All right, honey. I'll call you when I get settled in," she said as she reached out to me. Invited me into her. I don't want to let her go.

"How many days again?"

"Four."

"Why do you have to go again?"

"Because I want to be the best. Like you. Is that okay, Mr. DeCosta?"

I'm still hugging her. Until Jack "The Asshole" cop yells at me through his bullhorn. Wants to let the entire airport know that I need to move my truck. Idiot. I don't move. I hate cops.

"Honey, let's go. He's being stupid about this. I'll call you when I land, okay?"

I poke out my bottom lip. I don't even see Jack Asshole right now. All I see is Taiyler Richardson.

"Okay, baby. Call me, don't forget. I'll have my cell on all day. Or you can call the office. Or the house. All of my calls from your number are forwarded to my cell anyway. So I won't miss one." I thought about it. Guess I could say it again. Don't want to pressure her. But I want her to know I'm for real. I've said this and didn't mean it so many times, I guess it just feels good to say it from the heart. So I went for it.

"Love you."

She blushed. Kissed the bottom of my chin.

"I know," was all she said. And I'm glad that she does.

22

Nathaniel

Packing has never been one of my stronger points. I wait until the last minute to pack because I always end up needing everything. Pack my toothbrush so I won't leave it. End up having to dig in my bag to get it out in the morning. Along with my deodorant and other stuff. I hate packing, period. Especially this morning. I have a lot on my mind. Besides being way over budget for this year's Pharma Conference, which I desperately tried to discourage the higher-ups from sponsoring, I just found out that my boss is on the same plane as I, and he wants to talk. I don't have anything to talk to him about. And five hours to Aruba isn't the time to be locked into a numbers conversation. Besides, I need time to process these thoughts I've been having lately. And this is the perfect trip to do just that.

Unlike our company's national meetings and sales gatherings, this one is filled with lots of leisure time. Pharma companies and physicians are spoiled to death, meaning everything's paid for, and they don't want to be inside all day. So I made sure our meeting planners did their thing with the extras. Plus, I wanted to relax, too. Something that a senior financial business director never gets to do.

More than anything, I need to figure this Taiyler thing out. I've had several dreams about this woman. None of which I'm proud of having. One in the middle of which I ended up boning my wife. This is my boy's woman. And I don't even know her. So why she keeps popping up in my dreams is beyond me. But I'm going to put a stop to it. Immediately.

She must think that I'm crazy. Whenever we meet, I'm always either sweating, stuttering, or staring. For no reason other than I can't seem to control myself. I don't like her. I don't even know her. And although she is a beautiful woman, I have a beautiful woman at home. Who's given me an even more beautiful daughter. So these feelings, or whatever they are, have got to go. This trip is just what I need to make the shit happen.

We get to Aruba earlier than the masses. Early enough for me to check all of the logistics, make sure that everything is paid up. There are no glitches in the financial aspect of things. If there were, these guys would have a fit. On the plane, my boss seemed happy. If he's happy, I'm happy.

After my secretary checked everything out for me, assured me that all was well, I took a break. Went outside. Sat on the edge of the pier that was adjacent to the conference center. Pushed my thoughts from one side of the water to the other. I can't get the woman out of my head. For no apparent reason. Other than the fact that she's gorgeous and we've shaken hands. That's it. I've never been with her. We didn't have a relationship. We didn't go to school together. She's not a friend that I always wanted to sleep with but never had the chance. She's not even trying to give it to me. I've dealt with women who wanted me. She's not one of them. No sneak glances, no flirty gestures. And I'm not in the business of ruining my marriage for anything in this world, so there. It's solved. Ain't shit going on. Period. Maybe I'm starting to hit a midlife crisis or something. I'm barely thirty, but these days, with all of the fucked-up shit we eat, who knows?

I close my eyes. Inhale as far and as deep as I can. Let the salt water take control of my nostrils. Darkness take control of my thoughts. Until I am thinking of absolutely nothing. Exhaling anything that bothered me. Rattled me. Placed me in a dilemma. As soon as the smoke cleared, and I had reached that place in my mind where I saw only spots of color, I started to think about love. And life. And blessings. And the very image that I am combating at this point, that I have been avoiding since Garvin's party, emerged like storm clouds in the south. The things that I do to her make me sick. In such a good way. I imagined her sitting on my lap. Talking to me about the water, how beautiful it is. Me staring at her. Admiring how the combination of the ocean's blue and her eyes' gray make an awesome sunset. Make me want to run away with her. Spend days and nights sitting alongside the Nile, tossing jade pebbles, wondering if we were related to kings and queens. The Nile . . . Nile. Oh, shit. Nile. My daughter. I have to snap out of this bullshit. Right now. I have no other choice. Thank God I'm here. Away. So I can sort this out.

As I listened to our opening speaker give the most boring speech outside of balancing redox equations and plate tectonics, I wondered, who the fuck chose Bruce Jenner? As a motivational speaker? Get real. I already know our president's speech will be a snoozer, so we at least needed someone to offset that. Especially when Smith Barney, Inc., brought Quincy Jones down last year. Thank God we paid for everything. We should've after this. We're killing people. To make matters worse, our president was no different. Sounding just like Baby Bush did giving his first national address. Like he couldn't recall his own address. With that fake-assed faraway look in his eyes. Only this one here couldn't nab the rhythm of throwing the faraway looks into the audience with glancing down at the teleprompter. The shit was quite hilarious actually. The prompter was moving faster than he was. And he was skipping lines. *"I just want to say welcome to Aruba, the home of . . . and we are number one in financial services . . ."* Fucking idiot.

Our star speaker, Andrew Blumenthal, the cardiology genius from Johns Hopkins, is about to damn near fall out of his seat, laughing at the man. Or at someone in the audience. Either way, he's better than he was a few minutes ago, when he was falling out of his chair snoring. I engaged myself in one of the arcade games on my cell phone. Talk about bored. Asking God what could any of us possibly have done to deserve Bruce Jenner and our company president back-to-back. They'd better have Jerry Seinfeld, Bernie Mac, and Dave Chapelle speak after this shit. After about twenty additional minutes of torture, and five more games of cell phone poker, we were done. Ready to get to our respective resorts. Physicians at the Aruba Beach Club and financial downtown at the Renaissance Hotel. Me, I'm skipping the bus ride and heading over to some of the shops. Explore the town. Get the hell away from all the fake smiles and handshakes. First stop. Little Switzerland.

"Hello, welcome to Little Switzerland. May I help you, sir? Or perhaps you'd like to look around first?"

Wow. Refreshing. I'm being attended to and given the option to look around for myself without being followed. Yeah, I'm in a country of color.

"Thanks, I'm going to take a look around." See some nice watches. I buy Kendra a Philippe Charriol. Take a look at the Jaeger LeCoultre reversible face. Look at other overpriced metals and gems. Wonder if the natives digging in the gold and diamond mines in Africa and Brazil see any dough off of these rocks. And then I run into what I want for myself. A huge black gemstone globe, made of all types of natural stones. Different colors and textures. That'll look great in my office. I have to have it.

"Excuse me, miss. How much is this globe?"

"Oh sure, sir. It's made from the finest jasper, and over one hundred stones from all over the world—"

"Yeah, but how much is it?" I cut in. Now I know it's expensive. She's stalling.

"Twenty-two hundred dollars," she answered evenly. Damn. That's a lot. I walk away from the piece, give its purchase some thought. Then I'm told that someone else in the store wants it. Wants my globe. They're ready to buy it now. Well, it's mine until I decide I don't want to buy it.

"Don't you have others in here? Why do they want mine?" I asked. The saleslady was extremely nice, because even I didn't have patience for my bullshit.

"Yes, sir, but yours, as you put it, is the only one we have left made of Egyptian jasper. Would you like to make the purchase?"

"I'm not ready yet!" I was almost yelling. The older black woman looked at me like I had two heads. Then one of her colleagues came over to her, whispered something in her ear. She glanced at me and grinned.

"Sir, someone wishes to speak with you about the gemstone globe. Please follow me."

And that's what I did.

23

Taiyler

I'm in Oranjestad. And even though my eyes are having a terrible time adjusting to the exuberant sunshine, I can see that it's exceptionally beautiful. The people are smiling. Welcoming us to their country. I can honestly say that I'm happy I came. When the rep told me about it initially, I didn't want to be bothered. With my workload, I didn't think that I could swing it. But my partners said that at least one of us should go. And since I'm new, and not exactly broken in to the special treatment that we are given from pharmaceutical companies, they suggested that I take the plunge. They, after all, were used to it. Plus, someone had to go all the way to Aruba to gather information on these new cardio treatments. So that someone was me. And I don't regret it for a minute.

After the last two weeks, I couldn't ask for a better break. Ever since Derrick had that party, I've been having a hard time. I've spent nights and days trying my best to shut out thoughts. Bad thoughts. Thoughts that make me want to hang myself. Thoughts that leave me hung. Dreams. Good ones. Of Nat. I hate to even say it. But I'm so comfortable in them. I can't even bring myself to admit to what I'm feeling in them, the level of comfort, the relaxation. The conversation. It's so deep. So spiritual. Half the time I don't even remember what we're talking about. But we're always in New York. In Harlem. On the street. Under the moonlight. And I almost always orgasm in my sleep. But we don't have sex. It's weird. The orgasms are so strong, they wake me up. If Derrick is there, he's staring at me telling me that I was dreaming, asking me about it. I'm too embarrassed to bring it up. How do you tell your man you're dreaming about his best friend? And that it isn't sexual, but it leaves you wanting to have sex with him? At least in your dreams. There is no way. Other than to get control of this shit before I get back home to the man who loves me.

While waiting for my bag to come around, I decided to check in with Auntie. These roaming charges are going to kill me.

"Y-ello!" she screamed into the receiver. She doesn't have her teeth in. I stifled a laugh.

"Hey, Aunt Mae! I'm here!" I exclaimed.

"Ain't it beautiful!" She's fumbling with her teeth.

"Yes, it is, we're waiting for our bags now."

"How was yo' flight? None uh dem crazy moos-leums on it, eh?"

"Nah, Auntie, everything was smooth. What do you want, anything special?" I always ask the same question while I'm traveling. And she gives the same answer.

"Oh, naw, girl, just bring your red behind back safe. That's all this old lady wants."

I'm smiling a mile wide.

"Okay. Will do. Question. Isn't your appointment today?"

"It was yesterday." She sighed. Obviously gearing up for the steady stream of questions that I dump on her after a doctor's visit. I'm sorry. This is my auntie we're talking about. If I'm not there, I want to know everything. I'm going to call him when I get back anyway.

"What did he say? What was your cholesterol count?"

"Uh, ninety-eight LDL and sixty-five HDL." Good. It's within guidelines.

"Pressure?"

"Normal. One twenty over eighty."

"EKG?"

"All dem damn waves was normal, girl! Stop wearing me out wit' the same questions you gon' call and ask the docta' anyway!"

I had to laugh at her frustration. She's right. All I do is call the office anyway. I just want to make sure she knows her stuff. And she does.

"Okay, Auntie. You're off the hook."

She chuckled.

"I used to change your dirty drawers, girl. I ain't off nothin' but my Black behind makin' some dinner."

I had to laugh at that.

"Yes, ma'am!" I saluted. Realizing I was one of the few still waiting on her bag, I proceeded to wrap this up. "All right, young lady. I'll call you when I get back. And tell that doctor of yours his stuff better be tight. Or else he won't be able to feed his family." We said our good-byes, and I tried to pay more attention to the carousel as my bag had obviously gone around a few times already. Once I grabbed it off of the belt, I noticed a group of folks with red plaid shirts on pointing and directing groups of people to buses waiting outside. Guess that's us. We're the largest group here. Or so I was told. I joined the group and found a seat next to a man who looked as if he'd done this plenty of times. I extended my hand.

"Hi, I'm Dr. Richardson, Cardiology sub and Internal Medicine, outside of Washington, DC, in Silver Spring."

After looking me up and down, shooting his buddy a sideward glance, and tipping his head to the side, he extended his hand.

"Dr. Blumenthal. Hopkins. Cardio. Preventative. But you can call me Andrew."

I know this man. I can't put my finger on it.

"So you look like you've done this before. Is it as boring as they say it is?"

He laughed. So did his buddy.

"I hope not. Because I've been giving the talks here for the past three years!" He continued to laugh. His belly jiggling like Jell-O. I'm feeling like slum change. I do know him. Andrew Blumenthal. Fucking foremost authority on cardio catheterization, preventative treatment, and cholesterol management. Former Head of Cardiology for the FDA. He can probably completely balloon one of my arteries before we get to the Convention Center. He basically wrote the guidelines that I use to diagnose and prescribe . . . and I'm the greatest idiot on the face of the earth. Way to go, Taiyler. First day. Make it count. Make it up.

"Did I say boring? No, they actually said it was the next best thing to courtside at the NBA finals." I winked my right eye and sat back in my seat as if I saved the day. He obviously has a sense of humor.

"Oh, is that what they say?"

"That's it, sir. But you know, I had to come and see for myself. Had to see what this Blumenthal guy was pushing. You can't believe everything you hear. And half of what you see."

He is rolling. Holding his stomach. If he cut that thick-ass beard and lost that gut, he'd be a good-looking middle-aged man.

"Wow, that was a good comeback, Dr. Richardson. I will make sure that I *don't* live up to what you've heard."

"Thanks, sir," I said as I stepped down off of the bus into the middle of downtown Aruba. The front of the Seaport Convention Center. Our destination. I take a quick look around. This is quite the beach town. Gucci. Cartier. Chopard. Little Switzerland. Ralph Lauren. Restaurants. Theaters. And too many jewelry stores to count. I wonder how many of the people that live here could actually afford to shop here. I wiped the thought. Going into a sea of old White men, thoughts of slavery and capitalism need to be as far away from my mind as possible. To my right, I see what I've been longing for since we took off. The water. Even deep, it's bluest blue. When the sun hits it, the green is breathtaking. I stood there mesmerized by my favorite work of God. That is until one of the red-plaid-shirted ladies so rudely tapped me on my shoulder.

"Ma'am, you can't stand here. Our guests are trying to make their way inside, and you're blocking the entrance."

I took a look at her. Then at the sixteen doors that led to the inside of the Convention Center. Then imagined myself blocking them. And laughed inside. I'm going to play with this ignorant bitch.

"Oh, I'm sorry. I was just amazed at all the folks talking and chewing and walking around. What are they here for?" I asked, hoping that she really wasn't ignorant enough to buy in to my antics.

"Oh, hon, this here is a medical conference. Maybe you are looking for the local market over that way." She scurried her fingers toward the area where White tourists were bargaining with Black locals on goods that were already cheaper than the cheapest stuff we had at home.

"Really? Are you sure? Because the itinerary says that physicians go that way . . ." I pointed to the doors and watched her face turn beet red. ". . . but I wasn't sure." Gotcha.

"It's okay, miss. I know that outside of the lily white hills of Utah, you aren't exposed enough to know that all doctors aren't middle-aged White men or East Indians. It's a little like algebra; it takes time to get. Keep working on it, okay, *hon?*" I turned around and headed inside. This is bound to be an eventful four days.

What started out as the introduction for the motivational speaker, ended up as a personal catastrophe as the sponsoring company's president came out, face tight as a trampoline, and proceeded to give the most boring speech on the face of the earth. I sat up front as usual and managed to make eye contact with Blumenthal. Caught him snoozing. I pointed his way, made fun. He smiled knowingly. This is torturing us both. He moved jaggedly through his secretary-prepared script, proving that he obviously had no idea what he was going to say before he got on stage. I kept Blumenthal in stitches by mouthing the words of his speech from the teleprompter, as I could see them clearly from where I was sitting.

After we were literally bored to death, they decided to take no prisoners by taking an extra half hour to go over the itinerary for tomorrow. I was never patient enough to stay with the class. I skipped ahead. Wow. They have some nice stuff planned. Ecoexcursions, horseback riding, water sports, deep-sea diving and fishing, the works. And it's all paid for.

As they dismissed us, I decided to ditch the tour bus and explore downtown for myself. I can get a taxi back to the resort. First stop, Little Switzerland. Lots of watches. Lalique. Waterford. Tiffany. Go figure. I see what I want. The globe I'm standing right in front of. It's black. Egyptian jasper. With each country made of a different natural stone. I see globes of this caliber only in antique stores, and even they are not made of jasper, jade, quartz, and mother-of-pearl. I have to get it. They have one made of lapis. Navy blue instead of black. I want it in black. That's what I tell the saleswoman. She nods her head, goes over to her colleague. Whispers something. What's all the fucking hoop-de-doo over me wanting to get this? I know it's not the racism shit. The globe is twenty-two hundred dollars, but damn, these women are black. She makes her way back over.

"It seems as if a gentleman picked out the same globe as you did. Would you be interested in the one made of lapis instead of jasper?"

Hell no.

"Ask him the same thing, then get back to me. I'll be standing right here." I'm walking out of here with this damn globe today. She comes back over to me wearing an expression that I don't want to see.

"Ma'am, he is only interested in the one made of jasper," she said solemnly. That's okay. We'll see. I'll put a little sugar on him.

"Let me talk to him. Maybe I can persuade him." I winked at her. Obviously aware of my position, she smiled and went to retrieve my victim. I turned back around to finish admiring the piece that would set the telescope in my sitting area off just right. And then I heard it. The voice from my dreams.

"What's wrong with the blue one?" he asked, obviously unaware of whom he was speaking to. I know him. I don't have to see him to know.

"That's not the one I want," I said as I turned around to face him. Watched his jaw drop.

"Which one do you want?" he asked.

"The one that I'm drawn to. The one that suits me best. The one I'm standing in front of." I stood back, placed my hand on my hip, and decided that I wouldn't melt. I wouldn't give it up. Like I did the frosting.

"I have my eye on that one, too," he said softly.

"Well, I'm sorry, it's taken." I'm trying. Really I am.

"I was here first, but you can have it."

I'm staring at his heart. Trying to keep from staring into his eyes. It's hard either way. "No, you're right. You were here. Take it." I'm a traitor to myself. How terrible is that?

"I insist. You take it home. You want it."

Now the salesladies are looking at us like we're crazy. Both of them. Grinning. It's weird when people see things that you just can't, won't, or refuse to. Caught up in the moment, or in those feelings that came tumbling back, I spun around, determined to walk away from this thing. As I had in the grocery store. To my dismay, I couldn't. My card was still at the counter. At the door, I turned back around. Ashamed of what he might see in my eyes. Ashamed of myself.

"I forgot my card."

He reached over to the counter, picked it up, and handed it to me. Held that finger. Seconds pass. Feeling like an eternity.

"How's that cut healing?"

"Slower than I want it to. It was a deep one," I said. Totally unaware of the fact that he was still holding it. Unaware of us leaving the store, him asking me if I wanted to take a walk. Me saying yes. Him, still holding on to my ring finger, pulling me out of the shop. Us taking a walk that would lead us down a road that neither of us wanted to travel.

24

Nathaniel

I'm walking down the main street of downtown Aruba to a rhythm that I can't hear. To notes I can't play. With one mission in mind. To find out what's behind those eyes. Don't get me wrong, I'm in love with my wife, in love with my life, and will not trade that for anything. But right now, at this very moment, all that matters to me is this conversation. Maybe if I can get to the root of this, of her, I can return to life as lived. Although the way she glances at me from time to time tells me that she wonders what my motivation is for all of this, she doesn't hesitate. In fact, her hand fits comfortably in mine, regardless of the uncomfortable expression resting on her face. We walk for minutes that seem like days.

"Do you want to talk?"

"About what?" she said, her attention focused on the group of tourists across the street at Iguana Joe's doing what looked like the Caucasian version of the mambo. The offbeat claps are annoying me. I want her attention. There is something that I need to determine. Something I'm trying to figure out. And it's now or never. I can tell she's not very expressive. Typical MCAT mentality.

"Uh, about anything. Nothing in particular." I'm chickening out. And I think I'm finding out exactly what I need to know. There's no energy between us. Which is great. All the weirdness and crap that I'd been feeling has more to do with me than her. Probably some early midlife crisis phase. Or as my wife would say, Satan. I breathe a sigh of relief. This won't be as hard as I thought. Taiyler hasn't looked my way once. We pass the small marketplace filled with island goods and tourist paraphernalia. She stops, heads over to a small hut filled with original art. Gives the merchandise a quick once-over. Ah, La Princesa speaks.

"Is this all you have?" she asked the woman who was managing to watch television, a two-year-old, and braid a young vacationing teen's hair all at the same time. I didn't know White girls' hair could stay braided. Learn something new every day.

"No, ma'am. Look be-hine dere, you'll soon come ta more pieces," the woman answered. Taiyler kept sifting through the canvas works until she obviously came to one she liked.

"How much is this one?"

"One hundred fifty dollars, ma'am"

"It's beautiful. Who's the artist?"

"I dunno," the woman answered bashfully. I could tell that kind of rubbed Taiyler the wrong way.

"What do you mean you don't know?" she asked in a cynical, I'm-not-going-to-be-an-asshole-about-this, but-I-really-want-to-know kind of way. I could tell that she was a little more than aggravated. But she wasn't rude. She loves art. Doesn't know why everyone else doesn't love it as much as she. I forgot about that. Shit, I didn't know that I remembered. I watched her agonize over whether or not to buy the piece without having any info on its creator. I wondered if she was this calculating in making all of her decisions. Finally, she said more than two words to me. Or to the woman.

"You know what? I can make the spelling out of the name from the signature and look it up on the Net. I'll take it," she answered definitely. She said something else that made me realize how out of it I was.

"I have to pay for this," she said, looking down.

"Okay. So go ahead." What's the holdup? I wondered. Dollars are good anywhere.

She fumbled around a bit, glanced at the street, and took a deep breath. Okay, this chick is a little dramatic.

"You're still holding my hand," she said. Still looking at the street.

"I'm what?"

"I need to get my wallet. You're still holding my hand."

"Oh, shit. Shit. I apologize." I took a look at the hard, cold evidence. Pulled her hand up to my face. Fought the overwhelming sensation I had to kiss it. Let it go. Took a glance at my watch. We had been walking for at least ten minutes. She must think that I'm a shady-assed best friend for one, a half-assed husband, and above all, a damn idiot. She was probably testing me. My loyalties. I heard women do that.

"Thanks for your help." She tipped the woman a twenty.

"It's my pleasure, ma'am," the woman replied with enormous gratitude.

Waiting for her to roll up the canvas, I stood there shifting feet. Mentally recapping the last fifteen minutes. I do remember taking her finger. Holding it. Asking about the cut. Feeling her hand kind of slide into mine. I don't remember how our fingers got locked. Really. She must think that I'm a pervert. We walk.

"So talk," she let out. Without so much as a warning.

Now I'm the one with my tongue in the cat's mouth. My thoughts are glued to the roof of my own. I want to tell her to stay the fuck out of my dreams.

"About what?" I asked. Feeling like more of a moron than I did a few minutes ago. Not knowing how to jump-start this investigation. I want to know why I feel like this when she's around. Why my judgment plays hopscotch and hide-and-go-seek while I sit on the sidelines as a spectator, watching it get its ass beat. Since I'm sure that she doesn't feel anything remotely close to what I'm experiencing, especially based on the fact that she doesn't even look at me when she speaks to me, I'm not sure of how to gather that information without it sounding like a come-on. She must sense how uncomfortable this is making me. I'm not trying to gallivant with my main man's woman. I really just want some answers. So that I can go on with my life as it was. She broke the silence.

"You were right about the Coltrane thing. I checked when I got home."

"Oh, yeah?" When I got home, I was fucking her in Derrick's garage.

"Yeah. The name of the song was 'Pursuance'; however, it was on the *Love Supreme* album."

"So what, now you're taking my jazz points back?" I asked in mock indignation. She chuckled.

"No, not at all, I was just letting you know that *A Love Supreme* did have something to do with the overall concept."

"So I'm half right? You drive a hard bargain Ms. I'm-wrong-but-I-don't-like-to-be."

She's laughing for real now. No bullshit chuckle. Loosening up. Not enough to look my way, though. My mother always said that was rude. Not to look at someone while you were speaking to them.

"Ah, so you've found something out about me. One point for Nat."

"What, that you were wrong, or that you don't like to be wrong even when you are indisputably, unequivocally, and undeniably proven wrong as hell!"

She rolled her eyes at the wind. Irritated with it for playing flip-flop with her ponytail. Trying to control something she couldn't. I stopped walking. We're at my hotel.

"This is my stop."

"Oh, so that's what this was? A fancy way of tricking me into walking you to your hotel? And they say chivalry is dead."

That last line struck a chord with me. The chivalry thing. Takes me to a place that I don't want to be. The beginning of all of this. I'd rather be at the end. I brought it up.

"That's what you said while you were cursing me out at the grocery store."

"What?" Convenient amnesia.

"Oh, how soon we forget. 'And they say chivalry is dead' . . . remember? As you proceeded to tell me what an asshole I was."

She sighed. Teeth over her bottom lip. She's uncomfortable. Blushing. Embarrassed.

"My apologies for that. But uh, you were sort of lacking in the gentleman department that day."

"And today?" I feel my eyebrows rising. My lids getting heavy enough to stick together when they close. I'm flirting. Waiting to get smacked. Asking for it.

"Today? I don't know what to make of today," she said. More on the honest side than I can say I was ready for. Brought me back to reality. Quick. I straightened up. Got my shit together. Got ready to cut this off. At the hip.

"Listen, I'm by no means disrespectful. And I would never—"

"Don't say anything, Nat." She tapped her foot on the curb. I shuf-

fled mine. Stared at the small stream of water running right through
the center of the hotel. More uncomfortable than George Bush at a
project block party. Both of us. I wondered what was next.

"So this is your hotel, huh? Nice," was all she said. Interesting creature.

"Yours is better. Right on the beach. On one of the rough points of
the island, so the waves crash in a little harder. Very scenic."

"I see. Well, I'm looking forward to the relaxation . . ." she said as
she surveyed the scene at the Renaissance Hotel, ". . . and of course
the work." She was smirking. We both know trips like this are more
pleasure than business for physicians.

"Uh-huh. I bet. I'll be working; you'll be snorkeling, sailing, and ex-
ploring the countryside."

She laughed. She knows it's true.

"And did I mention horseback riding? And waterskiing? And uh . . ."

"Okay! Okay! Yes! We are spoiled brats! No need to rub it in. You
knew this before you brought us here. So don't act surprised!" she exclaimed. I stared at her. For a while. She knows I'm staring. She has
to.

"So, uh, see you tomorrow?" I needed to end this. At least for today.
I walked out onto Main Street, extended my arm into the air. A taxi
pulled right over. In a matter of seconds. Wow. The pleasure of a
Black man being able to hail a cab without pretense was surreal.

"How much to the Aruba Beach Club?" I asked the driver. Who
oddly possessed a striking likeliness to a young Bob Marley.

"Ten dollars," he answered. I gave him twenty. He looked at the
bill, looked at Taiyler, nodded his head, and smiled. It was his lucky
day. I helped her slide into the taxi, closed the door, gave the driver
some dap, and told him to get her there safely. She assured me that I
didn't have to pay for her ride, dug into her wallet, and pulled out a
bill that matched the one I gave Bob, Jr. Finally. Our eyes met. And
they laughed. And talked. And exchanged pleasantries like old friends.
And as the taxi pulled off, and I was thanking God for that warm, uncomfortable feeling fleeing, another one instantly took its place. A
sudden chill took over my entire body. A cold, empty feeling that I
didn't ever want to experience again in this lifetime flooded me. Made
me feel like I was on something. And I needed it bad. Like now. Standing
there, watching the taxi turn the corner, I wondered what that something was. And if it had anything to do with her.

25

Taiyler

I didn't get any sleep last night. When I arrived at the resort I checked in, unpacked, and headed straight for the water. Even though the sun was just about ready to set. My suite was on the first floor, facing the beach. I had a patio area that led right to the sand. So to my pleasure, I was literally about fifty feet from the water. Which I needed more than anything. I ended up floating on my back in the Caribbean Sea, trying to submerge my thoughts in salt water. It took all evening. All night for that matter. I couldn't get the day's events out of my mind. And today, I'm attempting to do the same.

I thumbed through the agenda for the day, anxious to see how long we'd be stuck inside the Convention Center. Anxious to find new ways to keep my brain occupied with anything other than Nat. I'm trying. I just can't believe that he affects me the way that he does. After yesterday, I'm beyond being able to say that I don't know where the feelings are coming from. I do. I know them well. I just don't know why I feel the way that I do. They have flooded my senses since the first day we met. It's messed up. The only good thing about it is that I know that he doesn't feel the same. And that helps me a lot. He doesn't stumble over his words and thoughts the way I do when communicating with him. He has no problem looking directly at me when we talk. I, on the other hand, am a complete basket case. Yesterday, I had to focus extra hard on not looking his way. When I look into his eyes, I lose it. Lose sight. Lose the ability to use good judgment. Lose it all. So I'd rather not look. It's hard as hell. But if I'm to ever have the ability to control this, I have to start with the obvious.

As I glanced up from the meeting agenda, I noticed him up front. Talking to one of the sound techs. Watching how he expressed himself with his hands. Wondering how they felt. Somehow, feeling comfortable in them already. Feeling their warmth. I closed my eyes and remembered how they felt locked into mine. Remembered them caressing my shoulders in my dreams. Remembered us on that Harlem street. On the corner. Under the moon. Holding on to happiness.

I held on to those thoughts through our cardio breakout sessions, through cholesterol absorption inhibitor training, through beta blocker and calcium channel blocker reviews and updates, and through closing statements. Until finally, we were getting ready for some fun and sun. This morning they had us choose our excursions and water sports for the day. I chose the Jeep ecotour which basically takes me all over the island. You kind of get everything in one. Water sports, history, and relaxation on the beach. It left in an hour. My eyes roamed the conference room until I spotted Nat. Wonder what he's doing today. I decided to ask him. Fuck it. I headed over toward the front of the room. He turned around as if he knew I was on my way over. It kind of startled me. I'm grinning. I know it.

"So, uh, what do we have planned for today? They don't keep you cooped up in here all day, do they?" I can't stop myself from flirting. Even if I force myself to think of Derrick.

"Nah, not today. I'm out in the sun. I'm a water person. Plus, I wanted to get in a little history, so I'm on the Jeep ecotour. What about you?" he asked. I was so fucking elated, I doubt that I hid it well.

"Me, too. That's the one I chose," I said, two seconds from shouting up and down the aisle like I'm on Sunday evening television. We're shifting feet again. He broke the silence this time.

"The Natural Pool and Baby Beach are great. I heard you can dive off of a small cliff into the pool and Baby Beach is relaxing as hell."

"Oh, yeah?" I answered for lack of anything good to add. I don't know anything about Aruba. I'm hating that right now.

"Yes. So leave all your problems in this room, Doctor, we are going to have a ball," he said. His eyes dancing a jig. If he only knew. He'd have to stay here. I'm staring my number one problem in the face.

"Well, guess I'll see you in like an hour," he said as he pulled his hands together in one huge clap. Looking just as excited as I was.

This is a trip. Literally. Me and the narrator of my dreams on the beach of life. This shit isn't funny.

When the tour van pulled up in front of the resort, all of the excitement that I'd built up over the last hour went straight down the drain. He wasn't in the van. I should be happy about that. But I'm not. I'm pissed. The tour guide made all sorts of jokes that would ordinarily be funny to me. Seeing that we were the only two Black people in the vehicle, I would usually help him out. Talk to him. Share some of the pressure of having to dance a mental jig for the spoiled American tourists that feel like the locals also have a duty to entertain them as well as transport them around the island. But not today. I don't want to help. Not this time. I'm heated. Staring out of the window. Seeing my anger fog up the glass. Noticing that we'd come to the tour headquarters. Saw the Jeeps lined up, awaiting their passengers. Saw something else. Something that put a smile on my face. Gave me a sigh of relief.

To my delight, as we pulled into the lot, I saw him stepping out of a van that looked just like mine. Feeling the huge smile creep across my face, I felt ashamed of myself. Almost like everyone knew why I was smiling. But I was excited nonetheless. I'm glad he came. As I stepped down onto the red clay, our eyes locked instantly. And told each other how relieved we were that the other didn't cop out on the tour. It was then that I realized that my feelings weren't just my feelings. I'm sharing them. So is he. That made me feel good.

"Thought you punked out," I said, watching him pull the camera off from around his neck. The urge to throw my arms around that thing threw me for a loop. I can make it through the day. I know I can.

"I thought the same, Doctor. You sure you and all of that Chanel swimwear, plus that manicure and pedicure, are ready for the deep blue sea? I know how spoiled rotten you are, and believe me, this is not for the pampered."

"Who?" I yelled, in that tone we women use prior to telling you where to go and fuck yourself. Thank God I spent countless summers with Solange in her family's time-shares on beaches all over the world. I'm talking a lot of shit, but I can back it up. I'm not mad at him, though. At least not about this.

"Who? Ain't no owls around here! You, Miss Priss! You ready for na-

ture with your little purse and your Evian?" He's obviously enjoying
this. Cracking on me. I stole a quick glance of myself from the reflection of the glass on the van and had to chuckle to myself. Everyone
else has on dollar flip-flops, water suits, fanny packs, and Ray-Bans.
Me? I'm in an ocean blue Chanel swimsuit and matching rimless sunglasses. I look like I'm en route to a Jay-Z pool party. I chuckle. Hope
he doesn't let the outfit fool him. I will tear him up in that water. And
that's what I tell him.

"Don't let the Chanel fool you, mister. I swim like a fish and will
whip your ass on a wave runner. Don't test me," I said, staring him
down. Ready for a challenge.

"Really?"

"Really. Name your sport." I hope he doesn't want to water-ski.

"Okay . . ." He's grinning. Looking at me like he knows I'm bullshitting. ". . . how about, uh . . . waterskiing?" Nat's reading my mind.
I swear he is. Mutherfucker.

"No problem. Waterskiing on Baby Beach. Done deal." I spun
around and headed for the old 4X4 that was waiting to take us to the
finer spots on the island. I heard him laughing in the background. I
remembered it from my last dream. I liked it. Liked how it sounded.
He sat right beside me. The laughter stopped.

"What?" he asked.

"What?"

"Why are you looking at me like that?"

Caught daydreaming about my night dreams.

"I'm not looking at you in any particular way." I'm lying. Trying to
figure this shit out. It hits me every now and then. What I'm doing.
Playing with fire. Burning to have a conversation that'll be good for
the soul. I ponder over it. Decide to go for the gold. Time to dig up
bones. Might as well. We're in the Jeep alone. Riding over rocks, being
thrown around by nature. I'm feeling strong for a change. I go for it.

"I was just wondering . . ." I started. But didn't have the strength to
finish. My body betrayed me. My stomach was doing somersaults like
a champ. I'm an undercover punk. Especially when it comes to expressing myself in awkward situations to someone I care about. I shut
down. Try to avoid addressing it. Did I say care about? Slow down,
girl. This is someone's husband. And you are his best friend's love.
Control this.

"Wondering what?" he answered aimlessly. He has no clue about anything. About these feelings. About my confusion. About my dreams. I'm wondering if I should tell him. I'm fighting with the possibilities of letting the cat out of the house. It could come back. Or it could get flattened by a sixteen-wheeler. I don't want either. I'm so confused.

"Nothing," I answered in a tsk. Turned my head toward the window. Focused on the trees leaning toward the wind and the water crashing the rocks below. Wishing I could wash these feelings away. I know it's showing on my face. I'm disgusted with me.

"Uh-huh." He doesn't sound convinced. I'm not convincing myself.

"You know, the window is not as good of a listener as I," he said as he pulled the bottom of my chin toward him. His touch is nauseating me. Making me want to vomit all of this pent-up energy. I want to tell him so bad. About everything. Bounce questions off of him. Search for answers. Dig into my spirit. Find what it is about him that ignites it. I focused extra hard on my manicure. If I don't look up, don't look at him, I won't melt. I'll keep it all together. He placed his forefinger under my chin and lifted it. Until we were eye to eye. The interrogation began. I, a pupil of circumstance and a victim of emotion, folded under questioning.

"I-I was wondering if you . . ."

"Yes?" he said softly, as if he already knew what I was going to say.

"If you ever in your life, felt something for someone, and you didn't know what it was. You didn't know how to control it, or if it even could be controlled. You know it's an emotion displaced, and you try your hardest to check it. Put it in the right place . . ."

Now he's looking out of the window. Straight ahead. Focusing on Black Stone Beach. The place where wishes are granted on this island. I wished to be returned to my normal self. Normally I have more self-control. I wondered what he wished for.

". . . and trying just isn't enough. So you do what you have to in order to preserve your sense of self. Your judgment. Your foundation. Yourself. And the more you do to sustain a sense of regularity, the less you can honestly say you've become someone that you recognize."

Now he's counting trees. Wild aloe vera. Cacti. Picking up where I left off. I extended my arm and placed his chin in between my thumb and forefinger. Pulled him toward me. A rhapsody of opposition. Fighting to maintain balance. Before it topples over and creates a mess. He has no manicure, so he stares at me. Looks at me sadly. He knows the feeling. He has to.

"Yeah. I've been there before. But I just shut it down before it gets out of control," he replied. I'm back at the window. The cat has been flattened. By all sixteen wheels. I'm crushed. I should be happy. He looks back over at me, sighs, and then looks past me. Toward Venezuela.

". . . But sometimes, you never quite get control. Although you try, you don't understand how to wrestle it to the ground and steal its power without raping yourself of the wonderful feeling that it brings . . ."

I leaned my head on his shoulder. He's my window. My escape. At least while I'm spinning haplessly into an emotional oblivion. While I'm hiding behind my thoughts. Dreaming of Harlem nights.

". . . and you wonder, for the life of God, how something so destructive can feel so good. Set your spirit at ease. Make you want to go to it. Wrap yourself up in the feeling like a homeless man does newspaper on Christmas Eve. Like it's your only hope. It's weird. But I think I understand it. Or rather I understand you. Where you're coming from."

By this time, we're both in our own worlds. Wrapped up in newspaper. Well, at least I am. Until our tour guide announced that we had arrived at the Natural Pool. We grabbed our belongings, hopped out of the Jeep, and followed the guide toward the water. This is it? I thought as I stumbled over volcanic rock and red dust as we walked toward the horizon. I don't see a damn thing. I noticed a stream of water, some rocks, a wild dog, and a few trees. The view was great because we were on the high point of the island, but overall I felt taken. I was expecting something way more breathtaking than this. That was until we trekked down the mountainside and walked toward the most beautiful cove I've ever seen in my life. Surrounded by huge boulders was the most crystalline water on earth. The ocean waves crashed violently up against the rock barriers, sending monstrous splashes spilling over into the cove. Creating a natural pool of water. It was so tranquil. So quiet. So romantic.

"This 'ere is the natural pool . . ." said the guide. "It is one of the most popular sites on the island. Especially for honeymooners like yourself." Nat looked at me, then at the guide.

"Honeymooners? No, man. We're just cool. We're with the medical convention," he replied.

"Yeah, we're not together," I added. The guide looked at me. Looked me up and down, grinned, and then shot a look at Nat. Some silent man talk, I'm sure. Because Nat grinned right back.

"So ya' tellin' me you here wit' dis lovely lady 'ere, but you not husband and wife, eh?" He obviously didn't believe us. I nudged Nat. I hate when men talk over me.

"Owh! No, we're not," Nat reiterated. The tour guide smirked, as if to say, *yeah, fucking right.* I don't know why, but I wasn't irritated. I just followed him down the rock path to the pool. Admired its beauty. Slipped in. Realized the shit was deep as hell.

"It's like twenty-five feet deep in the center!" Nat yelled from across the pool. He was sitting on a small rock. How he got over there so fast was beyond me. I swam right through the middle, past maybe about two or three couples who were either playing in the water or huddled up. The water was so warm. I kept going until I popped up right at his feet. Instead of pulling me up, he slid in.

"So, Doctor. Are you enjoying yourself out here in the deep blue sea?" he asked, treading water, trying to wipe the salt from his eyelashes. His lids were so low, I almost didn't think that they were open.

"Very much so. I needed this. Work can get stressful," I answered while floating on my back. There's an uncomfortable tension in the air. I watched him make his way deeper into the cove. Right into the small outlet that ran into the ocean. He leaned up against a small ledge made of multicolored rock. This place is really beautiful.

"You coming? It's shallow over here."

"It's dark!" I yelled back.

"You scared?"

"No!"

"So come on!"

I made my way over to where he was. Heart beating in a rhythm unknown to me. His back against the ledge, he reached out to me, pulling me into the small tunnel. Face-to-face again. I felt like jelly. I didn't think for a minute that I'd be able to control my actions. I only hoped that I was wrong about him feeling the same. That would be the only thing that could save me.

With both arms, he drew me into his space. He hesitated for a second. In a moment where he appeared to be questioning what he was doing. Wrestling with it. If he felt the way I did, he would be in just as much trouble. Standing on this small platform, staring at the man who floods my dreams with words of rose petals, is dangerous. Being this close is catastrophic. Feeling his arms wrapped around my waist and his energy wrapped around my heart is causing my legs to tremble.

This isn't fair. I'm trying so hard. So damn hard. But I can't continue to deny myself the opportunity to feel this. Secure. Locked. High. Sacred. Everything I've felt in every dream he's ever starred in. Every conversation we've ever had. I'm still trying, though. I'm strong. My grandma raised me that way.

I attempted to gain my composure by counting the colors in the rock behind him. Lord knows I can't take this. Being this close to him. I didn't know that I would melt down like this. I never have in my entire life. Not with Lance. Not with Derrick. Not with anyone. I'm longing for him. Aching. My body is losing the argument with my mind. My spirit making its presence known. It wants to be heard.

"Nat."

"Yes."

"I'm so sorry."

"Why."

"Because. I am, I'm . . ."

"I know. I am, too."

"I would never hurt him."

"I know. I'd never hurt her. I've tried everything."

"I can't sleep."

"I know."

"I can't eat."

"I know."

"Why is this happening?" I'm almost in tears. He gently placed my head onto his chest. I'm comforted. He's comfortable. We let the waves choreograph the dance that we do so well. If I close my eyes, and concentrate, I can predict the patterns of his heartbeat. Somehow, I remember them; they help me fall asleep. Help me dream. I felt his breath as he prepared to say the unsaid.

"You're in my dreams, Taiyler. In ways that make me despise myself."

My heart jumped a million beats. He is it. My reflection. My song. I'm seeing myself in his eyes. What is this? I'm scared to tell him that I dream of him also. I'm so overwhelmed that I can't put anything into words. An awkward kaleidoscope of nervousness, fear, and infatuation rushed through me. My body retrieved the remnants of each emotion instantly. It's shaking like a leaf. He's holding my bones together with his heart. I feel like I want to give him everything. Shake loose my womanhood and stick it in his back pockets. I have to tell him he's not alone. He may not believe me, but I dream, too. And it's ruining me. I begin to tell him just that.

"My dreams . . . we have these conversations. About places and things and love. We dance. We talk while we dance, take long walks under bright stars. We count them, name them. Aimlessly speak of love. Life. So many things. So many . . ." I'm rambling. Anything that I keep pent up inside me will surely pour out with a violence that can't be detained. Like spilled milk. Except this can't be wiped up. ". . . and we do things that I've never done. Say things that I've never said. And I wake up with your likeness in my skin. With your scent in my hair. And become ashamed. Embarrassed that I let it get that far. That my mind took a hiatus, and let my spirit wander into a dead end . . ."

He continued to stroke my hair. Holding me close. Silence danced in the light wind. Light and free. He let his fingers, the middle three, lightly touch the back of my neck. Counting hairs. Special. Separating my mind from my body. Understanding the reflection in his eyes for the first time, I reached up, placed my arms around his neck. My hands at the back of his head. And tried to keep his thoughts close to me. In the palm of my hand. Tried to keep myself inside of him. Wrapped up in newspaper.

"And I can't shake it. It's saturating me," I said, feeling purged. Unraveled. Let loose. Relaxed. As I let the beat of his heart lull me to our own spiritual spa, I realized that I may never be able to shake this. It feels so good. I may never want to.

26

Nathaniel

I think I'm asleep. I have to be. I'm waiting for someone, namely my wife, to wake me up from this. I need some regularity. This dream is lasting way too long. I start to make myself do things to test its validity. I feel everything. The pinches. The water. Her. It feels like heaven. Imagine my horror when my dream fails its litmus test. This is real. She's here. In my arms. Telling me things that I don't want to know. That she understands me. That our connection is real. That I'm not crazy. She's my mirror.

"So you know how I feel. You know."

"Do I?" she asked bashfully. After she let her thoughts cascade down my chest. I continued to stroke her hair. Hypnotized by her ability to be true to herself. To her spirit. She's much stronger than I. Even on my best day.

"Yes. You do."

"How is that? How do you feel?"

"I can't tell you."

"Why?"

"I just can't."

I refuse to let on to how I had her body pent up against mine in her man's garage. I won't do it. Reduce myself to emotional adultery. Somehow, I feel that if I don't acknowledge it, it's not real. The feeling won't exist. Even with my arms around her. I'm fighting a losing war. This battle, it's for idiots. I can't win no matter what. My will is

strong, but my heart has other plans. It's driving me insane. The ability to control, direct, and make the appropriate decisions make me a
man. She's robbing me of my manhood. A thief in the night. A beautiful one. The sparkle in her eyes propels the urgent need for me to
be honest with her. Ante up.

"Do you dream of me, Nat?" She looked up at me. I can't deny her
an answer. I can't deny her anything.

"Yes. I have at one point or another." I'm bullshitting. She sees it.
Blushes. We're there. No secrets. No hope. No control. Can't tell her it's
a few times a week. More like a few times a day. When I get up, when I
go to sleep. She's there. Her hand around my heart. Squeezing life
into me. Pumping it through my body.

"And you won't tell me."

"I can't."

"Fine," was all she said. Something about the way she held on to
me. Like she needed to hear it almost as much as I needed to say it.
Made me spill the beans. All over the ocean floor.

"Mine are intimate." Silence. I lost my nerve. Knew I should have
shut the fuck up. After about a good sixty seconds, La Princesa spoke.

"Intimate. How so?"

"Don't want to say."

"Try."

And that's just what I do.

"You are all mine. You make me do things that I've always wanted
to do. Like I always knew I could. When I'm inside y—" I couldn't. I
couldn't do it. She understands. She stroked my spine. Made it tingle.
Gave me courage. Made me a man. Truth is hard to swallow. The
buoyancy of the salt water is lifting burdens that would naturally be
three times heavier.

"When I'm inside you. I feel your troubles. Your challenges. Your
stresses. And all I want to do is relieve them. And I do. In ways that
make you curse me. You face me and tell me things that no one else
knows. My lap becomes our playground. And you play me like a brass
instrument. Then I can't face my wife in the morning. I can't face myself. The only face I can tolerate is yours." There. I did it. She shifted
a little, readjusting herself on this small platform that we shared.
Forehead to forehead. Creating a telepathic bridge for our innermost
thoughts to travel. I know what she's thinking. I know her. Inside out.
If we can just get out of here, we can avoid it. Avoid this. The disrup-

tion. The pain. The inevitable. Life is too good to us. God is, too. We will fuck it all up if we stay. I know we will. But I can't move. The weight of the scale is leaning toward holding her right here, in this very place, for an eternity. I can't think of anything else I'd rather do. Any place I'd rather be. Other than on this colorful ledge. Daydreaming of reds, yellows, and blues. Watching them dance across the bridge of her nose, vying for my attention.

"Let's go," she said.

We took baby steps off of the ledge and swam the width of the pool over to our belongings. And there was our tour guide, at the base of the Natural Pool grinning like a Cheshire cat.

"Y'all ready?" He's obviously amused by the fact that we're twenty minutes late. We were supposed to meet him at the Jeep.

"Yep!" I answered as I watched Taiyler slide her shorts and sunglasses on. He noticed.

"She's a beauty, sir."

"Yes, she is," I replied, my eyes on her. Behind her. Around her. Whatever.

"I'm talking about the pool, mon'. She is a beauty, eh?" This mutherfucker's playing with me. And I'm falling for it. Falling for a lot here in Aruba.

"Yeah, the pool is great. Let's get out of here."

"No problem," he said as Taiyler slid into the backseat of the Jeep. The guide adjusted the rearview, told us to hold on, and hit first gear like a pro. Seems like this entire island is an uphill venture. Guess I'm in the right place. I've been running uphill for a while now.

We decided to skip Baby Beach. For the best. I tipped the tour guide, had him take us straight to the Aruba Beach Club. I watched her gather her belongings. How she folded her towel, placed every object from her sunglasses to her wallet in the appropriate place. Such a calculated individual. Nothing like me. But the same. I hate to say this, but I want to see her again. Like this. I still have more to say. I refrain from asking for more of her time.

"So you had a good time?"

"Very much so. Had fun," she said, eyes sparkling. Standing in the way of the van's sliding door. Man, I don't want her to leave. But I grab every piece of strength I can muster up in order to keep myself from expressing that.

"So . . . uh, tomorrow is what, Innovative Therapy Introductions?" I asked. I'm stalling.

"Yep. That'll be interesting."

Her smile is killing me. The tour guide catches my eye through the rearview and grins. Makes me grin against my will. Sucker.

"What's so funny?" she asked me. Even her inquisitive looks are killers.

"Uh, nothing. Your man up front is a comedian. That's all."

"Okay. Well, I'll see you tomorrow."

"Tomorrow it is, Doctor," I replied as the guide pulled the sliding door closed. I sat there gawking as I had on so many previous occasions. Only to be interrupted by Def Jam up front.

"Mon', who ya foolin', sire?"

"Huh?" I'm the cat with the canary in its mouth.

"You not togedder, eh?"

"Nope." I'm not lying. We're not.

"You can't fight it, mon'. Let it happen. You can't fight love."

"I'm not, dude. I am married. I love my wife. She is involved. It ain't even like that," I answered nervously. My hands still jittery from shaking hers. He looked through the rearview again. Shook his head. He thinks I'm a freaking joke. I'm getting upset.

"Oh, yeah?" He raised his eyebrows.

"Oh, yeah. Nothing's there," I answered defiantly. Sensing my irritation, he backed down. Shuffled a few thoughts around. Got to the one he wanted. Spit it out.

"Well, the best place in Aruba to eat is La Trattoria El Faro Blanco. Near the California Lighthouse. On the eastern tip of the island. You know, fuh friends. In case you get hungry." He threw a coupon in my lap and hit a hard U-turn. We're in front of my hotel.

"Thanks, but no, thanks. I'm just going to order room service tonight."

"'Ave it your way. Hope the tour was good for you. May God bless you." The sincerity of the natives is touching. Even when they work your nerves. I had no choice but to give my man some dap. He's good people.

"It was great. Thanks a lot."

"No problem."

I hopped out, jetted through the overly air-conditioned lobby, got to my suite, and plopped down on the bed. No shower, no anything.

I'm thinking. About today. Everything was going so fast. I went from arguing with the sound tech to staring into the eyes of my weakness, in a sea of blues and greens. Standing so close, our thoughts became hues of yellow. I'm a man. I'm attempting to reassure myself of that. I'm a man with a family whom I cherish. I'm a man with the life that I've prayed for. The life that my mother worked for and wanted for me. This is the ultimate test of my manhood. I will gather myself. I will. My will is too damn strong to be sideswiped like this. I took my wallet out and flipped to the picture of Kendra and me in Rock Creek Park last year. I love her. No doubt. This is just some fluke of a situation. I'll get through it. I noticed the restaurant coupon sitting on my bed. Calling me. Whispering reminders of my day, how I spent it. Riddled. Wrapped up in her. Mentally unwrapped. I was lying on my bed, skipping rocks across rivers, being attacked by feelings with guns. I'm so fucking pitiful. I get up, make that call. I can't do this. Spend another minute without my fix.

"Aruba Beach Club, to whom may I direct your call?"

"Dr. Taiyler Richardson, please." I'm cold. Shaking. I get under the covers. The phone rings several times. She is not in her room. I feel duped. I hit zero for the operator. Try again.

"Front desk. May I help you?"

"Yes, Dr. Richardson didn't pick up." I don't know why I'm saying this stupid shit. It's not like the operator can help me. I have to turn this AC down.

"Would you like to leave a message, sir?"

"No. I want to try again."

She has to think I'm an idiot. I know I do.

"Sure. Please hold." It rings again. She picks up on the first ring.

"Hello?"

"Hello?"

"Uh, can I speak to Nat?"

"Taiyler there?"

"This is she."

"This is Nat."

"I hope you don't mind me calling," she said.

"I was calling you."

"No, I just called you. You picked up."

"Didn't you hear your phone ringing a few minutes ago?" I asked her. I'm blown by this.

"I was in the shower. I didn't hear anything." Quiet. I can hear her smile. Warmth replaces the chill inside me. I shoved the covers off.

"Uhm, so you had fun today?"

"You asked me that already . . ." She's chuckling. I'm a retard. ". . . is that why you called?" she asked coyly.

"Yup. Just making sure. Plus, I heard they had a *Coloreds only* spot that served nothing but fried chicken and watermelon, right up the way . . ."

She busted out laughing.

". . . wanted to know if you were down. They have colored water fountains and everything."

She let out a long breath. Her mind clicking. I can hear it. It matches the rhythm of my heartbeat.

"*Coloreds only*, huh? They have an outhouse?"

"Fully equipped."

"How can I turn that down? When and where do you want me?" she asked. Right now, the answer to that would be vulgar.

"How about I'll pick you up at seven?"

"Sounds good. I'll be waiting. Right out front."

We hung up. I hit the shower. Rinsed the sand off of my body. Tried to rinse the desire for this woman down the same drain.

Instead of taking a taxi, I decided to get a small rental from the hotel. Just in case I couldn't get a cab later on tonight. I jotted down the directions to the restaurant from the concierge and hopped into the car. I hope I don't get lost. Honestly, that would be an improvement. Since I seem to have lost myself some time ago. I navigated toward the Aruba Beach Club. It was a straight shot from my hotel. When I pulled up, she was waiting for me. Just as she said she would be. I saw my breath going up in cigar smoke. Again. As she walked toward the car, I couldn't even concentrate on what I was doing. She slid in. My head almost hit the steering wheel.

"So, mister. Where are we headed?" she asked. Me? I'm headed for the mental asylum. I'm just trying to get her to the restaurant.

"La Trattoria El Faro Blanco," I answered. She checked her reflection in the passenger mirror. Perfection.

"The best place to eat here," she said. Damn. She checks out everything.

"That's what I've heard. You eat Italian, right?"

"I love it. But, uh, you think I could still get my chicken and water-melon?" She glanced over at me playfully.

"Hey, this is no corner store mom-and-pop operation! You can get cheese with that!" I joked. She laughed along. We're feeling relaxed. The night breeze helped. I stole a glance at her. Her light silk blouse. Her linen pants. Her hair. The large curls cascading down her back. Flying out of the window. Meeting the wind. I wondered how some-one could be this beautiful. She let her right hand dance in the wind as we drove through small towns with no traffic lights, corners with no street signs, and over hills that looked never-ending. Until we came to a small restaurant, sitting on a large cliff. Basking in the sunset. Overlooking the entire island. Wow. The view was breathtaking.

"Oh, my God. This is beautiful," she said as we were escorted to a small table by a waiter with a wonderful accent. He seated us in the most popular and exquisite area of La Trattoria. The place where the sun blesses the patrons with a mirage of color. The terrace. He told us how reservations were usually booked for this area in advance, but since we were newlyweds, he'd be happy to serve us there. I didn't argue the point this time. I was too busy looking down the mountain-side. Out into the sea. The sunset. It was stunning. I thought back to the tour guide and decided that I would ring his fucking neck when I caught him. This is going to cripple me.

27

Taiyler

Sitting across from Nat, taking in the most beautiful view on the island, I wondered, what in Christ's name was I doing here? Earlier, when I got back to my suite, I had a message from Derrick. Telling me how much he missed me. How much fun we were going to have when I got home. He's everything I've ever wanted in a man. Fuck being rich. He's intelligent, cultured, sexy, and he'll give me his all. He's giving it to me now. And he claims that this is nothing. That it's the icing on the cake. I don't want for anything with this man. Listening to his loving message made me excited to get back home. I love Aruba, but I wanted to be close to my man.

I got into the shower, determined to wash this grit off of me. His boy's fingertips. His touch. His embrace. I wanted to shed it all. Get Taiyler back to being Taiyler. The one with the fine-ass man who loves her to death. I stood still, allowing the pressure from the water to massage the small of my back. Cascade right down the middle of me. I still felt them. His hands were all over me. Caressing my shoulders. Massaging my temples. Stroking my spine. Lightly. Softly. My frustration turned into hot tears. I wished I could burn this feeling. Singe it off of my skin. Watch it turn into light ashes. Washing the same area for about five minutes let me know exactly how distracted I was. Suddenly, another feeling invaded. Urgency. I had to hear him. So, to my dismay, I picked up the phone. And felt my frustration flee. Felt relaxed. We talked. Laughed. And now I'm here. At the beginning of a dream.

"Today's special is *fettuccini al salmone affumicato, gamberoni con rughetta* for appetizer, and *zuppa di verdure fresche.*" As the handsome waiter acknowledged the specials, I dug deep into my mental Rolodex for that Italian vocabulary.

"The fettuccini with smoked salmon, shrimp cocktail with arugula as an appetizer, and fresh vegetable soup. Sounds good."

Nat looked at me in sheer amazement. I learned the romantic language while touring Europe with Solange during the summer of our junior year. We were in Italy for two months. Her folks paid for everything. Including language lessons. As far as they were concerned, culture was priceless. And I was like their adopted daughter. So they spared no expense.

"You speak Italian?" Nat asked, obviously moved by my interpretation.

"A little. Enough to get by."

"Wow," was all he said. We both glanced at the menu again. The waiter waited. I skimmed through it, found what I wanted. The penne with fresh tomatoes, garlic, black olive, capers, and anchovies. That's what I order. He's still looking. I'll bet he wants the ravioli.

"I'll take the ravioli with seafood, black beans, corn, and cilantro." He motioned to the waiter. Damn. I was right. He gave his menu to the waiter. His eyes were on me.

"We're here," he said. To no one in particular.

"Yes, we are," I answered as I stared back. I'm not pretending anymore. I couldn't if I wanted to. I'm thinking out loud.

"What is this?"

"I don't know," he replied sadly.

"I wish I knew why, Nat."

"What can we do?"

"Whatever it takes. Whatever it takes to keep it in check." I'm speaking opposite of what I feel. Something my grandma and aunt taught me never to do. The words will always come back to eat you alive. Finish you.

"I'm not myself," he reasoned.

"I know."

"I hate what I've become. I love how it feels, though, Taiyler."

"I know. I know." I sighed. This is hard.

"I can't help it."

"Do you want to?"

"I don't know."

Our food arrived. Looking tasty. But my appetite was gone. My common sense followed it. I noticed Nat picking over his ravioli.

"Looks good," he said, referring to my dish.

"I can't eat," I whispered to myself. Thinking out loud again.

"Yes, you can," he said as he took a stab at his ravioli, leaned across the table, and invited me to taste. I accepted without reservation. Eyes half closed, I wrapped both lips around his fork.

"How does it taste?" he asked. I took a minute before answering. I was savoring the moment. Imagining his fingers in my mouth.

"Great," I answered as I picked up my fork, dug into my plate, and offered him a small mouthful of pasta. He blushed.

"You like it?" I asked him. He bowed his head, almost in prayer. Seemingly trying to shake off what it was he wanted to say. As he lifted his head, I saw those eyelashes sticking together. It made me weak. Made me want him.

"Nat."

"Yeah."

"Let's go. I'm not hungry." Not for pasta. He opened his eyes, jumped up like a hot potato. Left a hundred-dollar bill on the table and grabbed my hand. I didn't flinch. No acting. No remorse. I just let the naturalness of his touch envelope me. Send me first class to tranquility. He opened my door.

"Where to?" He looked feverish. I wanted to relieve him.

"Leave the car here. Let's walk," I suggested.

We made our way carefully to the bottom of the cliff, following the paved road we drove up on. The space underneath my stomach fluttering like a dove.

"You hear that?" he asked, looking around. The faint sound of drums, dance, and song in the background. I hear it.

"Yes. I do. Where is it coming from?"

"Over there." He pointed toward an area with smoke rising from its center.

"Are they having some sort of barbecue?" I asked. It sounded logical.

"I don't know. This looks like a very small town. It should be easy to find out. You wanna walk over there?"

"Why not?" I've been wanting to get out with the locals anyway. Experience Aruba in actuality. We turned down an extremely narrow street. Just large enough to squeeze in one compact car, one way. The music got louder. It's a celebration of some sort. I started getting excited.

"They are partying," Nat said.

"Do you think we'll be intruding?" I was concerned about that.

"Only one way to find out," he replied.

We made our way down the small street until we turned onto a larger one. Filled with people. Dressed in lively colors and costumes. Dancing. Singing. Having a hell of a time. It almost looked like a parade. We came up on a crowd of people clapping, chanting, having a ball. This was where I wanted to be. Until I saw something that resembled a chicken, or a rooster, being buried. First thought. Hell no. We done walked up on some voodoo shit. Nat tapped the gentleman directly in front of us. An older man.

"Sir, we're not from here. We just happened to find our way back here to the festival. May I ask what you guys are celebrating?"

"Oh, yes, most definitely . . ." The man was so congenial. "This is Dera Gai."

"Dera what?" Nat replied.

"Dera Gai, the festival of prosperity, the festival of rain. It is an annual Aruban tradition."

"It almost looks Spanish. Like a smaller version of Carnival," I interjected. My voodoo thoughts went flying out of the window. Americans. We're so judgmental. I felt humiliated by my own ignorance.

"So what's up with the rooster?"

I had to chuckle. Nat's reading my mind. The gentleman chuckled as well.

"It's not real. It's plastic. They used to bury a rooster, a real one, which was symbolic of life, prosperity, love . . ." he explained, looking directly at us both. "You are welcome to celebrate with us."

If we could only be this hospitable. This inviting. To each other at home. We'd be so much further as a race.

"But first, you have to visit one of the elders. Have him read you."

"Do what?" I asked. I'm not a regular churchgoer, but I'm not into that psychic shit either. I never want to see what's coming.

"Read you. It's not bad, really. He will just tell you how to keep from hindering prosperity in your lives. Everybody gets it. It's good luck to shake his hand. Please, if you would, follow me," the gentleman said as he led us about ten feet away from where we were, into a small, clean home. Smelled like a bushel of Indian incense. He rang a bell. Which was odd, because we were already inside. An elderly man with male osteoporosis crept out slowly from one of the back rooms. The gentleman spoke to him in their native tongue. Papimiento. Nat nudged me. Whispered in my ear.

"I wonder what language that is. Sounds Spanish."

"It's Papimiento. A combination of Spanish, Dutch, and English, they—" I was blatantly interrupted as the elder shouted something out all of a sudden.

Although he spoke directly to us, we didn't understand a word he said. It was all in the native language. The gentleman smiled, looked our way.

"What did he say?" Nat asked. He patted Nat on the back.

"Sometimes you get great things out of this man; other times, you get the obvious. Shake his hand. Both of you," the gentleman directed. We did as we were told and proceeded to head outside. Back toward the commotion. Back to where I wanted to be.

"Now you are ready to enjoy the festivities. Please partake of any food or drink that you wish. Clap, dance, do what you feel. You're celebrating life!" He started to walk away. Back toward the group he'd left. Nat yelled out to him.

"Hey! What did he say in there?"

The old guy laughed, looked our way. "Unfortunately it's probably nothing new to you guys; it's painfully obvious. He said that you were in love, you would always be in love, and not to fight destiny," the gentleman answered as he proceeded to walk away. That's impossible. It's impossible. I kept repeating to myself. I felt Nat squeeze my hand. He looked stunned. He said nothing. Nothing at all. We made our way around cars, dancers in big dresses, and children with colorful feathers in their hands, until we were at the end of the festival area. Standing in front of a man playing strings.

"Vallenato."

"What?"

"Vallenato. Cultural music of Columbia. The most romantic," I replied, allowing him to turn me toward him.

"Dance with me." His eyes were begging me. They didn't have to.

"Are you sure?"

"Very."

He pulled me into his chest. Slid his arms around me. Through me. My waist. My shoulders. My soul. My everything. He let his lips brush the edge of my eyebrow. If he weren't holding me so tightly, I would have passed out right there. My entire body is on fire.

"Please . . . Nat . . ." I want to feel him. I want to kiss him so badly. I can't hold it anymore. I feel like I've been holding this in for a lifetime instead of a few months. He's taken his fingers, all ten, and is massaging my scalp with them. Jesus.

"Every night. Every day. You're here, like this," he whispered in my ear. My body acknowledged his every word. Every vibration.

"Making love to you . . . it's cathartic."

"Tell me," I managed to say between breaths. He's rationing mine out to me.

"It's new. Gorgeous . . . unfair."

"Why?"

"It leaves me a raving lunatic when I wake, makes me crazy," he expressed.

"How do we put this off?"

"What?"

"This."

"I don't know. My heart is open."

"Mine, too. I want you all over me." That was an understatement. If I could become him, I would. Become a better version of myself. The possibility of a closer us aroused me. Made me think of him inside of me. Made me breathe quick breaths. Took me to an orgasmic height. I felt my body shudder. Shake. Just like in my dreams. We swayed to the sensual music, leaning on each other for strength. Two weak links. Broken by love. He tipped my head upward and began to feed my hunger. His lips. Oh, my God. I don't know how to describe their softness. They were for me. They tasted the way I knew they would. They conjured up a feeling in me so intense that I was willing to trade my life for another five minutes of rapture with him. I was lost in space for a moment. I blanked out. I know I did. Because when I returned, the sun was completely set, the instruments packed, and the streets emptied. The only things stirring were our lips, our caresses, our energy. For the first time in my life, I felt it. Felt whole. Full. Removed from my burdens. And as I continued to tell him how much this meant to me in coded kisses, all I could think of was Rachelle's song. I got there. I'm seeing it. The reflection of my heart.

28

Nathaniel

We're on a 757. Headed straight for reality. Real life. Real shit. Real things. I was caught between thoughts buried under boulders. There was so much on my mind. I wanted to spend each minute of this flight as we had the past few days. Talking. Laughing. Living. I told her enough about me to make a mint in blackmail. From the looks of it, she did, too. Told me everything. How she grew up. What her relationships were like with her family. With her friends. With herself. The trials she overcame. The tribulations she didn't. What's still haunting her. What she's let go of. I feel like I know her. In every sense of the word except the biblical. And how I managed that has more to do with God than it does me.

She's sitting three seats over from me. Every now and then I steal a frame of her face. Photograph her expression. Mount them on the walls of my imagination. Stand back and appraise my work of art. Gordon Parks couldn't have done it better. Times like this make you understand the true meaning of the phrase *"a picture is worth a thousand words."* Thinking, a thousand is an understatement. I've shared things with her that I didn't even know I remembered. That no one ever knew. My fears. Experiences that I was either too ashamed or too embarrassed to mention. My feelings toward my father. And now, reality is staring me in the face. This is over. My four-day eternity. It needs to be. Maybe in another lifetime, we'll do it again. I sure hope so.

"Please fasten your seat belts as we prepare for landing . . ."

I never understood the significance of wearing a seat belt in a vehicle that traveled five hundred seventy miles per hour. When this is over, it's over. There isn't a damn thing a seat belt can do for you. As a matter of fact, seems it'll only make things worse. The thing gets jammed, and there you are. Stuck. Watching some asshole hop his ignorant ass straight into your lifeboat. He's paddling away, while you're trying to frantically unlock your belt. One big splash, and that's a wrap. It's now all about who you were. I'm not fastening anything. I looked at the stewardess with an expression on my face that read *don't even fucking think about it.* Coming over here to tell me about this seat belt shit is a dead issue. The gentleman beside me passed me a red piece of paper. Folded in squares. I know who. It's from the woman who made me believe in asexual orgasms. As I unfold it, my heart skips a beat.

> There are some things that words cannot describe. Many of those things I've experienced with you. What we shared will always be a part of me. I can't help that. I don't want to . . .

My body is tensing up already. She doesn't have to be anywhere near me to affect me the way that she does. It's sickening.

> . . . you make me chase rainbows. I can see them clearly in your smile. But I know, I think we both do, that no one has ever gotten to the end of one. This is where we stop, Nat. I know you know . . . endlessly, T.

I glanced over to where she was seated. Determined to squeeze in a few more memories before the plane hit the ground. Made them terminal. I tried to get her attention. To my dismay, she wouldn't lift her head. She wouldn't look. I thought about getting up and going over there, but thought twice about it. In this day and age, they, meaning the passengers, would fuck me up for walking the aisle during landing. Like they did homeboy with the bomb in his sneakers. Whipped his ass like he owed them child support. I signaled for her attention with my eyes. It worked every single time in Aruba. It's not working now. Realizing that this was really it, that it would be the last time we'd ever share anything at all, a sort of desperation came over me. I was almost angry. Why won't she look at me? I thought about calling her name. That would be straight-up ghetto. Fuck it.

"Taiyler."

No response.

"Taiyler!" I called louder. Saw her reposition herself in her seat. She's uncomfortable. And at this point, I'm selfish. I want to stare into her eyes the same way I did at the cove. La Tratorria. The festival. Baby Beach. One last time. She wouldn't deny me that, would she? She couldn't. She can't. I spoke her name. Once again. A little softer. A little less urgent. Even though I'm burning inside.

"Taiyler."

She lifted her head, turned it to face me. I saw the water threatening to turn those gray eyes red. This is hard for her. Just as hard as it is for me. I slowed down. Don't want it to hurt. We shared a long, hard gaze.

"We've landed at Baltimore Washington International, the time is now seven twenty-three P.M. . . . *"*

As the passengers applauded our pilot for a safe trip, I held up the red piece of folded paper between my fingers. Caressed it the way you would a soft rose petal. I want to let her know that I understand her. That I always will. That even though we, of course, can't ever be more than associates, she is not alone. She's always with me. In my dreams. I mouthed that in the simplest way that I could.

"I know," I whispered. Hoping she was able to read my lips.

"I know you do," she mouthed back. Right before standing up, grabbing her knapsack from the overhead compartment, and making her way into the aisle. I was still sitting. I'd rather watch her go. I need a minute to snap out of this. Get back to life. Back to reality.

Walking through the narrow gate I saw something that brought reality right to my doorstep. My boy Derrick. And his woman. *His* woman. He's laughing, kissing her, swinging her around. He's happy. Suddenly the guilt hit me like a Mack truck. I despise myself tremendously. What the hell have I done? Who am I, or rather what am I, to steal his happiness, even if only for a few days? I know better. Emotional infidelity is just as sour as the physical. I watched him carry the woman that I felt so deeply for over the past few months. Past few days. Hours. Minutes. I watched her expression. Watched her watch me. Watched her dilemma unfold in front of both of our eyes. Now that I know what's behind hers, I wish so much that I didn't.

29

Shala

"So you think your father would disown you if he found out?" Dr. Henderson asked, legs crossed, rimless glasses hanging on her nose, with that interrogatory look in her eyes. She's so much different here. Much different as my doctor than she is as my friend. So stern. So professional. I had to think about that one for a minute. Dad? Disown me? Never. But then I thought it over. He loves me. The me that he raised. He didn't raise the person that I've become. What would he think of me now?

"I dunno," I answered matter-of-factly.

"Think about it," she replied. Determined to get some answers out of me. I always start off with a bunch of bullshit in my sessions. That is, until I'm broken down. Made to stare myself in the face. My last sessions ended with me feeling free. Liberated. Headed in a direction that wasn't popular, but it was me. I wondered where these sessions would lead.

"He wouldn't talk to me. He'd be too hurt. And too busy trying to figure out where he went wrong," I said.

"Even after you explained to him what you've gone through to get to this point?" she asked wholeheartedly. She knows what I went through.

"It wouldn't matter."

"Why do you say that?"

"You of all people know how it is. The church. Old and set in its ways. Let's get real. Would you tell my father, your pastor, that you were a lesbian?" I already knew the answer to that one. Fat Joe had a better chance of endorsing fat-free sandwiches from Subway.

She was quiet. Thinking. I know she wouldn't.

"As a member, no. As his daughter maybe."

Bullshit.

"Maybe, huh? Don't take this the wrong way, but when I was here before, I was trying to figure myself out. Whether or not I was going to act on feelings that were overwhelming me. I've been there. Done it. I love it. No question about it. Right now, this is a little different. As my best friend said so candidly, I'm searching for a reason—a damn good one at that—to leave someone and something that I love almost more than I love myself. How would that make you feel? To have to leave your husband. Right now. Because your daddy told you to."

Quiet again. This shrink shit is overrated.

"Shala. Has he said that?"

"Said what?"

"That he wouldn't accept you. Asked you to leave her."

"No, I haven't said anything, remember?"

"Exactly. So you have no idea what he's going to say. The difference between you and me is simple. He raised you. Loved you. You're his favorite. That's obvious. It would kill him to lose you in any way. Me? I'm just a member of his flock. He advises me. Separates love from logic. With you, he can't do that even if he tried. Love always wins," she said, uncrossing her legs. Leaning forward.

"Love wins in fairy tales," I replied.

"In life, Shala. In life. Love wins. No matter what you try to do. Love is the only thing keeping you from leading what you call a normal life right now. See how strong it is?"

I sat there. Thinking. Until she clicked her ink pen against her desk. Time's up.

"Next week?" she asked.

"Next week," I answered. I gathered my things and headed for the large cherry-wood door. Took a look at the picture on the bookcase.

"Kiss Nile for me."

"I'll do that," she said as we hugged tightly. If I could get my life together the way she has hers, that would be the shit. Right now, I just need to get back to work. I'm trying to get home early today. Watch TV with my girl.

* * *

I only had about three more doctors to see. Some days I hate this job. Most days, I love it. I can get a day's work done in two and a half hours if I work smartly. I'm sitting outside Taiyler's office building in Silver Spring. Call planning. Getting my presentation together, so I can deliver the current drug information and updates to these doctors as quickly as possible. I hope they don't have lots of questions. Today's Monday. Busy as hell. So they probably won't. As I packed my bag with drug samples, my phone rang. It's T.

"Bitch, you didn't tell me you were back." She must have seen me from her office window.

"You didn't tell me you were coming to the office," she snapped back. She must have seen me from her office window.

"I didn't know I was until a few minutes ago. Didn't feel like going downtown today. When did you get back?" I asked. It's not like her not to call me when she lands.

"Late last night."

"Derrick came to the airport?"

"Yeah," she sighed. Something's wrong.

"What's wrong?"

"Nothing."

"Fool yourself. You're not fooling me." A saying we both took from Auntie.

"Not trying to. Just having a hard day. Overloaded with patients. That's all." Qualifier. She's lying.

"You're lying," I said quickly. Sure of myself. I know my best friend. She's quiet. I'm leaning on the trunk of my car. Waiting for her to drop the bomb.

"I had a good time. It's hard being back," she said sadly.

"Damn. Was it like that, T? Did some fine island man give it to you real good? Or better yet . . . a finer woman?" I gasped. I'm joking, but I want to bring her here. Have her tell me what the issue is. In real time. Not in hers. I can tell she didn't even crack a smile. No chuckle. No giggle.

"No. Not at all. I just had fun. It was very relaxing. I discovered some things about myself." She's not ready to talk. When she is, she'll spill the beans. Before then, getting her to talk about anything is damn near impossible. Fuck damn near, it is.

"Okay. Well, I'm coming by this weekend. We can talk all about it."

She's not even listening to me. On my way to the office, I overheard her arguing with one of the nurses about a prescription that she just wrote for one of her patients. Alendronate 70 mg. Once a day. She's saying she didn't write that. The nurse is saying she did. Showing her the signature on the prescription pad. I ran that through my mental Rolodex. Alendronate . . . Fosamax, new indication . . . 70 mg . . . once weekly versus 10 mg daily. Oh, shit. Once weekly! And she wrote that for once daily? That's seven times the indicated dose! She's trying to kill that woman! She better be glad her nurse caught that. Whatever happened while she was on that trip is fucking her up at work. Taiyler never makes mistakes like that. She double-checks everything. Where's her head?

"Taiyler."

She doesn't hear me. She's still making her point to the nurse. She needs to be saying thank you to that lady.

"Taiyler!" I yelled.

"What! I'm talking!" she answered. Obviously aggravated.

"Calm your ass down and listen!"

"I have to handle—"

"Would you just shut the fuck up and listen!" Now I'm aggravated.

"What, Sha!"

"Alendronate. The prescription you wrote for it will kill that woman at that dose! You wrote it *q.d.* They're sampling the weekly version now. The daily version is older. Almost obsolete."

She got quiet. She knows I know my shit.

"Are you sure?" she asked.

"I am. Check it out. Right now, while we're on the phone . . ." I heard her steps clicking down the hall toward the sample closet.

"The new weekly dose is in the green packaging. The old daily dose, the 10 milligram tablet, is in yellow packaging. You gave her the green, T. You had to. They hardly even sample the yellow anymore," I reassured her.

"Oh, shit. Oh, shit, Sha. Oh, shit, shit, shit!" She realized it. I felt her anxiety. Felt her relief. My ace would have been in court by the end of the week. In jail by the end of the month.

"Twice the LD50. How could I?" she cried. She's fucked up for real.

"I'm coming over. Fuck this weekend. We're talking tomorrow

night. So get ready. You need to take your red ass home. Whatever happened in Aruba has you about to lose your license."

"Nothing happened."

I can see her at her desk, with her head in her hand. Beating herself up. She loves her patients.

"Whatever. I'll be there around seven. And I'm bringing chocolate Haagen Dazs. You haven't been this jacked up since you and Lance split."

"Nothing happened," she repeated.

"Okay. Then we'll talk about nothing. But I'll be there at seven regardless."

She sighed. Hung up. Before I got to say good-bye. This doesn't sound good. Doesn't sound good at all.

Great news to myself. I'm out of this bitch. Done. No more doctors for me. I watched the numbers in the elevator light up. Take me from torment to tranquility. As soon as I stepped out into the lobby, my phone vibrated in my pocket. Scared me shitless.

"Hey, Shala, how ya doin', girl?"

I looked at the caller ID. Private number.

"Who the hell is this?"

"It's D! Derrick! Taiyler's main squeeeeeeze!" He made me grin. He's always happy. I guess we all would be if we were loaded.

"How'd you get my number?" I really wanted to know.

"Nothing is off-limits in my line of work."

Yeah, I bet. He wants something. I thought back to his antics the last time I saw him at his metropolitan home. It's so funny. At the party, he sounded like a Blood or a Crip. Kicking it outside on the stoop with the homies, throwing the English language around like a cut cigar at a blunt party. Fucking it up for real. Today. I didn't even recognize him. His diction is beyond excellent. He sounds like he's not from anywhere. Definitely not from DC. I have to make up for my rudeness. Kill it with kindness.

"To what do I owe this honor, Your Majesty?" I asked him. I heard him chuckle. Like he's used to being called majesty. Go figure.

"Oh, now I'm Your Majesty, huh?" He laughed. "Now I know why you and my baby get along so well. Your attitudes complement each other," he concluded. Still chuckling. Arrogant mutherfucker he is.

"So you called to insult me?"

"Far from. I called to pick your brain."

"Wrong place. Anything that she didn't tell you is off-limits. Anything that she did say, well, you just have to remember, because that's Area Fifty-one, too."

"Area Fifty-one?"

"Off-limits, Brainy Smurf. Aren't you an attorney? I was told the LSAT was logic-based. Guess they gave you the Hampton version."

"Owwh! You always hit that far below the belt? I would let you have it, youngun', but I need you for something."

My curiosity's getting the better of me. I stopped playing around. Wondered if his call had anything to do with Taiyler's dismal mood.

"All right, playa. What's up? I'm all ears."

"From what I saw, you got that right," he belted out loud. Cracked himself up. I snickered to myself. I had it coming.

"Okay. I want to run something by you. You're Taiyler's best friend. And from what she says, the person who knows her best. Besides Auntie."

"Uh-huh."

"I want to buy her something nice. Of course I've chosen something to fit my standards."

"Oh, of course," I said sarcastically. A pompous, stuck-up, cool-as-hell, down-to-earth boy from South East. A weird combination.

"But as you know, Taiyler has eclectic taste. And it varies from day to day . . ." He's right about that.

"Some days we shop and I can pick up a seven-hundred-dollar Jimmy Choo, and she'll love it. Take it right to the register. Other days, she wants a seventy-dollar pair from Kenneth Cole. Confusing a brother like hell." He laughed. So did I. He seems to be used to getting women what they want. Taiyler has him going in circles.

"So what do you want to buy her?" I asked him.

"A pendant. Chopard floating diamonds. Dainty. Just her style."

"So what's the problem? She'll like that."

"I want to purchase something else for her as well."

"What is that, lover boy?" I'm losing patience. Anxious.

He paused. "A ring."

"A what?"

"A ring." He's waiting for my reaction. I don't give one. I waited for him to further explain this.

"Shala."

"What?"

"She's the one."

"Excuse me?" I'm wondering if I heard him correctly.

"She's it. The one I want to spend my life with. My afterlife. My everything."

"You sure, Derrick? It hasn't even been a year yet."

"I know. This won't be for another seven months or so. I know it sounds crazy. To get the ball rolling this early. But the ring that I want for her is precious and takes about that long to come in." He's dead serious. So he's not the reason she's upset. My mind is working over-time right now. Seven months from now will be well over a year. Not that there is a specific amount of time associated with making an en-gagement work, but knowing Taiyler, and how slow she is, I want her to be sure. It'll take about that long.

"You have to make sure she's sure, Derrick. Don't spring that shit on her. You know how she is."

"I know, Shala. I know. Which is why I'm going to wait. Even though I'm ready today. Right now."

Awwh. Behind all of that macho bullshit, he's a sweet guy. Really sweet. I inhaled deeply. Began to feel it. Excitement. Welling up in-side of me. Starting in the pit of my stomach. Moving its way up to the center of my chest. Until my eyes began to well up.

"Have you told anyone?"

"No. You're the first."

"When did you decide this?"

"When I first laid eyes on her."

"You are committing yourself to her well-being. Overall. Before yours. Her life, before your own. Are you ready for that, Derrick?" I sounded just like my father.

"No doubt," he answered without reservation.

"She's a lot to handle. And won't hesitate to drop your ass if you fuck up. Can you deal with it?"

"Most definitely."

"Can you deal with me? If you screw up, Derrick, I'm coming after your ass. She's my sister. More than that. If you fuck with her mind, I won't be able to think straight. Hear me?"

"Yes. I do. Believe me, I do."

"Then let's pray."

"Let's what?" he asked incredulously.

"Pray, Derrick. Not that you are, but you'd lie to me a whole lot faster than you'd lie to God. This isn't something that I'm willing to experiment with. It's her life. You are. Or you will be. Bow your head."

He was silent. A few seconds passed by. No response.

"Go ahead, Shala."

Oh. Thought he was still thinking about it. Homeboy beat me to the punch. I bowed my head, closed my eyes. Took a deep breath and started the prayer off like I had so many times before, so many years ago. Like I still do. During the day. At night. Hoping He still hears me.

"Father God, in the name of Jesus . . ." I felt a warmth move through me. ". . . I come to you as humbly as I know how, thanking you for your love. Your mercy. Your grace. I come to you on behalf of my brother Derrick, asking you to bless him, Father. Bless him with the mental clarity needed to make this lifelong decision, the visibility to have the necessary foresight to navigate as head of a household . . . head of a complicated woman. Be a part of all that he does. Be a part of this. He's asking to stand before you. In marriage. In truth. In peace. In spirit. Bless him with the wisdom, knowledge, and under-standing that he needs for a lifetime of love. Thank you, Lord. Amen."

I didn't hear anything.

"You still there?" I whispered. I forgot I was still in the lobby.

"Wow. That was serious," he replied.

"So if you mess up, you have to answer to God. And me. But I'd en-courage you to go to Him first. He may have more mercy on you than I will."

He laughed a hearty one.

"I'm sure. But we won't need all that. She's my one. My only. My gift. The Big Man Upstairs is looking out. He's not an Indian giver," he said sincerely. Yeah, I'm liking this. This may be it. I ripped him down; now it's time to build him up.

"So tell me about this ring!" I'm really excited now. So is he. I can hear it in his voice.

"It's a Harry Winston. Perfect emerald-cut. Six and a half carats. VVS1, A. Flawless. Not a spec of carbon, a crack, or hinge in sight. All of the facets are set perfectly. GIA couldn't ask for a more picture-perfect stone. It'll take a while, because it's on back order. But that's what I want for her. Only the best."

I was still on six and a half carats. This damn rock is worth more than my home. He's still talking. Trying to impress me. Not knowing that I was impressed a long time ago. When he expressed his love for her in front of all of his friends. His boys. His exes. What neither he nor Taiyler knew was that I had him checked out a while ago. He was handsome and all, but he was a notorious ladies' man. I mean, the shit was ridiculous. However, I knew that T could handle it. From the looks of it, I was right.

"Damn, D! That sounds like a boulder!"

"That's why I got an emerald-cut stone. I know she doesn't like gaudy jewelry. A round stone would hang off of her finger. Princess wasn't rare enough, and anything else just wasn't my style. I wanted classic, rare, and beautiful. Just like my baby."

"Emerald will sit just right on her. The surface area will broaden the girth of the stone. Make it wider instead of deeper. So it won't hang. She hates that." I offered my two cents.

"See, I knew you'd know your shit. That's what I'm talking about! Let me find out I should have paid more attention to y'all Spelman chicks before I got locked down!" He's stupid. Makes me laugh.

"Thanks."

"Nah, thank you! But, uh, that's not it. We both know that Taiyler is too smart for me to try to get her finger sized on a whim, so I'll need your help. I want this to fit perfectly, Shala. Meaning, I need her to try on the exact band. The one that I'll place on her finger. Not a replica."

"That will be impossible," I answered with assurance. Taiyler's a brainiac. It'll be hard enough getting her fitted period. And this dude wants to be picky?

"No, I got it."

"Got what?"

"The metal. The platinum. Just the bands, though. A few different sizes. From a five and a half to a seven."

"They gave them to you?" I asked. He must have clout like shit.

"I wish. I bought them all. Like five or six of them. Different widths, too. So she can choose the most comfortable one. I'm not into re-designing and upgrading shit. I want to get it right the first time. Move on, get her something else. You know what I mean?"

Actually, I didn't. But I acted like I did. This guy is serious. Taiyler's hooked up with Aladdin. As I continued to listen to him carry on about how he had this all planned out, I thought, wow. He is definitely a class act. As well as a perfectionist. This is what Taiyler wanted. A match made in heaven.

30

Nathaniel

"Come walk with me," she said as she took my hand, led me to that special place, the one she just spoke of not too long ago. I'm anxious. I feel it.

"Where are we going?" I had to ask.

"The Savoy," she answered.

"The dance hall?"

"Yeah. Unless you can't do it."

"Do what?"

"Dance."

"I can do better than that," I said as I picked her up. Swung her around, to the other side of me.

"Well, then, show me."

"Show you what?"

"Show me what you can do."

"For you? I can do it all."

"Sounds good. But is it true?" she asked.

"It always is, my dear. Love is always true."

"Is that what you call it?" she said, beaming.

I was, too. Inside. "That's what it calls me."

"What?"

"True. Love calls me by my name. True. When I'm with you."

"Well, then, what does it call me?"

"I don't know. You have to ask it." I laughed. So did she. We were in each other's arms. The possibility of us, dancing in each other's eyes.

"One more dance, madam?"

"Let me think . . ." She backed away from me, seemingly in appraisal of my suit. My looks. My soul. ". . . no, we've danced enough," she replied. I could dance all night with her like this. Dance the night away.

"This is soul food."

"What is?" she asked as I held her coat open for her.

"You are. Good to me. Good for me. Like soul food."

She blushed.

"I see," was all she said as she allowed me to take her hand in mine, place a kiss on the back of her palm . . .

"Mr. Woods? Mr. Woods! Are you okay?" My secretary's shaking the shit out of me. I must have been sleeping hard because I didn't hear her at all. Letting out a big yawn, I motioned to her that I was all right. No need to worry. I'm not on my way out.

"I'm fine. What time is it?" I asked.

"It's fifteen after ten. I just came in a minute ago, and you were wide awake! I thought something happened! Don't scare me like that!" she exclaimed.

"I haven't been getting much sleep lately." Really, I hadn't.

"Well, you need to, sir. Mr. West is on his way up. He wants to talk to you." She gave me a look that said she heard something. Something bad. Our signal for watch your ass. The one that Blacks develop in the workplace out of concern for others. Sort of like a corporate underground railroad. She keeps her ear to the ground for me. I appreciate it. But this time, I don't know what could possibly be wrong.

"Did he say anything?" I asked out of concern.

"No. You know he wouldn't tell me anything. But Ms. Johnson said that your expense report had some discrepancies. A major one actually. I don't know what else it could be," she said, appearing to be racking her brain as violently as I was mine. My boss will usually send a minor glitch back up through departments. He never comes in personally to discuss them. It's beneath him. Or so he thinks. This must be big.

"Here he comes," she whispered. I felt a twinge underneath my armpits.

"Nat."

"Yes, Mr. West."

"Can we have a minute?" He signaled over to where my secretary was standing. She got it. Made her exit quietly.

"Your current expense report. Everything is accurate, right? You double-checked?"

As far as I know I did. Even if I didn't, saying that I did not double-check things was setting myself up for the kill anyway.

"Yes. I did. I always do," I answered.

"Well, can you explain this?" he said as he handed me a copy of what I perceived to be my current report, with numbers that were unfamiliar to me.

"I'm waiting," he said impatiently.

Mutherfucker wait, damn it. I'm reading it. "These are not my expenses. Some of them are, but this one here—"

"The thirty-two-hundred-dollar charge, the one that you submitted a three-hundred-twenty-dollar receipt for?"

"Yeah."

"You know how we feel about skimming, Nat. Now, I'm not implying anything, but this looks bad. The two things you can be fired on the spot for—"

"Forgery and expenses," I interrupted. I know the policy well. I taught it. But I didn't steal over twenty-five hundred dollars. Even though that's what this report showed. From the looks of it, I added another zero to the dollar amount by mistake. Mistakes. Something that is intolerable in the world of number crunching. A decimal point can cost you a million.

"And you know that, so I'm going to assume that this was not intentional. I know it wasn't because I know my employees. When the money is transferred into your account, return it via certified check immediately to the firm. You hear me?"

"Yes, sir."

He doesn't have to do this. He's well within his rights to let me go.

"Sir . . ."

"Yes, Nat."

"It was a mistake. I would never—"

"I know. You submitted the receipt to go along with it. If you were trying to hide it, you wouldn't have done that. You're not stupid enough to do it knowing that we check every receipt that comes through the department. Don't let it happen again. I won't be able to cover for you next time," he said. I owe him. Big.

"Thanks a lot, sir," I said as I extended my hand. He grabbed it, shook it, and to my surprise, gave me dap. I had to laugh.

"No problem. You're one of my best. I'd fuck myself trying to replace you. Do you know how long that would take? Damn it, I just bought my summer home in Maine! You aren't going anywhere until I pay that sucker off!" He laughed, his belly doing the Harlem Shake over his belt.

"But, Nat, do me a favor."

"What's that?" He has my full attention. He just saved my ass, big-time.

"Get some sleep. Get some therapy. Or just get some. Whatever you're going through was about to cost you your job. You never make mistakes like that. I don't want to lose you over dumb shit. If you're going to make these types of mistakes, move a decimal point! Make an extra million! Shoot, I may go in with ya!" He's cracking up. Has me laughing, too. Even though I don't feel like it.

"No doubt, sir," I replied between breaths as he made his way out of my office, onto the elevator, and back upstairs to his office. Or penthouse. Whichever you prefer. I got my secretary on the intercom.

"Hold all of my calls."

"Mr. Woods, everything all right?" she asked. She's concerned, I can tell.

"Yeah, all is good. I just need a breather."

"You got it, sir," she answered. I have to give her a raise.

I leaned back in my chair. My hands behind my head. And thought. I did that report when I got back from Aruba. In the middle of the night. I couldn't sleep. So I decided to do something constructive. Something to get her off of my mind. Get her out of my house. And the shit almost cost me my job. Or rather she did. I can't stand her. So much that I reached for the phone. I've been fighting the urge all morning. If I could just hear her voice. Just once. I'll be good. Won't bother her anymore. I can get her out of my system forever. One more hit. The phone rang. And I felt that belt wrapping around my arm. Felt the pressure building inside. I pulled it extra tight. Waited for my main vein to answer. She picked right up.

"This is Taiyler."

I couldn't say anything. I was stuck on high. Stuck on good shit.

"This is Taiyler," she said again. "I know who this is. And I've been thinking about you as well." Her voice was low. Dreamy. And then she hung up. Cut off my supply. They say it's a thin line. I believe that. Because I hate her right now. I hate what she's doing to me. I have to get this monkey off of my back before I hit rock bottom.

"Mr. Woods. Mr. DeCosta is on line two for you. Want me to put him through?" my secretary asked cautiously. They call her "The Gatekeeper." Well, at least my boys do. When it's time to hold calls, you can hang it up. She's not letting you through. No matter what. I think she likes Derrick, though. I looked over at the clock. It's the end of the day. I'm feeling better and managed to get a few things done despite my condition. I need to talk to D. Maybe that'll chase this shit out of me.

"Yeah. What line again?"

"Line two."

"Okay, thanks." I pick up. Only to be surprised by my best friend doing a very bad DMX impression. Barking the hook to "Who We Be."

"The hurt, the pain, the dirt, the rain . . . (uhh!) The jerk, the fame, the work, the game . . . (come on!)." He's into it.

"What up, fake thug?" I snickered.

"What up, nigga! Oh, my bad, I mean what up, bruhua? I'm trying to stop using the N word."

"Since when, *niggaaaaa!*" I'm instigating. He's tried this before. It didn't work. It's too catchy.

"Since Taiyler said she wouldn't give me any if I kept using it." He laughed. I did, too. But inside I was crying. Why'd he have to say her name? I'm shaking off a Tyson blow to the chin.

"Oh, really? So you think you're going to stop for real, nigga? Huh, nigga? What? I didn't hear you, nigga!" I'm playing with him. That's been his word of choice since I've known him. He claims that he's taken the negative connotation of the word and used it positively. Taken its power. I can see that. Blacks have done it for so long. Taken scraps and used them for nourishment. Made the bad good. Innovate. We did it with food. Clothing. Why not with words? Nobody's screaming that cut-off shorts are damaging to our health as a race. Somebody just cut a hot-ass pair of denim jeans and made them short. So they could survive the summer. Survive the heat. So nobody could tease us for not being able to afford shorts. As a matter of fact, we made it trendy. The same way we did the word *nigga*. Made it acceptable. So that it doesn't hurt. At least that's what they say.

"Yeah, nigga. So I'm trying to cut down on that shit." He said it. And didn't even realize it. I laughed to myself. If I brought it up, he'd deny it.

"So we on for tonight?" he asked me.

"What's tonight?"

"Don't make me slap a pimp down with his pimp cup!" Okay. Now he's quoting Nas. This is South East Derrick with his former gang member vernacular. He must not be at work.

"For real. What's tonight?"

"Yo. It's Monday. Basketball. For the past three years. Does that ring a bell?"

Damn. I forgot. Too much on my mind. A game may be just what I need. Take my frustration out on some unsuspecting middle-aged man with his knee wrapped up. Find my Patrick Ewing and make him look like Patrick Ewing. I overheard him talking to someone.

"Yes. File those . . . please. Yes. Tell her I'll see her in about five minutes; I'm on a conference call. Thanks." So he is at work. Funny how he switches up his accent, diction, and speech patterns to accommodate his surroundings. Make everyone comfy. I've always admired that. We all do it. But he's an expert. He sounds like a completely different person.

"So yeah, man, I'm mad that I have to remind your bitch ass, but we do have a game tonight."

"I'm there," I replied. I got his bitch ass. Right there on the court.

"I want to run something by you. It's important. So we'll need a one-on-one."

"One-on-one?"

"Yeah. Got a problem with that?"

"No. It's just that our last one-on-one was—"

"I know. Mother's Day five years ago. When I was having issues with Mama not being around. This is different. It's good."

"Cool, bruh. So I'll see you later. And, uh, Derrick . . ."

"Yeah?"

"Bring your game with you this time."

He busted out laughing. Last time I sent him home with no pride.

"No doubt," he said as he hung up. This will be interesting.

* * *

"My ball!" I yelled out as Derrick shot and caught the ball in one fluid movement. He's frustrated. Oh, well. He walked.

"Your ball? Stop making those bitch-ass calls! This ain't the Gold Coast, nigga, this is South East! And we're on the muthafuckin' court with real niggas! Not them punk-ass corporate cornballs you play with in the suburbs!" He got in my face. Here it goes. It always ends like this.

"You traveled. You know it. All that fancy dribbling will get you nowhere. Gimme the rock." I attempted to reason with an unreasonable man when it came to ball.

"I ain't givin' you shit! Traveling? Bullshit! You were the only one traveling. Right to the ground when I shook you out of your shoes!" He's full of wisecracks.

"This isn't a fucking And One mix tape, Derrick! Real basketball has rules! We're not in the penitentiary!" Now he has me yelling. I'm irritated. I tried so hard not to let him get me there.

"Don't start with that basketball-is-a-functional-sport speech. I play with finesse. Like A.I. Like Kobe. Like real mutherfuckers. That stop-and-pop Larry Bird shit went out when he did. Get your game up, fool. Shoot for it." He launched the ball at my chest.

"Why should I have to shoot when I made a good call?" I asked him. He looked me up and down like I was an extra in the *Thriller* video. He thinks I won't make it.

"Because the ball doesn't lie, man." He glanced around the park for one of his boys. Found one that played for Maryland. Just won the NCAA championship. Got drafted to the home team.

"Aye, Juan!"

"Whassup, D!"

Here goes. He has to put on a show. Shit just can't be simple.

"Does the ball lie? Did it lie when you beat Duke's ass in the championship?"

"Naw, D. It didn't," he said, grinning.

"Did it lie when you dropped that thirty on North Carolina?"

"Nope!"

"Did you see me just break my man Nat down right over there? Behind the key?"

"Yup."

Punk-ass chump. He looks up to Derrick. He'll agree to whatever he wants him to.

"Well then, it isn't going to lie now. Shoot the shit, Nat. Stop being a bitch."

I don't know how he gets me painted into these corners. I pick the ball up. Head to the foul line. Shoot it. Miss it. Lying-ass ball.

"Whatever, man. You traveled. If you're going to do all of that fancy stuff, learn how to do it right," I said.

"All right. All right. Let's just shoot around. I want to get this out," Derrick said. I'm a little anxious about what could be so important.

"You've known me for how long, Nat?"

"Almost twelve years."

"And in those twelve years have I ever made a rash decision? Been impulsive?"

"Not ever."

"Have I ever jumped the gun on anything without being extra sure about it?"

"Nope. Never," I answered. So sure of myself. He's the slowest and most precise person that I know when it comes to making decisions.

"Good. Because I'm about to make a very important one. Perhaps the most important ever," he added seriously. Wow. He's going to do it. Leave his firm. Start his own group. He's been talking about it for a while. He became quiet. For the first time all evening.

"I'm listening," I edged him on.

"Okay. I have to take another deep breath. Because when I tell you this, you especially, then I know it's a done deal."

"That's usually how it works," I added. He bounced the ball a few more times. Blew imaginary smoke from his nose and mouth. He's in heavy thought. Suddenly, with the wind behind him, he let the cat out of the bag.

"She's the one, man."

"Who?"

"Taiyler. I want her to be my wife."

"What?" I felt like I was breathing through a straw, into a paper bag, right in the middle of an asthma attack.

"I need her in my life, Nat. She's my right arm. There's not much I can do without her by my side. I know this now. With her next to me, all I can do is grow. Become a better man. So I'm going to ask her to marry me . . ."

Oh, shit. The room is spinning. My stomach is turning. Nat. Get control of yourself. I feel nauseous.

"And I want you to be my best man."

Where's the garbage? Where is it? I'm scanning the playground frantically for the canister to catch all of this when it comes up. All of these feelings. All of Aruba. I found one. Stuck my face in it. Tried to vomit up her remains. Her touch. Her smile. Her laughter. I had to get rid of it for sure now. By any means necessary. If I have to become bulimic, so be it. I'll induce this until it's all gone. Derrick came running right over.

"Yo! You all right, man?"

"Bad . . . timing," I managed to let out between heaves.

"I'm not proposing tomorrow, and besides, I thought you of all people would be happy for me," he said. Sounding a little let down. I am happy for him. I just need to get my shit together.

"No . . . bad . . . timing," I said as I wiped my mouth off. Disgusted by the taste. I'm still tasting her kisses. They're a sweet addition to all of this acid. I reach deep into my adrenal cortex. Scan it for an easy lie.

"I ate Chinese for lunch. I was nauseated all through the game. It came right up. At the wrong time," I told him.

"Oh, man. You ate Chinese? Remember how you threw up in the back of my truck the last time you ate all of that MSG? I almost left you on the curb! I was pissed," he said, laughing. I joined him. I remembered. Downed a mouthful of water, swished it around, spit it out with the memory of how our fingers locked so easily. I pulled myself together. For his sake. For mine. Became an equal partner in the conversation.

"But anyway, back to the issue at hand. I know you are, D. Because I know you. But I have to ask anyway. You're absolutely sure about this, right?" He has to be. Who wouldn't want to marry her?

"Absolutely. Like my man Jay said, she's about to get all the keys and security codes."

"She already has them. You've been whipped. Don't act like this is some brand-new shit," I joked.

"That's beside the point." He punched me hard in the shoulder. A macho expression of love.

"Well then, when is the extravaganza? Because knowing you, that's exactly what it will be," I asked playfully. When Derrick's serious about something, he does it up. Real big.

"Oh, that will be months from now. I just wanted you to know that your boy is off of the market." He's beaming.

"There will be riots in sorority meetings, churches, and hair salons from here to Cali! And please, pleeeeease, let me be there when you tell Sharon. I couldn't stand her ass. Oh, and Tracy, too. She was a bitch," I added with a new-found strength. My boy is settling down. I've wanted this for D for a long time. I'm happy. Really I am. If I think of him, instead of her, I'm okay. He spit a mouthful of Gatorade out in hysterics. Even though I'm joking, he knows I'm telling the truth.

"As a matter of fact, the only woman that I've even remotely liked was Taiyler," I said, hyped off of my ability to fake myself out. Act like I wasn't fazed. Like I wasn't ashamed. Needless to say, that was way too much for me. My knees buckled. As soon as her name rolled off of my lips. Derrick caught me. Irony is a bitch that will fuck you twelve ways from Tuesday.

"How many women have I been with, Nat?" he asked seriously. Holding me up. The way you would the guy that's always been in your corner. Your best man.

"Is that a trick question, Dick 'em Down D?" I joked. Feeling my strength return in my legs.

"No, for real."

"Dude, you were going after Wilt's record. But I can say that you were extremely selective through it all. Always top shelf. Always the best."

"I've never been this happy before," he said, almost to himself.

"I believe you, man. But you have to be there for the good and bad times. And believe me, there can be quite a few bad times," I advised wholeheartedly.

"Nat, with Taiyler, I'm trying to be there until there isn't anymore time left!" He grabbed the ball off of the floor, threw it up at the backboard, dunked it, and left it for me to chase.

"Fetch the ball, man. You lost the last one. It's game time."

31

Taiyler

I'm stretched out on my living room floor. On my rug. Listening to Anita. Staring straight up at the ceiling. Calm. Still. Hoping the quiet will allow me to hear myself think. I've had a rough day. A rougher two days. And it doesn't seem to be getting any easier. I almost killed a lady today. Almost killed my relationship a few days ago. What next?

You bring me joy, when I'm down . . .

I love Anita Baker. Her voice is so soothing. So what I need right now.

I was so afraid, when your eyes said . . .
come to me . . .

Now that? That's definitely not what I need right now. Don't need any reminders of him. I gather the strength to get up, grab the remote, and change the disc. Ah, *Blue Train*. Much better. No words. I lay back down, stretched out, and took a deep breath. My cell phone's making the most annoying sound. My ringer's off, so that must mean that I have at least a thousand messages. I leaned over, grabbed it from underneath the sofa, and took a look at the small screen.

Sixteen missed calls. Nothing can possibly be that important. I hit the power button. Now it's completely off. Take that. I don't want to talk to anyone. About anything. I inhaled. Let the green tea aroma from my oil burner fill my nostrils. Nothing should be this hard. Especially not this.

I closed my eyes and let thoughts that have been waiting for me all day invade. If I can ever feel the way I felt last week with anyone else besides Nat, he will be the one. In a few days, he had my entire life story. Stuffed inside his jacket pocket like his favorite paperback. Right next to his heart. Things I haven't even shared with Shala, I was able to somehow find the courage to share with him. My heart spilled, all over the place, like rice. And he managed to pick it all up. Every grain.

I don't know where the comfort came from, but it was so easy to talk to him. I felt like he'd been there for me all this time. Through my mother's antics and grandma's death. Through pointed discouragement and lifetime disappointment. Through it all. I felt so clean. Like I had been born again. I wanted to give myself to him as a gift. In return for what he'd given me. Which seemed to be all of him. At least for a few days. It felt so right. That is until I stepped off of that plane and saw Derrick. Arms outstretched. Smiling from ear to ear. Waiting to wait on me hand and foot. And then it came. The guilt. Driving slowly through me. Like a sanitation truck on a one-way street. It wouldn't move. No matter how much I wanted it to. Until its job was complete.

So I stood there, feeling like the biggest asshole that ever lived. With Derrick's arms around me, the guilt began to suffocate me. Made me feel like even the air I breathed was dirty. It wasn't a good feeling. Not a good one at all. When we got to Georgetown, the feeling started to subside. Derrick, of course, went overboard with all types of food and goodies. Claiming that since we hadn't spoken, he didn't know what I'd be in the mood for. So he had his chef make all of my favorites. We ate a delightful dinner. And he ate an even more delightful dessert. With me lying on my back, twisting in as many directions as there are flavors of ice cream at Baskin Robbins. He is so damn good at that. It makes no sense.

I inhaled. Exhaled. Let my thoughts play Double Dutch in that playground they call a brain. Coltrane saw his way out, and the disc changer brought in another one of my favorites. Stevie. I've been lying here for a while now. *Blue Train* is not a short LP.

If it's magic . . .

As if on cue, my mind raced back to thoughts of last week. Of peace. Of solitude. Of understanding. Of Nat.

Then why can't it be everlasting . . .

Becoming frustrated with myself for relapsing, I wrestled with thoughts that left me twisted like a pretzel. My desire for him is so strong that I can't see past myself. Past him. I thought about our talks. Our walks. I've never felt like this in my life. So close to someone. Yet so far. This afternoon I didn't have to hear his voice to know that he was on the other line. With me. Thinking of me. In anguish. In fever. Hungry. Wanting no more than to share my space. Mental, physical, emotional. It didn't matter to him. Or me. I don't know how I'm going to deal with this. Right now, I feel like a widow. What's that noise?

"Taiyler, open the door!" That's Shala. Banging on my front door like the FBI. Why is she yelling?

"Hold on," I murmured as I headed in that direction with the speed of a tortoise. I unlocked the door. Saw her standing there arms crossed, foot tapping to the rhythm of her anger. She looked me up and down like I owed her money. She's not happy. I don't care. I'm sulking right now.

"Taiyler!" she exclaimed, my back already turned to her. The door's open. I'm on my way back to the place where being held in Nat's arms is okay.

"Taiyler Richardson!" she screamed. She's had enough. So did I with him. Enough to last me a lifetime. Or so I thought.

"What?" I answered dismally. Trying to hide the lifeless tone in my voice. It was a pointless effort.

"You're not answering your phone. I've been at the door for at least ten minutes. What the fuck is the problem? What's wrong?" Her tone softened when she looked into my eyes. Saw what I was dealing with. The soul never lies. Even though I wanted so much to tell her, I couldn't.

"I'm tired. The trip has me worn out. Going to Derrick's last night, then straight to work this morning was a bad move." I hope she buys it.

"Taiyler, don't play with me. You didn't hear the door. And you were right here." She motioned flagrantly toward the messy living room floor.

"I was sleeping."

"Really?"

"Yeah."

"Were you crying in your sleep?"

"No. Why would you ask that?"

"The tissues. Stevie. You know, shit like that doesn't allude to the fact that you're on your way to the club." She's so sarcastic. I'm not even in the mood to reply. Silence.

"Well, I'm calling Grai."

"For what?"

"I'm sitting here until you spill the beans. Period," she said as she removed her cell phone from her black Bvlgari bag. The one with the nickel front plate. One of my favorites.

"Have it your way," I said. As I headed toward the window. Needed an escape. I stared down into my pool from the huge picture window. A thought came to mind. Maybe I need to get out.

"Sha. Call Solange for me. Please?"

"Why?"

"I want to go out. Maybe to one of the jazz poetry spots downtown."

"Taiyler, you need to get this, this—whatever's bothering you—out."

"Shala, I need a drink. That's about it. So call her. Let's go to Bar Nun."

"You don't drink."

"So what! Stop giving me a hard time and set the shit up!" I jumped down her throat. Felt bad. An apology is in order.

"I'm sorry. Please, Sha. I just need to get out of the house. Be around my girls. Call her, okay?"

She hugged me tightly. My best friend. My girl. She feels my pain.

"Okay. Bar Nun, it is," she said as she dialed Solange's number. Maybe this will help. Something has to.

The thick smell of Jonaki's Nag Champa incense was as astute as the group of hungry artists at Bar Nun. Feeding off of groove gumbo.

It's a relaxing form of revolution. A place packed with problems and solutions. The questions to the questions. And the answers to match. Piled up in heaps of broken syllables and sentences. We walked inside, through a judgmental crowd that despised being judged. Priding themselves on their ability to live freely. The artsy crowd is a funny one. Dredded up, dashikied down, passing words and songs like marijuana around the crowded brownstone-turned-lounge on U Street and Fourteenth. We found three seats at the bar. Heard the knots and kinks of Black America being worked out in a grinding blend of percussion, brass, and strings. Just what I needed. Some jazz.

"I forgot how nice it was here," Solange offered. Eyeing a particularly handsome drummer up front.

"I know. Me, too. Good call, T," Shala co-signed. Her eyes traveling in a completely different direction. Toward an Ethiopian sister with short curly hair. Irony.

"So, ladies! How's life?" Solange asked candidly. I think I better let Shala answer that one. She gave me a look that said she wanted to know just as bad as Solange did. Guess that question's for me.

"It's good. Aruba was good. Cleansing. The works."

"Meet any fine island men?" Solange asked. I looked down, took a long sip of my martini, and told a bold-faced lie.

"Of course not! Not on a trip like that. Nothing but old White doctors fishing and scuba diving."

Solange bought it. I think Shala did, too. However, she is not satisfied overall. She knows that I'm not the same as I was when I left.

"So what else happened on the trip, Taiyler?" Shala asked. Her eyes almost daring me to tell another lie. I take her up on that.

"I played in the water all day. Hit a few spas. Read. Did the jazz thing at night on the beach." The jazz thing, that wasn't a lie. Nat and I lay out on the beach, listened to Miles, the night ocean waves, and our hearts. All at once.

"Sounds nice," Shala said.

"I came back so tired. The sun drained me. And I had a hell of a day."

"I bet." Shala. She won't let up. Not even for a minute. I signaled the bartender. I need another one.

Every time the bartender hands me a martini, both Shala and Solange look at me like I have two heads. I'm getting sick of it. Sick of all of this shit. Especially sick of my gat damn phone vibrating. Twenty missed calls. Who is blowing me up like this? For the first time since last night, I answered it.

"T."

"Who is this?"

"Drea," she answered solemnly.

"I didn't know. You haven't called me T in fifteen years. What's up?"

She was exceptionally quiet. As if she was trying to find a way to tell me something important.

"Drea, what? Spit it out." I'm becoming impatient. She must need money.

"Aunt Mae."

"Yeah?"

"She's gone."

"Gone where?" I asked. She's always going somewhere. That lady is always on the go.

"She passed. This morning, she—"

I hung up. I'm in no mood for cruel jokes. I don't believe that shit for a second. I spoke to her when I landed. And Drea hates me enough to play with my emotions like that. An eerie feeling crept through my body. Made me a little nervous. I picked up the phone. Pressed speed dial one. Shala and Solange are in deep conversation about something. Sha looked my way. Tilted her head. Like she was waiting for bad news.

I listened to the phone ring an absurd amount of times. Looked around for a window. Found one. Got up. Walked toward it. Hit speed dial number one again. Glanced down at my watch. She's got to be home. *Jeopardy* is on. It kept ringing. She must be at my older cousin Ella's house. They always visit each other. I located her number in my PDA. I know they have to be over there. Old folks are always at home during the evening. Gotta catch the news. The phone was answered on the first ring. That's unusual. Cousin Ella has what Southerners call a slow hip. She needs at least three rings to answer the phone. And forget about the doorbell. Give her about five minutes. And that's if she's wide awake.

"Hi, is cousin Ella there?" I asked nervously.

"She can't come to the phone right now. May I ask who is calling?" the young voice answered. Sounds like my little cousin Madison.

"This is Taiyler."

"Hi, cousin Taiyler. Grandma is in her room."

"Can you tell her to come out for me? I have to ask her something."

"She said she's not coming out for nobody today . . ." I overheard her mother trying to wrestle the phone from her daughter. Now I'm really nervous. My cousin Shawnie works nights. She should be at work. Not at her mother's house.

"Taiyler?"

"Hey, Shawnie." I tried to sound as upbeat as I could, considering I had a gang of butterflies running Olympic trials in my stomach.

"We've been trying to contact you all day."

Oh, shit. No. This isn't about to happen.

"What happened? My nephews okay?"

"Yes."

"My sisters?"

My phone vibrated again.

"Hold on, Shawnie, I have another call . . . Hello?" It was my oldest nephew. Mike. Screaming like I've never heard him before. Yelling about something he said his mother just told him. Something he feels is unfair. I have to calm this boy down. I clicked back over to my cousin.

"Shawnie?"

"I'm here," she said. She sounded worn out. Weary.

"Mike's on the other line. I have to talk to him for a minute. I'll call you back."

"Okay, T." Everybody's calling me T today. I clicked back over to the sound of my nephew breathing like he was running a rat race.

"Mike, honey, calm down and tell me what happened."

He doesn't cry like this. It must be serious.

"I-I wa-nt . . . my . . . au-n-tie . . . to see me . . . grad—" The end of his sentence was cut off by heaves and sobs that were so big. Too big for my hard-core nephew. He's a complete mess. My phone vibrated again.

"Mike? Hold on, okay, honey?"

He was still bawling like a baby. What the hell is going on?

"Taiyler, it's Drea. Don't hang up. Just listen, okay?"

In light of all the weirdness, I did exactly what she told me to.

"We've been calling you all day. Your cell phone, your home phone.

When we called the office, they said you'd left early . . ." She's using proper English. She's nervous. I tried to keep my mind from wandering back to the first call that I'd answered today. Hers. With news that I would never accept.

". . . and they found her in the bed. With the phone in her hand. Like she was talking . . ." she said, doing her best to hold back hiccups and minute sobs.

"Who did they find?" I didn't hear her. I hated to think it would be bad enough for me to block out. I know I do that from time to time. Shala came over to where I was standing. Gave me a who's-that look.

"Aunt Mae." Silence.

It's difficult to explain the whir of emotion that comes over you when someone tells you that the person you love most in life is dead. It's a mixture of shock, confusion, shock, and more shock. For me, the one that takes over is disbelief. She would have told me if something was wrong. I would have known. Would have made the calls. Would have been right there by her side. Me. Before anyone else in this world. Her baby. Her Muppet. I don't believe it.

"I don't believe that."

"She's at Brookdale. You have to come up, T. Dr. Shalom wants to see you. He's cracked up about it, too."

"I'll come up there, but when I arrive, I'll be happy to tell everyone 'I told you so,'" I answered matter-of-factly.

"Just come up, T. You're the only one listed as next of kin. Everybody's fucked up. We can't even see straight. We need you."

I haven't experienced this sort of kindness from Drea in over a decade. It's scaring me.

"I'll be there in three hours," I said, determined to prove everyone in the family wrong. I have a headache. I hung up the phone to find Shala staring me in the face. Waiting to exhale.

"Sha. I have to go to New York."

"Why?"

"They keep saying that Auntie died. I know that's not the case. She probably went to Atlantic City on a whim, and the woman that they found in the house probably resembled her, but she would have told me if she felt bad, so I know she is still here, probably out playing numbers or something or down the street at her friend's house, the one who grills the fish every Saturday, who gave her that oil for her feet, so I'll be there to find her . . . and we'll go grocery shopping and I'll take her to the drugstore and to the bank and to Sears . . ." I'm rambling. I'm jittery. Just because.

". . . and we'll go to Nathan's to get a hot dog and sit in the living room watching television while I eat all of the Riesens out of the candy dish. I knew one day she had to go, but I know it isn't today, so I just want to get up there and show everybody that I take care of my aunt. I take care of her, Sha . . . wherever she wants to go. I come home. Drive three and a half hours to take her . . ."

Now Shala is crying, too. Over my shoulder. Hugging me tightly. What's wrong with everybody? I said I'd find her! And this will all be washed away. We can go back to sipping martinis.

". . . so all the commotion is for nothing. She would have said something. I'd be the first to know." I must have run out of breath before I ran out of words.

"Oh, my God!" That's Solange. Screaming out loud. Figures. I must be the only sane one in the building. In the family for that matter. My aunt isn't dead. She would have told me. We're that close. I remember getting up in the middle of the night, in the middle of one of her acid reflux attacks. I went right into her room, found her bottle of Maalox, and took care of it. I just popped up out of my sleep. Because something was wrong. I could feel it. No questions asked. Death is much bigger than acid reflux.

"Listen, Shala. Solange. Both of you. Wipe your eyes. Auntie's still here. I'm going up there to take care of things. Prove everybody wrong."

They both stood there with tears cascading down their cheeks. Looking at me like I'd just been released from Bellevue. I know what I'm doing. I know my auntie. She'd never leave me here by myself. Not without some sort of preparation. And then something told me to check my messages. All twenty of them. I stepped outside.

"I'm going to get the car," Shala said. She's really fucked up over this bullshit.

"Cool. I'll be here. I have a ton of messages," I answered nonchalantly.

I skipped over quite a few. Messages from Derrick, Shala, Drea. Cousin Ella. Drea again. My little sister. My youngest nephew. He needs my account number to charge his plane ticket to JFK. No problem. And then there was the one that twisted the knife.

"Seventeenth message. Today, three twenty-five A.M.

"Hey, Muppet . . . it's me. It's late. I'm not feeling too well . . . " She's whispering. I can barely hear her.

". . . my chest is a little tight . . . I'm gon' try to call the docta' . . . " She's coughing. I'm tearing. Feeling the world cave in on all four sides.

". . . been hurtin' since yesta'day . . . didn't know if it was serious o' not, so I didn't say nuthin' . . . I knows how you like to worry . . . I didn't want you comin' up here in the middle of da' night . . . " The line disconnected.

Message eighteen. Three-thirty A.M. *". . . I ain't goin' ta no docta' this time a night. I'll wait till the mornin' time. Hey . . . I love you, Muppet. And stop worrying about me, this ol' lady's gon' be okay. I'm in God's hands . . . You are, too. I'll call you tommorah'. Auntie."*

Just then the possibility hit me. This could be true. The mere thought of it caused the ground to move from underneath me. From side to side. It made me dizzy. And then my phone rang again. I looked at the screen. Cousin Ella.

"Hey, cousin Ella." I was managing at my very best to sound like I didn't believe the shit they were pushing.

"Hey, baby." She sounded tattered. Torn. Like the quilt she made me so many years ago.

"So is it true?" I asked. Not wanting to know.

"Yes, sweetie. It is. She left this earth this morning 'round seven. They said you didn't believe nobody. So I called myself." She wouldn't lie.

"How?"

"They said it was something like a heart attack."

Oh, now I know she's lying. I took care of my aunt's heart. "Where's Dr. Shalom?"

"He got to the hospital before the medics did. We should'a got him to take her in. He didn't waste no time. When he called, he was very upset. Never heard an old Jewish man cry like that."

"How long did the ambulance take to get there?"

"I don't know, baby, but she made it to the 'mergency. She just didn't make it through the surgery. It all happened so fast."

This is a mistake. Got to be. I'll handle it when I get there. The calls, messages. Coincidences happen. I couldn't have lost two people that I love in the same day. Shit doesn't come back that hard on anyone.

"She wrote something out for you. She used to tell me that every time she tried to talk about stuff like this, you would clam up and start crying. So she left instructions for you. Said you were the only one who could handle it. The funeral, that is." And there it was. The magic word. Something about the way my cousin Ella said *funeral* that did it. Brought years of nightmares and anxiety to me on a platter made for homeless dogs. I couldn't breathe. Instead, I hyperventilated. Scared the shit out of her. She started wailing. Shala made a beeline for the curb. Parked. Jumped out. Grabbed a paper bag. I couldn't hear myself over my own tears.

"Taiyler, sweetie, calm down, please calm down . . ." I heard cousin Ella saying as I focused intently on the colors behind my lids. The softness of black. The comfort of the dark. As a matter of fact, I heard so many voices saying so many things. Solange shouting out medical directions to Shala. My mother telling me and my sisters that we weren't going to be shit. My school counselor calling me, telling me that I had to go home, that my grandma had passed. *Hey . . . I love you, Muppet. And stop worrying about me, this ol' lady's gon' be okay. I'm in God's hands . . .* Forget about God. He's obviously forgotten about me. I felt myself succumbing to the best feeling that I'd experienced all day. Nothingness. And the sound of the last voice that I could remember. Telling me that he understood me. That he'd always be with me. In his dreams. I let his soft kisses lull me to a place with no pain. And he held me in his arms until I passed out.

32

Nathaniel

Home sweet home. I've had a hell of a day. As the garage door eased up, I was greeted by the sweetest little angel heaven ever let loose.

"Daaaddeeee!!!" she screamed.

"Hey, princess!" I yelled through the driver's side window. "Move back so Daddy can park, okay?"

"Okay!" she replied, while responding with the little dance she does when she's happy. She's so damn cute. And she knows it.

"I've missed you!" she said as I scooped her up. She threw her small arms around my neck, placed a huge zerbert on my cheek. I smacked one right back on hers. I've missed her, too. When I got in last night, she was fast asleep. So she hasn't seen her dad since he left for a trip that he'd like to forget.

"So what did you do while I was away?" I asked her. She smiled even brighter. I already knew. She had a hell of a soccer game. And even better spelling test scores. I keep up. Those were the first things I asked Kendra about when I returned.

"Guess what, Daddy?"

"What?"

"I scored two goals in soccer!"

"All by yourself?" I instigated.

"All by myself! And I got a one hundred on my spelling test! The hard one with the long words! And Mommy bought me this! . . ." She raised her arm to show me yet another bracelet. This one with streams of pink and blue charms dangling. Making five-year-old music. This girl loves jewelry. I feel sorry for her future husband. Husband? Perish the thought.

"Wow! I'm so proud of you, Nile! Daddy's baby is a genius!"

She beamed. Patted me on the head as I carried her inside. I know she wants to know what I brought her back from Aruba. But she never asks. She hardly asks for anything. She has everything that she along with every five-year-old from here to Botswana could possibly need or want.

"Want to see what Daddy bought his little princess?"

She squealed an absurdly loud yes as Kendra came up the stairs from the laundry room with her hands full of whites and coloreds. Looks like she's having an average African American day.

"Hey, honey!" She gave me a very healthy kiss on the lips. Emphasis on *very*. She looked radiant. I wondered how she managed that with her schedule. We stood face-to-face. Taking each other in. Admiring the qualities about each other that sent us down the aisle eight years ago.

"Babe, you look good." I winked. She batted her eyes, ran them down the length of me, stopped at the place that she calls her own, and made a reservation for later on tonight. I grinned.

With Nile in between us, rummaging through the tissue paper that her natural gemstone tiara was wrapped in, we stared at each other. Her wanting to rescue me from what I'm sure she could tell was a hard day, and me just wanting her to rescue me from myself.

"So how was it?"

"I had a crazy day," I answered. Nile let out a stream of laughter and screams that indicated how pleased she was with my gift. I know my angel. Both of them.

"I know. But the trip. How was it?" she asked.

"It was business. On the beach instead of at the office," I offered weakly. She didn't push. Probably thinks that I'm just fed up with work in general and don't want to talk about any of it. If she only knew the half. Honestly, I just need to feed off of her beauty for a while. Allow her to remind me of how urgent it is that I get my shit together. Of why I need to give her all of me all of the time. Sell Nat to Kendra for more than the twenty-four dollars the Indians made off of Manhattan. While Nile tried her tiara on, I dug through the red-and-white-striped Little Switzerland bag and handed Kendra her gift from me.

"You know you didn't have to, babe."

"I know. But I think you'll like it," I said as she carefully untied the perfect silver bow wrapped around the box that housed her classic Phillipe Charriol timepiece. The look on her face said it all. Made me happy as hell.

"Oh, my Lord . . . but I never told you I was looking at this one. How did you know?" she gasped, two rows of beautiful white teeth creating a frame for an equally matched pair of lips. Only a fool would risk all of this. Not even a fool.

"A little birdie told me." I looked at Nile proudly, who at this point couldn't care less about anything that wasn't related to her tiara. I took her to one of our favorite jewelry stores downtown a while ago. Asked her what she and Mommy look at when they come. Because I know they do. And she pointed this one out. Can't believe the girl was fucking right. She's going to be a mess when she gets older. We've created a little monster.

"Thank you, sweetie. Thank you so much. You won't regret this either." She gave me one of the sexiest looks that a woman could possibly give a man. The one that leaves your mind totally detached from your dick. She noticed mine jump. Signal for her to come on over. Have a drink or two. She chuckled at that outward display of feminine power. Decided to put me on ice.

"Dinner is almost done, Nat. Wash up. Nile!" she called over toward where a pint-sized version of herself was sitting.

"Huh?" the little jeweler answered without looking up for even a second.

"Put your tiara away and come help Mommy set the table!"

I heard Nile let out a huff. She hates that. But she doesn't complain. She doesn't have a choice. Kendra will check her little ass immediately. I watched her solemnly rise, trek to her room, and back to the kitchen like she was a candidate for death row. And it was her turn. I had to laugh to myself. Guess she takes after me in that sense.

I plopped down on the sofa, kicked my feet up on the ottoman, and relaxed. Allowed the aroma from the kitchen to calm my spirit. There is no doubt in my mind that I will get control of this situation. I have too much to lose. And I don't have a choice. Even if I did, my family means the world to me. And as a man, I will preserve their safety at all costs. Physically and emotionally. There's nothing else to say about it.

I'm in the basement. After dinner. Reclined in my recliner. Horn in hand. Fingering through mental pages of age-old bebop. Resting on the standard that suited my mood. "Alabama." Trane. As I raised the cold brass to the challenge of a grueling two-minute, twenty-seven-second masterpiece, the mouthpiece fit my lips perfectly. Just like those of a particular woman that I remembered. One that I struggled to forget.

I inhaled. And exhaled what I hoped would be the remainder of an equation that I could not solve. The dreariness of my mood came floating out in a collage of some of the world's best arranged notes. Coltrane. His life was not nearly long enough. I transitioned from "Alabama" to a more melancholy "What's New" to a purging "After the Rain." Thinking back. After her words brushed my ears with colors of spring, I became brand new. Against my will. She had my heart. Fucking thief. Enter anger. Enter Bird. I moved to a tormented "Be Bop." Measure after measure. Letting my wrath pour out of my lungs through the vessel I called Lucille. Until it tumbled out in staccato notes furious enough to antagonize the air. Chase it around the room.

She felt like heaven. I felt like hell. "Blue in Green." A masterpiece. Miles was too much of a perfectionist. I broke stride on some of the Miles-specific notes as I let my mind take me to my own hard bop lounge. Where I was allowed to fuse my thoughts and beliefs with those of the greats. Contortion. My confusion fucking the erratic emotions of tormented talented trio. Twisting all types of music and song, theirs and mine, I played to an extremely rapid rhythm. One that called my fingers to move so fast that it gave me no choice other than to focus on them rather than her. That was my preference. Not to think of her in that way. Ever again. I'm almost there. Although I'm glad, the notion of it is disparaging. Sort of like the way it felt on the plane. No one likes good-byes. Whether I liked it or not, upon my leaving this room, it will be official. Taiyler never happened to me. I'm working this all the way out. And that's urgent as hell.

Using three fingers, I sketched her face on canvas made to hold the most vivid expressions of love created in music. "In a Sentimental Mood." Her favorite. My thanks to her for an inviting week. For a cleansing weekend. For peaceful moments. For exotic seconds. For opening my mind to piano ideas. Saxophone thoughts. And organic percussion. In heartfelt measures. Played just for her. All in quarter notes.

"Nat!" Kendra came tearing down the narrow stairway that led to my haven of reflection. I put her down. Both women. Lucille and Taiyler.

"Yeah?"

"I've called you five times! Derrick just called. Upset about something! Something major!"

"Did he say what it was about?"

"No. He sounded really down, though." She sympathized with my boy who never shows his emotions outright. Especially to women. At least not that she knew of. I could tell she felt bad.

"Okay, babe. I'll find out what the problem is," I said as I located my cell phone on my pool table. Getting some rest for a change. I scanned the ice-blue illuminated panel. Hit the right button for Derrick. Speed dial number six. His line number. The ringer sent waves of uneasiness through my abdomen. I wondered what the problem could be.

"What up, D?"

"What up, man? Shit is fucked up."

"Kendra said you sounded down. What happened?"

"Shala called me. Taiyler's aunt died early this morning."

"Damn." I felt like I'd been kicked in the chest.

"She won't talk to me, dude. Shala said she was fucking hyperventilating and shit and that they took her to her office so that one of her partners could monitor her asthma . . ."

She has stress-induced asthma. She told me that she needed to refill her albuterol or whatever she called her medicated spray pump while we were away. I wondered if they took care of that. I wondered if Derrick knew. The struggle to resist asking was beating down on me harder than the news of the death. I hoped she was okay. At least functioning. I can't even imagine how she's feeling. I pulled my gray HU sweatshirt over my head. Headed for the front door. I need some air. More than that, I needed to see for myself that she was okay. The more I digested the description of her emotional digression, the more urgent that need became. I fingered the business card that she gave me in Oranjstad. Located the address. Thought about it. She's hurting. More than anyone would ever know. I know because I feel it. With that, I hopped into my truck. At that point, there was nothing I could do to stop myself. Believe me, I tried. As the cool breeze hit me hard in the nostrils, I continued to listen to Derrick spill the beans.

". . . and now she's home. Shala was with her making arrangements for them to fly to New York, but Taiyler's partner said that she was in no condition to fly anywhere and told them that she couldn't go until she saw him tomorrow morning. She's fucked up, man . . ."

He sounded so distraught. I didn't know how to help. I was feeling woozy myself. I shook it off. Concentrated on what was in front of me. Scrolling upward like credits at the end of a film. On one of our live conversations abroad.

> *"My aunt Mae is my bread and butter. She'll be in the front of the fridge when it's full, packed with groceries . . . and when it's empty, she'll be right there in the back. Next to the spoiled milk. The only thing left that'll feed you . . ."*

In light of heavy thought, streetlamps can be mesmerizing. As I watched cars go by me in whirs that seemed to resemble colorful laser beams, I realized what this meant for her. And felt that sever my already severed heart. As much as I'd hate to admit it, I'm hurting for her. Her bread and butter. She probably loved that woman more than she loved herself. It looked like three o'clock on my speedometer. I needed to slow down before Prince Georges' county police found a reason to put a bullet in the back of my head. Once you hit one hundred miles per hour, anything goes. A flash of Taiyler hyperventilating reflected off of the glare of my windshield. And I floored it. Fuck the police. I felt that uncanny tug at my spirit as all of the compassion that I could muster was funneled in her direction. I forgot Derrick was still talking. I have to snap out of it. He's upset, too.

"And she won't talk to me, man. *Me.* She hasn't said more than a few words to Shala since she came to."

Whoa. Came to? Okay, she's strong. This I know. But this may actually be too much for her. I wiped my eyes on the back of my lint-balled sleeve. This sweatshirt is on backward.

"She passed out?" I asked weakly. Delivering way more emotion in that reply than I wanted to. It went unnoticed.

"Yeah. A few times. Shala said she was okay, though. Said she sleeps most of the time. I went over there. Knocked. Called. She's not coming to the door. Not answering my calls."

I watched the streetlights go by in a collection of seasons. Feeling like an entire year before I got to where I was headed.

"So she's nonresponsive," I said to myself. Thinking out loud.

"Yeah. I don't know what to do," he answered as my phone signaled that someone else needed my attention. I wondered who.

"Hold on, D. I have a call," I said as I ran up the huge brownstone-style steps. Taking two at a time, I got to the top and waited. When I realized the implications of what I'd done with my boy on the line, I got nervous. Began to panic a little. I was scared of myself.

"Nah, man, you go ahead. I'll just keep trying," he said as we disconnected. I hit the FLASH button.

"Hello?" I answered expectantly. Found myself waiting again. No response.

"Hello," I offered again. I know who it is. I spent all of last week studying the rhythmic patterns of her breathing. I don't need to hear her. Just the rhythm. No sharps or flats. Just quarter notes.

"I know, Taiyler. I heard. You don't have to say anything. You can't describe it. Don't worry. You don't have to," I said as I pulled the phone away from my ear. Glanced at the screen. Private number.

"Taiyler."

Nothing. Nothing at all. I just wanted to know if she was okay. Breathing easy. If not, I'd be happy to lend her my breath. For as long as she needed it.

"Open your door."

"She was all I had," she whispered weakly. Finally. La Princesa speaks. She sounded exasperated. I was crushed.

"Open your door." This is not a dream. This was real. Knowing that she was on the other side of that door, without me being able to see her, made me itch. I'd rather bathe in poison ivy.

"She was everything." Another whisper. Stronger this time. The dead bolt turned. Lamp came on. My heart soared. Sored.

"Open your door."

"It is open," she said as she swung the large wooden plank wide open and stared at me. Eyes puffy. The red overwhelming the gray. No sunset today. I wanted her to know that I wasn't referring to the door that physically separated us. I meant the door to her heart. I want her to let me feel this with her. Alleviate some of what I'm seeing in that sea of clear crimson. It took a minute, but eventually she understood. Because she fell into my arms and cried a bayou. And I cried a river. For seasons that felt like years.

"It wasn't supposed to happen like this . . ." The interpretation from the muffled sounds coming from the groove of my neck seemed to be accurate.

". . . I didn't answer the phone . . ." she mumbled almost incoherently. I understood, though. I understand everything racing through her right now. Because I feel hopeless. Overwhelmed. Confused. I feel it all. With her almost lifeless body dangling from my arms, I navigated through her foyer, and then what I believed to be her den or living area with ease. Almost as if I had been here before. I sat on the sofa. With Taiyler still in my arms. Holding her like a newborn baby. Until she cried herself to sleep. And woke up. And cried again. Rediscovering her slumber in between gallons of tears.

"I have to . . ." She attempted to alert me to a detection that I'd already been privy to making. She has to throw up. I know. I've by now carried her to the bathroom. Held her over the toilet. Wiped her still beautiful mouth and lips. Even with her lunch smeared all over them.

"I'll be okay," she said. I know she will. That's what I tell her.

"I know."

"You can go if you need to," she said in between small sips of chamomile tea. I like how she's become comfortable in my lap. Balled up like an Eskimo in an igloo. I continued to spoon-feed her sips of warm tea.

"Take these." I offered her a few different chemical compounds. One for her headache. One for her asthma. One to help boost her energy. She smiled a weak one. But it was a smile nonetheless.

"Thanks."

"And you know when I'll be ready to leave."

"I do?"

"Yup. When you tell me about your last dream." I wanted to divert her attention away from reality. Take her back to a place where she's free to be. She smiled. A real one. She fidgeted a little, making herself more comfortable in my arms. I adjusted my embrace. Sometimes I hold her too tightly.

"Where were we?" I asked. Decided to help out.

"In Cairo," she replied. Her voice was so hoarse. It reminded me of what she was facing tomorrow. I cringed. Decided to make tonight paradise. I used my fingertips to massage her scalp. All ten of them.

"What happened to Harlem?"

"I don't know. This time we were far away . . ."

I watched her eyes roll at half-mast. She squinted, as if struggling to retrieve the content of the dream without fault, amidst the fury of relaxation that she was experiencing.

". . . and we were doing the unthinkable."

I smiled slyly. Finally, she had a sexual dream about me. She tilted her head upward. Smirked. She was still striking. Even with puffy eyes and asthma.

"And no, not *that* . . ." she said, referring to sex. Reading my mind as usual. She continued.

". . . we were having breakfast. Watching the sunrise. In the Valley of the Kings. And you gave me this," she said as she held her arm up to display her favorite silver cuff. The one she told me she bought from a Harlem street festival years ago.

"Wow. Guess I have good taste," I joined in.

"Uh-huh."

"So what else?"

"You told me a lot. About your family. About your aspirations. A lot of the stuff I already knew," she chatted away. I enjoyed the smile in her eyes. My plan worked. At least for now. But I knew it would. I knew her.

"And did I say anything else?" I asked. She paused. Looked at me intently. It flushed a warmth through me. For real.

"Now, *that* I can't tell you," she said as she cupped the back of my head. Extended her neck upward. Placed an even kiss on my lips. I was so excited that my dick couldn't even get hard. Not that I wanted it to. I was ecstatic just holding her. Seeing her smile. Carrying my share of her burdens on my back. I lay horizontally on the sofa. Allowed her to stretch out on top of me. Spread herself all over me like jelly. She's so much smaller than I. I'm amazed at how it seems as if she covers every square inch of me.

As I helped her move and shift and stir herself into comfort, the sandman called. He wanted to fight. I didn't. So I gave in. And began delivering the contents of my own dream. Live. Direct. In full color. She was there as usual. But we were far away. And I was telling her that

I loved her more now than I ever had before. While she tugged and pulled at that silver cuff on her arm. The outline of a butterfly marked in stones of the earth. Jade, turquoise, amber, and quartz. She said thank you a thousand times in a thousand different ways. Lying atop me, using my heart as her pillow. Allowing the rise and fall of my chest to lull her to a place with no pain.

33

Shala

I hate funerals. The last one I attended had to be my grandma's years ago. I was four years old. And all I remembered was the fact that she didn't look anything like I remembered. All of the rhetoric about her being in a better place and resting in peace went over my head. How could she possibly be better if she looked worse? I made a four-year-old promise to myself not to attend any more funerals. For the majority of my life, I've stuck to that. However, this one is a major exception. Aunt Mae was like a grandma to me. So I had to go. I wanted to. No doubt about it.

"How are you doing?" I looked over at Taiyler, who was doing about ninety on the New Jersey Turnpike.

"I'm okay. I just want this over with."

"Cousin Ella gave you the list she left, right?" I asked. Saw her eyes well up again. She's been crying for two days straight.

"Yeah," she answered while I reached into the glove compartment for more tissue. She's not going to be able to do this alone. I need to see that list. Get started on some of the less personal items.

"Where is it?"

"What?"

"The list."

"It's in the side pocket of my bag. The Kieselstein. I jotted it down while she read it to me over the phone. It's sloppy as hell," she said as she motioned to the backseat of the BMW truck. I wished that she would have let me drive. She said that she needed to. That the road gave her something else to concentrate on.

"This is it?" I asked as I unfolded a yellow sheet of paper.

"Yeah," she said as I allowed my eyes to scan the list of to-do items. Mine welled up after reading the first three words. *Armstrong Funeral Home.* I took notice to any task that didn't involve a signature or special approval and scribbled my initials next to it. The rest I'd leave for Taiyler. I wanted to help her out as much as I could. Especially after yesterday. She scared the shit out of me. At first, she went delirious. Didn't believe that it had even happened. Then she hyperventilated. I thought that I could handle it, but when she kept passing out, I decided to take her to her office, where I knew her partners would still be.

She wanted to leave on a flight out last night, but Dr. Samuels prohibited it. Said she needed rest first. And vitamins. And a loading dose of asthma medication to help prevent an attack. So I took her home, prepared to stay the night. Make sure my home girl didn't join her aunt before her time. To my surprise, she wanted me to leave. Said she needed to be alone. And that she would call me in the morning. Taiyler had to almost physically kick me out. I just couldn't see leaving her in that state. But when she's made up her mind, that's it.

I spent the rest of the night packing, canceling appointments, and on the phone with Derrick, who was going crazy. He spoke to Taiyler once, but she had since turned off her phone and was not coming to the door. I felt sorry for the brother. Needless to say, she must have needed that time alone, because she looked one hundred percent better this morning. Like she had been refreshed overnight.

"I don't know if I can do this," she said as we turned onto Linden Boulevard, crossing the Canarsie-Brownsville border.

"Taiyler, you can make it. God will strengthen you," I replied as we made our first stop at Brookdale Hospital. I wished that I was as confident as I sounded. I know her. She needed time to process something like this. We parked up front. She threw on her lab coat and headed for the building that she claims kills more people than it saves. At first, I wondered why we stopped here first instead of at the house. But I know Taiyler. She wants to get to the bottom of things. Get it all straight from the horse's mouth.

"I'm Dr. Richardson here to see Dr. Shalom. He's expecting me," she said without the slightest indication that her world was upside down. Before the man could even be paged by reception, he'd made his way down the ninth-floor corridor and into Taiyler's arms. She was not moved. She won't be until she gets the truth.

"What happened?" she said flatly. She's ready for the kill. He looked at her carefully, absorbing her anger in gulps and blinks. She wants to slit his throat. He knows it.

"Come with me," he said as he took her hand in his. Leading her down the hallway to a reality that she was not ready to face. None of us were.

We lined up outside in the rain. Cousin Ella, Taiyler's sisters, nephews, Solange, Michelle, myself, and a few older relatives. Behind us was a line that rivaled that of the Million Man March. Family and friends galore. From all over. Florida, South Carolina, Virginia, California, Germany. Tennessee, Chicago, Kentucky, Georgia, and Connecticut. Bishops, English teachers, Civil Rights activists, janitors, musicians. Charter buses and vans. David Dinkins, Al Sharpton, Bishop Brown, Priscilla Wooten, Cornerstone Baptist Church, Berean Baptist Church, the People's Baptist Church of Brooklyn. Mount Zion Baptist of Mississippi. Israel House of Prayer for All People. Elohim Sabbath Temple. And that was what I could count myself.

Then there was Taiyler. Sitting inside. Alone. First pew. First seat. She'd been here since seven this morning. The viewing didn't begin until twelve. I leaned over the white velvet ropes, past the strong-faced Fruit of Islam brothers who volunteered to guard the body. They'd been out here since seven yesterday evening. And hadn't moved an inch all night. Dressed in white. Seven of them. Three on either side of the wrought-iron gates, one blocking the entrance. All this for the woman who came to visit them in prison, supported their causes in the community, bought every single issue of the *Final Call.* Even though she was Baptist. I strained to see inside. I was anxious to see if the powder-blue dress that I picked out for her fit. That's the color she wanted. Guess I'd find out soon enough. I held my stomach as a swarm of killer bees invaded it. I don't know if I'm ready for this. I felt a tap on my shoulder. Almost caused me to jump out of my skin.

"How is she doing?" It was Derrick. Looking like he had slept just as much as we did.

"Honestly? I don't know. She's been in there for five hours."

"By herself?"

"That's what she wanted, Derrick."

He was quiet. Thinking.

"I'm going to get back in line. I'll see you inside," he said as he headed back to his place in the quadruple doubled lineup.

"Okay, D," I answered. My eyes still inside the funeral home. Suddenly, as if they knew exactly what we needed, one of the church groups started singing. Clapping. Rejoicing. And it spread down blocks, around corners. People sang out of windows, from the inside of bodegas, basketball and handball courts. All types of people. Old, young, Black, Spanish, Jewish, Italian. Celebrating Auntie's eighty-six years of life. She knew, loved and helped everybody. And everybody loved her.

> *I dun' lived my life fo' Christ (well),*
> *Ma' three score and ten lived right (well) . . .*
> *I'm . . . gon' . . . be wit ma' Jesus,*
> *I'm gon' be wit ma' Jesus,*
> *In my mansion in the sky . . .*

They went from that to "Take Me Home, Lord" to "Jesus is the Light," until the funeral director signaled that they were ready to begin the processional. Mike, Taiyler's oldest nephew, slid onto the organ. His younger brother sat right next to him. Both took turns playing their hearts out for their great-great-aunt. All of her favorites. While folks poured out by the thousands to say their good-byes. The boys were out of tissue, and we hadn't even started the service yet.

"Aunt Shala. Can I have another box?" That was Travis, the youngest one.

"Sure," I said as I reached underneath my seat and grabbed a box of Kleenex for him.

"Thanks," he said sniffling. Wiping his eyes and nose. Taking it over to the organ. Sliding the box across the top for his brother. Okay. This is going to fuck me up. My leg started trembling. I'm doing my best to hold back the storm of tears welling up inside. I looked over to where Taiyler was sitting. And that did it. Sent those tears cascading down my face faster than I could wipe them. I've never seen her look so tattered. So broken. Out of all of the things in her life that could have broken her, this did it. She just sat there. Almost as lifeless as the woman lying seven feet in front of her. Gazing at the white-and-silver casket. With the little old lady inside. Powder-blue dress, still smooth skin, and all of Taiyler's spirit. Bound up in the pine that encased her.

Taiyler looked like a widow. A miserable combination of Coretta, Betty, and Jacqueline. Victims of the ultimate heist. The unexpected loss of a most prized possession. A most valued gem. A life lived in love. And for the first time since I've known her, I'd determined that this may be the one thing that she'll never get over. I just hoped that I was wrong. Her sister Drea was a complete mess. So was her younger sister. Cousin Ella shed her tears as the older generation usually did. With dignity.

People got up. Told tales of Aunt Mae's love. Of times she took them in when they were homeless. Fed them when they were hungry. Stopped fights with kind words. Visited all of her friends in nursing homes, while their own families neglected them. They spoke of her candor, her wit, her ability to say the right thing at the right time. Mike's turn to play his last song for his aunt was the straw that broke the camel's back. Donny Hathaway. As soon as those hundred or so light keystrokes fluttered into the air from the organ, people lost it.

I've been so many places in my life and time . . .

I know your image of me, is what I hoped to be . . .

There were no vocals. But we were all singing it. The recessional. As cousin Ella held her running mate's hand for the last time her frail frame shook. Drea almost passed out again and had to be carried outside. Dr. Shalom's face was as red as a tomato. Aunt Mae was one of his first patients right out of medical school. Forty years ago. Travis walked up there, took his platinum and diamond chain off, placed it around his aunt's neck, and walked out. His eyes barely open. And Taiyler. She just sat there.

It was the saddest thing I'd ever seen. When her turn came. Everyone had been up, paid their respects. Except for Auntie's favorite. Her Muppet. As Derrick and I helped her toward the front, everything finally hit her. And she stopped walking. Started sliding her feet across the floor. So we carried her. And she fought us the entire way. She didn't want it to end. Because then, it would all be too real. As long as she sat there, first pew, first seat, she could pretend it was all a dream. I know her.

"She's not moving her feet," Derrick whispered to me.

"I know. But she has to do this. Just hold her up," I whispered back. As we approached her everything, she did allow her feet to move. But it wasn't to aid us. It was to prevent us from getting closer. She kicked and punched and resisted as much as she could. Tried to wiggle her way out of our grasp. Until we got right up on her bread and butter. One good hard look at her. And then it stopped. The fight. The resistance. The world did. And it allowed them to have their last conversation. In spirit. She leaned in and tried to hug her. After a few attempts, she settled for a kiss on the forehead. My heart is breaking. I couldn't make out what she was saying to her. I was barely able to hold myself up at this point. All I know is that we were still there two hours later. All five of us. Mike on the organ. Derrick and I on either side of our girl. And then there was Aunt Mae and Taiyler. Talking like old friends over tea.

My phone rang this morning with a jubilance that was unwelcome. I had to wake Taiyler up, get her into the shower, and get her to the burial. I cracked the door to her aunt's bedroom, peeked inside. She's sleeping peacefully, with Aunt Mae's housecoat wrapped tightly in her arms. I hated to have to bring her back to reality. Decided to stall that. Answer this call.

"Hello," I answered softly.

"Hey, Shala. It's Derrick."

"Hey, D. How are ya?"

"I'm okay. How is she?"

"Good now. She's sleeping."

"What about you?" he asked.

"Me? I'm doing as expected. It hurts."

"I know. I went through something similar with my mom. Taiyler did a better job than I did," he said as if he were reminiscing on the entire event at this moment. I didn't know his mother was deceased. And that he took it that hard. All that macho. A façade.

"Wow. I'm sorry."

"It's okay. Listen. I called to tell you that I'm going to propose to Taiyler sooner than we talked about."

"Really? What brought about the change?" I asked.

"I know that she has you, but I don't want her to suffer alone through this. Focusing on her family being dismantled instead of acquiring the joy of working on a new one. That's what I did. I sulked for years. Until I met her. Besides, she'll need something happy in her life. To offset the tragedy. I'm ready. I just hope she is."

Shoot. I hope so, too, I thought.

"When do you want to do this?"

"As soon as I get the ring. I checked today. I just have to pay an extra hundred or so to jump the wait list."

"Hundred dollars?" I asked like an idiot. He chuckled.

"I wish. Naw, hundred thousand," he answered like it was a hundred dollars after all.

"All right, let's talk about this when we get back. I actually think it may be a good idea, as long as it isn't too soon. Maybe half the time. Three months instead of six," I assured him. Heard him let out a huge breath.

"Thanks, sis."

"No problem," I replied to my future brother-in-law. He's the one. I'm sure of that.

"You ready, T?" I asked as I put her X5 into reverse. I'm getting her out of here. No burial for Taiyler today. She can't take any more. I decided that as soon I witnessed her on her knees in the shower. Nope. Enough is enough. She nodded her head up and down in response to my question. And kept nodding. Didn't wave to the fifty or so family members who were outside of her aunt's Brooklyn home waving to her. Seeing her on her way. Southern tradition is strong. Even in New York City.

"Okay. You know everything is taken care of, and these things usually don't last longer than five minutes, so don't feel bad, all right?" I relayed, attempting to assure her that it was okay not to attend the burial. She nodded incoherently again. She understands. Besides. Aunt Mae had everything taken care of. Everything paid for. All of her paperwork was in order. There were no outstanding debts. At all. It was almost like she knew her time was almost up. Anything that Taiyler couldn't handle, cousin Ella did without reservation.

As we pulled off, she finally raised her arm and waved in their direction. She had long since lost her voice. I watched her mouth *good-bye* and *I love you* over and over before finally concluding that she wasn't referring to any of her relatives. Her stare was aimed at the top porch. At the wooden rocking chair that floated back and forth in the wind. The one she bought for her aunt years ago. I slowed down. Realized that she still needed time. While she mourned, I rummaged through piles of old ideas, sayings, and parables. Searching for the right one to make things all better.

"T, she's still with you, you know that, right?" I reasoned. She shook her head back and forth in a violent series of no's. I have to get her into Dr. Henderson's office as soon as possible. Like tomorrow. She may actually snap.

"Taiyler, God won't place any more on you than you can bear." There. I heard my mother say that one all the time. She continued to shake her head. Meanwhile, I'm running out of ideas. God, please send some help, I prayed. Hoped He'd hear me.

As if on cue, Taiyler's cell phone rang. And this call she actually answered. As soon as she heard the voice on the other end, she smiled. The first one I'd seen in days. And then she broke down. Cried from the Verrazano Bridge to the Delaware Memorial. Slept in between spells. And whoever this was stayed on the phone with her the entire time. Whether she was sleeping or crying. Sometimes they talked. Sometimes they didn't. The sparkle in her eye was oxymoronic. I wondered where the fire came from. I wondered who this was. Who could touch her like this? Whoever it was, she'd never mentioned them to me. And I wondered why.

PART FOUR

34

Derrick

Interstate 95 was the shit today. No traffic. No buses. No anything. Just me. I broke out the platinum Ferrari. Topless. Taiyler hasn't even seen it yet. I keep it stored in the garage underneath my home. Cruise it when I'm feeling special. Today is a special day. I picked up her ring. Celebration is in order. Next Saturday evening, Taiyler will be mine. For real. As long as she says yes, it will be all good. Right now, I'm on a victory tour. I'm calling and visiting family and friends like it's my first Thanksgiving home from Hampton. I pulled out my cell phone. Dialed K's number. He answered on the first ring. That's a no-no. I have to school this brother.

"Yo-Yo!" I belted out our frat call.

"Yo' girl, yo' wife, yo' ho!" he called out in response.

"If she ain't on a leash and you left her alone . . ."

"We fuckin' her on our flo'!" We both finished in unison. The good old frat days. We lived them out as long as we could; now it's time for real life. And as my man Morris Chestnut said, real things.

"To what do I owe this honor? Shouldn't you be boning that beauty of yours?" K asked me. It unnerved me to hear him refer to Taiyler in that way. I mean, we always have thrown our sex lives around like an old football, but she was different. I was, too. My guess would be that it would take a while for the guys to see it. Rome wasn't built in a day.

"Hey, hey, don't talk about my future wife like that!" I was trying to clue him in to the reason behind my call.

"Future wife? Only if you're Solomon. And from the looks of it, D, you're coming damn close!" Kalonji belted out. He's laughing. I'm not. Damn. Was I really that bad?

"I *was* coming damn close. I'm a changed man now," I protested.

"And I'm from the show-me state," K challenged.

"Nigga, you're from Alabama. And you live in Jersey. And I've changed. For the better. Taiyler's changed me," I said earnestly. I forgot. Nat's the only one who's ever seen this side of me. Earnest. Humility. Honesty. I have to give K a minute. Only a minute, though.

"Well, if she can do that, then she must have an *S* engraved on her pussy."

Okay. That's it.

"Mutherfucker, don't you *ever* refer to anything on my fiancée's body again. Ever. Or my foot will be so far up your Black Power ass, you'll be flossing with Timberland laces. Hear me?"

He got quiet.

"You're serious."

"I am."

"You know you called her your fiancée, right?"

"I am aware of that. I'm holding a ring in my hand worth more than some of the buildings I own. I am well aware of it." I let him digest that for a minute before continuing.

"She's the one, K. I'm going to ask her to be my wife next weekend at my house. And I want you and Garvin to be there." Had I told him in person, I would have had to check for a pulse. He was too quiet. Until it hit him. I'm giving up the life.

"You are dead fucking serious! What did it, man? Why her?" he asked in a voice that told me this was hitting him hard. It was okay, though. That was an easy question to answer. The words came tumbling out of my mouth like gymnastics.

"She complements me in every way. She's brilliant. She's insanely beautiful. She can and will take care of me without me having to spell shit out. I trust her. She's spiritual, and I don't mean in the fanatical churchy type of way. She knows and loves art. Latin authors. Cuban revolutionaries. African American revolution. She's old school. New school. She can walk any supermodel right off of the runway. She looks great in Gucci. But won't hesitate to buy something funky from a thrift store. She always leans over to unlock the driver's side door for me. She's thoughtful. She has her own shit. She's never asked me for anything. She appreciates what I give her. She appreciates what I don't. She stops to smell the roses, man. And because it's time." I could go on, but the notion was coupled with the fear of him falling asleep on me.

"Wow," was all he said. He's in shock. I should be the last one of the crew to do this. I know that. I just met the right one.

"So, next Saturday evening. My house. Be there at eight. It's a black-tie. Bring a chick that you're trying to fuck. That type of shit turns them on. She'll have her panties wrapped around your face before you can even get to the corner."

He snickered. Guess I'll pass down a few pearls. I won't be needing them anymore.

"Congratulations, man. I just can't believe it. Hey, you told Nat, right?"

"Of course. A while ago. He's the best man."

"Cool. So do you need anything?"

"All I need is for her to say yes, K. That's all I need in this life right now." As I rounded the corners of my old neighborhood, I thought about what I'd just said. Those were the truest words I'd ever spoken. I scanned the streets in between a group of young guys playing football and girls braiding hair on stoops. I didn't see Tony. I *really* need him to watch my car. Fuck five dollars. He'll get a fifty spot today. The smell of money must truly be intoxicating. Because the six-foot-two, one-hundred-forty-pound dude came tearing around the corner. A thirty-year-old impersonation of the Roadrunner. Dopeheads. The shit is funny, but it ain't.

"De-rrrrrri-ck! Lemme watch cho' caaaaa!"

I had to laugh. I enabled the motion detector on the vehicle. You never know.

"What up, Tony?" I dapped him up. Pulled him to my chest. We grew up together. He's a man. Dopehead or not.

"Yo! You straight cuuurrry-in niggas wit' dis, mane!" Tony motioned toward the Italian racing masterpiece.

"You're foolin', T. Just watch it for me," I said while sliding a fifty to him in the give-and-go hand-to-hand motion I learned while selling the shit he was on when I was young. Thank God for Hampton.

"Oh, shit! Thanks, D!" he exclaimed while looking down at his hand as if I'd given him a rare rash.

"Get some groceries with that."

"Oh, fo' sho'," he said sincerely. I hope he meant it. Reminder. I have to put him in rehab before the fall comes in. I swung the door open to the shop. From the smile on my face, interrogatory glances erupted from patrons and barbers alike. In the hood you can keep a scowl, but niggas want to know what's up when you're smiling from ear to ear.

"It's a beautiful day in the neighborhood . . . a beautiful day for a neighbor . . . would you be mine?" I sang, slapping Willie on the back.

"Boy, I ain't inta no gay shit," he exclaimed, expelling laughter from each of the large leather chairs.

"Guess what, Willie?" I asked, sounding like Nile.

"What, boy?" He couldn't care less.

"I'm doing the damn thing. I'm getting married."

The shop gathered an eerie silence. Clippers were turned off, throats were cleared. They're all looking at me like I'd lost it. Was I *really* that bad?

"Boy, it's too late in the day to be comin' up in here actin' foolish!" Willie scolded. I had to chuckle. Damn. Maybe I was that bad. I reached inside my jacket pocket. Pulled out my proof. Cracked the box open and watched the shop's volcanic eruption. "DAYUM! WHAT THE FUCK! YO, D, WHAT TYPE OF SHIT IS THAT! THAT SHIT CAN'T BE REAL! SHE MUST BE A SUUUPER FREAK!" It was so loud in here, with so many different responses, that I hadn't even noticed my pops sitting in the back right corner. With his jaw dropped.

"Pop!"

"Derrick!" He raised himself out of his chair. Placed one hand in mine. The other around my back.

"I just called the house. You weren't there."

"'Cause I was here, fool!" he answered impatiently. With a smile on his sixty-one-year-old frame.

"Pop. I found her. I'm going to marry Taiyler." And for the first time other than my mother's funeral, I saw my pop's eyes line with tears.

"She's wonderful, son. We have to talk."

"Yeah, I know," I answered to both comments.

"I'm proud. I knew she would do it."

"Do what?"

"Break you, Dot." He's the only one that still calls me Dot. I was a frail boy. With a big head. Resembling a large-sized dot. I replayed his comment in my head. Finally, I got it.

"Break me out of my shit. Like Ma did you. Right?" I was still a humble chap in his presence. My father took care of me in every way imaginable. He taught me how to be a man. He let me know it was okay to cry like a girl when we lost my ma. He cried, too. He hustled to get me through Hampton. Sold boot-legged liquor. Did what he had to. I owe him happiness. Grandchildren. Whatever. However. I owe him my life. As I watched him raise his handkerchief to his eyes, I felt my own tears hit my shoes. I'm happy he's happy.

"Allllll right! With all of the sentimental shit!" Willie broke the silence. "It's time to party up in this here! Derrick wit' one woman! This damn near needs ta be a national holiday!" Willie exclaimed as one of the young Howard boys cranked up the volume on the speakers. I couldn't believe it. Niggas—I mean brothers—actually started a mini soul train line. They were cutting up something serious. Celebrating the news like it was their own. If I had ever sensed a connection with my brothers, it was then. A huge hand slapped me on my left shoulder. It was Kane.

"Yo. Hop in the chair, D. It's on me," he said, displaying the first full smile that I'd ever seen on his usually apathetic face. Whoever said that Black men don't support one another obviously wasn't Black. Or never did anything worth supporting. If anyone in this world will support you while you're down, it'll be your brothers. Just ask Magic, Jordan, OJ, Iverson, and even the King of Pop himself. Michael. We just do it in our own way. And you just have to work a little harder to gain respect in our hoods. Our stakes are higher. And so are our standards. The Howard young buck came up to me cheesing.

"So she had everything. Right?" he said, his usually hardened stance melted by admiration. It was then that I realized we were being watched closely. Especially by the younger generation. He thought all of my bed hopping was cool and shit, but *this* was what he admired. What he looked up to. I could tell by the glow in his eyes. And instantly, I wanted to snatch back every torrid story I'd told about how I fucked and freaked a woman. Even if she was trifling.

"So I know we're all invited to the wedding."

I turned around to face the direction the voice was streaming from. I'll be damned. It was my boy. My real boy. Before Nat. Before

Hampton. Before the crew. We'd saved each other's lives too many times to count. In drug wars. In gang fights. Our life was a struggle. I hugged him like the long lost brother he was. It's been too long.

"Trey. What's up, man? Where you been?" I asked him. Ashamed that I had to.

"Doin' my thang," he said as he motioned to the front of the shop. His Ferrari was identical to mine. Except his was black. Mine was silver. We always did have the same taste. The only difference was that I had the opportunity to get out. He didn't. So he made the best of what he had. To feed his family. Hustling is nothing but untaxed capitalism. IBM. Phillip Morris. Pfizer. The block. Same shit.

"Oh, yeah. You're in the wedding, man. I didn't give a shit if I had to send out a warrant for your ass. I would have found you," I joked.

"Warrant? Nigga, you foolin'." He laughed. We walked outside together. Compared stats on our vehicles. A favorite pastime of ours.

"So tell me about this woman. Because, if I know you . . ."

Damn. Him, too? I shook my head. I was bad. Really bad. I remembered it clearly now. He almost shot me for looking at his sister. Made me promise to stay away from her. He looked at me with raised eyebrows.

"Nah, I'm just thinking back, man . . . just thinking back . . ."

My last stop of the day. Shala and I are having dinner at a restaurant in Georgetown near my home. Sequoia.

"So you got it?" Shala bopped up and down in her seat, squealing like my five-year-old goddaughter. Women. They get so emotional.

"Yeah. It's in the box," I said, pointing to the medium-sized box and bag sitting on top of our table facing the water. The breeze felt good.

"Oh, my God! This is gorgeous! But I thought you chose an emerald cut?"

She gave me a quizzical look that helped me answer the question quickly. She must be looking at the pendant.

"Check the other box," I directed. The look on her face said it all. She got it right this time. She held one hand over her mouth. The other was holding my baby's ring. Shala hasn't said a word.

"So do you like it?" I asked nervously. She has me shaken. Maybe it's too big. Too gaudy. If she doesn't like it, Taiyler damn sure won't. And it will go right back to Harry Winston in a New York minute. In what took her all of about sixty seconds, she finally gave me an answer.

"Derrick . . ."

"Yeah?" She's killing me.

"I've never seen anything this beautiful. Oh, my God . . ." Her eyes were the size of saucers. Lined with French coffee tears.

"So you think she'll like it?" I asked in affirmation. She was still staring at the rock.

"Oh, my Lord. D. This is straight out the mines. Straight from the Motherland. This is an actual rock. Like, it's equivalent to the size of the ones on the streets," she evaluated. Her eyes were parachuting from the top of the emerald-cut stone to the bottom. I'm happy she loves it. We can move on.

"So everything is straight for Saturday?" She didn't hear a word I said. Women's fascination with diamonds. It's a weakness.

"Shala!"

"What! Can I have some time with the rock, please!" she answered mockingly. She's going to be fun to have as a sister.

"Saturday, Sha. Is everything good?" I really wanted to know.

"Yeah. Don't worry. It'll be easy. She isn't getting out of bed for anything other than therapy. She'll be there. I'll pick her up. Make sure she's presentable." She was still gawking at the ring. It filled me up with pride. She's a hard one to impress. Like her best friend.

"Now, let's replay this. I'm going to tell her that I'm out to London on business. So that she won't suspect anything," I stated as I began drawing out the battle plan in my head.

"And I'll remind her that you want her to look in on your house while you're gone," Shala joined in.

"Why would you have to accompany her to my house to do that?" I asked.

"You're right. That was idiotic. Scratch that. I'll figure something out. Don't worry, I'll have her there at nine," she assured me.

"Are her sisters and nephews coming?" I asked. I was converting the rooftop of my home into a model of the top floor of the Eiffel Tower. I'd contacted the best waiters and maitre d' in the city. A few of my partners from the New York Philharmonic were looking me out. So was Will Downing.

Even with all of the hype, I still preferred the event to be quaint. Private. Only family and extremely close friends. Especially at a hundred fifty dollars a plate. More than anything, I wanted her folks to be involved. They were going to be my family, too. I wanted to holler at her nephews. Let them know that I planned on taking good care of their aunt. Her sisters, I figured I could deal with; the youngest, Dion, and I hit it off while I was in New York. Her mom, well, she declined the invitation. I was actually surprised when her older sister, Drea, accepted hers. Since Taiyler really didn't deal with her father, Aunt Mae would have been the one whom I'd ask for her hand in marriage. But that fell through, of course. So I sent up a short prayer. Asking God to tell her that Taiyler was in good hands.

"Yeah. I believe so. I told them that you were paying. That was all that Andrea needed to hear . . ." She pulled out a yellow legal pad. Went down a short checklist. I can see why she and Taiyler are close.

"Everyone's flights are confirmed, you have the catering, Nat has the wine and music, right?"

"Right."

"The guests get in at eight. If anyone important is late, i.e. flights delayed, they'll call me. I'll call you. We'll wait."

I love efficiency.

"Okay. So it looks like we're on. Six days from now," I finalized. Felt a twinge on my upper lip. I'd broken a minor sweat.

"Don't worry, D. She'll say yes." Shala glanced at the colony of beads gathering on my brow. I'm shaken. She gave me the reassurance that I needed to get up from my seat.

"I hope so, Sha. In my mind, she's already said 'I do.'"

35

Taiyler

I'm staring at an alarm clock that I've never had to use. Blinking. Flashing reality in my face. No more wake-up calls. To my left was a full bowl of cold chicken soup that Derrick had sent over for me. His favorite. I hadn't eaten anyone else's soup other than Auntie's, and I don't plan on starting.

Derrick has been really sweet through all of this. He's made sure that I've eaten every day and checks on me in person during work hours. His lunch hours, breaks, and any extra time he could find has been spent over here. Pampering me. When he threatened to cancel his business trip to London yesterday, I made him go. No sense in all of us losing our lives to this. Mine was still at Cypress Hill Cemetery where I'd left it. Besides, I needed time to myself. Away from people. So that I could try and get my mind right.

My fleeting thoughts landed on Shala. Lord knows I wouldn't have made it without her. I'm so glad that Sha thinks on her feet. There was no way I could have watched them place my bread and butter in the ground. No way. I would have ended up doing something extreme like jumping in there. And thinking that it was okay to be at the bottom of a six-foot ditch, sitting on a pine box. As a niece, I was just mourning my aunt Mae's sudden death. As a physician, I was showing strong signs of temporary insanity. I know that for sure. I was incoherent. Delusional. Confused. Rambling. By DSM-V guidelines, I could probably have killed someone and gotten off. I guess Shala noticed, too, because she scheduled and paid for all of my therapy. My appointments started three days after we returned from New York. Even though she had to drag me there kicking and screaming, I can't say that it hasn't helped. Dr. Henderson is wonderful. Attentive. Had I seen her after my grandmother passed, I would have healed much faster. Wow. I still can't believe it even happened.

I fingered my aunt's white-and-red-monogrammed handkerchief. My nephew's rendition of "A Song for You" running circles around my mind. Chasing salt water out of my eyes.

We're alone now, and I'm singing this song to you . . .

Although therapy is helping, on days like this I couldn't move if I wanted to. The feelings that I've experienced during the past few weeks are in such severe divergence that I truly feel ripped in half. Loss and love. Love lost. It has been entirely too much. Even for superwoman.

I shifted around in a bed that was damp with optical dewdrops. It used to house pleasant dreams. Pleasant thoughts. Now the only thoughts that my spirit danced a happy jig to were the ones of Nat. Of us. Of him massaging my scalp. Raising that warm spoon to my lips. Collecting my tears. Relieving tension that would have been the cause of my demise. I can't believe that he came over. I can't believe that he did it before I asked him to. I felt myself smile inside. For the first time since I'd last heard his voice.

In the beginning, I questioned whether or not he felt the same way. Mentally. Physically. Spiritually. Did he tremble when I walked by? Did the room spin when I looked into his eyes? I questioned my own faculties. Why couldn't I control myself around him? Why did it seem as if my mind, the one and only thing that I've ever relied on to control my heart, had turned against me? In the middle of all of this chaos? Right now, my heart is in the driver's seat. And my mind is leaning out of the passenger side window headfirst, like a cocker spaniel. Letting the fresh air hit it right in the face. I've been dealing with this for six months now. Trying to fend off thoughts of us together. Of him. What he's doing while he's not talking to me. Laughing with me. Finishing my sentences. What he thinks of when he sees me with his best friend. If he dreamt of me every night. Thought of me every day. If he tried as hard to forget me as I had him. And why it was so damn hard. Why couldn't I kick the smell, memory, taste, and touch of a man with whom I'd never slept with? I wondered if he thought the same thoughts. Who am I kidding? Of course he did. I fingered the buttons on my phone. Studied his number in Braille. Placed my fingerprints on each one. So they could trace him back to me. Back to us. The time between rings is testing my patience.

"Hello there," he answered. I can see his smile. I'm sure that he can see mine as well.

"Hello."

"How are you today?"

"Better."

"Because?" He posed a question that made my heart drip honey.

"Because I know you care."

"And?"

"Because you know I do, too." I heard him breathe a bright row of thirty-two teeth. I can't take it. I need him here. I need a healing.

"You like strawberries, right?" he asked.

"You know that."

"And green grapes?"

"Yes. You know that, too," I answered. My body calling for more than a massage from this man. He can make me forget myself. I struggled not to. I changed the subject. For once since things came tumbling down, I could do small things like that. I could think.

"Tell me about your last dream." I borrowed the million-dollar request of his from weeks ago. The one that made me smile in the eye of a storm. He laughed nervously. I know that his are more vivid than my own. Especially in the physical sense. It's his turn.

"I'm at work."

"So what. You can tell me. There or in person." I didn't care.

"And you know that my dreams are very . . ."

"I know."

"Are you ready for that?"

"I was ready at the grocery store." I'm being bold as hell. I want him. I want to feel him so damn bad that I'm ready to risk it all. Just for a chance. Even if it is in third person. If I have half of the effect on him that he has on me, he wouldn't be able to tell me no.

"All right," he surrendered. I felt his heart quicken while he rummaged through colorful thoughts of us. Of me. I decided to help him out.

"Where were we?" I asked him. Superimposing his question. Making it my own.

"On the One."

"On the what?" I asked.

"The One. Pacific Coast Highway. Malibu Beach. You wore a white silk scarf. Like the one you wore to La Trattoria."

"And what else?"

He didn't say anything. I felt him grinning from ear to ear. It made me blush. Guess that's the answer to my question.

"The scarf was amazing," he said in repartee. I blushed. So he's seen me naked. No wonder he's never asked me to take my clothes off. I wanted him to.

"Was it? And what else was amazing?"

"The sea. We rode through the mountains. Admiring the sunset. And then you asked me to pull over. The road was too narrow to do that. But you couldn't wait . . ."

I watched my breasts rise and fall. Envisioning the fingers of a trumpet player all over them.

". . . so you faced the sun. And I faced the mountains. And you drove me crazy." He stopped. As if he were close to gathering the sanctity of the moment, rescuing it from the past. Bringing it to the future. To the here and now. I can help him with that.

". . . I thought we'd crash, but we never did. I drove you like Earnhardt. From Malibu to San Diego."

"How was it?" My questions were bolder than ever. But I needed him more than I'd ever remembered.

"I don't remember. I passed out," he said feverishly. Made me want to pull my hair out by the roots. Remember what Langston said about a dream deferred. Enough with the dreams. I wanted to wake up with him. Tonight. Tomorrow. Forever.

"Nat."

He was still quiet. Basking in the afterglow.

"Yes?"

"I have a space for you next to me." Silence. And that was all that I needed to hear.

The soft knock on my front door made me dizzy. The sight of him made me irresponsible for my actions.

"You never answered me," I said, taking his hand. Drawing him into me. Feeling his bones play pitter-patter with one another. Forehead to forehead. Again.

We were wound up in the smell of sacrilegious thoughts and hopeless passion.

"Answered what?" he responded in a wave of hot kisses. From my forehead to my eyelids, to the roof of my mouth.

"How . . ." Oh, my Lord. His kisses took me back to our night in Aruba. At Dera Gai. But this time, I wouldn't be able to stop the inevitable. He picked me up. Placed my back up against the wall in my foyer. Allowed me the pleasure of positioning myself on the spot that made me want to give him the keys to my house.

"How . . . did it feel . . . Nat?" I feared that would be the last complete sentence from either of us tonight. He stopped his lips from running their ragged race all over me. While I struggled to lick whatever was left of his essence off of mine, he brought his eyes to me. On priceless china. He has something to say.

"Let me dress you. I want you to get out of the house."

He's a lunatic. Out of the house? Now? He was obviously unaware of the fact that my nipples were about to burst into flames. I don't know how. He was staring right at them. Leaving me out of the conversation. Men.

"Excuse me?"

The man whose girth I could feel whether he was inside me or not jolted, averted his eyes. He seemed to be able to get his game back. Guess I'm losing mine.

"You've been in this house for weeks. Auntie wouldn't have wanted that. Let me dress you." He was serious. Carried me on his back up to my bedroom. This is the wrong place for me to have him right now.

"Where are you taking me?"

"It's a surprise," he said as he waltzed into my walk-in closet. Fingering the numerous wooden hangers, he pulled out a dark brown, linen, half-sleeved top and the matching crop pants. Good choice.

"I have to get into the bathroom. It's been a while." He didn't hear me. I turned up my nose to my own pungent scent while he fumbled around in the most intimate space of my home. I watched him grab towels. Turn knobs. Peak his head out of the small steam-filled room.

"You ready?"

"For what?"

"To wash that ass of yours. I'm not going anywhere with anyone who prides themselves on practicing French hygiene." Oh, now he's full of jokes. I noticed how his smile could light up my entire bedroom. It was interesting. I hurled one of my pillows at his head.

"So that must mean that you'll be joining me." I couldn't hit the brakes. Not today. I'm not in the driver's seat. My heart's racing tonight. Without a helmet.

"You'll see," he said as he lifted my gown over my head. Tied my hair up. Laid me down. In a small sea of boiling water and bath crystals. I monitored the burning of the sage-scented candle behind him. Nat. His name rang bells up and down my spine. Tonight's the night. I can feel it.

"Lie back." He sat on the side of my Jacuzzi-sized tub. I did as he said. Saw the softness in his eyes. The concentration. The way he separated the beads of perspiration on my brow from the drops of bathwater. Brushed them into their appropriate places. As if he could tell the difference. His eyes stopped at mine. I recognized the look. The look of love.

"No more dreams, Taiyler. We have to figure this thing out," he said as an array of lush green grapes and plump strawberries emerged from beneath him. I longed for the grapes. So that I could sneak a taste of his fingertips.

"You're right. We can't continue like this," I relayed between bites. The water was perfect. So were his fingers. I stood up. Let him continue to wash my body of all common sense. It was surreal. The water cascading down my thighs. My loofah has never known me so well. The lathered mesh of soft plastic ran a slow race all over my body. He cleansed me. Shaved me. I saw the fever in his eyes. He's enjoying it. As much as I am. It's amazing. How focus, willpower, determination, and self-control suffer the same type of death as Amadou Diallo. In the presence of love. We both know what we need to do. We're strong. What happened to our strength?

"Tell me a secret." He wrapped me up in one of my oversized Lauren towels. Placed me on the edge of my bed. Ran his shea-buttered hands up and down me freely. I'm in awe.

"You know all of my secrets," I replied. The articulation of the phrase itself exhausting me. He stood me up. Slid my linen top over my head. Laid me down. Pulled my pants on. Massaged my feet. Picked out my sandals. Brushed my hair. I didn't have to do a thing.

"You're keeping one from me." His piercing stare ripping through me. I searched my brain for an intelligible answer. I had none.

"I don't know, Nat," I said as we skipped down the stairs. Pausing to collect my image at the life-sized mirror in my foyer, I was pleasantly surprised. I haven't looked this good in a while.

"Yes, you do," he said as he turned the key to the ignition. Instinctively, I turned to the window. But this time, my escape, my comfort, was on the opposite side. My eyes found themselves at the left corner of my lids. Staring at the nape of his neck.

"A secret," I thought aloud. I could tell him that I love him. I refrained.

"A secret," he replied. Sometimes lying's easier.

"I used to pee in the bed." I laughed out loud. At the absurdity of the comment. He did, too. We turned into the parking lot of what looked to be a small nightclub. I'm a little confused.

"You said you knew how to step." He noticed my confusion.

"How to what?"

"Step. Chicago style. Don't cop out now." He toyed with my pride. Dancing. It's intimate for me. I do it well with someone I like. Even better with someone I love.

"No cop-out here. Just make sure that you can keep up," I said as a couple in their mid-forties sauntered past us. Drenched with sweat.

"Oh, believe me, I can," he replied, heading straight for the dance floor. Surveying the room, it seemed to be filled with older couples. People who looked like they had weathered the storm. Together. I watched the floor become crowded as the midtempo stomp-and-clap beat of "Kwah" hit us hard. Right in the chest. You have to move to music like this. Anthony Hamilton's voice makes you want to plan a family reunion. Just so y'all can dance.

I wanna tell you what you mean to me . . .

Nat grabbed both of my hands. And on the downbeat, we both dropped. Our feet shuffled to the rhythm. His strong hands guided me as he spun me around to the circular melody of Roy Hargrove's horn. We were in sync. In harmony. Balanced. I didn't have to look anywhere other than into his eyes to know that he had me. I wouldn't trip. I wouldn't fall. We've done this before. I was having a ball.

He blushed as I mouthed the words to the soulful tune. I was singing to him. It felt nice. Natural. The next line was mine. From him. I watched his lips move. Watched him mouth words that allowed me to see his feelings on sheet music.

I would do anything for you . . .

I had to laugh. He delivered the words right back with sincerity, but with a playfulness that had me captured. Sweating, dropping, and grooving, the last verse was ours for each other. I got down like my auntie taught me to.

I had to figure out how I was going to tell Derrick. I had a lot to figure out. My cell phone buzzed in my bag. After a few seconds of playing cell hide-and-seek, I found it. Saw that Shala was calling.

"Hey, girl," I said as Nat dragged me by the hand to an adjoining room with a small band performing on an even smaller stage.

"Hey. You talk to Derrick lately?" Reality is a ton of bricks.

"No. Not since yesterday. Why? Is he okay? He's not due back from London until Sunday." I was rambling. Nervous. I should be. I'm cheating on him.

"First of all, calm down! Second of all, where the hell are you?" she asked. I had no answers tonight. Not even for myself. This is fucked up. Well, at least I am, for now.

"I'm not exactly sure." And that was the truth.

"What?" I could tell that she couldn't really hear me over the sound of the band. And I was thankful for that. Because it was my out.

"I'll call you back, Sha. I can't hear anything."

"I can't take any calls; I'm at a pharma dinner. But listen, I need you to be dressed tomorrow night by eight o'clock."

"Why?" I yelled back.

"Just because. Don't ask," she answered as she hung up. Wow. Guess she wants to get me out of the house as well. Nat looked like he wanted to know who it was, but was too ashamed to ask. For obvious reasons. I obliged him.

"It was Shala. I think she's taking me somewhere tomorrow night. Wants me dressed by eight." I replayed the audible contents of the conversation to him. Witnessed his expression turn from inquisitive to utter alarm. The upper lip I loved so much quivered. I wanted to know what was bothering him. I had to know. His anguish has become my agony.

"What? What's wrong, Nat? What's on your mind? Please. You can tell me." I cupped both hands around his face. I wanted him to look at me. But he wouldn't. He was willing himself not to. I couldn't read his expression. At first. But I did know one thing. What I saw I didn't like. He looked surprisingly distressed. Like he'd remembered something important. Something close to being forgotten. Something he almost wished that he hadn't known.

"Nat." I called his name as I had so many times before. As I wanted to tonight. He appeared to be stunned. Staring at the stage. I demanded that he tell me why. Immediately. All of a sudden, as if instantly brought out of a strong hypnotism, he snapped right out of it.

"Taiyler. I have to get you home." His voice was arctic. Acidic. For the first time ever, I felt removed from him. Distant. I wanted him back. I wanted whatever was taking him away from me over with. I was still under the gun. Still hypnotized by his presence.

"What? Tell me what the problem is, Nat."

"We have to go. Now," he said, his hurried stance almost knocking his chair over. And that was it. He said nothing else. For the rest of the night.

36

Nathaniel

It's Saturday morning. I tossed and turned all night. No dreams. No sleep. No anything. Today's the day. The proposal. And to think that I actually forgot. I'm beyond asking what's wrong with me. I'm beyond wondering what my problem is. I'm beyond misunderstanding my feelings. I know what they are. Where they come from. What they're doing to me. I know love. Never in a million years did I ever think that I would fall in love with anyone other than my wife. Never. But here it is. Strong. Deep. Pushing me to my limits. A strange love it was. Selfish. It didn't care about me. My family. My friends. It just stormed me with all of its artillery, while I sat peacefully on the banks of the Ivory Coast. Trying to find new ways to make myself more of a man for my family. It betrayed me. Confused me. Shackled me. Knocked me out. Trapped me in a vessel that would transport me to a land that I would be forced to notice. Build. Claim. I felt stripped of my roots.

I flipped my pillow over. To the cold side. The hot side was damp with tears. In the past few months, I've teared up way too many times. Like a homo's first time. She ripped a hole through me that left my heart bleeding when I wasn't with her. She fucked me. And I somehow became a bitch in the process. I couldn't be a man. Men don't lose control like this. I felt Kendra shift her body. Move it closer to mine. She had to have noticed my despondence. She waved her ass around my hot spot in circular motions that indicated she was ready to begin our Saturday morning ritual. Mr. Magic is still lying there. Looking out of place. Like an extra on a video set.

"Baby, can I have you this morning?" She's in a playful mood. I'm not. She climbed atop me. Mr. Magic is a punk. He'd have to be a little harder to even be considered flaccid. Kendra took one look at me. Slowed her roll. Stopped it.

"What's the issue, Nat? What's wrong honey?" she asked sincerely. And it killed me. How do I answer this?

"I don't know . . ." I don't want to hurt her. But I want to be honest. I owe her at least that.

"You've been in a slump for a while now, baby. Is it work?" she inquired. I shook my head.

"Your mom?"

I shook it again. How am I going to tell her? She caressed my forehead. Made me hate her for loving me so much. Made me hate myself.

"Nat. Ever since you came back from Aruba, you haven't been yourself. Whatever it is, you can tell me, baby."

That was it. That was all he needed to hear. Aruba. Mr. Magic gave Kendra's dark, thick pubic hair the ol' salute. She took that as a sign of her getting through to me. I know she did. An image of the sunset in someone else's eyes flashed before me.

"Uhmm . . ." Kendra moaned as I entered her. Visions of that someone's mental and physical nakedness ran marathons through my mind.

"Nat . . ." My wife of eight years breathed my name as if she owned me. I wanted her to. But I'd sold the rights to someone else. As I held on to the roundness of her ass, she pumped like her life depended on it. And visions of Taiyler's body pent up against her foyer wall, leaned backward in her tub, of me tracing her loofah around her most sensitive parts, flooded my psyche.

"Baby . . . oh, that feels so good!" Kendra screamed. I tried to focus on giving her the pleasure that she so deserved. But my own thoughts were being held captive in small spaces. I couldn't shift them. I couldn't move them. They were centered on Malibu Beach. On Taiyler riding me into oblivion. I let all of that tension loose. Emptied it into my wife. And felt an all-time low. I've hit rock bottom.

"Honey, guess what?" Kendra asked. Bright eyed and bushy tailed. She needed that release.

"What?" I asked dryer than powdered eggs.

"I have a new patient. A woman. She's actually a physician."

"Really?" I attempted to mask my indifference. It worked.

"Yes. A Black one. Very accomplished. About our age. Reverend Matthews's daughter's best friend."

"Uh-huh."

"Well, anyway, she's a very strong woman. Suffered some heavy losses. She seems to rebound quickly. I guess she had to. She's provided for her entire family for so long . . ."

I listened to her go on about her new patient as she usually does when that person has touched her heart in some way. When she accidentally forms a bond with that person.

". . . and she's been through so much in her life. I see so many people with problems. Some are more critical than others. But this one. She could write a novel."

"Really," I stated more than asked. I was still basking in my indifference. Selfish mutherfucker.

"Really. Well, I think that I've located her problem. It's not what she thinks. I'm excited about that."

"That's great, hon."

"I know it is, listen. She came in for one thing. She's dealing with multileveled loss. Attachment issues. They extend throughout her childhood. But her issues in the present have more to do with love than anything else. She's deeply in love. She can't express it. She can't act on it. She won't. Even as it's eating her alive. She won't. Because of the way that she was raised."

"Uh-huh." I'm listening. But I'm not. She continued.

"The guy is married, and from the looks of it, the love is a two-way street. He's just as much crossed up in it as she. The things that he'll do for her . . . even as a professional I have to fight back the urge to run out of there. Come home and tackle you . . ." She chuckled in embarrassment. "But neither of them seem to be scandalous enough to sleep together. And it's ripping her apart. Causing a cascade of issues. Although it's honorable it's heartbreaking. To find your soul mate and not be able to love them. It's sad."

"What are you going to suggest?" I decided to add a little more to the conversation than I had been.

"As her physician I'm not going to suggest anything. But I will help her find her way to a solution. She needs to confront this thing head-on. Make some decisions. Because the direction that she's headed in now will only add to her ruin. She needs to be honest with herself. And acknowledge the direction in life that she wants to take in love. It's evident that she's done it professionally. But she needs to reassess some things personally. That I'm sure of. He seems to offer her that no-holds-barred love that she became comfortable with as a child. And that's more of a *personal* observation than a professional one," she added for clarity.

"Well, it sounds as if you have your work cut out for you," I assessed. She's so diligent in her work. In her life. I'd rather hurt for the rest of mine than to hurt her. Period.

"Actually it's not that bad. I discovered that one of my stockbrokers has serial killer potential," she said and laughed. I did, too. My attention shifted back to the matter at hand. Tonight.

"Kennie. Are you coming tonight? You know Derrick's getting engaged."

"Oh, my! I forgot! This will be a landmark. I have to bring a camera. No one's going to believe me. Yes, I'll be there. But I have to turn in early. Get Nile ready for tomorrow. It won't be late, will it?"

"No. Eight o'clock. That's when it's supposed to go down," I answered.

"Great. I can stay for an hour or so. Leave Nile at Ma's. Hopefully they'll begin on time." She popped up, threw the comforter off of her, slipping her panties back on one leg at a time. And I developed a funny feeling in my stomach. I knew that tonight would be it.

Derrick is a genius. As I peered upward from the rooftop, maybe about a good seventy feet north was the pinnacle of the Eiffel Tower. As we browsed around the brown steel appendages, no one could figure out how he had it done. And he had the nerve to borrow DC's most premier fine dining establishment for the evening. The waiters were familiar faces from The Palm. As were the staff and maitre d'. He said that he wanted to whisk her out of the country, but feared that no one would believe that he had actually asked her to marry him. So he brought Paris to us. With a little touch of Washington to make us feel at home.

Butterflies the size of hawks circled my abdomen. I was nervous as hell. For him. For her. For myself. Either way, I was walking away from the situation. Derrick deserves his happiness untainted. Since I couldn't add to it, I settled for not taking from it. Bringing Kendra along was the icing on the cake. Introducing her and Taiyler would seal my commitment to making things work. The right way. I'll get over this. Somehow or another.

Kendra grabbed my hand.

"This is so romantic. I honestly didn't know that Derrick had it in him," she acknowledged.

"I know. He went crazy with it. Check out the New York Philharmonic." I pointed out the gentlemen of classical music dressed in their finest black-and-whites.

"And, babe! Look! That's Will Downing!" Her eyes grew large with surprise. Oh, shit. Now, that's a surprise. I didn't know Will would be here. And he's going to sing? That's some shit. I located Derrick sitting in the corner. Looking like he did right before we crossed the burning sands into our fraternity. Scared shitless.

"Kennie. I'm going to go over there and see about D." I navigated carefully through each of the white-linen-covered tables, the instruments, the fountain. He looked up.

"Nat. My main man." He dapped me up, and to my surprise initiated our secret fraternal handshake.

"My back," I said, feeling like Judas. I gave his woman a bath last night. She won't open up to anyone but me. I know her thoughts before she thinks them. Her words before they're spoken. I love her. And so does he. But he has the right to. I don't.

"So it's here. And I have to say, Nat. I couldn't have come this far without you. You made it okay to be me. Backed me up when I needed it. Held me down. I just want to say thanks, man." That made my stomach turn.

"No problem." In light of the situation, that was all I could offer. What do you do when you despise yourself? Just then, what had to be Taiyler's sisters were escorted to one of the nine tables surrounding the Philharmonic. The looks on their faces said it all. This couldn't *possibly* be someone's home. Derrick noticed them being seated.

"Be right back, man," he said, heading in their direction. I watched him pull a seat up and charm the pants off of a younger version of Taiyler and her older sister. He made them feel at home. That's D. Knows how to handle the ladies. Before he left the table, he and the older sister were doing the bump. From Taiyler's description of the two boys, what had to be the eldest of her nephews, Mike, waltzed in.

Gave Derrick a pound. He was a tall one. D directed him to a seat in the far corner. Ten minutes later, Travis, a shorter version of Mike, with Taiyler's eyes, appeared at the round table of manhood. And they lamped about in what ended up being over a twenty-minute conversation. Derrick is doing this the right way. I need to follow suit. Man up. My observations were interrupted by a sly hand traveling across the back of my neck. Kendra wants to dance. The horns. The harp. The light percussion. The striking view of the city. I have to admit, it was all intoxicating.

"Wow. This is bringing back memories," Kendra reminisced. The sway of her hips. Her arms thrown carelessly about the back of my head. She was relaxed. It felt good. I can do this.

"Yeah. It does. Remember when I asked you?" I did. I recognized the familiar twinkle in her eyes.

"Of course. We were in New Orleans. Had left Sweet Lorraine's, were on our way to Decatur Street . . ." she recalled.

"We hopped out of the cab. Walked the cobblestone, right into the middle of the French Quarter. Right into the middle of the street. Where the Second Line was playing." Remembering makes me warm. "I got on one knee—"

"Both knees . . ." Kendra interrupted. I always forget that part.

"And asked you to spend the rest of your life with me. Right outside Café du Monde. In front of only, say . . . a few hundred folks." I recollected memories old enough to have begun the fourth grade this fall. She nibbled on my ear. I felt a shiver of delight run through me. And I thanked God for it. I was coming to terms with myself. With my reality. We danced a slow groove. An old one.

"Honey, what time is it?" Kendra asked me.

"Eight-fifty."

"I have to leave in a few. I told Ma that I'd pick Nile up at nine forty-five."

"They should begin shortly," I assured her. My heart jumped at the notion of Taiyler walking through that door at any minute. I wondered how she would look tonight. I suspected pure radiance. Derrick had Shala take her to B Natural, for an all-day spa treatment and shopping at Tyson's Galleria. She's under the impression that it's a girls' day out. Ending with her presence at one of Shala's black-tie pharmaceutical dinners. I wondered how she would take the truth.

"Hey, everyone . . . they're downstairs!" Kalonji yelled. He was ap-

pointed the rooftop lookout for the evening. Just in case Derrick's
phone lacked reception from the roof and its new-found appendages.
I shot a quick glance at D, who was sharing a quick moment with his
pops. He nearly jumped out of his skin when his phone rang.

"Hey, Jean!" he yelled out at the maitre d'. "Please escort my lady
upstairs. You know the rest." As everyone scrambled into their appropriate positions, I began to feel queasy. I gulped that shit back down.
I'm a man. My wife appeared beside me with an anxious look in her
eyes.

"Wow. I'm so excited for him. Nat, what's wrong?" I guess she noticed my barflike glaze.

"Nothing. I'm just nervous for my boy," I said, studying the second-
by-second illumination of the elevator lights . . . 2 . . . 3 . . . 4 . . . 5 . . .
6 . . . The pixied ding of the floor-arrival alert alarmed me to no end.
Here she comes. Her emergence from the steel box was no less than
defunct. It wasn't them. Derrick looked let down. He pulled out his
cell immediately. Meanwhile, Kendra insistently tapped me on my
shoulder.

"Nat. Nat. Hon! I have to go. It's almost nine-thirty. It's at least a
forty-five-minute drive to Ma's from Georgetown. I'm late. And it's
past Nile's bedtime. Plus, we have an early service tomorrow. Tell
Derrick I'm sorry that I missed it."

I placed a kiss on my wife's cheek. Damn. I need her here to do
this.

"All right. I'll tell him," I said as I fumbled with the keys to the
truck. I can get a ride home.

After her hurried exit, I sat down. Spent some time alone. Assessed
my feelings about all of this. My capabilities. Weighed will against ability. Character against desire. Wondered which of the quadruplet
would prevail. Which ones I still had control over. I've never possessed the will, character, ability, or even desire to cheat on my wife.
Ever. To love another. With or without sex. Somehow, all of that got its
ass beat voraciously. The longer I go without seeing or hearing from
Taiyler, the more ravenous I become for her spirit. For her touch.
Feels like I've been holding my urine from Maine to Miami. When
I'm not around her, it hurts. I wondered how I would be able to force
these feelings down the toilet in a plastic baggy. Wondered if they
would ever resurface.

I wasn't exactly anxious to see my fate unfold in front of me. When the elevator surfaced with the guest of honor, I made myself busy. Tried to ignore the surprised gasps and laughs between family and friends. I didn't want to know how close or far she was from me. So I focused on the red blinking light coming from the Washington Monument. To no avail. I was able to scale the distance between us easily. I didn't have to look. My senses were being led by a Seeing Eye dog trotting in the wrong direction. Each step placed me closer to kryptonite.

I can imagine that this is how it feels to be pregnant. Each sense heightened tenfold. I could see the outline of her shadow. I tasted yesterday's strawberries on the tip of my tongue. I heard her calling my name. In various pitches and tones from varying realities. Yesterday's kiss. Last night's dream. Playing both sides of the fence between the spiritual and physical elements of love. If in inhaled deeply, I could smell the delightful combination of Spanish Dutch salt water and her perfume. I felt it. It made me tingle. And when she passed me by, I felt her aloofness. Her distance. Her detachment. She was cold. Her stare was defiant. Unforgiving. I had never experienced that. Didn't know how to handle it. Then I remembered yesterday. I left her hanging. Man. The clinking sound of silver on crystal faded my reflection.

"Family and friends . . . tonight is a very special night." The rooftop quieted in anticipation.

"I have loved this woman since I first laid eyes on her . . . She has been everything to me. I don't know how I've made it this far without Taiyler in my life . . ." A cascade of *awws* paraded around and about the small tables. ". . . she has made me realize what it truly means to be a man. And how empty my life was before she became my angel . . ."

Tears already. Shala. Drea. Dion. Derrick. Me. I'm happy for him. Really. And Taiyler, she wouldn't even look my way. I was glad about that. Following his proclamation, he got on one knee. And I saw it. No one else did. But I know her. She's confused. Twisting that silver bracelet, she vied for Shala's attention. But Poca was caught up in the moment. She looked around for someone who would understand. And when all were evaluated, and the final cut was made, her eyes landed on me. And that selfish, self-centered love reared its ugly head. Despite that, she still said yes. And I couldn't take it. I've never felt so hopelessly and desperately in love. As I watched my line brother slide the most obtuse expression of his love over her left ring finger, I realized that I would never in life feel this again.

"That was so sweet!" Shala said. She was standing right next to me. Beaming. "They are made for each other!" she exclaimed. I watched them dance. Watched Taiyler watch me. And I realized that Shala was right. We were.

37

Taiyler

Shala raised her arm at least a foot and a half above her head and snapped like an old drunken woman to the music. Stifled snickers and chuckles tumbled out of B Natural's client waiting room. The spa wasn't ready for her today.

Yeah, you hurt me, but I learned a lot
Along the way . . .

Beyonce Knowles was singing the hell out of this song. Even though Shala's wolf-cry attempts were far from authentic, she hit a note or two herself. I never thought the young Diana Ross was that great. That was until Shala made me watch her shake all that her mama gave her on the BET Awards. She got some points from me for her Tina Turner resurrection of a performance. That's hard to do. Tina is not easy to impersonate. Plus, the girl *really* can sing. And Shala can't get enough of her. For more reasons than one.

"T! Today is a beautiful day, don't you think?" She is happy as hell this morning.

As the receptionist called our names for our spa treatments, Shala got up, shook her hips in response to Beyonce's soulful chorus, took a few steps forward, and to the spa's surprise, backed her ass right back up. She was getting down this morning. In rare form. I cracked up. She did, too. The first hard laugh I'd had in over a month. We undressed, lay facedown on the warm tables, and waited for our respective massage therapists to enter.

"This is what started it all," she said.

"Started what?"

"Zadia, India, Zori, Marin, and Grai . . ."

Oh.

"It all started right on one of these tables," she recollected.

"Do you regret it?" I asked. I always wondered if she did. It didn't seem so until recently.

"Sometimes, yes. Sometimes, no. Depends."

"Explain," I requested as two very different therapists entered the candlelit room. Mine male, hers female.

"Oh, shit . . . mmmh. Hold on, T." She squirmed as the female masseuse pressed her fingers into her lower back. Shala is so emotionally responsive. If it feels good, you'll know. If it doesn't, you'll know that, too. I envied that. She moaned like this girl was putting it on her something serious.

"All right! Enough already! There are two other people in here!" I yelled in mock disgust. Both she and her masseuse let out a laugh. I could tell that Shala was happy to have her friend back. If it weren't for her and someone else, I would still be curled up in bed with softballs of Kleenex surrounding me. She began her explanation.

"No, in that I've experienced pleasure and love in its rarest form. I'm uninhibited. True. Understood. It's cleansing. Makes me wonder how I ever lived without it."

"And no?" We're supposed to be quiet in here. We never are.

"Yes . . . hmmm. When I realize that I may not be involved in the most society-oriented, morally correct expression of that love, the realization is coupled with a reminder of the love that I knew prior to this, and sadly, it fails in comparison."

"Uhm-hmm." I'm listening. Trying to draw lines between her feelings and mine.

"And then you're faced with yet another decision," she added.

"Which is?"

"Whether or not your spirit, your psyche, can even handle the retreat."

"Retreat?" I think I know what she means. Just being in Nat's presence makes me wonder how I ever loved anyone else. It's the feeling of the moment. I will it away when he's not around. Sometimes it works. Most times it doesn't.

"Yes. Retreat. Turning back. You wonder if you can love below your threshold. If you can live without the spiritual feeding that you receive from your soul mate. Or if you'll dry up, turn into a pillar of salt. Like Lot's wife."

Damn.

"So is Grai your soul mate?" I was quizzical. Intrigued. Impressed by the knowledge of my best friend. Thankful that she was so insightful.

"She is as close as I'll ever get."

Wow.

"How do you know?" I'm full of questions today.

"When a person has touched you spiritually, the question more so becomes how do you *not* know?"

"So what can be done about something like this? Being in love and not being able to see it grow to its fullest potential?" I asked. I've given too much away. And Shala knows me too well. She raised her head off of the table. Raised her eyebrows along with it. With her silky black ponytail still at her waist, her stare pierced every lie, every cover-up that I'd managed to dig up. She's on to me.

"What do you mean? You're in love with Derrick, right?" she asked as if she could answer that on her own.

"I'm being general."

"No, you're not."

"Yes, I am."

"Bitch, don't play with me today." She's serious. Looking at me as if her life depended on me answering the question affirmatively. I toyed with telling her about Nat. There has never been a time in which I felt that I couldn't tell Shala a secret. This time, I felt the same way. However, shame overtook me. I fucked around on a good man. A great one.

"I do love Derrick, Sha." I've known that for a while. But in the way that you love someone who you know would never hurt you. Someone who deserves your love. Nat is different. He takes all of me. Whatever I try to hide, he finds. Pockets. Until he's placed my entire being into his. Until we share breaths. Heartbeats. Like Siamese twins. The chances of death are way greater when they're severed.

"And you're sure about that?" she asked. Her eyes scanned mine for any uncertainty.

I decided to speak truthfully about my man from the heart. "How could I not? He's perfect. All that I've ever said that I wanted or needed in a man. He takes care of me. He's worldly. Strong. Intelligent. Thoughtful. Humble . . ."

She snickered.

". . . well, humble when it comes to me." I had to laugh at that one. Derrick is cocky as hell. I liked that. I continued.

"He is at my feet before I ask. He's not embarrassed or ashamed of his love for me." The longer I spoke of him, the warmer I felt inside.

"Would you spend the rest of your life with him?" She threw that out like she was Johnny Cochran's prize student. I thought long and hard. Would I? If I were able to erase Nat's touch from my memory, yes. Yes, I would.

"Yes. I would, Shala." But the obvious had not occurred as of yet. Nat was still a million points of light scattered about my being.

"Great!" She let out a burst of air. She had been holding her breath. I wondered why.

Our girls' day out was tremendous. I promised Shala that I would accompany her to one of those black-tie pharmaceutical dinners that she hated so much. So we're back at my house. Getting dressed. And from the looks of it, getting ready to stop the show as well.

"Put some lotion on your hands, Taiyler!" she shouted from the guest bathroom. What the hell did she think I was doing? I have to use my hands to lotion my body. She's tripping.

"Just get dressed! We're running behind!" I yelled back. Good thing we both got our hair done this afternoon. One less caveat. She pranced out of the bathroom in a strapless Elie Saab couture gown. Split from her ankle to her waist. Black Manolo Crepe d'Orsay shoes. She really wanted to make an impression. If so, mission accomplished. Shala was ready for the world.

"Let me see." She whisked me around in a full circle, scrutinizing my wears. The V-lined center of my Valentino creation started at my neckline and plunged headfirst to my tailbone. Something Derrick bought on a whim. I wish J.Lo *would* step out in this dress tonight.

"Nice. Very nice. And the shoes?" She reached for my foot. This is a joke, right? She has to be kidding.

"Giuseppe Zanotti, Shala. Fall '03." I'm not a rookie.

"Uhm. Hmm. Sexy Valentino, jeweled dragon sandal by Giuseppe, you're ready to hit the catwalk, missy."

What is her problem tonight?

"I'm not seven years old, Sha. I have this," I answered. She's annoying me. She knows it.

"Sorry. You just never know who you may see."

No reply. I just want to get there and get back. I have some heavy thinking to do. I still have no idea why Nat left me out to dry the way he did last night. He had me begging him to talk to me. And he didn't even call after he brought me home. That shit pissed me off. He just dropped me off like he fucked me and didn't know my name.

"Taiyler! Snap out of it! We have to go! And remember you still have to stop by Derrick's first!"

Damn. I forgot. I had to disengage the alarm system for the carpet cleaners tomorrow. I thought about how much Derrick trusted me. How he revered me. How Nat is a happily married man. And about how I stooped below what I'd been taught. I'm nobody's sloppy seconds. Period. At that moment, I convinced myself that my love for Derrick's best friend was transient. I would make it so. At least until I figured something else out.

Georgetown was its usual Saturday night buzz. We rode down M Street feeling free. Two Black women. Basking in the glow of overcoming the odds. Doing it. And doing it well.

"Is that new?" Shala motioned over to the funky new restaurant lounge, Mie'n Yu.

"Yeah. It opened up a few months ago." Derrick and I had staked our claim in one of the Moroccan-style lounge areas when it first opened. I loved the way he was always up on the latest cultural activities. As we pulled into my baby's driveway, I noticed the glow from an unfamiliar light source on the roof.

"Come on!" Shala was extra excited about me and this damn ADT code.

"I'm moving! Relax!"

She was trying so hard to contain a smile that wouldn't quit. Derrick must have left a surprise for me upstairs. Got her involved. She loves stuff like that. Surprises. I decided to play with her.

"All right. We're ready to go. The alarm is deactivated."

T.P. Carter

The look on her face was too much. She almost fell out.

"No, T! Uh . . . I mean . . . hold on." She answered what was the fifth call to her cell since we left Bowie.

"Yeah. Yeah . . . In a minute, damn it!" she exclaimed. Whoever it was had just plucked a nerve. I chuckled.

"Taiyler, while we're here, I need to grab my cell phone cover. I left it upstairs. During Derrick's last party."

Good one, Sha. I have to give it to you. That one came straight from *Hell Week*. You're on your toes tonight. I laughed inside.

"Can you come with me? I don't know my way around this . . . this museum."

This time, I laughed out loud. She left no room for me to be difficult. My girl.

"Sure. Let's take the elevator." As I witnessed my best friend's eyes turn into sparkling rows of fiery diamonds, I wondered what I was in for.

It all went so fast. First it was Drea. Then my little sis, Dion. Then Travis on the trumpet. Mike. Solange. North was a replica of the Eiffel Tower. How in the hell did he do that? Will Downing. A million stars. A clear night. I'm dizzy. Kalonji. Garvin. Waiters. Black ties. White tablecloths. Strings. Brass. What in the hell is going on? Oh, my God. Chopard. Floating diamonds. I love this pendant. He's so damn fine in that tux. Derrick, baby, give me a kiss. He did one better and got on one knee. No. This can't be happening. Not yet. Oh, shit.

"Dr. Taiyler Milan Richardson, will you be mine forever? Will you marry me?"

He's serious. Shala's smile is blinding me. I need her to stop. I need to talk. Need some telepathy. She can't stop herself. She's not reading my eyes. I need her to concentrate. What the? Oh, my Lord. Harry Winston. It's huge. Never seen anything like it. Ever. Faces. Eyes. They're all on me. Decisions. Millisecond memories. The first day we met. Our first dinner. First trip together. First conversation. First kiss. I loved every first with this man. His eyes were pleading. Begging. He doesn't have to do that. I know he loves me. I can see it in his eyes. I can see behind them. I said yes. In spite of all that.

Everyone loves me right now. Even Drea. Whisking me around the room. Shala and the lotion. She's a fanatic. Someone calm her ass down. Let go of my hand. I need to talk to him. Get some shit out. For real. He can read them. The ones that I give. Signs. Virgo. Capricorn. Catcher and pitcher. Venus and Serena. French Open. It'll all be over before you can say love.

"So you knew?" Fury and hurt mixed together in my stomach like light and dark liquor. We're both in the kitchen. He read the signs correctly.

"Yes."

"And you still allowed yourself the pleasure, huh?" I'm throwing crossbows.

"You said yes." He's not answering me. I'm annoyed.

"And you're married." Stay on track, Taiyler. Don't melt.

"And so are you."

"I *hate* you." I do. I really do.

"Ditto." He's throwing darts. Crossbows. Darts. We're killing each other.

"Fuck this," I spun around, ready to get back upstairs. Get back to being loved. He grabbed my arm. I can't believe this shit.

"You said yes, Taiyler." He's rubbing it in. So what? So what that I wanted him like I've never wanted anyone in my life?

"Anyone that says yes . . . do they—do they get what I got?"

I'm fanatic right now. I've never been this angry.

"Calm down."

"No, you calm down!" I was whispering. But I was screaming. On the inside.

"Not yesterday. Not weeks before. Today. *Today* you said yes."

I'm pissed, and he wants to riddle. I'm in no mood for games.

"So fucking what?" I was irate. He knew about all of this. And still made me love him. Each call, each word, sent me crashing to the floor. And each time, I picked myself up, dusted myself off, and bandaged up my heart. Just to crash harder. One word. One thought was all it took. Bastard. I felt like an open-chested dear on Route 66. He sighed. Looked at me like he could wring my neck at any second. I didn't flinch.

"Listen to me, Taiyler. Listen to me well. *You* did this. *You* fucked me up. Fucked up my entire life. Everything that I've worked for. Everything that I know. You make me so fucking sick! Every time I think of you. You make me sick. And I stay that way. Until I can touch you. See you smile. Hear your voice. And then you said yes today. And now I can't stand you. For making me fall. For making me love you, Taiyler. This is *your* doing." His eyes were bloodshot. I fingered the engagement ring from my fiancé. Stared my soul mate in the face. No forehead to forehead today. No anything. I can get used to it. I willed it. It hurt like hell.

"Taiyler! Come on! We have a soul train line going on up here, babe!" I heard Derrick shout downstairs in excitement. It startled us both. Jarred us to reality. Nat fingered a folded red piece of paper. I knew it well.

"This is where we stop, right?" His eyes were beyond glistening. Beyond what I could stomach at this time. I averted my own. I was unable to speak.

"This is where we stop. I know. You don't have to say it. Maybe next lifetime, huh?" His glare softened to a gaze so warm, so loving, that I wondered how I could live another moment without it.

"Maybe," I replied. One-word answers were a hot commodity right now.

"I hope so." He said it with so much sincerity. As if he could wish its existence. I looked down at our fingers. They've always had a mind of their own. Their ritualistic lock-and-key pattern was too symbolic to ignore. I don't remember taking his hand. The look on his face suggested that he didn't remember taking mine either. He wiped my eyes. He shouldn't have touched me. Those points of light scattered about in a million directions. Like broken glass.

"I have to get upstairs."

"I know."

"So I'll see you around."

"See you, Taiyler." Something about the way he said my name. Like it was too precious to be spoken in English. Too fragile to be broken into twin syllables. It rolled off of his lips like honey. Brought me back to the Natural Pool. La Trattoria. Dera Gai. The night of Aunt Mae's death. My foyer. My bathtub. The fund-raiser. The grocery store. The feelings flooded me. Drowned me. I love this man. But I also loved the Man Upstairs. I'm not an adulterer. I prayed for strength.

"I . . ."

"Say it, Taiyler. Please say it." His stare was hysteric.

"You already know, Nat." Too weak to return the gaze, I took each stair with penne legs. My limbs were weak, but I'm strong. Amidst all of this turmoil, where is my strength?

38

Shala

Months later . . .

"So!"
"So?"

We were in her office. Having lunch. On my company. Taiyler mocked me in the same way she usually did when I was excited about something that she wasn't.

"So what have you decided?" I was antsy. Carrying the conversation at the top of my lungs. It's not my fault that Taiyler isn't a wedding type of gal. She never has been. All she needs to know is what time the service starts, and she'll be there. I'm different. I love it all.

"Shala. I don't know. This shit is beginning to work my nerves. Derrick is the big event junkie. I'm not. I swear, if you two don't leave me alone, we're getting married at the justice of the peace." She's aggravated. So what?

"Uh. You are insane. The man basically gave you a blank check and turned his head. Told you to do whatever you wanted. All you've decided on is what you'll be wearing." This is blowing me. She cracked up at my irritation. I always knew it would come to this. We've argued about this since the good old Abby Hall days. One of the few ways in which we differ. Weddings.

"And so you think that I should just hit every bridal boutique in town? We can use the money to invest in something else. I'm thinking of having a small wedding. I always said that I would if Auntie wasn't around to see me jump the broom."

I could tell the words still stung. The glossy gray was too obvious to miss.

"Taiyler. Don't do it. The Sorors will have a fit."

"Fuck the Sorors."

Okay. Try, try again.

"And all of our Spelman girls."

She didn't even bless that one with a reply. Her six-carat declaration of love sent coded signals of light to UFOs.

"You're so busy reprimanding me that you haven't inquired of my more astute findings." A half-moon crept slowly around the top of her chin. She's done some research. Underneath her Tod's midsized shopper were a series of magazines, catalogues, and brochures. She cares. As my mom says, *"Thank ya!"* To her delight, I ravaged them like a hungry teenager.

"I was thinking of getting married overseas. Morocco. Ivory Coast . . . I dunno." Her tone indicating that she'd given up before we'd even started. I sorted through each of the travel brochures. This may be a good idea.

"Thanks to Mr. and Mrs. Hanks—"

"Who?"

"Solange's parents. Thanks to them, I've already traveled to half of these places." She slid the slim Paris brochure across the fiberglass desk. She's obviously tired of going over it. After reviewing them myself . . . Milan, Madrid, Amsterdam, Ibiza . . . yup. She's right.

"So you're thinking about Africa?"

"I don't know what I'm thinking. But in spite of your chastisement, this gal has been doing her research. It's just hard for me to do all of this when I have real work to do. You and the wedding planner can have it. Just set my alarm for me. Let me know what time you want me there."

I was amazed at her ability to chuckle at something like this. The wedding is literally months away.

"Taiyler, I always knew that your wedding would be the death of our friendship." I was half kidding, half serious. This is important.

"Then don't sweat it, Sha. You already know how I am about these things. Besides, Nat will love me whether we marry in Curacao or City Hall."

Who?

"Who?" I asked.

"Who else? Derrick. He may act like it, but he doesn't care where we do this."

"You didn't say Derrick."

"Yes, I did."

"No. You said Nat."

"No, I didn't." She paused. As if she had to think about it. Whether she'd inverted the names or not. Why did she even have to think?

"Freudian slip. Why are you thinking about Nat?"

She looked at me as if I'd hit a nerve.

"It was a mistake. That's all." Qualifier. She's hiding something.

"That's all, huh?"

"Damn it, that's all, Shala! I made a mistake! Derrick, Nat, you knew who I was speaking of, so why all the drama!" She shifted, tapped her glass with her straw. She's *lying*. We sat in silence. If I know her, and I do, she needs to talk. She's needed to for quite some time. I wondered what was holding her back.

"Taiyler."

No response.

"Taiyler."

She's daydreaming.

"Taiyler!" I was being loud. Unrelenting. I felt left out.

"What, Sha? It was a mistake, okay?"

When her gaze returned to my own, it was lined with emotion. We need to talk. Now.

"T. I'm going to say this once. You are my best friend. My sister. There is nothing in this world that I wouldn't do for you. However, if you don't tell me what the issue is, I'm going to have to resort to drastic measures. Now, what was a mistake? You saying that Nat will love you or something else?"

She toyed with my words for moments that made me realize that this was more serious than I'd originally thought. Raw emotion elbowed its way to the front lines of her forehead. This is a biggie.

"Are you sure you want to know?" she asked timorously, her usually confident persona overdrawn with hesitancy. She's nervous. And taking it out on her bracelet.

"Taiyler Richardson. Enough with the bracelet. Look at me."

She raised her head. We were eye to eye. A draw.

"Spit it out."

Slowly but surely, the words came. Their arrival paired with passion. Fever. A hysteria that was unbeknownst to Taiyler. Words that she owned, and ones that she didn't, came crashing in like the Red Sea.

"I'm fucked up, Sha. I can't eat, I can't sleep. I'm crying all night . . . at work. I want to stop thinking about him so bad, but I'm so weak. What am I going to do? I wanted him. I still do. I know what he's thinking. Even right now. I don't understand how this could happen . . . When he kissed me that was it. It was where I wanted to be . . . His arms were made just for me . . . his hands . . . his lips . . . all of him. I want all of him all over me all of the time . . . I would give so much just to feel him for five minutes . . . almost give it all, really. I'm so fucked up. I don't know if I can do this. Don't know if I can live without him, Sha. I'm hurting right now. I hate him for doing this . . ."

I listened carefully. Extracting tidbits of useful information from her torrid description of the past year. She met Nat first. Although she wanted to, she couldn't control herself. Still can't. The grocery store. The fund-raiser. Aruba. They were in love. Maybe more than that. I was amazed at the transformation. She's crippled. I've never seen her like this. Ever.

". . . so we stay away . . . and the longer we do . . . the harder it gets. I'm starving myself," she concluded. I'm speechless. Minutes passed. I waited for the old Taiyler to emerge from the gun smoke left by a love that insisted on an unfair fight. She never did. It's killing her.

"T, you have to excuse me; I'm digesting all of this." And that was all I could say. She was dangerously in love with a married man who happened to be her fiancé's best friend. I sat still, the only pliable sound emerging from the tapping of fingers and feet.

"Say something, Shala," she pleaded. Words were scattered about my brain like a school of guppies.

"Okay." I let out a sigh that matched the burden at hand. What do I say? I cleared my throat. Here goes.

"For the record, this is by far the singular most scandalous shit I've ever encountered in my almost three decades of life."

Our eyes met for a moment. And we both fell the fuck out. She laughed. I laughed. Sometimes you have to laugh to keep from crying. As Auntie used to say.

"So you love this man."

"So much, Sha."

"And he loves you."

"Yes."

"And he's married."

"Uh-huh."

"And you've kissed."

"Yes, we have." A smile brighter than the sun illuminated her face. Brought one to mine.

"And had sex?"

"No."

I didn't hear that right.

"Excuse me?"

"We've never had intercourse." Astonishment flooded her features. Almost as if she hadn't realized the former herself.

"But you want to, right?"

"My God, yes."

"You have to do something about this, T."

Silence. Illogical illusions.

"I'm marrying a man who loves me more than anything on this earth. That's what I'm going to do."

"You're an idiot."

"Excuse me?" Those eyes narrowed into slits. The old Taiyler is back. Good. Now we can be rational.

"I didn't stutter. You've met your soul mate. And you're letting him live life without you. Denying yourself is one thing. Denying your spirit is another."

She paused. Inhaled oxygen. Exhaled fiery darts.

"Really?" Her sarcasm was unmatched.

"Really."

"All of this from someone who is willing to live her life without the one she loves, just to fit in. To please another."

"That other is my father." I felt like a hypocrite. She didn't have to call me one, though.

"And my other is my fiancé." Two meteorites approaching each other head-on. When analytics clash.

"And God," I added. She can't dispute that.

"And adultery is pleasing to the Most High?" Her rhetorical question blinded me. I slapped my poker face on. It's do or die.

"As you offered in a past discussion, neither is lying at the altar in marriage. I *dare* you to lie to Derrick in God's face." I see you T. And I raise you five.

"The eighth commandment, Shala."

"He hates liars, Taiyler."

"Remember that when you leave Grai. When you walk down the aisle with him. Whomever *he* may be."

"Exactly." I won. Gimme my dough. Saw those wheels spinning. She's in a corner.

"I am vowing to love Derrick. To honor him. To respect him. That will be the truth. Nothing but." She won't lose. Neither will I.

"Honor him. Go ahead. Honor him by screaming out Nat's name while you make love. Make babies. Do it. Honor him, Taiyler. You seem to have this all figured out." Shit. I'm frustrated. Tired. My last comment was a bit much. But the truth hurts. She looked away. I prevail.

"I don't know what to do. Nat has a family, Shala. A daughter who loves her daddy. Something I've always wished I had. Who am I to rip that apart?" She has a point. This is hard.

"Have you spoken since the engagement?"

"No. We decided that it was best not to." Her eyes beseeched a solution. She's been over this a million times. I boiled down. Determined not to let my best friend leave this table without the much needed direction she required. A soft knock on her office door startled us both.

"Come in," Taiyler answered reluctantly.

"Dr. Richardson? You have a very special guest." Lucy beamed.

"Who is it?" she asked.

"He wanted it to be a surprise . . ."

"Hey, baby! I thought I'd surprise you! I had lunch with a client nearby, and I thought you might be hungry!" Derrick emerged from the hallway, toting Caribbean goodies from Negril. He almost ran all of us over trying to get to Taiyler.

"Hey, honey . . ." Taiyler placed a well-deserved kiss on his lips. She didn't even break a sweat.

"Shala brought lunch. We just finished."

He looked heartbroken. For all of the wrong reasons.

". . . but I tell you what. I'd love to spend a few minutes with you. Let me grab my coat. We can stroll Rock Creek Park."

His eyes lit up. Taiyler was his Christmas.

"Okay, sweetie." Derrick stood patiently. Like a child awaiting Halloween candy. I don't even think he knows I'm in the room.

"Sha. We'll talk later," she said, without yielding the slightest indination of her emotional status just a few minutes before. I was in awe.

"All right, T. Later." I watched Derrick help her with her coat, grab her hand, lead her outside to his four point six chariot horses, and couldn't stop myself from thinking they were the perfect pair. Love is a mutherfucker.

I'm exhausted. Whoever said that pharmaceutical sales was the easy way out, obviously didn't have a clue. My evening dinner program was stellar. Today's midday conversation with Taiyler was stressful. And I'm holding all of the tension in my neck and shoulders to prove it. I'm not going in tomorrow. I never do after a late night.

"Graaaai . . ." My thunderous cry was greeted blankly. I forgot. She's in Chicago. Lushena Books. Another signing. I miss her. I plopped down on my sofa as if I couldn't care less that the leather was beaten by hand. I'm beat. And I'd love more than anything to curl up with my baby right now. I hate it when she tours. Hate making my own tea. Running my own bath. Tucking myself in. I'm a spoiled brat.

As I sulked and cursed for having to rub my own feet, I reminisced over the content of today's conversation. The true. The false. The accusations. My part in all of this. My happiness. Taiyler made strong remarks. Striking ones. Comments that forced me to reevaluate my position on love. On life. If nothing else, the events of this past year prove that life is changing. Times are. I'm staying the same. Refusing to acknowledge truth. Refusing to grow up. To grow. What an adversarial stance on a soul's progression. Decisions were trapping me into the corner of public school yards. Threatening to blacken my eyes. Prevent me from seeing peace. Truth. Solitude. Understanding. Or was I the bully? Wearing the appearance of strength. Hiding behind life. Behind decisions.

If I had the leisure of procrastination, I would indulge. As I have done so effortlessly through the year. But that isn't an option anymore. Even if it were, I'd ignore the opportunity. It's time to decide on me. My fate. My love. My life. The alternatives were wrenching my brain like crazy. No pen. No legal pad this time. No Taiyler. It's time for me to do this.

Eyes closed, I absorbed the quiet of the night. Inhaled the fresh sound of raindrops running splintering steps across hardwood. My life before me in plain view, I swayed back and forth between the realms of reality that each choice held. Life without Grai is unimaginable. That's factual. Everything about her is about me. Our qualities intertwined over the past few years like roots of age. She makes me feel safe to be. Period. To release myself from that, from her spirit, was accepting the dismal possibility of dying a spiritual death in love. Was I ready for that? To stage a suicide of the heart? The rain continued to fall. And I continued to think. In the dark. Hoping to shed some light on what has become a potentially hopeless situation. I love her. She loves me. That should be all that matters. But it isn't. The blaring of horns startled me. Who the hell is in my house? Playing *Love Songs*? Thunder clapped. I let out a high-pitched shriek to rival Miles's best treble clef adventure. And fell right into Grai's embrace.

"Hey, babe." Her words slipped through teeth that displayed her content. I'm happy to see her, too.

"You scared the heck out of me. I thought you were signing in Chicago."

"I was."

"What happened?"

"I cancelled."

"Why?"

She let her eyes roam the longitude of my navy pinstripes. Let her lashes tease one another into a frenzy.

"Come and see." Grai can be so mysterious at times. The life of a writer is filled with cubbyholes and trapdoors. Often subjected to living lives that trail the vivacity of their live-wire imaginations, they create vivid works to fill dismal gaps. Putty for personality. Grai. She's quirky. Elusive. Quiet. Playful. Sexy. Moody. Uptight. Loose. Loving. All of that sometimes and none of it all at once.

"All right," I surrendered, allowing my love to lead me by the hand, one stair at a time, to the hot stream awaiting the chance to flirt with my skin. My bath. I needed it so badly. Grai already knows that. Because she knows me. She removed my blazer. My blouse. My bra. And guided me inside the cleansing pool of hot water, salt pebbles, and soap.

"Baby. I needed this so much," I said as we sank into the abyss of steam that allowed her legs to slide around mine without effort.

"I know." She poured a slender glass of piñot noir. One for me.

One for her. I'm so filled with pleasure, my body doesn't know whether it should bother itself in arousal, or realize it's been beat by relaxation.

"And when I came in, I thought of you."

"I know that, too." She grinned. Kissed behind my ear. This feels great. My back lying gently against parts of her that called me names in words that I seldom understood. I wanted to hear those names tonight. Our legs slipped around and about one another. Trading signals of wanting. Needing. While the thunder roared, I allowed the buzz of the wine to soothe me. No tears. No confusion. Just us. Bathing in love. Allowing it to splash about us frivolously.

"So tell me about the tour. How was Atlanta? Seattle? San Francisco?" I was excited. Interested in her. She loved that about me. I felt her smile spread across the back of my neck. Felt her heartbeat.

"It was great, babe. I had no idea that the book would affect so many people in the way that it did. I mean, there were all types of folks at these signings. Handing out testimonies about love. Spiritual love. About how the novel helped them to realize its true power."

"Like Luther," I said. She laughed. I joined her.

"Yeah, babe. Like Luther. The big one . . ." The remnants of her purr echoed out to the tips of my fingers. It tickled me.

". . . I could tell that I'd struck a chord with some. Mainly the ones who believed that love was solely a mental or physical entity. That it could be manipulated by the strong willed. Controlled by the righteousness of mind. But the majority, I'm happy to say, were converted. They accepted the love of my characters for what it was. Wild. Strong. Disobedient. I'd made them believers . . ." she pronounced triumphantly.

As she continued to enlighten me with love tales in tankas, I'd sunken deeper into thought. Into her. And realized the truism behind her work. She'd written about spiritual love. In literature as in life. She'd written about us. Of the struggle behind our love. Of the desperation. The rampage. The insanity with which I loved her. Of times she wanted to leave but couldn't. Of places. Spaces. Days. Nights her body followed her mind. Her mind followed her heart. And her heart followed her spirit. Of the true meaning of *my other half.* Of souls divided. And brought back together. All of which I didn't understand. All of which I did. She'd compensated for my weaknesses. She'd written about me.

"So what did they do, baby? The characters. How did they handle all of that?" I asked, student to teacher. In adoration's classroom.

"Oh, it was never up to them, Shala. They did what they could. Love did the rest." She sipped from her glass. And that was that. I decided to face her. Stare love down. See how bad it really was. As the tip of my tongue traced the outline of her tender lips, she gazed at me without reserve. Her eyes said it all. I'm no match for the tyrant. I'm no match for love.

"I love you, Grai."

"And I love you." And that was all there was to it. Period.

39

Taiyler

The rain sang songs of its arrival on each and every one of my sky-lights. Reserving rhythmic odes of adorn for listeners who welcomed its verses into their homes. Into their hearts. Simply stated, tonight is a night for love. With each unrelenting crash of thunder, I thanked God for blessing me with an outpouring of love throughout my life. My grandmother. My great-aunt. Loved me without reserve. Without condition. Introduced me to love in its purest and rarest form. I thank them. Although I know in my heart that I couldn't have saved my aunt Mae, that she had made her peace with her Lord, I bled with sorrow. There is no love like unconditional love. Familiar love. Love that saves lives. Love that survives. Love of the spirit. Tonight, reflection is in order.

A sip of spice tea, Rachelle Ferrell, an ink pen, and my journal. All the food needed for my spiritual journey. The words are packed tightly in cerebral knapsacks equipped for the long haul. It's been a long year. I need to write.

Taiyler Richardson, M.D.
Friday, November 21, 2003, 9:15 P.M.
Entry # 113: Reflections of my heart

It's amazing how time and space are not familiar to anything other than love. Over time, I've recognized spaces in life reserved in pockets of love. No more, no less. My childhood years were filled with times that were either over-joyed with love or not. My grandmother loved me. My mother didn't. My aunt did. My father didn't love me enough. Space in my heart is reserved for those who've showered me with love. For those who haven't, I don't share space. Mental. Physical. Or spiritual. Fortunately, I've shared life with those who've loved wholly. And for those who haven't, I've spent very little time.

Reflection on this past year proves to be quite an adventure. I've loved. I've lost. I've loved again. The death of my great-aunt hit me hard. It represented the beginning of the end. The end of love as I'd known it. The portion of my childhood that was to be remembered. Revered. The space in time for which I was loved absolutely. All that I represented. All that I've come to love about my-self. My upbringing. Values. Comfort. Security. As far back as I could remem-ber, for as long as I could remember, that love was there. Same address. Same telephone number. No invitation required. I was free to love as hard as I wanted. As long. As strong. Free to fill space in my heart that had been left gaping with uncertainty and insecurity. Free to fill it with times of watermelon slices and Sunday dinners. Of family stopping by to say hello. Of down South stories and up North dances. Of card parties and birthday celebrations. They were masters of disguise. How else could they shroud selfishness, jealousy, and ruin? Make it palatable for the soul. Feed us love on silver spoons. My fear to love extends from the fear of never being able to love like that again . . .

My pen is moving slowly. Deliberately. Ensuring the inclusion of all that is important to my existence. To my spiritual growth. A complete understanding of myself. I've penned many an emotion in my day. Many a difficult situation. However, when it was time to embark on the road less traveled, on the path reserved for experts, the dampness under my lids forced me into a break. I raised my aunt's teacup to my mouth. Dedicated to completing my journey, I determined to rest for only a minute. Mental cramps were not welcome here. I needed to finish. I needed to understand. I needed to be shown the way back to my treasure chest. Love, truth, freedom. Solitude, peace, hope. And understanding. I needed to find the way back to me. Briefly inter-rupted by the silence that accompanied the end of the disc, I got up. Pressed PLAY. Reintroduced thoughts of love in strings and octaves. Listened to Rachelle sing my song.

I felt it. The feeling that I no longer questioned. It's been months since we've spoken. I wondered how he was. Longed to hear him. To feel him. Even now. As every single day since we last touched.

There's a strange familiarity
About you and me . . .

Instead of ruminating on life without my love, I began to fantasize about our life together. Our love. What it was. What it will be. I stretched it out on my floor. Held it down with wild words. *Forever. Eternal. I do.* Studied the blueprint of souls brought together in love. Built sandcastles. Brownstones. Built us. From the ground up. Lying on my back, I wondered if he'd accept my invitation. To live in the space erected for him. In my heart. I wondered if he'd walk with me in parks where old trees bore rings of age. If he longed to see me at sixty. At seventy-five. At eighty. If he knew "Poem No. 3." And that it was Sanchez's. From *I've Been a Woman.* And if he knew that it was my favorite. That I'd gathered up each sound he'd left . . . breathed them . . . become high. These thoughts. These raindrops. This thunder. They all raced through me like liquid electricity. Like Watts in riots. Gathering up whatever they could of what was left. I've made my decision. And I'll live with it. Hoping that times like this will come often. Or as needed. Allowing me to recite the words written by the rain on my rooftop. Blinded by my ability to be smitten, I decided to write a haiku love note.

This dream of mine
    Will you cross over
        Until you've lived my afterlife?

The blatant and annoying ringing of my telephone stifled what was scheduled to become a masterpiece of an entry.

"This is Taiyler."

"Dr. Richardson. This is Dr. Henderson. How are you?" My psychiatrist.

"I'm doing well. Now, I've asked you to call me Taiyler. How are *you?*" I asked in return. She's helped me tremendously. I faulted myself with my aunt's death. And now I don't. Because of her.

"Oh, I'm just fine. Cooking for my bigheaded husband and his twin daughter."

I chuckled at that one. I couldn't imagine coming home off of rounds and staking my claim in the kitchen. Superwoman.

"To what do I owe this honor? House calls are a privilege, Doctor!" I exclaimed. Happy to hear from a woman who has eased her way into my heart. Helping me patch up holes along the way.

"I have to cancel our appointment for Monday. You can reschedule for later during the week. I have a few minutes if there's anything pressing on the brain."

I heard her scolding what sounded like the cutest little girl. She's busy. But making time for her patients. You have to respect a physician of that nature. She's a rarity.

"No. You go ahead. Everything is fine here. I'm just sitting here, jotting notes into my journal."

"Great. Writing is excellent therapy." She paused. "Taiyler, may I ask you something?" Her voice lost its professional edge and took on a more personal tone. I wondered what it could be.

"Sure."

"We've spoken on many issues during our sessions. Many of which have to do with your past. The more torrid ones occurring in the present. Especially the ones reflecting love."

"Uh-huh."

"I-I wanted to run something by you . . ." She got quiet. Almost seemed a little nervous. "In one of our sessions, you spoke of a man . . ."

"Yes."

"Who touched your heart deeper than anyone ever had . . . I was wondering . . . if you'd ever made your feelings known to him."

"In some ways, yes." I wasn't exactly sure of where this was going.

"Has he to you?"

"Yes."

She sighed deeply.

"Does he love you, Taiyler?"

"Yes."

Another sigh. She needs to spit it out already.

"Would you accept some personal advice, Doctor?"

"Depends on what it is."

"Purge yourself. Tell him. Or your life in love will be filled with roadblocks. Don't be afraid to reach out to the type of love you experienced as a girl. As a teen. That type of love still exists, Taiyler. Even as adults. What you have is rare."

I was stuck. Inside a whirlwind of decision and possibility. I wanted to so badly. To rush into his arms. Carrying my heart in my hands. Present it as a dowry. For his eyes only. But something inside me brought all courageousness to a standstill. When it came to love. I love him. That I do know. Hard. Just like my grandma loved me. What if he can't? What if he can't love me in that way? I'd be crushed.

"I'll consider it, Doctor. Thanks." That was all I could offer.

"You're very welcome, Doctor."

Silence. I got up. Pressed REPEAT on the disc changer. Left Rachelle on. Someone has to find myself. Lying on my back, stretched out in octaves high enough to stop the sun.

I have a craving for strawberries. On a night where raindrops are cascading down my windshield like Niagara Falls, I realized how insane it is for me to be out. It's cold. Rainy. I glanced up at the small square-shaped timekeeper. Eleven-thirty P.M. I need to get in and out. Get back to my mental spa. I'd started my night of reflection with words accompanied by sounds of distillation. It's a slow process. I'll be at it all night. But in the end, I'm clean. Fresh. Light. Like spring water. My left-hand turn into the grocery store parking lot was met with a torrential downpour. Shit. Cats and dogs. I parked. Sat inside my vehicle for an extra few. When the water calmed, I slid both legs out of my truck, cracked open my umbrella, and headed inside. If anytime is the best time to shop, it's after hours. And on a night like tonight, only the mad tried their luck on slick streets. Guess that means me. Because it's empty in here. And I'm glad about it.

Cruising the produce section proved to be low hassle. All of the fruit was fresh. The grapes. Apricots. Kiwi. I located the strawberries. Nestled comfortably in between one another like siblings. I sifted through the green mesh boxes, searching for the ones that would give me the energy needed to pull through the remainder of the night. Grabbed a bunch of green grapes, a few plums. Fresh pineapple. I'm ready. Wait. No, I'm not. Honey. For my tea. I made my way through wines and cheeses. Through matzos and olives. Through ginger and rosemary. Until I'd arrived at aisle three. Where we'd made each other's acquaintance. I shared an inside secret with myself at the abundance of lemon frosting available. Had it been so a year ago, we wouldn't have met. My phone vibrated.

"Aunt Tai."

"Hey, Mike. Baby, what's up? What're you up to?" My nephew.

"Just checkin' on ya."

"Checkin' on me, huh?" I had to laugh. He's so protective of me.

"I have a physiology exam tomorrow. Pullin' an all-nighter. So I called my Aunt Tai for good luck." He's going to be a physician. Just like me. Smiles.

"Are you ready?"

"Yeah."

"You're in a study group?"

"Nah. I do it my own way."

We're almost like twins. It's funny.

"What organ system?" I asked.

"Neuro. Some muscular."

"That's a hard one." Where the hell is the damn honey?

"I got it. Don't worry."

"I believe you."

"So I gotta get back to the books. Just wanted to make sure you were doing okay."

My heart filled.

"Keep up the good work, Mike. I'm very proud of you. Call me if you need anything."

He laughed.

"What?"

"I can't."

"Why?"

"Because you always know. You always call first. Thanks for that, though." He chuckled. "I love you, Aunt Tai."

"I love you, too." We disconnected. It's great to know that you're thought of. His call sealed my heart. Filled it to the top with emotion. Until another feeling crept in behind it. I wasn't alone.

"Do you?"

"Do I what?" I didn't turn around. I was afraid to. His fingers resting lightly on the base of my elbow were enough to drive me mad.

"Do you love me?"

Silence.

"Taiyler." He said it with such passion. It made me drip. "Face me."

I'm fighting a losing war. My words wrapped in white flags, he surrendered the effort. Sighed.

"How have you been?" His eyes were unreadable. His stance stale. It's been too long.

"Fine . . ." Miserable. "And you?"

"I'm doing well," he responded without the emotion that I was so used to. I played tennis with the balls of my feet. "How's the wedding planning going?"

"Good." I want you. I love you. I need you.

"Great."

"Great." Tonight. Right now.

"So tell Shala I said hi."

"Will do." I can love you, Nat. Any way you want. Any way you need.

"Okay."

"Okay."

"See you later."

"See you."

We both stood at the beginning of us. The beginning of this. Glued to the floor. The sounds of afterlives, of children, of grandchildren, ringing clearly in our minds. We knew how it would be. We've been here before. The decision was made on this very spot almost a year ago. We could feel it. Blessed. We were standing on holy ground.

I drove home, my thoughts a mass of burning bushes. I felt his fire. All over me. I wondered why I was such a coward. As I climbed each one of my stairs, I realized that I couldn't do it tonight. Spend the night, the week, the year . . . the rest of my life without him. I'll tell him. Tell him everything. I couldn't pick up my phone fast enough.

"Hello?" His voice traced velvet tales of our love through my veins.

"Hello?"

"Hello, Taiyler?"

"Nat?"

"Taiyler, I was just calling to say that it was great seeing you tonight."

"Nat. I just called you. You picked up." We shared a moment. Recalling a similar occurrence. In Oranjstad. On a night made for love. Like this one. I cleared my throat. Prepared to give all of me to him. In jazz time. I was interrupted.

"Don't do it."

"Do what?"

"I want to be able to look into your eyes when you do." He knew. I couldn't hold it. Just the thought of spending even one minute with my love drove me crazy. Made me hot. One at a time, I removed all garments of restriction. Mental and physical. As if they had been ignited. My shirt. My sweats. Indecision. Fear. My bra. Panties. Doubt. Pain. They were scattered in smoke. Round about the hardwood. When that familiar knock teased my ears with pleasure, I was naked. Open to him. To the truth. To me.

"Oh, my God . . ." His jaw dropped. I could see the thickness of the man that I loved, calling for me. As they usually did, our fingers found one another. And so did our lips. And our love. We were hungry. Urgent. With my back up against the wall, legs hanging loosely on either side of him and his hotness on my neck, I unzipped him. Took his size into my hand. And prepared myself to take in all of him at once.

As he frantically unwrapped the small package, I realized there was no turning back from this point. Penetrating me in one long, deep stroke, he let out a gasp that was unreal. Loud. Pubescent. "T-T-Taiyler . . . b-ba-by . . . uuuuuuhhhhhmm!" My moans were caught up in my throat. In my gut. In my memory. I was shaking. Shaken. All it took was one stroke. Orgasm. We came together. As we did everything. My hands wrapped tightly around his head; he nuzzled his head between my breasts and breathed heavily.

"I . . . I'm sorry . . ." he said bashfully. I was still shaking. Still shuddering. Still a live wire. Still alive. I couldn't stand for him to touch me.

"Pl-pl-please . . . N-N-Nat . . . d-don't . . . to-touch . . ."

Smiling mischievously, he brushed the length of his erectness along my hot spot. Chased my nipple with his tongue. Wiped my overflowing cascade of tears.

"Baaby . . . Oh, my God . . . oh my God oh my God oh my God . . . I-I can't . . ."

My hands slipped around his sweat-beaded brow. The back of his head. His face. I was a madwoman. In three minutes. He'd reduced me to whimpers. I wanted to lie down. Do it again. I'm a punk. I couldn't speak. All I could do was point toward the stairwell. He carried me up three flights of stairs. Laid me down. Made love to my lips. Removed his shirt. His pants. Lay down beside me. Traced the outline of my nakedness with his eyes. My insistent jerks and clenches predicted whiplash if I continued. I needed him on me. Near me was not enough.

"Nat." I was barely audible.

"Yes?" He wrapped his strong legs around me. Held me in place. I wriggled a bit. Coveting the proximity of his dark, thick pubic hair to his penis. That spot. It belonged to me. I wanted to ride him. Desire clouded every word, every sentence. I couldn't remember what I opted to say if my life depended on it. I was focused. Intent. The rain our tambourine, we stomped, clapped, and sang songs of lives lived yearning. Craving. Longing. Overcome with emotion, I witnessed our gratification transform universal parallels. Physical. Mental. Spiritual. Celestial. Until we died and were born again between breaths.

Nat was the single-handed cause of my ascension. I soared until my back hit the ceiling. Until my spirit left my body. As if it had to see for itself what its own eyes couldn't believe. That we'd become one. Casting my eyes downward, I could see me. And Nat. Enjoying heaven. I could feel myself giving up. Giving in. To the light. To the calling of my name. In tandem, we traveled that tunnel of peace. Making miles of music along the way. *Love Songs.* My body toiled. Twisted. Turned. Until I saw blue in green. Until I saw hope. Truth. Freedom. Solitude. Understanding. In the eyes of the one I loved. Between light hiccups and sobs Nat held me. Rocked me. It was amazing.

Although I was still in pleasure shock, I found myself capable of certain acts. I could contract. I could hold him hostage inside me. I loved the sensual look on his face. The thirst in his eyes. I knew I'd have it as long as I lived. I'd have him. It was good to know. Allowing my hands to roam his rippled chest and abdomen, I took heed to a rhythm I owned. One that he obviously recognized. He moved with me. As if he knew every wall, every crevice, every aspect of my womanhood. My eyes filled again.

"B-baby . . ." he burbled. His stutters synchronized with his strokes.

"T-tell . . . m-e about y-your . . . l-lasss-t . . ." His eyes crossed vigorously. His breathing quickened. I wondered if he could stand me. Nat held my ass still.

"St-stop . . . Taiyler."

"What?" I knew what I was doing.

"J-J-Je-sus . . . stop. I don't wanna . . . co—" He tried so desperately to hold me. His eyebrows were taut with concentration. One more time. I gave him my back door. Let him slide into the deepest part of me.

"Ohhhhhhhhhhh . . . shhhhhhh . . . ahhhhhhhh!   Shheeeeiiiiiit!" His scream pierced me. Eyes squeezed tight, he exploded. So did I. Again. Attempts to avoid the inevitable proving useless, we toppled onto the rug. I couldn't hold him. He couldn't hold himself. Exasperated, I fell onto his chest. We lay still. Absorbing the reality of the unreal. This was too good to be true. The rain playing background to Rachelle's reflections on seeing each as a mirror for the other, I couldn't think of any time or any place that I'd rather be.

With him still inside me, we laughed. Flirted. Kissed long kisses. Finished each other's sentences. Argued points. Massaged temples. Teased tongues. Made love. Slept. Fucked. When nature called, he picked me up, trekked across the room, and relieved himself. With me on his back. We were exposed. Mentally unwrapped. Wrapped up in newspaper. In sheets. In each other. We were Siamese. Tonight. Tomorrow. Forever.

"Nat."

"Yes, my love," he answered. Eyes closed, heart open.

"The sun is coming up."

"I see." He's sleepy.

"I have something to say."

His eyes popped open. He smiled. He knows. He's been waiting for quite some time. We repositioned ourselves so that I straddled him. Eye to eye. Forehead to forehead. He pulled the comforter over my goose-pimpled shoulders. Pulled my hair around and about his head. Played in it. Wallowed in me. I prepared myself for words that carried meaning far beyond what I could comprehend. I was nervous. Not cold. I could never be cold in his arms. He slipped that warm tongue into my mouth. Wiped it clean of roadblocks. Stop signs. Hurdles. That was all I needed.

"I . . . uhmmm."

He kissed me harder.

"I . . . lov . . . yes . . . this . . ." I was incoherent. Jumbled. Rambling. Temporarily insane. He stopped. Planted a fat one on my lips.

"Go ahead, Taiyler." He's beaming.

"You know this. But I'll say it anyway. I love you, Nathaniel Woods. I've loved you from the moment our eyes met. Before then. After now. I love you without reservation. Without condition. With all of me. You're a dream come true."

Satisfaction showered his face with dimples. Lined his eyes with tears.

"And I love you, too. Until death. After life." He kissed my forehead. And we made love as if our lives depended on it. Our dreams crossing over. Living their own words. In broken haikus.

40

Nathaniel

I used to play in red clay. All summer long. Down in the delta. Whenever I visited my grandparents. Although simple, it was an act that above all childhood memories staked its claim in color. I remembered the feeling of freedom easily. I could run it through my fingers. Squeeze it. Get deep in it. Dirty. Smear it all over my face. At seven, that was where I wanted to be. Ripping. Running. In red. Last night, upon seeing the love of my entire life standing alone in our aisle, instantly, I envisioned running my hands through her hair. Through her. Through red clay. I saw us in mud fights. Spreading it all over our lips. Our stomachs. The insides of our thighs. I was seven again. I was free.

This morning, I gazed at her beautiful sleeping form. Amazed that I could love like this. Beyond borders. Outside the realm of possibility. Bewildered by our journey around, about, upside, and under each other. How much we knew. How much we didn't. Recalling the passion of last night's love in slow motion. I am spent. Mentally. Physically. Spiritually. My body waterlogged. My spirit damp with the dewdrops of new life. Of old love. I wondered what she thought about us. She stirred.

"Hey."

"Hey." Yawn. She was exhausted. Rightfully so.

"Good morning, sunshine."

She rolled her eyes at me.

"I can't move." She's mad. Happy. All or none at once.

"Do you want to?" I replied. Smiles. My answer. She threw her leg across my waist. Tapped my shoulder. She wants me to lift her onto me. She wants to talk. Quickly, I researched the most effective way to slide her beautiful body across mine, without losing contact. Her warmth baked me into a contagious bliss.

"Nat. We have to talk."

I'm in love with the way she brushes her lips across mine while she speaks. It tickles my spine.

"I know."

"You're married."

"And you're engaged." The actuality of what I'd stated—of what we'd created—bore gifts of Taliban soldiers.

"So how do we do this?" she asked. The physician wants to reason. Draw analytical maps. I can't do that right now. Her blatant stance was a lot to digest. "Breaking the engagement is one thing. Loving a man's best friend is another . . ."

I was speechless. The implications of events to come filled my mouth with saltwater taffy. All of a sudden, nervousness shook me. Punched me hard in the chest. My family. My best friend. All that I know. What have I done?

"Nat. Talk to me."

I couldn't. I was settling matters in the way that men do. In our minds. I could tell that my attention deficit toward such an important matter caused her blood to boil.

"Don't do this, Nat. Don't."

I wish she could hear my apologies. With the wind knocked out of me. My little girl . . .

"Nat . . ." She vied for my attention once more before dismounting me. Rolling over. Creating a division between us that reminded me of why I was here in the first place. I need her. To live. It's sad but true. Fifteen inches between us is almost unbearable. I extended my arm, pulled her slender frame back into me. My space. My air. My everything.

"Truthfully. We do it truthfully." That was my best and only answer. She nestled her head comfortably in between my head and chest.

"You'll lose a lot."

"I know."

"What about your daughter?"

I wasn't ready for the interrogation. My guess was that I should be. Considering I'm naked and not at home.

"I'll still be there. I just hope she understands." My eyes welled.

"And your wife. I haven't met her. But I suppose she's a wonderful woman."

"That she is."

"I have to tell Derrick," she said quietly. His name made my heart hurt.

"This is unreal."

I nudged her scalp with my chin.

"No, it's real. That's the problem."

We hugged. And thought. Pictures of people who loved us more than anything running circles about our heads. Was I prepared to do this? The look on Taiyler's face displayed all of what I felt. I'm hurting. Loving. All at once.

"Come here." She drew me a bath in her bosom. I cried.

"Baby . . . it's okay . . ."

The heaving of my chest warned my breath to shorten its wavelengths. I'm wounded in a lesser of evils. It would seem as if I'd chosen Taiyler over Kendra. Over Nile. But that was hardly the case. For those who could comprehend, I chose life. Either way, it hurts. I've taken so much from them over the past year. And I would have continued to take if I had stayed. My focus. My attention. Was elsewhere. Ever since Aruba. Ever since the grocery store. Maybe one day they'll understand. Regardless of whether or not I did.

"I love . . . them both . . ." I managed to express between chokes of tears. I'm not bitching out. I'm hurting.

"I know." She rocked me back and forth. Rubbed my back. My head. Kissed my face. Our tears meeting for a hot, wet session of sex. She stopped suddenly. As if she'd remembered something key.

"Are they waiting for you?"

"No. They're at her mom's house. They left after dinner."

"Oh." She almost seemed relieved.

"Is Derrick?"

"Is he what?"

"Waiting for you."

She exhaled certainty in one long, steady stream.

"Probably. Last night was a night of reflection for me. A night where I come to terms with the obstacles and illusions of life. Scatter them about. Write them down. I told him about it. And that I needed solitude. I needed to be alone. He'll want to see me today." She was definite. Examining her manicure, she raised her ring finger to my lips. Chased the tail of my tongue with it. Stirred my soul. My nature responded accordingly. So did she. Running the tips of her wet fingers across my peak of sensitivity, I let her guide me back to her birth canal. To where I'd been born again. She felt like a virgin.

"You . . . feel . . . so . . ." She tried to accompany her pleasure with a description that failed the sensual look in her eyes. ". . . good . . . to . . . me."

Ditto.

We flew first class on magic carpets. To places we'd visited together in dreams. Discovering new ones along the way. The arch in her back narrating her approval, her appreciation for each one.

I couldn't see. Couldn't hear. I didn't hear the front door opening. Or closing. Or the sound of keys. Or footsteps. Or him calling her name. Or water running. Or anything. Consumed with ecstasy, her hearing suffered impairment as well. All appeared mute except the jagged sounds of wrought iron waltzing with metal screws. She was screwing my brains out. So much that she didn't hear him knock softly. Hear the knob of her bedroom door turn. Hear me call her name. Feel me tap her. Notice that we weren't alone.

"Naaaaat!!!! Oh-oh-oh-ohhhh!!! Ahhhhh, baaaaaby! Uhhhhmmmmh! Shiiiiiiiiiiit . . ." She came all over me. Hard. Her body stiffened, went limp, and she fell face first onto my chest. With Derrick standing in the doorway, white lilies in one hand, forehead in the other. Shaking his head in disbelief. This is not the way it was supposed to happen.

"Y-y-your . . . you left the door open downstairs, babe," Derrick offered softly. He doesn't see me. He doesn't want to. I wanted to hide my face. I tried to. She was still in orgasm. Moments. Millennia. They're all the same right now.

"Wh-what's goin' on?" he asked. I didn't know who should answer him. Taiyler, his fiancée, or myself. His frat brother. His front. His best man.

"Did y'all hear me? What the FUCK is going onnnnnnn in this bitch!"

That did it for her. Taiyler jumped straight out of her skin. She heard that. Derrick paced the floor. Back and forth. Back and forth. He was making me dizzy. I had to man up. I had to handle this.

How was more so the question.

"No. No. No . . . no . . . this ain't happening. This shit ain't happening . . ." He looked at us. Strongly. Severely. Shook it off. It was a nightmare to him. At least he'd hoped.

"I can't . . . believe . . ." His head turned toward us again. "Hell no. No. This ain't real. This is a fucking figment of my imagination. Wake up, Derrick. Wake up, man. This is false . . ." He studied the scene. A half-humorous smile teasing his lips. "All right, muthafuckers! Allllll right, y'all! K! Garvin! Y'all can come out nowwwww! Ha, ha, ha, ha, haaaaah! The joke's on me! Y'all got me . . ." He babbled. Clapped his hands. Paced. Occasionally glancing in our direction. Me on the bed. My feet on the floor. Head in my hands. Taiyler with her back up against the headboard. She's speechless. Fuck.

"Taiyler, baby? That's not you, right? This is a fucking cruel-ass joke, T! You got me, okay? It can stop now . . ." He took baby steps toward her melancholy aura. "Please tell me that's not you . . . Where are you, Taiyler? Where's my baby?" He tore up her bedroom from the floorboards to the ceiling. Looked for her in the closet. Under her bed. In her drawers. Derrick is mad. Fanatical. Extreme. Dangerous.

"Derrick." Her glum attempt to divert his attention from destroying everything proved ineffective. It triggered something else. Rage. Viciousness. Ferocity. They were severe understatements. He looked at her. Then at me. Then back at Taiyler. It clicked.

"You fucking baaaaaaast-ard!" He lunged across the room. My back to him, I threw Taiyler off of the bed and took the brunt of his landing. We wrestled. Punched. Threw shit. It was ugly.

"Oh, my God! Derrick! Stop! You're going to kill—" Taiyler tried. But Derrick was determined to beat my ass into a fucking pulp. I forgot. He was a boxer.

"Mu-ther-fu—ck-er . . . you . . . fucked . . . my . . . wife . . ." While he expended his energy cursing, I gained balance. Threw punches. Tried to see out of eyes that were swelling. Then all of a sudden he stopped. Stared at his fiancée. My love.

"Okay, babe. What did I do? What did I do? We gon' work this simple shit out. I ain't do shit . . . but if one of those trifling bitches told you some bullshit, just tell me and I'll kill her. Okay? And we can get back to normal. Go shoe shopping and shit. All right? Okay? Okay? How you feel about that, baby?" He was on his knees. His arms wrapped around hers. Mutherfuck me.

"Derrick. Honey, it wasn't you . . ."

He wasn't listening. He was hysterical. In tears. Pulling her down to him. Taiyler's eyes met mine. Told me that everything would be all right. Shala raced in. Cell phone in hand. Stopped short at the scene.

"Oh, shit. Oh, shit. Damn." She surveyed the mess. Glanced at me. I was still naked. I grabbed my boxers. She grabbed Derrick. Pulled him up.

"Thanks, Sha," Taiyler mumbled.

"No prob. Derrick . . . Derrick!" Her voice was strong. Stern. He leaned on her. Cried like a baby. She was caught in between a rock and a hard place. Here for her best friend. For her sister. But she was too much of a human being to let Derrick suffer like that. I wondered what that made me.

"Stand up, D. I can't hold you up. Stand up," Shala said, helping him initiate steps toward the hallway.

"What . . . did I . . . do?" He repeated the mantra over and over again. Down the stairs. Through the foyer. The garage. Into the passenger seat of his truck.

"Are you okay?" Shala hugged her best friend tightly.

"Nope." Taiyler was tired. Overwhelmed. We both were.

"I'm driving him to his father's, T. Give me the directions." Shala's a smart one.

Taiyler grabbed a pen from inside and jotted them down. As they rounded the corner, she raised her hand to my swollen eyes. Inspected them. Pulled me inside. Iced them. We sat still. Silently. For hours.

"Your turn," she said. And she was serious.

I sat outside my home long enough to see Kendra come in. Watch the living room lights come on. See my little princess bounce around the house after her mommy. See a minivan full of five- and six-year-olds pull up. Watch her bop down the driveway, Black Barbie knapsack and sleeping bag in hand. Nile kissed Kendra on the cheek, hopped into her sea of sleepover friends, and pulled off.

I've been here for over two hours. I still couldn't find the words. I didn't know if she had spoken to Derrick or not. I didn't know how to approach my wife of eight years. What do I say? I've seen this on television. Heard of it amongst friends. Swore to God that I'd never. I'd never be that heartless. I didn't even have it in me. And now what?

I'm here. I'm leaving. I replayed the past eight years over and over again. What the fuck am I doing? I reviewed the past year. The past few months. She had to notice something. I was distant. Despondent. She kept asking me what it was. I kept denying the truth. If nothing else, I can give her that. Give her truth. No matter what she'd heard. What she thought. I'd give her the truth. That I loved her. I always will. I wanted to be there. For birthdays. Christmases. Recitals. I will be there. For my little princess. I went over my finances in my head. Yup . . . I could afford to live off of half of my earnings. Shit, a quarter if that's what it took. I still want to take care of them. Then it hit me. I sure do want a lot for a man who's leaving his wife for another woman.

I pulled into my driveway. Noticed the lights were off. Glanced down at my watch. Two-thirty A.M. I've been out here for six hours.

"Kendra," I called. No response.

"Kendra."

Still nothing. I felt around for the light switch in the living room. Noticed something. A trail of light extending from our bedroom. By memory, I took each stair as I had on plenty occasions. Stopped in the guest bathroom. Checked my eyes. They'd gone down some, but were still purple. I sighed. It's now or never.

"Kendra. You up?" My whispers echoed down the hallway. I felt like I was at the bottom of the Grand Canyon. Small. Big. Calling out to someone. Anyone who would hear me.

"I'm up," she said. Her voice filled with distress. Shit. She'd talked to him. I don't even know where to start. Don't know where he finished. I reached over to the night table. Clicked on the bed lamp. To my surprise, Kendra was sitting upright in our king-sized bed. A mass of paperwork about her. Patient charts. She looked drained. Took a fleeting look at my eyes and didn't even flinch. She knew. We sat in silence.

"You have a message," she relayed blankly. As if all of the emotion inside of her had been sucked through a vacuum. I glanced at the flashing light on the machine. Prepared myself to hear Derrick spite me through the small speakers.

"You have no new messages . . . You have three saved messages. Message one . . . November twenty-first . . . eleven forty-five P.M." "Do you? . . . Do I what? . . . Do you love me? (silence) Taiyler . . . Face me . . . How have you been?"

Beep.

"Message two . . . November twenty-second . . . twelve twenty-seven A.M.*"*

"T-T-Tai-yler . . . b-ba-by . . . uuuuuuhhhhhmm!!! (silence) I . . . I'm sorry . . ."

Beep.

"Message three . . . November twenty-second . . . twelve twenty-nine A.M.*"*

"Pl-pl-please . . . N-N-Nat . . . d-don't . . . to-touch . . . Baaby . . . Oh, my God . . . oh my God oh my God oh my God . . . I-I can't . . ."

We sat in silence. Until she was ready. I didn't have the right to speak in my own home.

"How many times have I told you to use the key guard on your phone, Nat?" Her eyes were red. Raw. As if she'd cried herself dry. I was empty. Just hours ago I was full. I have no practice in something like this. I have no idea of what to say. How to move. How to act. I would never cheat on her. Not like this. Not like anything. She wouldn't understand even if I tried to explain. The dreams. How I fought them. The thoughts. How I pushed them out of my mind through my horn. Every night. Every other day. How love did it. How it fucked me. I sent a search warrant out for the right terms. The right expressions. Came up with nothing.

"So you love her. What—how, Nat? What in Christ's name did I do to make you love her like that? In your dreams. You take her places that I've always wanted to go. Places that we've talked about. How? What did I not do? I cooked. Cleaned. Saw patients. Gave you a little girl . . . made love to you . . . what did I *not* do? I gave you everything, Nat. I gave you all of me . . ."

I had no answer other than I don't know. And Kendra deserves more than that. Wait. How did she know about the dreams? My obviously confused expression plastered across my face like a billboard, she slid one of the open charts across the bed. Four months of depth. Width. Dimension. Tied together in SOAP reports. I read and reread everything. Taiyler was the one. Her patient. Her patient who'd been smitten by love. Notes of our asexual love affair, although in bits and pieces, were spread out on the bed. Our kisses. Our talks. Her dreams. Things that I knew. Things that I didn't. She did have sexual dreams of me. For confidentiality's sake, I closed the manila folder. Let out a long breath. Kendra opened her up. For me.

"You love her so much, Nat. You make me want to be her. If I become her . . . if I can do that, will you love me like that? Will you? I fucking hate her. I *hate* Taiyler. And I hate you. I hate you! I haaaaaaaaate yooooooooou!" She hit. And slapped. And smacked. And kicked. And punched. And wept. And cried. And cried. And I held her. Tightly. Until her howls turned to hiccups. And her screams to whimpers.

"I do love you, Kendra."

She pulled away from me. She didn't believe it.

"Well then, do this. Stay here. With your family. Promise to never see her again. Not once. Ever." She stared at me defiantly. Challenged me to overcome my weakness. To kick my habit. My phone vibrated. Interrupted our draw. We both jumped. I considered her offer. The implications behind it. Never to see, smell, taste, touch or hear Taiyler again. My senses would rot from the inside out. Until I was a corpse of sorrow, buried six feet under her smile. Kendra scanned my eyes until she found what she was looking for. It would kill me. Literally.

"Then get the fuck out! Get the fuck out, Nat! Now!" A confetti parade of reports, analyses, and charts formed a paper trail behind me. And I answered my phone on the way out. Drugs. They call your name relentlessly. All times of the day and night.

41

Derrick

The most inconsiderate alarm clock in the world. A fucking rotary phone. Early in the damn morning. I tried my best to ignore the shit. But it's almost impossible. It's hollering. Over and over and over. And the volume can't be adjusted. At all. Piece of shit. I wish Pops would use the phone I bought him. Wait. Rotary phone? What am I doing at my old house? At my pops's? I choked the earpiece with my left hand. Eager to shut it the fuck up.

"Hello." My voice was groggy as hell. Why was I so tired?

"Yo. What's the deal, man?"

"Who is this?"

"Trey."

I wiped the sand out of my eyes. Wondered why he was calling at this time in the morning.

"Yeah, man. What's up? It's like seven in the morning."

"What's up? Nigga, what's up wit' you? You're the one getting carried into your pops's house by some chick, all slumped over like you got your ass kicked. The hood is talking, man. Saying that you stumbled in there fucked up. Crying and shit. Nigga, you tell me. What the fuck is the problem?" He was dead serious. Although it took a minute, it all came back. Showering large drops of open sores about my chest . . .

* * *

"Taiyler . . . Babe," I called out to a mass of papers spread about and clothing scattered around in a hot mess. Her night of reflection must have been pretty damn good. She has shit all over the place. I have to tell her about leaving this front door open, though. I don't care how safe it is in this neighborhood. She needs to keep this thing locked.

"Taaaaaiyler! Baaaabe! I'm downstairs!"

No response.

I know she's here. Both cars are out there. Oh. Okay. She's upstairs. Hammering. That's cute. My little contractor. The last time she tried to bang something into a wall, she almost hacked her fingers off. I had to laugh. She just won't give up. I took the lilies I bought her out of the vase. Skipped stairs. I can't wait to hug my baby. See the look on her face. She loves lilies.

"Sweetness! It's me! Your Prin—"

What the? Nah, that isn't her. That isn't Taiyler. Aight. If she cheated on me, I'd take her back. I've already decided on that. Karma has to catch my ass somehow. She'd have to have a good reason, though. Which I'm sure she would. She has cold feet. Or she's scared of commitment. Or she's not good enough for me or some bullshit. I'm screwed up. This I know. Let me think. I did get out of the bed . . . leave the house . . . get a haircut . . . pick up the tickets to the art show for later . . . stop by the florist . . . and yeah. Yeah. I came over here. To Taiyler's. So that is her. On some nigga. Fucking his brains out. Whoa. Not so. Damn. It is. Oh, that shit hurts. She has to have a good reason. Has to. She's not that type. Fuck! What did I do? Oh, my God . . . oh, shit . . . no. It can't be. It's *impossible*. Nat? Okay, Derrick DeCosta. Shake this off. Maybe you didn't leave the house this morning. Maybe you're still asleep.

"Naaaaat!!!! Oh-oh-oh-ohhhh!!! Ahhhhh, baaaaaby! Uhhhhmmmmh! Shiiiiiiiiiit . . ." Did she just . . . with me in here? There it is. I see it. My heart. My manhood. Hanging from an oak tree by its wrists. Whipped. Lashed. Lynched.

"This is a fucking figment of my imagination . . . Wake up, Derrick . . . Wake up, man. This is false . . ." I hear me shouting out loud. Reasoning with myself. With them. The outsource of this nightmare. I'm pinching the hell out of myself. Nothing's working . . . come on, man. Not you. Not you. I trust you. With everything. You're the godfather of my unborn child. The succulent taste of strange fruit is a godsend to the tang of treachery. So it is true. Damn . . .

I loved Taiyler more than I'd loved anyone on this earth. I still do love her. She felt so good to me. So great. I would have given her anything. Everything. I'd already given her all of me. And I still spent hours. Days. Months. Searching. Trying to find hidden gifts behind doors. Between couch pillows. Under beds. I still wanted to give her more. More than just Derrick. More than just me. I don't see how she overlooked that. The extravagance of my love for her. How could she not see that I would have sold all of my homes? All of my cars. All of myself. Just to have her. I wanted to celebrate this with her. Taiyler. Derrick. Beating the odds. Raising themselves up. Out of the hood. Through college. Professional schools. And into love. Into life as it should be.

Yesterday she was so quiet. As if she were observing herself outside of herself. I wanted to wait awhile. Wait for her to come back to her senses. Wait for her to snatch those lilies out of my hand. To jump into my arms. Smiling a row of Arizona blue skies. I was ready for that. For her to tell me about her patients. A new print she saw and liked. A book that she'd just finished reading. I wanted to wait. For her eyes to shine while I presented her with garments or footwear that she'd just casually mentioned in passing. For her sun-scraping smile to wrap itself around my neck like a noose while she tried them on in front of me. And they were the perfect fit. The perfect pair. Damn. I wanted to wait. So that she'd see how much attention I paid to every word that fell from her lips. Every thought. Every wish.

That's what I wanted. To wait. Just a few more minutes. Until she saw that I was her prince. Her Aladdin. Her genie. And that I'd kill myself to ensure that her heart's desire fell into her hands. At all times. At all costs. I would wait. That was the plan. For her to come back to her. To me. To play fights. To ruining shoes in showers. To soft kisses and foot massages. To her challenging my legal decisions. Questioning my choices. Making me better. Making me.

What happened? When did I lose track? Shit. I just proposed to this woman! When did she stop loving me? And Nat. He was there. All along. Offering jack-o'-lantern smiles with each fraternal handshake. I would never in my entire life have guessed it. Bearing witness to his hands racing up and down her spine while she spun deliriously into sexual oblivion was at the very least unbelievable. I didn't believe my own eyes. Nor did I want to. All I wanted to do was switch places with him. Love her all over. Deal with his backstabbing ass later. How selfish could he possibly be? All of this time, I was out to get what he already had. Family. Future. The ultimate success. Fuck all of the money. The mansions. The cars. What I bled for. What I sweat and cried for. I'd found it in Taiyler Richardson. And he took it all. Pulled the rug out from under me. Life couldn't possibly be this unfair.

As I passed blood through my pores in anger, in hurt, I listened to Trey go on about how much of an ass I'd made of myself after I saw my wife-to-be straddling my best friend. Fucking him like she's never fucked me. And she had the nerve to have an orgasm. In my face. I hope they rot.

". . . Yeah, so they said you was all fucked up. So I was callin' to check on a bruhua. Figured some bitch jacked up your ride for getting married." Married. What a joke. He was all laughs. I wasn't.

"Nah, man. That ain't it . . ." I contemplated telling a lie. Unfortunately, I lacked the mental capacity to think of anything else at the moment. "Taiyler cheated on me, man." I could hear utter shock roaming the optics through his silence. All he could say rolled off of his lips in one word.

"Word?" He was all ears. I know. It's unbelievable. Derrick DeCosta. Being on the receiving end of some bullshit like this. Shit, I still can't believe it.

"And that's not the worst part. I caught them. In her bed. She was fucking Nat. My best man."

Dead silence. A few seconds passed with nothing but breath exchanging between us. Trey's speechless. That's a first.

"Oh, so you *were* crying and shit?" And that was it. Ice pick through the heart. I felt it. Cold. Detached. Less than a man. Enraged. As I gave Trey a rundown of yesterday's events, he didn't want to talk problems. He wanted to talk solutions. I forgot who I was dealing with.

"So how do you want to handle this, D?" He's never been one to play around with being disrespected. It's all he has. His image. His respect.

"I don't know, man."

"Whatchu mean you don't know?"

"I mean I don't fucking know right now," I answered truthfully.

"Shit. Unless you plan on taking her back, there's only thing to do."

Silence. My brain was over- and underworking itself simultaneously. Maybe we could work this out. She and I. Fuck Nat.

"Nigga. Answer me. I know you ain't trying to hear no bitch-ass nigga getting away with fuckin' up yo' future. Your seed. Especially when it's a nigga from your own camp."

I counted how many times he said the word *nigga*. Three.

"So you down? Ride or die, nigga. Ain't no muthafucker gettin' away wit' no shit like that. Fuck that." Four. I'm not paying attention. I'm still there. Standing in the doorway. Watching her beautiful body move like fine silk in light wind. Seeing her collapse onto his chest. Exhausted. After an orgasm that I've never seen before. Never heard. Never been privileged enough to bring her to. My all wasn't enough. It's funny. A man's pride. When it's on the line, there's no telling what we'll resort to. Fame, fortune, career. Fuck it all. When you feel like you have nothing to live for, why care?

"Yeah."

"Aight, mane. I'm on it. Him, her, or both?" He wanted answers. I had nothing but questions. In my mind she was still lying there. On top of him. On top of the godfather of our firstborn. Panting. Trembling. Numb to the world. Even after he tapped her. Alerted her of my presence. She wouldn't get off of him. She couldn't. She just lay there. With her ring finger in his mouth. The eternal symbol of my love for her dangling from his bottom lip. At this moment, rationality is foreign to me. Everything in my childhood home appeared infrared. The color of raging bulls. The color of love. On autopilot, I gave a swift answer that made me feel like I had pocketed at least some manhood. He takes from me . . . I take from him.

"Him."

"I'm on it. Be ready when I call."

"I will be."

"One."

"One."

Time passed in shadows of itself. Hours. Minutes. In a matter of them all, I was a darker version of Derrick. An outline of how destitution can dim even the best of men. Sunken in an enclave made for failures, I spent each of those minutes in a parade of numbers. Names. Faces. One hundred seventy-eight. Women. I've fucked them. Loved some. Adored one. Karma. It doesn't come back like this. It can't. Who would come back for karma? Make its life a living hell for the fucked-up shit it's doing to me? This isn't real. My best friend. My frat. My best man. And my woman. The only one I've ever adored besides my mother. I wonder what Ma would think about this. I glanced down at the bluish gray tombstone, brushed the dirt off the crest with my sleeve. Decided to ask her myself.

"Hey, Ma. Hope you're doing well. Your son isn't. Remember the woman I told you about? The one that I said reminded me of you? Well, she doesn't anymore. She did some messed-up shit, Ma. She slept with my best friend. I know. I know. You've always told me to watch my friends around my women. I know I shouldn't date 'em so pretty. But Dad did it. Why can't I? You were the shit, Ma. Sorry for cursing. I really didn't want to believe it. So I went back over there late last night. Saw them together. Laughing. Laughing at me, Ma. Yeah, I know it's foul. Nope . . . no . . . I'm not. I'm not letting him get off easy. I know what I have to do. I'm a man, Ma. I have to. Hope you're not upset. He deserves it. Yeah. I love you, too. Till next time . . . Tell Grandma I said what's up. And Happy Thanksgiving."

The blaring of the horn fucked up my concentration.

"Aye yo, Deeeeee!" Trey hollered my name at the top of his lungs in the damn cemetery. He still lacks home training. He doesn't have any fucking respect.

"Aight, Ma. I have to go." I placed a kiss on the hard cold stone and trekked toward the '86 Caprice. Trey wasted no time.

"They got 'em."

"Who?" I asked. I was out of it. In and out of daydreams and flashbacks of the scene that let me know I could rely on no one in this world for anything.

"Your faggot-assed boy and the bitch. They over at the Union Station. We only got a few minutes, though."

Although it somehow still unnerved me to hear Trey call Taiyler out of her name, I let the shit ride right over me. I had no choice. I was focused. Electric. On edge. We were high on that drug called adrenaline. The one that enables fifty-year-old women to lift compact cars entrapping grandbabies. You get that way. In the heat. I hopped in the old classic, heart beating a mile a minute.

"Here. Hold this." Trey threw the cold metal in my lap. He drove. I rode. Like old times. I analyzed the high-powered rifle from handle to barrel. This was some serious shit. We turned up South Capitol, passed the park, cut through New Jersey Avenue. Mob Deep's "Shook Ones" about to shatter the windows.

"You wanna pull or you want me to?" he asked. No answer. Concentration. On the reality of what I was about to become.

"D. Lemme know so I can pull over and we can switch spots." He said it as if we were driving long distance to our annual family reunion. Has life become that much of a nontopic? I thought about it. I don't want to kill him. He has a daughter. I want to teach him a lesson. A good one. Don't fuck with me.

"I'll do it," I replied, examining the contours of my newfound pride in my lap.

"You sure? It's been a while." He was worried. I got this. Besides, there's no need to pull him in any further than he already is. The nigga has a rap sheet longer than *War and Peace*. I'm a man. I handle my shit.

"Yeah."

Trey nodded, increased focus on the road. I know him. Multiple escape routes. He always has them. He would have made an excellent attorney.

"Where you wanna hit?" he asked. He always did. Trey has always been a sure shot. Sort of like a hood sniper. And shooting, somehow, has always been a game to him. A gamble. He wants to place a bet. See how close I come to my intended target. I thought about what I was just asked. Honestly, I'd begun to have second thoughts. That is, until we cruised the roundabout across the street from the station. And I saw them. Outside.

Standing.

Snuggling.

Laughing.

Talking.

Who the fuck does Nat think he is?

"Aight. This is the deal. The silencer . . ." As Trey handed out imperative directions on his Talon TX magnum, I saw a lot of shit. Shit I didn't need to be seeing.

Infrared.

"And you cock it here . . ."

He's been holding her since we got here. Let her the fuck go!

". . . now the scope . . . you adjust it like this . . ."

She's laughing. What the fuck is so funny? I can't breathe. I'm choking on jealousy. On envy. On my rights as her husband-to-be.

"Derrick! Muthafucka pay attention before you fuck shit up!"

The look that I gave him must have been brutal, because his tone fell a few decibels. Quickly.

"Aight. Listen, so steady it on the seat of the window . . . so you hit."

He picked her up. Swung her around. Like he was used to it. I can't believe this. He's *used* to it. She kissed him. Deeply. With so much passion. No regret. I leaned in to get a better look. In hopes of seeing another couple, a different pair, amidst all this red. I squinted. Maybe it's not them. Yes, it is. Yes, it is. His hands. Her hair. His arms, her . . . where are her arms? Oh. There. Her arms are inside of his jacket. Wrapped around him for dear life. Why won't she let go? Why is he all over my woman? As my neck hit the rear of the headrest, I felt them both. My wife. My fraternity brother. All over my face. Each one the sole owner of bundled hot teardrops. Pouring out of me. Out of my soul. Onto my sleeve. Like morning coffee. That's it. That's fucking it.

"Give it to me," I snapped.

"Hold on. Five-O." Trey lifted his eyes to the rearview mirror.

"I don't give a fuck about no damn police! Give me the shit! Now!" I'll show Nat. I'll show his ass. Real good.

"Derrick . . . calm your ass down so you can hit. You start missin' muthafuckas when you're hyped up, nigga . . ."

"GIVE ME THE GAT DAYUM GUN! FUCKIN' NOW!"

Trey looked at me like I needed an exorcist. So what? Maybe I did. He handed the rifle right over. It felt good in my hands. Just as good as Taiyler felt in his. Fuck you, Nat. Fuck you for robbing me blind. You think you're a man? Huh?

"Derrick! Pipe down, mane! Wait a fuckin' minute! The muthafuckin pol—" Trey yelling. Blue lights. Red lights. One . . . two . . . three. Seeing red makes your target much clearer. I see you. And I raise you. Who's the man now, Nat? Yeah. Take this, bitch-ass nigga . . .

42

Nathaniel

Walking down my driveway, away from Kendra, away from life as I knew it, made me feel like shit. That's an understatement. But somehow, walking up those brownstone-style stairs made me feel like I was at the tail end of a bungee jump. Bundling up with Taiyler on the terrace of her master bedroom, overlooking her ink-colored pool, gave me even more of a rush. The cool, crisp November air hit my nostrils like a six-month supply of Altoids. She nestled close to me in the midst of cold air and brisk winds, oblivious to the fall forecast. We were wrapped up in blankets. Gazing at the conclusion of sharing dreams. Without sharing space in the womb. Sipping berry tea.

"Taiyler. How many cups are you going to have? You've been drinking tea all night! I'm not carrying you to the bathroom one more time tonight!" I felt her body shake in laughter.

"It's herbal," she answered between stifled laughter.

"It's an addiction. Do I have to place you in a T.A. class?"

"T.A.?"

"Tea-drinkers Anonymous."

She folded in laughter.

"I'll tell you . . . but don't laugh . . ." she started with a twinkle in her voice. I repositioned myself so that I could see her face more clearly. I love her eyes.

"When I was young, my grandmother only went shopping at the beginning of the month. She'd fill the cabinets with everything we could possibly need and want to eat. However, being the greedy-assed ghetto children that we were, we ate everything all day. All night. Like food was going out of style. Grandma purposely went to make groceries . . ."

"What?" I asked. Amused at the candor of which she spoke of not having.

"Make groceries. Don't act like you don't have some country-assed family members. You're from the South. *Make groceries.* Go shopping. Same thing. Anyway, my mom drank tea. Lots of it. So at the end of the month, when there was nothing left to eat, at least nothing we could make as kids, we'd shift gears to my mom's herbs. Drink cup upon cup of tea. Every day. All day. Summertime. Winter. Fall. It didn't matter. Little five- and six-year-olds with big-assed mugs of tea. Walking around like they were the shit . . ."

I felt her toned stomach contract while she chuckled. I wanted to put something in there.

". . . so I guess I just got used to it. I drink tea with everything."

"Fascinating, Doctor." I'm hard. All it takes is the sound of her voice sometimes.

"I thought it would be," she answered squarely. Smugly. She knows. Positions herself right there.

"So . . . Mr. Woods. Are you okay?" She wants to talk about my experience with Kendra. At five in the morning. While we were awaiting the sunrise. And I'm about to implode. She's funny. When she wants to talk, she'll talk. And you'd better be ready.

"Depends on what you mean by okay."

"Don't dance, Nat. What happened? How did she take it?"

"How was she supposed to? She knew more about us than Derrick did."

Taiyler raised her eyes to mine. She's confused.

"Taiyler. Your psychiatrist. Was her last name Henderson?"

She paused. Thought. And surely as the sun began to rise, the revelation seeped through her like rainwater on the roof of an outhouse.

"Oh, my God. Nat. No. That was Kendra?"

I nodded. We sat quietly. Admiring the start of a brand-new day. The security of each other's arms. It's weird. I know that this woman will be mine forever. There is no question. Karma, even if it did call itself coming for me, would get its ass kicked by love. Like I did. A hard morning breeze ripped through our makeshift tent of blankets and body heat. She moved in a little closer. Held me a little tighter. I tried to figure out how to shave millimeters off the distance between us.

Feeling her tongue tickle the corners of my lips made me smile. The affectionate way she rubbed the back of my neck made me weak. All the love I had to give on this earth, balled up the way she was in my lap, made me warm. The soulful duet by Lauren Hill and D'Angelo about one being a part of the other's identity made me think.

"Hey, this is unfair." I hate to say so, but it is.

"What is . . . babe?" she whimpered like it hurt to speak in between kisses. She didn't want to talk now. Spoiled brat. Although it was difficult, I continued.

"If you die first, you take me with you." That got her attention.

"How so?"

"Have you ever known anyone to live without a heart?" I paused. Wondered if she got it. She did. Wrinkled her nose. Brushed it off. Went back to blessing me with berry kisses.

"So. You'll do the same."

"Do what?"

"Take me wherever you go when you leave me."

"No, I won't. Women outlive men."

"I can't live without you. So what does it matter?" she offered nonchalantly, like it was everyday news. I'm smiling now.

"When did you come to know this?" I asked.

"Known it all my life."

"Impossible. We just met."

"Nothing's impossible."

The organ. The percussion. It soothed us. Whisked us into the reality of what we'd been forced to create. I'd found my way to the deepest part of her. It made me glad.

> . . . *there's no place I'd rather be*
> *Cause nothing even matters, to me* . . .

Taiyler sat up. Faced me. That familiar sparkle in her eyes. Spread herself open on my lap. Slid her hands underneath my gray HU sweatshirt. Allowed the organ and strings to choreograph a dance that told stories of love griots. She moved slowly. As if she had all night. All year. All of her life. All of the next. To craft legions of love. Precious oil on canvas. Sacred sculptures. Of our tale. Consciously moving like a serpent, she took an account of our romance for our children. My breaths were long. And deep. There was no need to rush. Forever is a long time. She picked up speed, as if fearful of our time being cut short. She called me.

"Nat . . ."

I felt her body give me all of what was left. I wanted to slow her down. I wanted her to feel forever. She erupted with the viscosity of a Hawaiian volcano. Gradually. Deliberately. As she held on for dear life. Forehead to forehead. We played cat and mouse with verbs and adjectives. Trying our best to describe what we were feeling.

"Nothing even matters . . . to me . . . to me . . . Nothing but you . . ." Beads of sweat appearing on the bridge of her nose, she smiled. Whispered the words to the ballad. Read the writings on the walls of her heart. Of her soul. Tickling my lips with hers. I was so satisfied. If I never lived to see another day, I would have lived life entirely.

"Good morning, sunshine . . ." I sang like my mom did while waking me for school. Amidst that all-white down Lauren comforter was an angel that did her best work at night. Taiyler was not a morning person.

"Let me sleep, Nat." She was irritated. I thought it was cute. As I gently placed a lush green grape at the brink of her lips, she managed a smile.

"Do you have to work this week?" I asked. I hope not. I'm off. She stirred. Tried to salvage remnants of sleep between my insensitive commentary. I can't help it. I want her up. I miss her.

"No. I always take Thanksgiving week off," she said, sucking the grape from my fingers.

"Really? That's great, because I take this week in vacation, too!" I was like a five-year-old on Christmas Eve. With the expectation of opening gifts all week long. I slid in bed beside her.

"So what does that mean, Mr. Woods?" she asked coyly. Sat up, haplessly threw her leg over my waist. Placed another grape in between my fingers, so that I could feed it to her. Oh, she's definitely up now. I'm thinking. I need to get away. Relax. Regroup.

"Let's go somewhere."

"Where?" She sat up. Excited. I gave it some more thought. Got it.

"Malibu."

She grinned.

"You're crazy! Are you serious! A flight to Los Angeles this time of year with this sort of notice?"

"Crazier has happened."

She blushed. Pun intended.

"All right. I'll call my agent." She's so used to taking care of things.

"No need." I pulled our itinerary out of my back pocket. I already called.

"Uh-huh, I see . . ." My addiction examined the papers. Trying so hard to contain herself. "And what if I couldn't go?" she asked. Grinned.

"What if? I don't know. Guess I would've driven the coast alone," I conveyed with a pitiful frown. I wanted her to feel sorry for me so that she'd kiss it and make it all better.

"Not in this lifetime, babe. I want to know how many times I can satisfy you before we reach San Diego. Only one way to find out."

We packed and ate in haste. Despite my apprehensions, I called the house to check on Kendra and Nile. To my surprise, Kendra let me speak to my little princess immediately. My guess was that she didn't want to be anywhere near the sound of my voice. Nile wanted to know where I was. I told her that I was away, but that I would be back to see her holiday dance recital. And that I'd take her to the Rainforest Café. That was all she needed to hear. All else will have to be handled when I return. I looked around the house that love built. Determined to find a way to sneak Taiyler onto my lap for one more round. Her scent does it to me sometimes. Fuck it. Her scent. Her voice. Every damn thing about her turns me on. On a hurried trip down the stairs, I grabbed her. Scooped her up in my arms. Used to our rhythm, she allowed her legs to swing open pendulum style. So that they landed on either side of me. Perfect. I smothered her. Hoping that she could breathe between kisses. I'll find out in a minute.

"Baby." She pulled away slightly. I sucked on her bottom lip. On her chin. She let out a slight moan. Came right back to me.

"Nat. Baby. We . . ."

I know we have to go. But I'm stuck in caramel.

"Tai-y . . . ler . . . sweetie . . . just one more, please?" I begged. She smiled devilishly. Tipped her head to the side. Slid down the side of me. Wiggled one foot out of her jeans. Pulled me out of mine. She couldn't help herself either.

Minor victories.

We sat together at the top of the stairs. Straddled in impromptu positions. Triumphantly, I brushed my lips over her white baby tee. Dampening the spot that caused her to sit up straight. Throw her head back. Mr. Magic knew the way. He jumped right in there. We enjoyed her hands on top of our thighs. We liked the way she moved them up and down our back. Across our neck. Down our chest. Grabbed our ass. Smacked it. Put our hands on hers. Picked up the pace. Uttered hoarse nothings in our ear. Allowed me into her deepest space. Gat dayum! This shit is good. Whoever said quickies were heartless fucks evidently has never known love completely. We made beautiful love in less than ten minutes.

"Babe. We really need to get out of here," she advised after we slowed our stride. Settled into deep breaths and hot flashes. She glanced at her watch. I licked the remaining beads of sweat off of her upper lip. Her body tightened. Made Mr. Magic happy as hell. "I still have packing to do." An afterthought. I chuckled. It took everything for me not to begin guiding her hips with my hands into that sweet uptake of rhythmic soul she seems to be so good at putting on me.

"What do you need that you can't get there? Let's just roll!" I was gung ho. Irrational. She laughed.

"My scarf. The one you seem to love so much." And that ended it. She had me. I let her go.

Given the time allotment, my agent could only secure a red-eye to LAX from New York. So off to Amtrak we go.

"Don't forget that scarf, babe." I grinned.

"Got it, sweetie. Do you have everything you need?" she asked. Yup.

"All I need is you." I swung her around by the waist.

"What time does the train leave again?" she asked between joyous giggles.

"In an hour and a half."

"We'd better make a break for it." And that's what we did.

Due to inclement weather, our train was delayed about an hour. Good thing our flight left late. We decided to walk around Union Station for a bit, take in the cheer of the beginning of the holiday season.

"Nat. I want to go outside. Listen to the guy on the sax." She motioned to an older gentleman playing his heart out in the cold. Surrounded by passersby. Folks who wouldn't stop to appreciate his efforts to feed himself. We waltzed past Thunder Grill hand in hand, through doors that have seen Rockefellers and kings. Standing out there, bundled up, her back leaned against me, felt great. We swayed to the hypnotic melody of the sidewalk jazz artist.

"Can you play like that?" she asked.

"Oh, hell yeah. You didn't see my name in the hall of fame? You know, Miles, Coltrane, Monk, Woods?"

She threw her head back in laughter. Allowed me to see the slender curve of her neck from where I stood. Mmmh. I don't know if I can wait to get to Cali.

"Taiyler."

"Yes?"

"Face me." I turned her around. Drew her in by her scarf.

"I love you so much. Really, I do. More than I can express. More than I can ever play."

"And I love you, Nat. Maybe more than life itself."

We were serious. I picked her up, swung her around, let her light chuckles wet my ears. Let the moistness of her mouth warm me in the cold. Whoa. What was that? She leaned into me.

"Babe. Did you hear that?" I asked her. Her eyes at half-mast, she nodded.

"Taiyler. Hey, babe. Did you hear that? Sounded like a whistle or something. Went right by us."

She leaned on my shoulder. The weight of her body surprised me. She's playing around.

"Taiyler. Come on. Let's go inside. There's some weird shit going on out here."

Silence.

"Babe. Come on."

Nothing on this earth could have prepared me for what I saw. Blood. It was everywhere. On my hands. On the back of her coat.

"Taiyler! I'm cut! I'm bleeding!" I yelled as I pulled her off of my shoulder. I checked my hands, nothing. Stared into her eyes. Her sun was setting. People were screaming.

"Taiyler, baby, what's up. Stop playing. Okay? We gotta go. The train is going to leave soon. Baby. Come on."

Her eyes fluttered. She blinked super fast. Blood was pouring out by the gallons. Oh, shit. It's her. My baby is hurt. The stabbing pain in my chest was too crucial to ignore. I hurt. Like hell. But I clenched my teeth. Bore it with all my might. Tried to suck up all of her pain. I had to take care of her. I had to take care of my bread and butter.

"Hellllllllp! Someboooooody get help! Get an ambulance. She's bleeding! Please! Please! I need a doctor! Nowwwwww!"

My love. My Sun. My Earth. She's bleeding all over. Asthma. Wait. No. Asthma doesn't make her bleed. Her period. Shit. No. Maybe I'm holding her too tightly. She's moving her mouth. She has something to say.

"N-at."

"Yes, baby. Yes, baby. We're getting you to a hospital, okay? Just hold on, T. We're going to Malibu. Okay?"

She attempted a nod. Stared into my eyes. Offered a smile. My heart was pounding.

"I . . . do . . . lov—" She started to cough. I started to cough. Her body shook violently. My body shook violently. We stared into each other's eyes through sirens and screams and paramedics and ambulances and Derrick and handcuffs and questions and answers and sand and sunsets and Aruba and the fund-raiser and the grocery store and Rachelle and Miles and Trane and Vallenato and dances and kisses and hugs and dreams. Through Malibu and Cairo and Paris and Rome and Ethiopia and Polynesia and Brazil and Costa Rica and Sydney and Fiji. Through the Valley of the Kings and the Eiffel Tower and the Grand Canyon and the World Trade Center and the Savoy. Until we'd arrived. At home. In Harlem. Walking nights of Tunisia. Down streets of a love that never slept. Never died.

"Tai—you-you can't do this . . . bab-y . . . I-I can't . . . brea . . ." My sobs were wild. High pitched. Uncontrollable. No one could understand why I wanted to lie alongside her in the stretcher. If they had to revive her, they'd have to revive me. I just wanted to be ready for things to come.

"Sir. You have to get up, sir. You can't lie there . . ."

I heard voices. But I saw only her. Smiling. Telling me what a wonderful time she had in Aruba. Last night. How much she was looking forward to Malibu. To the coast. This is unreal. It is. It has to be. She's my everything. My body. My bread. My blood. My spirit. My soul. My life. My death. My resurrection. She is mine. She is me. I nuzzled my head into her space between her head and shoulder. Kissed her neck.

While they poured and plumbed every plastic tube and apparatus ever made down her throat, through her veins, her nose. I felt every probe. Every prod. We're one and the same. We're old. We're new. I was born to see the day that I could watch the sunset in her eyes. In her arms. God knows. He has to. He did this.

"Sir. Are you her next of kin?" the cold voice asked. We'd arrived at Georgetown University Medical Center.

"Yes. I am," I said as he helped me off of the stretcher.

"I'm going to be honest with you, sir. She's in bad shape. She's one of ours, so we're getting her the best. Her partner is one of the best cardiac surgeons in the country. He's in there fighting with her."

I nodded. I was here and there. On the pavement and in emergency surgery. All I cared about was her being alive. Nothing else. I knew that she was, because I was. I sat in the waiting room. Monitoring her progress by the inflection of my own breathing.

"How is she?" A red-eyed Shala appeared with another very attractive woman. I couldn't answer her. She seemed to understand that.

"Nat. Look at me."

I glanced at my love's best friend. Still in a trance-induced nod, I feared turning completely. Didn't want to break rhythm. I had to concentrate. Taiyler needed every breath she could get.

"She loves you more than anything," Shala said. She took my hand in hers. I know. I couldn't say it. But I knew. Because she loves me like I love her. I continued to nod. To breathe. My eyes welled with tears that I wouldn't allow to hit the concrete. I couldn't afford to lose anything that she might need. I sucked them up. Delivered them to her in red boxes with white ribbons.

"She'll make it, Nat. She's strong," Shala reassured us both. I nodded. We sat there. Hand in hand. Willing every breath, every bit of strength we could gather, from ourselves to Taiyler. All I could do was be thankful that she was still alive. I knew she was, because I was. Fourteen hours. Seemed more like fourteen years. Chest pain. Asthma attacks. Numbness. I felt it all. Because she did. We stood.

"Sir. Ma'am . . ." A youngster in blue scrubs appeared through the double doors. Looking like he'd just given the performance of a lifetime.

"Dr. Samuels is a bit overwhelmed at the moment. He asked me to come out and tell you—"

I had to catch Shala before she hit the floor. In my heart I knew she was still here. She was still with me. Because my heart was still beating. Hard. Fast. Furiously.

"We didn't lose her, but she is in extreme critical condition. No one can see her. No family. Friends. Dr. Samuels is canceling all of his appointments. He'll be attending to her around the clock. He wanted you to know that he's prepared to stay here for as long as it takes . . ."

I didn't hear anything other than the fact that I had to go another minute without seeing her. That would kill me. And if it did, then she wouldn't make it. I was almost sure of that.

"When will I be able to see her?" The first words from my mouth in fourteen hours tumbled out like broken Spanish.

"As soon as we can stabilize her, sir."

Shala was doubled over. Her cries were loud. Flagrant. Aching. I wanted to help, but I was more interested in the matter at hand. If I could get back there, I could help her. I could bring her here. Just like I did the night Aunt Mae died. Why don't they understand that?

"And so when will that be?"

"It's hard to predict," he answered, his focus on helping the woman scrape Shala off of the cold tile. I couldn't accept that. I wouldn't. My chest tightened. Moments passed. I leaned up against the wall as it became increasingly harder for me to breathe. I had to see her. This shit isn't happening.

"Sir! Sir! Where are you going! Sir . . ." The voice faded into green walls and white uniforms. I turned and twisted down corridors. Through hallways. Around extra-large beds and machines. Around the sick. And the well. Until I had come to the place where my love, my heart, my well-being was spread out in a mass of pumps and tubes. Gently, I took her hand in mine. And told her my life story. Through sunrises and sunsets. Days and nights. Visits from family. Flowers from friends. Shala. Drea. Dion. Mike. Travis. Cousin Ella. Solange. Dr. Samuels. Colleagues. Nurses. Children. Patients. People she touched in this lifetime. And when I'd gotten to the place in my story where I had fallen deeply for a woman whom I'd already loved for an eternity, she smiled. Lightly squeezed my hand. Used the flickering of her lids to jump in where she could.

"N-Na . . . t." The light tickling of my eardrum caused me to almost fall out of the chair that I'd slept in for months. Fearful of it being another dream, I hesitated to look at her. I couldn't bear my hopes being shattered once more.

"T-tell . . . me . . ." She coughed.

I smiled a thousand beams of light. "Yes, love." There were no words. Those two were a miracle.

"a . . . bou-t . . . you-r . . . la-st . . ." About my last dream. That was easy.

"We were somewhere. I don't know where . . ."

She moved a little, held my hand for dear life. Those charcoal eyes teasing me. Taunting me. Dancing for me.

". . . and you were in my arms. I carried you . . ."

She smiled. I smiled.

"In . . . to . . . th-e . . . w-a-t . . . er . . ." she added slowly. As if she were remembering herself.

"Yes, babe. Into the water." Wait a minute. How did she know?

"An-d . . . ki-s-sed . . . my . . . be-ll-y . . ."

As tears flooded my face, I listened to Taiyler recall my last dream. Color for color. Memoir for memoir. Word for word. It was then that I realized that this life, this love, was only a snippet of what we'd experience together. And I wasn't scared to lose her. Because I knew it was impossible. To lose myself. As Dr. Samuels raced in with his team, pumping and praying and cutting and cursing and crying his partner back into existence, I didn't scream. I didn't panic. I held her hand. And prepared myself, for I knew my own time was near. Who can live without a heart?

"And I played for you . . ." While the best of the best challenged God in a series of beeps, breaths, and big words, I continued to recall memories that would transcend lifetimes. And watched her smile. Remember things that we couldn't remember. Things that we knew, but didn't. Things that made us who we were. Who we are. Who we'd become.

Through all of the commotion those eyes remained fixed on mine. Through them, she asked a very simple question. One she already knew the answer to. Yes. I'll be there. Kissing her eyelids. Caressing her shoulders. Massaging her scalp. Feeding her strawberries. And green grapes. On long rainy nights that would never end. I'll be there. For always. Forever. We inhaled. Exhaled. I held her hand. And willed myself to a place where our love would last. Where it was free.

Our love was made in heaven. Preserved in pyramids. Painted in murals. Locked in time. We loved in the spirit. Loved as one. And that is as good as forever. So amidst all of the crying and weeping and wailing, I did the only thing I knew to do. I wrapped my arms around her and held her. Until we both stopped breathing.

Epilogue

All Zoe wanted to do was get this book finished. She'd spent the last seven months reading. Writing. Editing. She was sick of looking at the damn computer screen. Determined to freshen her source of inspiration, she set out to change locales. Sitting at her desk was getting old. Borders was alive. Filled with activity. And right across the street from her apartment complex. She scanned the environment for something. Anything. Anything inspirational. Anything that would shake loose her ability to think candidly. Create. Be the artist that she knew she was. She glanced over to the area near the window. Her escape. Toiling with the thick silver bangle on her wrist. The outline of a butterfly, marked in stones of the earth. Jade, turquoise, amber, quartz. She stared at the stones until her eyes crossed. Edging them on to bring her back to where she could unwind. If she could just relax, she could write. A tap on her left shoulder proved that effort ineffective.

"Excuse me. Is that Raheem DeVaughn? And his band?"

Okay. She wasn't exactly busy. But she'd looked it. You'd think folks would respect that. Leave her alone.

"Yes, it is," she answered, without so much as a glance in the direction of the voice. She was being rude. But so was he.

"Oh, okay. Thanks." The voice faded into the small crowd. She looked around. Couldn't place who'd just come over. Borders was filled with twenty-somethings. Poets. Photographers. Painters. Writers.

Renaissance. Raheem brought out the artists. Feeling the music, she decided to close her laptop, slide it into her knapsack, and enjoy the moment.

Enjoy being.

She made her way through a hodgepodge of people. Some she knew. Some she didn't. There was her boy. So eloquently named after the Duke, W. Ellington. There's K. Alyn and Munch. There's Corey J. the drummer. All here for a sociopolitical run of smooth rhythm, bass, and brass from a young Marvin Gaye. Spread out in a utopia that could only be created by the type of music that can be felt in your neck. In your back. Zoe felt it. She let it run all over her. She wanted it to. It made her ears wet.

> *Is it possible for you to see*
> *That maybe you and I could be . . .*

Enjoying life as it was meant to be lived, Zoe threw her head back. Let it linger on any side of her that it wished. Let the keys tickle her ears. The clap of drumsticks on the high-hat arch her back on time. And the teasing of violin strings wind her waist like water. She was free. Racing through tall grass and green pastures. Top speed with her arms stretched, on boats made for more than slave trade. She was herself. All or nothing. All the time. Especially today. Whether she could pen a chapter or not. Taking a hiatus from her groove-induced trance, she allowed her eyes to roam the room once again. She saw some handsome brothers. And they saw her. Almost all in sync. Noticing the sea of resistance-inspired, twisted and buttered hair, she was thankful that her waist-length locks were red. Naturally so. She was different. And glad about it.

Fighting off the dogs was not as hard today as it could be. The artistic crowd is typically a pretty respectful one. The hardest thing to do here is separate the *"Queen, you are truly God's gift to the Black man and the earth and sea, and can we read poetry and walk together looking like righteousness, and by the way can I fuck you with no strings attached"* bullshit from the men who truly are. Men. She gently extended her arm. Snapped her fingers. Allowed the music made from her thick silver cuff bullying the smaller bangles around and about her wrist to sit in with the band's percussion section. That boy is singing tonight. That tap on her shoulder came again. At the wrong time.

"Are you enjoying yourself?" It was the same voice from earlier. And yes, she was until he so rudely disrupted her groove. She decided to tell him just that.

"Yes. I was unt—" Stopping midsentence was not in the plans. Come on, girl. Tell him. Tell him to respect your space. She tried. But her mouth was a wad of cotton. She felt warm. Nauseated. Faint. The moment she looked into his eyes. Her mind was spinning at dizzying speeds. She had to sit. Now.

"Please excuse me, but I'm not feeling too well," she said, averting her eyes. Avoiding his. The effort exhausted her. He took her hand. Led her by her ring finger. To a table nearby. One by the window.

"Neither am I. Guess it's going around. May I ask you something?" he asked.

"Sure." She felt lighter. Softer. There's something about him. Something that she can't place.

"What name could possibly be beautiful enough to belong to you?" He was serious. She blushed.

"Zoe. Zoe Michaels."

"Zoe." He said her name as if it were a sugar covered peach sliver. Melting on the tip of his tongue. He smiled at the sight of a honeycomb. The sound of sweetness buzzing about his breath. The taste of love.

"And yours?" She wanted to pucker up. Prepare to kiss the possibility of endless combinations of syllables that would make this man a permanent fixture in her mind. She'd know his name. And feel him on her instantly. It was something she could predict.

"Mahiri."

"Just Mahiri?"

He blushed.

"No. Mahiri Lamont."

"A man with two first names." Zoe made fun of him in lieu of her own discomfort. Although in conversation, she'd spent the last few minutes trying to figure out where these bizarre feelings were coming from. Mahiri laughed. Smiled his coast-to-coast smile. Obviously smitten by her beauty. Her wit. Wrestling with feelings of his own. In the moment, tracing her personality from her fiery eyes to the tips of her

red locks was his passion. He couldn't place it, but she looked familiar. She felt like family.

"Have we met?" His stare pierced her in places it had no business
knowing existed. Zoe shook it off. Thought about his question. The
one that he borrowed from her. She was sure they hadn't.

"No."

"Are you sure?"

"Yes," Zoe answered, not really sure at all. She was scanning her
brain for possibilities. Trying to figure out why their fingers were
locked and how they got that way. Something about him felt so good.
Like sharing a heart-to-heart with a deceased parent in a dream. Like
a first home. Like soul food. Their eyes met again. And she saw it all.
Everything that made her a woman. Screaming. Raging. Shaking.
Wanting to ball up in his lap, wrap themselves in blankets of possibility.

"So, Zoe. Are you seeing someone?"

Actually she was. She was just having a hard time remembering his
name.

"Yes," Zoe answered. Her admirer shifted. Smirked.

"I knew that," he answered.

"How so?"

"Your eyes said it."

"When did they say it?"

"When we walked over here. Sat down."

"I was smiling while we walked."

"Yes, you were."

"So how did you know?"

"I am him. I am your someone." He laughed. She did, too.

"Wow. That came so soon. And all you know is my name."

"That's all I need to know. I've made my decision."

"And when was that?"

"When you first walked in. And then when I came over to you. And
then again while we walked. And spoke. And now."

"How can you be so sure of yourself?" Zoe asked questions that she
seemed to already have answers to. She turned toward the window.

Mahiri extended his arm, placed her chin between his forefinger
and thumb, pulled it away from the window. Toward him. He wanted
her attention. Oblivious to what had come over him, he continued to
hold her chin with his fingers. Visions of sunsets, of crystal blue water,

of multicolored rock and sand dunes, flashed before him. Memories of precious moments. Sacred seconds. The scent of her hair. Her skin. He's already run his hands up and down her thighs. Her back. Lotion. His hands. The back of her knees. A special place. He knows. When he touches her there. It makes her squirm. Zoe. He can feel her leg thrown lazily across his own in bed. He likes the way she calls him. The way she picks up the pace when she's almost there. He sat there next to her. Remembering things he couldn't remember. Holding her by the waist. Swinging her around. Loving her laugh. He's done it. All. He knows this. He just can't recall when. Or where. It's confusing as hell.

Typically, he's a shy guy. If a woman wants his attention, she has to come over to him. Today he felt unleashed. Unruly. He didn't know himself. But he felt as if he knew Zoe completely. Her concerns. Her favorites. Her fears. Her aspirations. The way she moved. The way she wanted him to. He would have bet forty acres on him knowing. Knowing her. It was shaking him up. He shook his head. Determined to shake this feeling. It was all he could do not to sweep this beautiful creature up. Whisk her away. Tease her lips with grapes on stretches of uninhabitable land. She felt great to him already. Her presence. Just to touch her. Touched him. Everywhere.

"Zoe."

"Yes," she answered. Half there. Half not.

"Face me."

She had long since forsaken the window, and maintained her focus on the band. Mahiri wanted her to look at him. Directly. He needed her to. She raised her eyes to meet his. Flabbergasted, he soaked in the radiance of her smile. Of her fragrance. Watched the beginning of sundown in her eyes. Her beauty had yet to be matched.

Zoe took a good long, hard look at the gentleman. There was something so familiar about him. She longed to feel his fingers on her scalp. Massaging her thoughts. Her temples. She felt him carrying her across violent waters. Bearing her burdens. On his back. It was a lot for her to digest all at once. The fact that she could taste him. His fingers. She could feel his sweat trickling down the small of her back. His strength. His hands. On her shoulders. Her calves. All over her. All at once. She was used to it. Already. How? The proverbial nature with which he stared at her. The way he said her name. It did something to her.

Like deep bass.

She felt it in her neck. Her back. It made her want to sing. Hum. Move. She took a deep breath. Held it. Admired the way his scent took her from Borders to her bathtub. The piercing crack of bare wood on metal jolted her. Brought her back to life. Back to reality.

> *Hit cho' stick up 'gainst that drum,*
> *Boom, clack, boom, clack . . .*

No. No. No, Zoe. Have some control . . . she thought to herself. She glanced away from him. Examined her manicure. Only to find that she was still hopelessly intrigued. Interested. In Mahiri. His hair. His hands. His skin. She wanted to discover things about him that he divulged only in dreams. All of this, all of a sudden. It didn't make sense to her. The way he held her finger. Played with it. Used it to trace psalms on his palms. She wanted to know what made him think he could do this to her. More than that, why didn't she stop him?

"Would you care for a beverage?" Mahiri asked. Praying that she would. He needed just five more minutes with her. And in that five, he would borrow five more. Bank them. Cash them in for a better understanding of himself. Of this. He suspected she was a tea drinker. Chamomile.

"Yes, please. Tea. Chamomile," she answered. His inner self shivering with the release of her hand, he raised himself from his seat, determined to hurry his way back to the warmth. The comfort. The tenderness. The familiarity. The soothe that was Zoe Michaels. Chamomile. Damn. He was right . . .

ACKNOWLEDGMENTS

Life is filled with persona. Personality. People. As a person of art, literature, and love, my twenty-five years of living has been filled with lots of everything and nothing. All at once. Every day. All of the time. Through all and naught, my people have been there. Carrying the spillover while I was filled, overburdened, overjoyed. And searching for pieces of me to pick up, while I was sprawled out on the floor. Shattered. Feeling like there was nothing left. For these people. These personalities. This group. I thank you. For adding to the persona that is Tamara P. Carter.

God. Only you know. Thanks would be too little to offer. My love. My heart. My soul. My life. That's all I have. Hope you'll accept it.

Grandma Gillis, Grandma Nina, and Aunt Ida. Although it hurts even to see the letters that once housed smiles, hugs, and homemade meals dance across my screen, while not being able to reach out and touch you, I'd like to thank you with all that I have. All that I've become. All that I will be. Thank you for your lessons in life. In love. Thank you for loving me unconditionally. Without reserve. I know that God is love. Because I know you.

Mommy. We laugh. Joke. Cry. You had my brothers and me while you were still a young woman. Struggling. You never gave up. Never quit. Thank you for going hard. Loving harder. No one thought that you would be able to do it. Raise three knuckleheads. Three ghetto children. Three buzzer beaters. But you trusted in the Lord. And we're here. We're successful. You beat the odds, Ma. As Rabbi used to say, *"He'll make them honor you one day . . ."*

Cor and Mikey. My bad, you're not Mikey anymore. You're at Hampton. You're Big Mike *smiles*. We are closer than the average siblings. We've grown up. Physically. Mentally. Spiritually. Together. Through Brooklyn, California, West Virginia, Hampton U. (Yeah, they're getting all of our money right now). Up the street, down the street, across it. Back at 842 Hopkinson Ave. Back at Grandma's. No sweat. All we needed was a hot cup of tea. Ramen Noodles. And each other. Life is lucky to have known you both. So am I. Thanks for adding to a soul's progression.

My pastor. Proph. B. Odino. Thanks for praying hard. Long. Strong. Thanks for connecting with the Lord on my behalf. When I couldn't find the words. While I was breathless. Speechless. Choking on tears. Thanks for lending me your heart. While mine attacked me. Raced about my soul, looking for love. Peace. Solitude. Understanding.

Dad. You are the most intelligent man I know. Thanks for helping me understand where I get most of my habits, humor, sarcasm, ambition, drive, honesty, bluntness, arrogance, analytical skills . . . quantitative and qualitative, inquisitiveness, procrastination . . . I only have so much space to list the qualities that make me your "twin daughter." Thanks for the long talks, Dad. And the DNA!

My friends. Wow. To be able to say it and mean it in this day and age is priceless. Koshala. My analytical counterpart. Thanks for being you. Being a bad B!@#$. Based on the first words that tumbled from your mouth upon our initial meeting, *"I want my white CLK . . . ,"* I certainly couldn't have predicted that we'd be true friends. Thanks for your cutting-edge honesty. Advice. Understanding of life. Understanding of me. If the book sucked, you would have been the first to tell me. I appreciate that.

Danielle. Soror. Friend. Now will you make me some basil chicken? Look! I've written a novel and everything! *smiles* Thank you for your undying passion and dedication to reading and reading and reading and reviewing and reading each chapter. Thanks for your e-mails. Messages of encouragement. Your critical eye. I knew if I could get this past you, I'd get it past national security. Thanks for crying at the end.

Gia. Sometimes my little sister. Sometimes my big sister. Thanks for trading spaces with me as needed. For conversation. For realism. For viewing life through untainted eyes. Thanks for challenging me. My opinions. For holding my beliefs up to the light. Examining them for flaws. For listening. For offering perspective. Thanks for knowing how to.

Shelly. We connected immediately. You've been able to pinpoint my growth like no other friend. You were the first friendly face at HU, and you are still my friend. More than that, you are my sister. Thanks for the honesty, the loyalty, the editing skills, and . . . THE SPARE

ROOM! When a sistah didn't have a dollar to her name, thanks for being all that I needed you to be.

Hampton University. My friend. You cultivated my strengths. Strengthened my weakness. Weakened my rigid outlook on life, as it was when I'd arrived as an arrogant freshman from the "bottom" of the socially, politically, and culturally challenged zoo they call Brownsville, Brooklyn, New York. (Sidebar—Where are our rights? Where are the textbooks for the kids? How are we supposed to compete?) Thanks for humbling me. Taking me to the top. Thanks for the experience. Whatever I owe you will be paid in both of my brothers' tuitions. (Can y'all let up off of my brother Mikey's aid please!) Spring 2006. We're even.

My extended family. LaToya. We've grown in directions that complement us both. Thanks for being there always. My Sorors. Alpha Kappa Alpha Sorority Incorporated's finest. Erica (my big sis), Katrice (my line sis), Ayisha (the sweetest sis ever). You guys remind me of why I pledged in the first place.

To Jeff Woodruff (cover design) and Raeshawn Smith (cover photographer), for the independent revision of BTE. THANKS FOR PUTTING UP WITH ME! I'm anal. I know it. But so are you both! That's why we work so well together. Thanks for redesigning and reshooting and redesigning and reshooting . . . until we got it. Thanks to Kristin Mills Noble for the published design, you're very talented.

Thanks to my girl, Heather Austin, the first one to edit BTE. You made me learn the language and do these hundreds of pages by hand! The feedback was invaluable. As was the experience.

To the ones who've come before me. Terry McMillan. Sonia Sanchez. Toni Morrison. Octavia Butler. Alex Haley. Langston Hughes. Zora Neale Hurston. E. Lynn Harris. Eric Jerome Dickey. Bebe Moore Campbell. My favorites. I'd never taken a class, or a seminar, on "The Effects of Literary Freedom and Creativity on the Soul." My professors of penmanship were always housed in shelves that never saw dust. In books that were read over and over in anticipation of my next opportunity to take long trips through imaginations that never slept. Never died. You made me laugh when I felt like crying. Wipe tears born of laughter that wouldn't quit. Even when I wanted to. You reminded me that imagination, solitude, and depth are to be cherished. Your works helped me unveil what was hidden inside. Enabled me to understand the reality of fiction. Its purpose. Its position. You helped me understand. For that, I am eternally grateful. Thanks for the blueprint.

All right. My brother's telling me to wrap this up. My HU friends for life. Camille and Loretta, for opening me up. Letting me know it was okay to discover me from the inside out. The HU class of '98, Dr. Roy, Ms. K. Weatherly, Mrs. Amanda Murray, Mrs. D. Spells, Mrs. Friday, and Mrs. Costa in financial aid, for those *"Do you do you have ten thousand dollars? . . . Nope! . . . Well, you can register anyway . . ."* days, and all of the names and faces of those who made my experience genuine. We are truly a subculture! The entire Townes family, (From New York to Florida) Lynn Hobson, my publicist (for working with a sistah). Mike Walker, Mahiri Jones, and my man Star (for holding me down). To K.S. and H.S. I got y'all. Marc Barnes, Rene, and Lois "The Chef" (for feeding me). Al Flowers, Mike McQuerry, Rob, Darryl Huckaby, Iran, and Rashaan Casey . . . Thanks to all who accepted me. Accepted my work. Saw the fire. The spirit. Saw what was behind those eyes.

BEHIND THOSE EYES

T.P. CARTER

ABOUT THIS GUIDE

The following questions are designed to facilitate discussion in and among reader groups.

DISCUSSION QUESTIONS

1. In the case of Taiyler and Nat, their love was born centuries ago. In modern times, the theory of kindred connection is debatable. Is there a such thing as a soul mate? Or do couples work together to create the love that Taiyler and Nat had?

2. In the first few chapters of the story, Shala is facing a dilemma with sexuality. In the African American, African, Latin, as well as most other communities, same sex unions have typically been taboo. Especially as it relates to the church. Should Shala tell her father about her female partner? Is she right to consider "going back to men full-time" in order to feel more a part of society? What is the best solution to her problem?

3. Derrick has been a ladies' man for most of his life. In the beginning of the book, he makes references to how professional Black women set out to "capture" their male counterparts. Is his perception of women accurate? Or is there really a shortage of suitable partners for this group that prompts such behavior? Did he deserve what happened to him in the end?

4. At Garvin's birthday party, Taiyler's passionate rant on the lack of visibility and connection between educated middle- and upper-class Blacks and their poorer misdirected counterparts is met with opposition. Is there a lack of visibility of professional Blacks in our more indigent neighborhoods? Why don't the majority of us spend more time in poorer areas providing direction to those who need it most? Is there a divide between the working class and upper middle-class brothers and sisters? If so, how do we bridge the gap between the two?

5. The connection between Taiyler and Nat was genuine. However, it led them to make decisions that affected innocent people, namely Derrick, Kendra, and Nile, Nat's five-year-old daughter. Both characters tried to do the right thing initially, but ended up forsaking their families and friends to be together in the

end. Is love really that strong? Or is it used as an excuse for poor behavior?

6. Have you ever met someone, friend or lover, and instantly felt a special connection with them? Share examples of what was felt and exchanged between the two of you.

Dear Readers,

Thank you for reading my first work of fiction. I've written this book on the premise of reincarnation. This one is written on a debatable premise as will be future works. As I grow as a writer, my next book will hopefully be better but no different as it relates to addressing these sorts of topics. I want to bring things to the table via characters that we often neglect in modern-day society. Every issue in this book is debatable. There is no wrong or right. Just sharing. I hope Nat and Taiyler's story (as well as Shala's) has opened your minds and spirits to consider different types of love, and I wish love, peace, and open-mindedness for each of you. They all lead to happiness!

Till next time,

T.P. Carter